Now Leah, Paige and Morgan are home—
finally reunited—and each with a story
that will unfold…

Rocky
Mountain Brides

A heartwarming, emotional trilogy from
favourite author Patricia Thayer

Rocky
Mountain Brides

PATRICIA THAYER

First published in Great Britain 2012
by Mills & Boon, an imprint of Harlequin (UK) Limited,
Eton House, 18-24 Paradise Road, Richmond, Surrey TW9 1SR

ROCKY MOUNTAIN BRIDES
© by Harlequin Enterprises II B.V./S.à.r.l 2012

Raising the Rancher's Family, *The Sheriff's Pregnant Wife* and *A Mother for the Tycoon's Child* were first published in Great Britain by Harlequin (UK) Limited in separate, single volumes.

Raising the Rancher's Family © Patricia Wright 2007
The Sheriff's Pregnant Wife © Patricia Wright 2007
A Mother for the Tycoon's Child © Patricia Wright 2007

ISBN: 978 0 263 89688 6
ebook ISBN: 978 1 408 97097 5

05-0512

Printed and bound in Spain
by Blackprint CPI, Barcelona

RAISING THE RANCHER'S FAMILY

BY
PATRICIA THAYER

Dear Reader,

I love beginning a new series. I had so much fun creating the small town of Destiny, Colorado, and the people who live and work there, where families are the foundation, and the roots run deep in the close community.

Tim and Claire Keenan were blessed years ago when three little girls were left in their care. Morgan, Paige and Leah Keenan are the basis for these stories.

The first is Leah's story, *Raising the Rancher's Family*. When photographer Leah Keenan returns home from a tragedy during her travels, she runs headlong into stubborn rancher Holt Rawlins. The sparks fly, but so does the compassion as they help each other heal.

Then there's Paige's story, *The Sheriff's Pregnant Wife*. After being jilted, and ending up pregnant, attorney Paige Keenan moves home to open a law practice and be with her family to raise her baby. Soon, her once-boyfriend Sheriff Reed Larkin is hanging around, playing the part of stand-in daddy.

In the third story, *A Mother for the Tycoon's Child*, Morgan has emotional scars from her past. Now the mayor, she is doing everything she can to bring revenue into town. When tycoon Justin Hilliard arrives in Destiny to invest in a resort, he becomes twice as appealing when she meets his five-year-old child. In no time the father/ daughter duo work their way into Morgan's heart.

I hope you enjoy visiting all the places in my stories that make Destiny so special.

Thanks for reading,

Patricia Thayer

Originally born and raised in Muncie, Indiana, **Patricia Thayer** is the second of eight children. She attended Ball State University, and soon afterwards headed West. Over the years she's made frequent visits back to the Midwest, trying to keep up with her growing family.

Patricia has called Orange County, California, home for many years. She not only enjoys the warm climate, but also the company and support of other published authors in the local writers' organisation. For the past eighteen years she has had the unwavering support and encouragement of her critique group. It's a sisterhood like no other.

When she's not working on a story, you might find her travelling the United States and Europe, taking in the scenery and doing story research while thoroughly enjoying herself, accompanied by Steve, her husband for over thirty-five years. Together they have three grown sons and four grandsons. As she calls them, her own true-life heroes. On her rare days off from writing you might catch her at Disneyland, spoiling those grandkids rotten! She also volunteers for the Grandparent Autism Network.

Patricia has written for over twenty years and has authored over thirty-six books. She has been nominated for both the National Readers' Choice Award and the prestigious RITA®. Her book *Nothing Short of a Miracle* won a *Romantic Times* Reviewer's Choice award.

A long-time member of Romance Writers of America, she has served as President and held many other board positions for her local chapter in Orange County. She's a firm believer in giving back.

Check her website at www.patriciathayer.com for upcoming books.

CHAPTER ONE

SHE was finally home…

Leah Keenan drew a shaky breath as she drove the narrow road that led up the mountain. To the safe haven of Destiny, Colorado, where she'd grown up surrounded by love and the security of her two sisters and their adoptive parents. It had been twenty-seven years since the day when she, Morgan and Paige had been left at the Keenan Inn.

But she wasn't the same idealistic, fun-loving girl who had left the small town three years ago. The cruelty of the world had managed to change her.

For the past month she'd fought the recurring memories, but with no success. Memories of the Middle East where she'd been photographing the horrors of war for *Our World* magazine. She'd seen so much horror—the bombs, the gunfire, the death and destruction. She just finished filming the earthquake and seen the hundreds of thousands of homeless.

And, oh God, the children…

At the sound of a horn, Leah swerved just in time to miss the oncoming car. Shaken, she pulled her rental car to the side of the road and shut off the engine. In the silence Leah could hear the sound of her pounding heart. She had to get herself together.

After a few minutes, she climbed out and drew in a breath of clean mountain air. She slowly began to relax as she eyed the familiar area. White Aspen trees lined the road, their new growth and rich green leaves promising spring had arrived in southern Colorado. Her gaze rose to the San Juan Mountain Range, the Rocky terrain blanketed by huge pine trees. At the very top were patches of leftover snow from the previous winter.

Leah smiled, suddenly feeling adventurous. As a kid she'd hiked through these foothills as if they were her backyard, and her daring spirit had driven her parents crazy.

Luckily on her flight from Durango she'd worn her standard work clothes—a cotton blouse, pullover sweater, khaki pants and lace-up boots.

Grabbing her trusty camera off the seat, Leah marched to the fence and a sign that read, No Trespassing. Since the landowner, John Rawlins was a friend, she ignored it. She easily climbed over the wire fence, decided the direction she planned to go and set out on the narrow trail.

Leah made her way through the trees toward

the mountainside. A doe appeared in the grove of trees and she paused to snap a picture. The serene beauty of this place helped to soothe her. Eager to reach her destination, she picked up her pace. After another fifty yards, she could hear the sound of water.

In the shade of the trees it grew cool, but she let nothing slow her until she reached the clearing. She stared in awe at the sight and sound of water rushing over the sheer ledge of mountainside into the rocky bottom of the pond below. Years ago, she'd named this special place Hidden Falls. Since adolescence, this had always been her private retreat, her escape where she could daydream.

A sudden movement caught her eye. She glanced toward the base of the falls to find a small child squatting down on a rock and washing in the water. He looked about eight years old, she thought as she snapped a picture of him, then glanced around to look for anyone else in the vicinity. Like a parent.

Not another person in sight.

Leah moved closer and the kid suddenly jerked around and caught sight of her. There was fear in his eyes as he stumbled backward, then regained his footing and took off.

"Hey, wait," she called after him. "I'm not going to hurt you. Are you lost? I have a phone in the car."

The kid didn't stop. He darted through the trees like a mountain lion. Leah followed, but the youngster was too fast. "It's going to get dark soon," she yelled, but the boy was gone.

Okay, he so wasn't going to come to her. Refusing to give up, she continued through the trees as she checked her watch. It was after three o'clock.

"He didn't even have a jacket," she murmured, knowing how cold it would get after nightfall.

Then in the distance she spotted a figure on horseback. As he approached she could see he was a large man with a black Stetson pulled low over his face. Suddenly her attention was drawn to the rifle he held across his saddle horn. She suddenly felt fear, something she'd thought she'd left behind.

"Hello, maybe you can help me," she said a little too breathless. "There's a boy—"

"You're trespassing," he interrupted.

She blinked at his rudeness. "Not really," she said, trying to recognize the man, but his sandy-brown hair and startling green eyes were unfamiliar. "I know the landowner. I'm more worried about the young boy I saw. I think he might be a runaway."

"I haven't seen any kids," he insisted. To her relief, he slipped the rifle back into the sleeve. "So you need to leave."

"I said it was okay, I'm Leah Keenan. John Rawlins has let me hike here to take pictures for years."

"That's not going to be allowed any longer."

Leah wasn't used to people around here being unfriendly. "And why is that?"

"John died about six months ago." She was close enough to see something flash in his eyes, sadness, vulnerability...

Quick tears stung her eyes. "Oh, no, not John. I didn't know." The rancher had been about her father's age. He was also someone she'd loved and enjoyed seeing and talking to.

"Well, now you do." He shifted the big gelding and pinned her with startling green eyes. "So you can leave the property."

"I can't. There's still a lost child. He could be hiding out in one of the caves. That could be dangerous."

"Then I'll ride around and check it out."

His offhanded promise didn't reassure her. "I know where all the caves are around here. I could help you look."

"I don't need your help."

Leah worked hard to hold her temper. "There is no reason to be rude. I'm only worried about the child."

"That child is trespassing, and so are you. Now leave."

Her temper got the best of her and she jammed her hands on her hips. "Just who are you?"

"Holt Rawlins."

Leah's gaze combed over the shadowed face, and finally recognized the strong jaw and the familiar cleft in his chin. The difference was the sandy-colored hair, and those piercing emerald eyes.

"John's son," she whispered. "I didn't know John had a son."

A bitter smile creased his wide mouth. "That makes us even. For years I didn't know I had a father."

Holt Rawlins slowly followed the intruder on horseback and watched as she made her way to the fence and climbed over it. Leah Keenan got into her car and finally drove off.

He breathed a sigh. The last thing he wanted was another resident of Destiny telling him what a wonderful man John Rawlins was. If the man was so great why hadn't he seen or spoken to his only son in nearly thirty years?

Holt's parents' divorce had been a bitter one. For years his mother had told him that his father was a selfish man, that his family hadn't mattered as much to him as his precious Silver R Ranch.

With the notification of his father's death four months ago, Holt had now returned to the place of his birth. To live on the land that rightfully belonged to a Rawlins.

And he was a third generation Rawlins.

He turned the chestnut gelding, Rusty, toward the picturesque waterfall, letting the tranquil sound relax him as he looked through the rows of aspen trees toward the majestic mountain range. Though he was a New Yorker who thrived on the energy of big city life, there was part of him that got a different kind of rush from this place.

He attributed it to the fact that his life was in turmoil right now. He'd ended a long-term relationship with a woman whom he'd thought he wanted to be his wife. His career wasn't the exciting challenge it once had been. So when the lawyer called and said his father had passed away and left him a ranch, Holt knew he needed to come back. At least to learn about the man who was his father. So far, all he'd discovered was that everyone around here had loved and respected the man. His chest tightened. Then why hadn't he had time for his only son?

Holt thought back to the numerous birthdays and Christmases when a small boy had waited for a present, or letter. Just a phone call. But there had been nothing…ever.

He pushed aside the memories and glanced toward the road. All evidence was gone of the petite blonde with the big doe eyes. But something in those deep, chocolate depths told him she didn't give up easily. He doubted he'd seen the last of her, or heard the last praise of a man who to Holt had been no more than a stranger.

Leah drove down two-lane First Street, the main road through town, past the row of buildings that made up the small community of fifteen hundred residents. In the historical town square was the bank, the sheriff's office, City Hall and the mayor's office. Leah smiled. The mayor was her older sister, Morgan.

Leah drove past the large tiered fountain that spouted clear mountain water…for now. Over the years the water mysteriously changed color according to any upcoming holiday.

Not much had changed in the pleasant town she and her sisters had grown up in. That gave her comfort, comfort she needed to help heal her body…and her heart.

She slowed at Pine Street and turned left. Just a block up the road she saw the huge brick and wooden structure she still called home. She pulled up in front of the decorative white sign posted in the yard of the historic bed and breakfast, the Keenan Inn, Tim and Claire Keenan proprietors.

Leah climbed out of the car as her mother rushed out of the house. Right behind her was her father.

"Leah, you're home." Claire Keenan wrapped welcoming arms around her daughter and held on tight. Leah fought her emotions as she inhaled her mother's familiar rose scent.

She kissed Leah's cheek then pulled back to examine her again with concerned blue eyes. "You look tired—and you're too thin."

Leah laughed and brushed away a tear. "Gee, Mom, thanks."

"Step aside, Mother, I need to hold this lass in my arms to make sure she's really my baby girl." Tim Keenan pulled her into a rough embrace and whispered in her ear. "You're home now, Leah, and you're safe. My prayers were answered."

Her father had always had the power to know what she was thinking and feeling. What she needed. The big, burly Irishman had dark good looks with an easy smile and big heart. And from the time Leah had noticed boys, she'd compared everyone to him. Not one of them had ever measured up.

Suddenly Holt Rawlins came to mind again. There was something about the man she hadn't been able to shake. As a trained photographer she'd prided herself on reading people, but not this man.

"Tim, let the poor girl get a breath," Claire said. "Let's go into the kitchen." She took her daughter's hand and squeezed it as she blinked back tears. "It's so good to have you home. You've been away too long."

"I know, Mom."

They walked up the steps to the Victorian house. The large porch was trimmed with baskets of colorful spring flowers. Two wooden swings hung by chains on either side of an oak door with the oval beveled glass inlays. She stepped across the threshold into a wide entry and honey oak hardwood floors. A burgundy carpet runner led to a sideboard that was used as the hotel's front desk. The high white ceilings were trimmed in crown molding. The pocket doors to the parlor were partly closed, but Leah could see two guests sitting at the window enjoying their afternoon tea.

Her mother said something to the girl behind the desk, then escorted Leah past the winding staircase that led to six guest suites upstairs on the second floor.

They passed the library with the fireplace and the big comfortable, overstuffed wing chairs and the shelves loaded with books. Next was the formal dining room with the floral wallpaper and oak wainscoting. Several tables were already set for tomorrow's breakfast with fine china and silver and colorful napkins.

They walked into the kitchen. This room was different from the rest of the house, mainly because it was strictly for family. No guests were allowed in this area. The same went for the Keenans's living quarters on the third floor

Her father led her to the big table in the alcove lined with windows facing the backyard. "Now, tell us about your travels."

As Leah sat down she felt her heart begin to pound, but before she could speak, her mother spoke up. "Tim, leave the child alone. She hasn't even had a chance to catch her breath."

Leah touched his rough hand. "Dad, I want to know about what's been going on here. That Morgan was elected mayor is so cool. I bet that ruffled good old Hutchinson's feathers."

The Hutchinsons had always been the wealthiest family in town. It was their great-grandfather, Will, who first struck it rich with the "Silver Destiny Mine," and had helped found the town.

Claire looked sad. "I think Lyle is more concerned about his father. Billy Hutchinson is failing badly. It's a shame he had to be put in the nursing home."

"I'm sorry to hear that." Billy Hutchinson had to be well over eighty.

Her father stiffened. "Well that didn't stop his son, Lyle, from trying to undermine the election, by strong-arming his employees to vote for him. Lyle wants what's good for himself." Tim nodded. "Morgan will do what's good for the town."

Claire carried a big tureen of potato soup to the table, then filled bowls for everyone. She handed the first one to Leah.

"I have to say, Mom, I've missed your cooking," Leah said.

Claire beamed. "Well, I hope that convinces you to stay longer. Both you and your hotshot lawyer sister."

Leah didn't want to talk about leaving again. She just wanted to think about pleasant things. Like home, and family. "How is Paige? I haven't been able to e-mail her in months."

"She works too hard," her mother said, "but we're hoping to get her home for the celebration."

The familiar voice called out from the hall. "Hey, where is everyone?"

"We're in here." Leah jumped up and went to the doorway as tall, willowy Morgan came in.

Her auburn hair was long and curled around her shoulders. A perfect frame for her green eyes. Morgan and Leah were as opposite as two sisters could be.

"Leah, come here, squirt." Morgan hugged her tight in a comforting embrace. "I'm so glad you're home."

"And I'm glad to be here." Tears prickled Leah's eyes as her sister held her close. So many times while she'd been far away from home, she had relied on her big sister's love and support.

"Come eat, you two, before it gets cold," Claire called.

They walked hand in hand to the table and sat down. After a short blessing, the family began to eat.

"I heard that John Rawlins died," Leah said. "Is that true?"

Her father nodded. "It happened so fast. A heart attack." His gaze met hers. "How did you find out?"

"I stopped by Hidden Falls and ran into a man

who says he's John's son. A Holt Rawlins." She didn't mention that he was good-looking, but not all that friendly. "I didn't know John had a son."

Her father nodded and leaned back in his chair. "Years ago John met his wife, Elizabeth, when she was here on vacation. They fell in love and were married just weeks later. But she never took to being a rancher's wife, and Elizabeth took the boy back East to her family."

"Why didn't Holt ever come here to visit John?"

"John tried, but Elizabeth's family had money and she got full custody of their son. She refused to let him come back here even for a visit."

"Well, he's here now," Leah said.

Her mother sighed. "John left him the Silver R Ranch."

"Is he going to stay?"

"Not sure," her father said. "The word is he's a financial adviser in New York. Why so interested?"

Leah shrugged. "I guess I'm curious as to what kind of man he is," she said honestly. "I noticed a little boy at Hidden Falls. By the looks of him, I'd say he's a runaway. Mr. Rawlins wasn't too eager to help me look for him."

Morgan looked up from her soup. "I haven't gotten a report from the sheriff about any runaways. Are you sure he's not just a camper who strayed? John's property borders the Mountain View Campground."

Leah had seen too many hungry street kids not to be suspicious. "Could be, but tomorrow, I'm going back to look for him whether Rawlins likes it or not."

Her parents exchanged a look. "Maybe you should let the sheriff handle it."

"The sheriff can't do anything if he can't find the child, if he's hiding out. But don't worry, I can handle Holt Rawlins." She thought about the intimidating man with the rifle and hoped that was true.

But she thought wrong.

The next morning, Leah parked her car in the same spot and followed the trail that led toward the falls, but she didn't make it undetected. Mr. Rawlins met her on the trail.

He looked better than a man in a pair of old jeans and a Western shirt that looked like he'd been working for hours had any right to look. He wore his Stetson like a shield, low, concealing a lot of his face.

"I thought I told you I would take care of this," he said.

She raised an eyebrow. "I decided you could use some help," she told him.

He leaned forward, resting his arm on the saddle horn. "You're still trespassing."

"And there's a young boy who could be lost."

"Or he could be running from the law."

"Either way, he's just a child." She folded her arms over her chest. "I'm not leaving."

"I could remove you, or call the sheriff."

"I'll still report seeing a child," she challenged right back. "He'll get a search party together and comb this area."

Holt stiffened. The last thing he wanted was more people coming on the property. Curious residents of Destiny, wondering about his business here.

"Of course with a lot of people searching," she continued, "it could drive the frightened boy into more danger."

"I'll give you two hours. If we don't find anything, the search is over." He held out his hand. "Climb on."

Leah Keenan's big brown eyes rounded. "You want me to ride with you?"

"Since I don't have another mount, and I doubt you can keep up with me on foot, I'd say this is your only option."

She squared her shoulders, bringing her height up to maybe five foot two. He'd always been attracted to tall, leggy women. Of course he couldn't deny he'd noticed her shapely, petite body. At this stage in his celibate life any woman would spark his interest.

"Okay," she relented. "We'll start with the caves."

After his reluctant nod, she marched toward the

horse. He slipped his foot out of the stirrup, and she put her boot in, gripped his forearm, pulling herself up behind him. He had no doubt she was an experienced rider.

"All set?" he inquired.

"I'm set." She grabbed the edge of the cantle on the saddle. "Head toward the hills. I know two caves there. I'm hoping he's holed up in one of them instead of an abandoned mine."

Holt tugged the reins to change Rusty's direction. The transition didn't go smoothly and Leah gasped and grabbed on to Holt to stay on the horse. He tried to ignore the feel of her hands on his waist, but her touch was like a brand burning into his skin. He found he'd missed it once they got on the trail and she released her hold.

"If you need to hold on…"

"I've ridden all my life, I think I can manage to stay on a horse."

About twenty minutes later they finally reached the edge of the rocky hillside. Leah was eager to get off the horse. She was becoming far too aware of the close contact with this man.

"Stop here," she called and dismounted before he could offer to help. She took off up the slight grade of the slope, feeling Holt behind her. She heard him slide in his leather sole boots, but wasn't about to help him. He didn't care about any lost kids. Let him keep up with her. She finally made it to the ledge, and kept going around the rock formation. Years disappeared recalling it had probably been since high school that she'd scaled this rocky terrain.

"Hey, wait up," Holt called to her.

Leah stopped and waited as he came up beside her. For a city guy, he handled the climb like a local. Four months of ranch life had benefited Holt Rawlins in other ways, too. She couldn't help but admire his developed shoulders and chest. Suddenly her breathing became a little rough and she quickly blamed it on the altitude.

"You can wait here if you're claustrophobic," she told him. "The space is kind of narrow."

She couldn't ignore the intensity in his green eyes. "Just lead the way."

She walked around another group of rocks, made it to the other side where there was an entrance to a deep cave. She leaned down to make it through the opening. It was empty and there weren't any traces of it recently being inhabited by a human.

"He's not here," she said disappointed.

Holt sighed and tipped his hat back. "So what's next? Are you ready to give up?"

"No, I'm not giving up," she insisted.

Leah marched out with Holt close behind her, too close. She continued her trek along the wide ledge for about thirty yards. She had hiked this area during her teenage years when she'd first taken up photography.

"How do you know about these caves?" Holt asked.

"I used to come here to take pictures. John told me as long as I stayed away from the old silver mines, he'd let me have the run of the place." She paused and a breeze whipped at her hair as she looked around.

They were surrounded by the brilliant colors of the mountains. Above, a rich blue sky topped each peak, and below, a lush green meadow was spotted with cattle.

"Why did you stop?"

She glanced back at the man. "Just enjoying the view. Your view."

"I don't have time to stand around."

She sighed. *Save me from New Yorkers.* "We're almost there." She went around another group of rocks to the entrance of another cave and she ducked inside the cool space. That's where she saw several empty water bottles. Holt came around her and took his own inventory of empty food wrappers. "It looks like the kid is also a thief."

Leah placed her hand on his arm. "Please, Holt. Your thief, as you call him, is only a boy." She glanced around. "Look how he's had to live."

"He shouldn't be living here."

"Maybe he has nowhere else to go," she insisted. "Have you ever thought about that? He's a child and he's living in a cave." She blinked back sudden tears. "Looks like he has moved on anyway."

For a split second she saw something in his eyes that gave her hope. Holt relented. "I won't have a thief around."

"You won't. I'll come back and find him." She reached into her vest pocket and pulled out two energy bars and placed them on the log. "In case he returns here." She walked out and Holt followed her.

They made their way down to the horse. "What did you mean you'll be back?" he asked.

"The boy isn't going to survive out here for long. The weather could change, and it could freeze. I can't stop looking for him."

"Okay, then come by the ranch and you can have your own mount."

"So, you've changed your mind about the boy?"

"I've only decided it would be safer if he's found."

Well, Leah decided. This man might have a heart after all.

CHAPTER TWO

IN THE bedroom, later that evening, Leah sat on the bed with Morgan, reliving memories of their childhood.

"You'd still be stuck in that tree if I hadn't found you and got you down," her older sister told her.

"It would have been okay if I hadn't got my jeans caught on the branch," Leah recalled. "Mom wasn't happy that I destroyed my new pants."

"That wasn't all she was worried about. It was your lack of fear. And now, you're out there traveling from continent to continent."

"I can take care of myself." At least physically, Leah thought as pictures of forgotten kids flashed into her head. She shook them away. "Mom doesn't need to worry."

"As if she would ever stop," Morgan said. "You're her baby."

Leah had felt secure in the arms of her family. Unlike her sisters, she couldn't remember any life

before coming to live in Destiny. She considered the
Keenans as her parents. She hadn't been as inquis-
itive as Morgan and Paige about her biological
parents, or why their mother had given up her three
young daughters. This was home and now, that
meant more to her than she could explain.

"Please tell me you're staying for a while."

"I told you I would be here to help with the town's
celebration, and Mom and Dad's anniversary. I don't
have to report for my next assignment for six weeks."
For the first time since she started photographing
third world countries, Leah wasn't eager to return.
The constant sight of famine and war had taken its toll
on her. Suddenly another picture came to mind. That
of the young, thin boy she'd seen at the waterfall.

"What's wrong?" Morgan asked.

"I'm sorry, I'm just worried about the lost boy."

"I can understand," Morgan conceded. "But the
sheriff is looking into any reported runaways. Reed
Larkin is an ex-FBI agent, and he's good at his job."

Leah wasn't worried about the sheriff. It was
Holt Rawlins's attitude that troubled her. "What do
you know about Holt Rawlins?"

"Just what Mom and Dad told you." Her sister's
green gaze showed concern. "A few months ago he
took over the running of the Silver R. He's come
into town a few times, but pretty much keeps to
himself. Speculation is that he's waiting until after
the roundup, then he's going to sell the place."

"Why would a New Yorker spend so much time here?"

Morgan shrugged. "A lot of people want lifestyle changes. Just because you're a globetrotter doesn't mean some of us don't like life in a small town."

"Well, whether he goes or stays, he isn't going to keep me away. I'm headed out there in the morning to continue my search."

"It seems to me you're keeping a pretty close eye on the guy."

Leah stiffened. "Only because Mr. Rawlins seems to have a chip on his shoulder. I don't think he's going to look for the boy."

"So it's Leah to the rescue." Her sister smiled.

Leah only nodded, but knew her track record wasn't that good.

The following morning, Holt came out of the barn to find a compact car pull up at the house. Leah Keenan climbed out and walked toward him. She was dressed in a white blouse, a pullover red sweater and a pair of jeans that molded to that curvy little body of hers. How could someone no bigger than a minute have such long legs?

His gaze moved to her face. Her shiny, wheat-colored hair was pulled back into a ponytail, exposing flawless skin void of any makeup. She walked toward him and her rich brown eyes slowly widened and her full mouth creased in a big smile. Something in his chest tightened when she took off running then he realized her attention wasn't directed at him.

"Zach," she cried as she flew into the arms of the old man standing in the doorway of the barn.

The ranch foreman, Zach Shaw, took her into his arms and hugged her. "Leah," he said. "I heard you came home." He stood back to look at her. "Well, if you aren't still the prettiest girl in town. It's about time you came to see me."

"And if you aren't the biggest fibber ever." She sobered. "I'm so sorry about John. I hope he didn't suffer."

Zach shook his head. "No, it was his heart. He was gone in minutes." The old guy blinked, then smiled. "John talked about you a lot. And he sure enjoyed all the postcards you sent him. He said you'd gone to places whose names he couldn't even pronounce."

"I couldn't pronounce them, either."

They both laughed as Holt watched her wipe stray tears from her eyes and he suddenly felt like the intruder. His own father had known this woman, but never had taken the time to know his own son.

He'd had enough of their friendly chatter. "If you two are finished reminiscing, we need to get started." He walked past them into the barn.

Leah followed. "Just tell me which horse you want me to saddle," she said.

He stopped at the stall. "It's already done."

Zach came up behind them. "I thought you'd do best on Daisy."

Leah patted the mare's neck. "You're a pretty girl," she crooned, then glanced back to Zach. "You didn't have to saddle her."

"I didn't," the old man said. "Holt had her ready before I got the chance."

Holt led his mount toward the door. "I thought it would save us time."

"I'm ready," Leah insisted as she opened the gate, grabbed the reins and followed close behind. "Zach, you want to go with us?"

"No thanks, darlin'." He glanced at Holt. "I'd say this is a two-person job. I'll hold down the fort here. Besides, the little rustler might decide to come back here and steal again."

Leah's gaze shot toward Holt. "Are you sure it was the boy?"

Holt shrugged. "We're short a couple of blankets, a flashlight and some food. What do you think? He came right into the house when we were out with the herd."

"The kid is pretty careful about not being seen," Zach said. "If he's running from someone, that probably means he isn't being treated right."

"And we need to find him," Leah said as she climbed up on Daisy.

"Just be careful, you two," the old man told

them. "Holt, you can handle a horse just fine, but there's a lot in this country you don't know. Leah does. She can lead you to the caves."

Holt nodded. "We should be back in a few hours," he said.

Zach glanced from Holt to Leah and grinned. "Well, if I was a young buck again and had such a pretty companion, I wouldn't be in such a hurry to get back."

Holt grimaced. Damn if the old man wasn't matchmaking.

Leah hadn't realized how much she'd missed riding along a trail in some of the prettiest scenery in the world. She was definitely a mountain girl. She loved everything about the high, jagged peaks that seemed to reach up and touch the sky. Oh, she wished she'd brought her camera.

At least she'd have something to do. She glanced at the man on horseback next to her. Although she'd tried to make polite conversation, Mr. Rawlins wasn't the chatty type. They'd already returned to the cave where they'd found evidence of the boy living there. Everything was gone today. No signs were left of the child.

"Is it just me," Leah began, "or are you like this with everyone?"

He seemed taken aback by her question. "Like what?"

"You haven't said more than a dozen words to me since we left the ranch."

"I didn't think it was required of me to carry on a conversation."

"No, but would it hurt to be cordial?"

He continued to stare ahead. "That all depends on what you want to talk about."

"Well, for starters, why didn't you ever come to visit your father?"

He tensed. "I'm the wrong person to ask that question." He finally turned his green-eyed gaze on her. "I'm sure you or anyone in Destiny knew more about John Rawlins than I did. I haven't seen the man since I was four."

Although Holt Rawlins worked hard to hide it, she caught a flash of sadness in his eyes. And as much as she tried to fight it, his vulnerability got to her. "But John was your father."

"Says you," he said, then guided the horse through a group of trees. "Maybe it would be safer if we concentrated on the task at hand, which seems to be protecting this kid you're so worried about." Even through his gruffness, there was also an undertone of softness in his voice.

"All children need protecting," she said.

"Then, let's find him," he said. "Since he's run off from the cave do you have any idea where he'd go?"

"My biggest fear is that he's holed up in one of

the abandoned mines." She pointed upward toward the foothills.

Holt knew this was a mistake. He should have let the sheriff handle the search for the boy, and then he wouldn't have to deal with Ms. Keenan.

He knew her type. She was out to save the world. Everyone was her friend, and everyone liked her. What wasn't to like? She was beautiful. With her engaging smile that drew you in, it was impossible not to react to her. Those tawny-brown eyes of hers seemed to look too deep…too far inside to see what you didn't want anyone to see.

Yes, he needed to stay far away from the woman. Too bad he hadn't taken his own advice. This morning he'd been up early, waiting and willing to do her bidding.

Holt made a clicking sound with his tongue and the gelding picked up the pace. The sooner they found the kid, the sooner the tempting Leah Keenan would be off his land and out of his life.

About thirty minutes later they reached their destination. Holt followed Leah's lead as she climbed off her mount and tied the bay mare to the tree branch. "The Sunny Days Mine is up there."

Armed with flashlights, she started up the rocky grade with Holt close behind her. To his surprise, she managed to climb with ease. They reached the landing, then another twenty feet they located the mine. The entrance was boarded up and a Keep Out sign nailed across the front. A closer look showed that the barricade had been loosened, making entry easier.

"This is a popular place for teenagers," Leah explained. "It's kind of a rite of passage. They come here to drink and…be with their girlfriends."

Holt pushed back his hat, and rubbed his hand over his unshaven jaw. "This gives Lover's Lane a whole different meaning," he said.

"And it's a whole bunch more dangerous."

He pulled off two loose boards to allow them better access. With flashlights on they ducked into the dark mine. The temperature was a good ten degrees cooler inside and a musty smell assaulted their noses.

Holt directed his light toward the floor, showing dusty evidence of past parties.

"Typical teenagers, they never pick up after themselves," he said.

"We should report this to the sheriff so he can notify the owner to seal the entrance."

"Do you really think that will keep out curious kids?"

Leah ignored Holt's sarcasm. While he examined the main room, she started off toward one of the tunnels, praying she wouldn't find any traces of the boy living here. She ducked through the entry to the tunnel framed by huge wooden support beams. There were old mining tools and stacks of rotten lumber. Just as she walked around the beams, a rat scurried across her path. She gasped and jumped backward tripping over the rotting wood. Unable to regain her balance, she hit the dirt floor as the stack began shifting.

Dust stirred the air and Holt rushed to her side. He swept her up in his arms and carried her out into the main room. Setting her down against the entrance, his large body shielded her from any falling debris. Finally silence filled the air, but he didn't release her. She was trembling, feeling Holt's breath against her ear, his large body against hers.

He looked down at her. "Are you all right?"

She managed to nod.

"Then let's get the hell out of here." He took her hand and drew her outside.

Once in the bright sunlight, he held her at arm's length and did a closer examination. "Do you realize what could have happened to you?"

She was still trembling. "Yes, but I'm okay. Thank you."

That seemed to make him angry. "I don't want your thanks. You could have been seriously hurt or…or…" He turned away, jerked his hat off and combed his hand through his hair. "Dammit, Leah."

Now she was angry with herself. "I know. I shouldn't have gone into the tunnel. I guess I wasn't thinking. I just wanted to find the boy."

"Are you this reckless as a photographer?"

He didn't know the half of it. "They hire me to do my job," she insisted. She started down the slope when he grabbed her wrist and pulled her back. They stood inches apart.

"I'm not taking another step until you promise me not to do anything that crazy again."

The last thing she wanted to do was kowtow to this man, but after he'd rescued her, she owed him one. "Okay, but you need to accept that I mean to find that boy." She glanced up at the sky as the sun suddenly was shadowed by threatening clouds. "We should hurry because we're running out of time." She started down to the horses.

"We're finished for today."

She stopped to argue, but decided it wasn't worth it. "Then I'll go myself."

He gave her an incredulous look. "After what happened in the mine shaft, I'm not letting you out of my sight."

Twenty minutes later they rode back to the ranch, but not before the sky opened up and soaked them before they got into the barn.

The rain pounded against the roof as Leah took Daisy to her stall and began removing her tack. She placed the mare's saddle on the railing, then started wiping down the animal. Once her horse was settled, Leah went to put the saddle away.

"Let me get that," Holt said as he came up behind her.

"I can manage." She glanced at him. He removed his hat and for the first time she got a good look at his handsome face. His sandy-colored hair was wavy and fell against his forehead, and his startling green eyes were framed by long dark lashes. "I…I know where everything goes."

"As do I." He took the saddle from her and continued down the aisle. She went back for the bridle and blanket and hurried to catch up with him in the tack room.

Leah hung it on the wall. "Well…I guess that's it." She turned around to discover Holt watching her. The direction of his heated gaze was on her rain-soaked blouse. At first she resisted the urge to cover herself, but then a clap of thunder shook the barn along with the pounding of the rain. She shivered and crossed her arms over her breasts.

Holt couldn't help but stare. Even soaking wet Leah Keenan was far too appealing. His protective instincts took over and he reached for a blanket. He went to her and draped it around her shoulders. Then he made a big mistake and looked into her big brown eyes. "I think you should wait out the storm here."

"Okay," she whispered. "I'll stay out of your way."

"I have a better idea. Why don't you come up to the house and get out of those wet clothes?"

Her eyes rounded. "I'm fine right here."

"Don't look so frightened, I'm not going to attack you."

She straightened. "I never thought you were. I just didn't want to put you out."

"It's a little late for that," he said as he took her elbow and guided her toward the door. "Come on, the rain has eased up a little."

Together they headed for the house. By the time they reached the porch, they were both soaked again. Holt pushed open the back door and let her inside the mudroom.

"We better take off our boots, or Maria will have our heads for tracking up the kitchen."

"Maria Silva?" Leah looked up from unlacing her boots. "She still works here?"

Holt nodded. "She cleans once a week, and prepares some of the meals."

"Lucky you. She's a great cook."

"I can cook, but after a long day of work, it's been nice not to have to." He went into the main part of the house. He grabbed a towel—and the only thing available for her to change into—one of his flannel shirts. He returned to her.

"I don't own a robe, so this is all I have. While your wet clothes are in the dryer put this on."

"I don't need to change."

"You're shivering. Do it or Zach will kick my butt for letting you catch cold."

"Okay." Leah took the shirt and followed him through the kitchen and down the hall.

He pointed to a closed door. "That's a bathroom." "If you want you can take a hot shower."

Holt climbed the stairs to the second floor of the large ranch house. He definitely didn't need a hot one, he thought as he went into the master bedroom that once belonged to his father. The large sleigh bed was a dark mahogany covered in a multicolored quilt. The small print wallpaper had faded over the years. A braided rug partly covered the hardwood floor that Maria kept polished to a high gloss.

There weren't any pictures of family and none of him, even as a boy. Holt tried to push aside the memories of a man who wanted nothing to do with his son. His only child.

There were three other bedrooms on the second floor, but Holt told himself the reason he stayed in this room was because of the connecting bath. He began stripping off his clothes and heard the water go on downstairs. Great, that was all he needed, the image of a naked Leah Keenan in his bathroom. He got in the shower and turned on the faucet to cold.

But ten minutes later, he went downstairs and found Leah in the kitchen. He swallowed hard. She was dressed only in his shirt. Her face was scrubbed clean and the blond hair pooled wet against her shoulders was beginning to curl.

"Hi," she said. "I hope you don't mind, I fixed some coffee."

She'd made herself at home. "Sounds good," he told her. "I take it you know your way around here."

Leah sipped from her cup. "I'm sorry, it's just that while I was in high school, I used to spend a lot of time here taking pictures."

He tried not to look at her legs, but it was impossible not to, even for a saint and he wasn't anywhere close to being a saint. Her smooth, shapely calves and trim thighs made his mouth water as the edge of his plaid shirt cut off any more view. He took a gulp of the hot coffee, nearly scalding his throat.

He went to the refrigerator and pulled open the door to the cool air. "How about some lunch?"

She came up beside him, too close and smelling of his soap. "Only if you'll allow me to fix it."

Holt stepped back. "Sure. There are cold cuts in the meat bin. I'll get the bread."

She touched his arm to stop him. "I can do it. Please, Holt, go and sit down."

He nodded, went to the large oval table, pulled out a chair and sat. He couldn't help but watch as she moved efficiently around the kitchen. She laid out the bread on the white-tiled countertop, and layered the cooked ham on top, then added lettuce and tomato. He was handling things just fine until she went to the maple cabinets and reached up for plates. That was when the shirt rose high, exposing the back of her smooth rounded thighs.

Damn. He glanced away. A man could only take so much. Suddenly the back door slammed and in seconds Zach appeared in the kitchen.

The old foreman glanced around the room. His hazel eyes sparkling as he grinned. "Well, if this doesn't look cozy."

CHAPTER THREE

LEAH realized what her being half naked and standing in the Rawlins's kitchen must look like. But she pushed aside her embarrassment, put a smile on her face and went to greet Zach.

"You're just in time for lunch," she announced. "Do you want a ham or a turkey sandwich?"

The foreman glanced at Holt. "I don't want to interrupt…"

"Since when has that ever stopped you?" Holt told him. "You might as well sit down. We're just killing time until Leah's clothes dry."

"So you two got caught in the storm?"

"We were headed back," Leah said. Why was she feeling guilty? "Sure you don't want a sandwich, Zach?"

"Well…if it's not too much trouble." The foreman went to the table and sat down across from Holt.

Leah smiled. "Not for you."

"I take it you didn't have any luck finding the boy," Zach said.

"No, but I'm not giving up," she assured him. "He's out there somewhere." She turned back to her task at the counter.

"I think he's moved on," Holt said. "We haven't seen any sign of him since yesterday morning."

Leah placed the sandwiches on mismatched plates from the cupboard and carried them to the table. "That doesn't mean he isn't out there." She went back and poured two glasses of milk, staying busy to keep calm. "I have some places to check tomorrow." She sat down next to Zach, tugging her makeshift robe over her knees. "I thought I'd try the old Hutchinson mine up on the south ridge."

"That's a thought," Zach said. "There's water close by and even though the cabin is old, it's still in good shape." He bit into his sandwich.

"Hey, don't I have a say in this?" Holt asked. "I can't keep traipsing around the countryside looking for a kid who doesn't want to be found."

Leah tensed. "Then I'll go by myself."

"Not without my permission."

She caught his determined gaze, but she wasn't intimidated. "I'm sure the sheriff could get some volunteers together within an hour and search until nightfall."

Holt glared. "I don't like being threatened."

"Not any more than I like to think about a child

being left out there alone." She got up from the table, went to the mudroom and slammed the door behind her.

"Well, you've done it now," Zach said as he looked at Holt. "Maybe where you come from people don't care about other people, but around here we take care of our own. If you won't go with Leah, then I will."

Holt tensed, knowing it wasn't true that everyone in Destiny took care of, *their own*. His father hadn't. Something tightened in his chest. Even Holt wasn't so callous as to let a kid roam around the wilderness.

"Will you stop grumbling? I didn't say I wouldn't go." Ignoring the gleam in the old man's eyes, he stood and went to the mudroom. He opened the door just in time to see Leah pull her jeans over those long smooth legs.

Damn. His body suddenly stirred to life.

She jerked around and fisted the shirt edges together. "Do you mind?"

Holt leaned against the doorjamb as if the intimacy of watching her didn't bother him at all. Like hell. He forced a smile. "Not at all."

Leah turned her back on him and fastened the jeans. "I'm going back to town now. I'll get your shirt back to you."

"Keep it as long as you want. It looks a lot better on you anyway."

She ignored him and pulled on her boots, then

grabbed her blouse and bra off the dryer. "I'll be back tomorrow."

He nodded. "I'll have the horses saddled about eight."

She froze. "But I thought—"

"I only said I couldn't keep doing this all day…every day. I do have to help Zach with chores, and we're trying to organize the roundup."

"I know." Her expression softened as she came closer. "Holt, I appreciate your time and help, especially after the mishap in the mine."

She looked young…and innocent as she flashed those big brown eyes at him. He felt the reaction deep in his gut. She drew more than protective instincts from him. "That's why you shouldn't go into those mines alone."

Leah nibbled on her lower lip. "So…I guess I'll see you tomorrow morning," she said.

Holt nodded, not trusting himself with saying anything more.

"Goodbye," she said, then darted out the door and down the steps. The rain had slowed to a soft drizzle, but she seemed to hardly notice it. Leah raised her face skyward and drew a deep breath before she got into her car.

From the window he watched her drive off. Had he ever been that carefree? He knew the answer to that. He'd been driven all his life. His mother, Elizabeth Pershing, had expected certain things from her only child. He had to uphold the blue-blood old Boston Pershing family's name. And being the son of a Colorado rancher had already been a black mark against him. As hard as he tried, Holt never felt good enough to be a Pershing. He'd once overheard his grandparents say that Elizabeth had made a mistake marrying, and having a child with John Rawlins. Holt never doubted that he was the "mistake."

The one difference between himself and his mother was he'd finally stopped trying to please the family. When he'd heard of John Rawlins's death—and even with his Grandmother Pershing's threats to disinherit him—Holt had quit his job and moved to Colorado to take over the ranch.

He walked away from his career and from the woman he supposedly loved. Melanie was everything a man could want. But when she wanted to settle down and start a family, he couldn't take that step.

He wasn't sure if he was capable of love.

"Leah, did you hear what I said?" Morgan asked.

"What?" Leah glanced at her sister, embarrassed that she'd been caught daydreaming.

"I asked if you think the church hall is big enough for Mom and Dad's anniversary party."

"Well, you should know better than I do. How many people will the place hold? Are we inviting the entire town?"

The always organized and composed Morgan looked anything but that today. "I'm not sure," she said. "It's just that we've got the town's Founder's Day celebration at the same time."

Morgan was the only one of the Keenan sisters who had stayed in Destiny. Leah had taken off to photograph the world. Paige, with her law degree, took a job with the D.A. in Denver. Morgan's dream had always been to teach school. But while she'd been student teaching in an inner-city school, she'd suddenly come home. To stay. She'd said that she'd changed her mind about her career, then soon after opened a gift shop in the Keenan Inn. Since then Morgan hadn't traveled any farther away from Destiny than Durango. She'd been the one here for the family, especially her sisters.

Leah decided it was about time she and Paige helped out.

"When did you say Paige was coming home?" Leah asked.

"Not sure. The last time I talked to her she was working on a big criminal case. She's hoping she'll make it by the end of the month."

Leah frowned. "That only leaves us two weeks before the party."

"I'll take whatever I can get." Morgan smiled. "I'm just glad you could get so much time off. Three years is too long to be away."

Guilt made Leah blush. "You always knew I was

an eager kid with big dreams. I had to grab an opportunity when it was handed to me."

"Are you sorry?" Morgan asked.

"Of course there are times," Leah began, "that I missed the family." So many nights she'd cried herself to sleep after she photographed all the pain and suffering. It was what hadn't gone into print that truly haunted her. She sighed. "But *Our World* magazine gave me an opportunity I couldn't pass up." For the last three years, she'd led Morgan to think her life was so glamorous, but the faces of the children she had to walk away from would bother her always.

Leah forced aside the memories and smiled. "I wish I'd had better accommodations. Most of the places I went didn't even have running water, or toilets." Or any respect for life.

"Well, we for sure can give you better living quarters. I just hope you don't get bored."

On the contrary, Leah welcomed the peace and quiet of her hometown. Her thoughts turned to Destiny's new resident, Holt Rawlins. He hadn't exactly made her feel peaceful. "I think I can stay busy enough."

"If you're talking about the runaway boy, maybe I should give Reed a call. As sheriff he could get together a lot of volunteers."

"I'm just afraid that we'll drive him deeper into

the woods. Maybe it's better if Holt and I go out tomorrow alone."

"You've been in town for only a few days and you've seen more of our new resident than we have in the past four months." Morgan's eyes widened. "What's he like?"

Leah shrugged. "I see a strong physical resemblance, but he's nothing like John. Has he made friends with anyone in town?"

"Outside of the few times I've seen him at the grocery store or the trading post, he's pretty much kept to himself. He's cordial and polite. Maybe you should invite him to a town meeting and introduce him around."

Leah wasn't sure Holt wanted to make friends. "Doesn't it seem strange that John never mentioned a son?" Leah asked. "Why he never had a relationship with Holt?"

Morgan shrugged. "Could be the divorce was a bitter one, and it's difficult to keep a long-distance father/son relationship going."

Leah drew a breath. "It's still hard for me to imagine John Rawlins ignoring his own child."

"It happens," Morgan told her. "Look at us. Our birth mother never came back to get us."

It was no secret that twenty-seven years ago three girls—two toddlers and an infant—were left at the inn for the childless Keenans to raise. There had never been much discussion about the girls' biological parents. Why would a mother just leave her daughters?

Morgan looked at her sister. "Sometimes parents can't keep their promises."

The next morning, although the sun was shining, the weather was still chilly. It was a perfect day for a ride. Leah brought her camera this time and tucked it away in her saddlebag. She wasn't going to waste this incredible scenery.

Riding Daisy, Leah followed behind Holt on the trail. They'd already checked out two abandoned mines. Only this time, Holt had her stay outside while he looked around. As much as she wanted to protest, she knew better than to push him anymore. So she busied herself taking pictures.

As they headed back they approached the water-fall. Holt reined his horse and turned toward her. He pushed his hat back exposing his handsome face. "How about we take a break?"

"Sure why not."

Leah climbed down and retrieved her camera. She started toward the rushing water, feeling the temperature cool. The fresh mountain air was re-freshing and a fine mist caressed her face as she climbed over the rocky base to find the best angle to shoot a picture. Poised with her camera, Leah was in her own world when she shifted and began to slip. She gasped. Suddenly a pair of strong arms circled her waist and kept her from falling in the water.

Leah regained her footing, then looked up into Holt's green eyes. Her heart raced. "Sorry, I lost my balance."

He gave her a hint of a smile. "Seems that's been happening to you a lot lately."

"I'll try to be more careful." She regained her footing, and climbed onto a big boulder to look around. "That's where I first saw him." She pointed. "At the edge of the pool."

Holt took in the incredible sight of his own piece of Shangri-la. Crystal-clear water sheeted over the granite that protruded from the mountainside. Several large boulders circled the small pond below, its bottom covered by colorful rocks. He heard a clicking sound and glanced back at Leah. She was taking his picture.

"Surely you can find a better subject than me."

"Maybe, but right now you're all I've got." He caught her sly smile. "Just don't turn grumpy on me."

He surprised himself and smiled. "You're pretty sassy for…a kid."

She moved and took another picture. "You need your eyes checked. I'm not a kid."

"There's nothing wrong with my eyesight." He flashed back to yesterday with her in his shirt. Her long legs. "You might be full grown, but in years, you're still a kid."

"And you're so old."

She lowered her camera and he caught a flash of sadness in her eyes. His chest tightened and he wanted to go to her, but decided it wasn't wise to pursue it.

"What do you say we have some lunch? Maria made sandwiches."

He made his way to his horse and returned with a saddlebag and blanket. He found a big flat boulder and spread out the blanket. Leah sat down on the far edge…keeping her distance. Was she really so afraid of him? Maybe she was wise to be afraid.

"Is there anywhere else we should look?" he asked, handing her a wrapped sandwich.

Leah was getting discouraged. Where had the boy gone? She prayed he was safe. "I can't think of where he'd go."

"He must be a pretty bright kid to outsmart adults," Holt said.

She looked him in the eye. "Or he doesn't trust them." She took a bite of her sandwich. "Maybe they've let him down. But surely his parents would put out a missing persons report."

"Not all parents are like yours," he said, looking at her. "Some don't have time for their kids."

Leah saw the pain on his face, the sudden distant look in his eyes that suggested his childhood wasn't ideal. Before she could speak, he moved toward her.

"Don't turn around but your little friend is hiding just behind the falls."

Leah gasped as Holt's arms encircled her shoulders. "I'm going to try to get a better look, so go along."

She nodded. "Okay, but don't frighten him off."

Holt smiled. "Then you better help." His head lowered as his arms went around her back and drew her closer. She tried not to react, but he radiated heat, and there was the feel of his muscular chest. When he nuzzled her neck she had to fight her response.

"The little thief is moving closer to the edge of the water."

Holt shifted so his mouth was close to her ear. She could feel his warm breath, the brush of his lips as he spoke. Agonizingly sensitive to even such a slight touch of his mouth, the delicate outer curve of her ear seemed to tingle and burn.

"You were right, he's only about eight or nine, dirty blond hair."

"That's him," she whispered. "How are we going to convince him we're here to help?"

His lips moved to her cheek, then her jawline. She shivered as an ache started in her chest and began to shift lower. She didn't need this complication. A man like Holt wasn't good for her. "Is this a good idea?"

He raised his head just inches and stared down at her. "I'm not sure...you tell me." Just then his mouth closed over hers.

Leah was totally lost in the kiss as Holt drew her closer against his body. Wrapping her arms around his neck, she forgot everything but the feel of Holt's mouth against hers. Then slowly he lifted his head, breaking the intimate contact. He sucked in a shaky breath as his eyes drifted open and locked with hers, revealing the heat in the emerald depths.

Suddenly he blinked and turned his attention over her shoulder. "Damn. He's gone."

Before Leah could clear her head, Holt took off after the kid. She scrambled to her feet and hurried along the edge of the pond behind Holt. There was no sign of the boy.

"We lost him."

"I thought you were watching him," she said accusingly, hating that she let this man affect her.

He combed his fingers through his hair. "I was until you decided to be a participant in the kiss."

"Me? You're blaming me for distracting you? It was your idea."

He came up to her, displaying the heat in his eyes. "Yes, and it was a really bad idea."

Holt was silent all the way back to the ranch. Fine. Leah wasn't taking the blame for losing sight of the boy. And she was still blaming herself for losing herself in the kiss, no matter how incredible. But just because there were sparks didn't mean they should do anything about it.

Outside the barn, they dismounted. "Okay, now I have to call the sheriff," she told him.

"Go ahead, but I'm telling you that kid doesn't want to be found," Holt argued.

"Then we're going to have to persuade him we want to help him." She tugged on the reins and led her horse into the barn. Once in the stall, she began to unfasten the cinch straps, then she lifted the saddle off and put it away in the tack room. They'd had three days, and hadn't been able to find one young boy. It was time she called the sheriff.

After putting everything away, she returned to the stall. That was when she saw Zach and Holt at the other end of the aisle and went to tell them of her plans.

Holt took her by the arm. "We need to go up to the house and talk." He started to walk, pulling her along with him.

Leah resisted. "What do we need to talk about?"

His eyes narrowed. "Things."

This time Zach joined in. "Yeah, things."

Leah allowed the two men to lead her outside and up to the house. Once in the kitchen, she swung around.

"You're not going to talk me out of calling the sheriff. We can't find the boy on our own, and it's going to be pretty cold tonight."

"He's living in the barn," Holt said calmly.

"You're kidding." She could believe their good luck. "Really?"

Zach nodded. "I had to go up to the loft earlier. I found a blanket, some clothes and a stash of food."

"That kid has been stealing things right from the house," Holt said accusingly.

"He's trying to survive the only way he can," she pleaded, wondering if this man actually had a heart.

"Well, he can't do it in my barn."

Leah shook with anger. "Of course not. That would be too much trouble for you. That child needs help and you're only worried that he's taken a few of your precious things. I bet you didn't even miss them."

Holt glared. "You know I'm getting tired of being the bad guy. I just meant that a barn is no place for a kid to live. Go ahead, call the sheriff and tell him to come out here." He walked out, letting the back door slam shut.

She looked at Zach. "What's he going to do?"

"Nothing as bad as what you're thinking. He's probably going to find the boy."

"Great," she grumbled and had started after him when the phone rang.

Zach answered it and called her back. "It's your sister."

Leah took the receiver. "Hello, Morgan."

"Leah, the sheriff is on his way out. There's a report of a missing boy from Durango. The boy that fits your description is Corey Haynes. He ran away from his foster home."

"He's been hiding in Holt's barn, in the loft. I've got to go."

Leah hung up and ran for the door. "His name is Corey," she called to Zach.

Running down the steps, she saw Holt with Corey in tow. His hand was around the boy's skinny arm, pulling him toward the house. His clothes were filthy, shirt and jeans were torn, and his white tennis shoes nearly black. The child cursed as he resisted their forward progress.

Leah ran to meet them. "Corey, it's okay. You're safe now," she told him.

He continued to fight Holt. "Just let me go and I'll leave."

Holt finally managed to get the kid into the kitchen. Pulling out a chair, he parked him there, but he jumped up. Holt pushed him back down, feeling the tender spots on his shins, knowing he'd probably have bruises tomorrow.

"Sit down, or I'll tie you down."

Fear filled the kid's blue eyes, but also defiance. Then surprising Holt, he sat down. Holt grabbed another chair, swung it around and straddled it in front of the boy. "Okay, kid, I need a name and where you came from."

"I'm not going to tell you shi—nothin'." Head bent, he stared at the kitchen floor.

"Is it Corey?" Leah asked. "Corey Haynes?"

The boy looked at her and blinked those innocent blue eyes at her. "I don't know any Corey."

Leah squatted down beside the boy. "Corey, you don't have to be afraid. We're here to help you."

"Yeah, I heard that before," he muttered. "Just let me go."

"No way," Holt said. "You can't live in caves."

"Why not? It was a lot better than where I was." Tears flooded his eyes and he swiped them away.

Leah gave Holt a pleading look. He could see she'd already lost her heart to this kid. "Were you mistreated?" She touched the boy's arm and he didn't pull away.

"What difference does it make? Nobody cares."

"I care, Corey," she insisted. "I want to help you."

He looked up and his dirty face was streaked with tears. "Why?"

"Because you deserve better than you're getting." She moved in closer and pulled the child into an embrace. Her nurturing touch seemed as natural as her next breath. "No child should have to live in a cave, or a barn. You should feel safe and secure. And clean." She wrinkled her nose. "You don't exactly smell too great."

She rose and looked again at Holt. "He needs a shower. Is it okay?"

How could he deny her? "Sure…why not."

"How about I take him?" Zach said.

"Will you go with Zach, Corey?"

The boy hesitated. "Will you be here when I get back?"

Smiling, she brushed his shaggy hair off his forehead. "Yes. Just scrub from head to toe."

"I'll make sure he does," Zach said as he led the boy down the hall and into the bath.

Leah turned toward Holt. "Oh, I never thought to ask, do you have anything Corey can wear?"

"Zach will come up with something."

The last thing Holt wanted to do was get involved with this kid's problems. But from the moment he'd found Leah on his property, she'd managed to draw him into her search. He'd followed her around, looking in every cave and mine shaft for a kid who didn't want to be found. He'd gotten far more involved with her than was good for him, especially after the kiss. Not one of his best ideas.

"You think just because he gets cleaned up that's going to make things better?" he told her.

"It's a start," she said, folding her arms over her chest stubbornly. "And I'm not going to abandon him."

"Looks like you might not have a choice," he said. "The kid's a runaway. And once the sheriff gets here he'll have to go back to his foster home."

"The kid's name is Corey Haynes. And he'll never go back to an abusive home. Not if I have anything to say about it."

"You don't know anything about his situation. And you won't have anything to say about whether or not he goes back."

She stood there and stared at him. "What in your life has made you so bitter?"

He didn't need her snooping into his private life. "Not everyone has had a life as secure and charmed as the Keenan girls."

Leah started to speak when there was a knock at the back door. Holt went to answer it.

"Hello, I'm Sheriff Reed Larkin," the man standing outside said.

Holt shook his hand. "Holt Rawlins."

"I knew your father," the sheriff said. "Sorry for your loss."

Holt responded with a nod, and motioned for the man to come inside to the kitchen where Leah was waiting.

"Hi, Reed."

"Hello, Leah. Looks like you've been busy since you got home."

Leah caught the good-looking sheriff's grin. Tall and muscular, Reed had nearly black hair and dark brown eyes and he'd always been crazy about her sister Paige.

"You know me, Reed, I get bored easily."

"You still should have called me to let me know about the boy." He pulled out his notepad along with a grainy picture. "This is the runaway, Corey Haynes, age eight."

"That's him," Leah agreed. "But we can't send him back to his foster home. The boy has been gone nearly a week. Why didn't the foster parents report him missing until today?"

Reed nodded. "They're being investigated, so the boy has a reprieve…for now. But he'll have to go to a shelter for a few nights."

"No," Leah said, her gaze darted back and forth between the two men. "I promised Corey that I wouldn't let you take him back."

"Leah, there isn't much else I can do," Reed said. "His mother is deceased and his father's in jail on a robbery charge. There's no one. And foster homes are overcrowded."

"He'll just run away again," Leah said.

The sheriff was about to argue when his radio went off. "Excuse me, I need to take this." Reed stepped onto the porch.

Holt watched as Leah paced nervously. He knew from the beginning how involved she'd gotten in the boy. He told himself that he'd done his duty by finding the kid. That there was a nice foster home that would care for him. But seeing the frightened look on the boy's face, he knew that wasn't true.

They both turned to the sheriff when he came back in the door. "Sorry, that was Social Services…they were letting me know that there are no foster homes available. So that means I have to take him to Durango to a group home."

"No, you can't," Leah cried. "Maybe my parents will let Corey stay—"

"He can stay here…" Holt interrupted her. "We'll give it a try anyway."

Leah's gaze darted to Holt. "Here?"

"No offence, Mr. Rawlins," the sheriff began, "but I don't know you. And if I were to recommend you for temporary foster care say for the next few days, I'd need more—"

"I know him," Leah jumped in. "We've spent the last three days together searching for Corey. And…Zach's here, too. He'll be around."

Holt watched as Reed contemplated the suggestion. "And Leah will be staying here, too," he added.

"You sure about this?" Reed Larkin asked.

Leah tried to hide her surprise at Holt's suggestion. She would do anything to keep the boy safe…even live under the same roof with this man. "It's time Corey started believing in someone," she said. "Besides, until we find a suitable home for the child, this is the best solution."

Reed looked at Holt. "I'll get in touch with Social Services and they'll be contacting you." The sheriff paused. "Are you sure this is what you want?"

Leah held her breath waiting for the answer.

"I'm sure," Holt said.

"They'll probably send someone out to your house."

"That's fine. I have nothing to hide."

Just then Corey came into the kitchen. He was scrubbed clean. His hair was two shades lighter, and he was wearing an oversize white T-shirt that hung past his knees with a pair of socks on his feet. The boy's smile disappeared when he saw the man in uniform.

Leah went to him. "It's okay, Corey. This is Sheriff Reed. He's going to let you stay here with Holt for a few days. Is that okay with you?"

Corey looked at her. "Will you be here, too?"

"Sure, for as long as you and Holt need me."

CHAPTER FOUR

LEAH rolled over in bed and opened her eyes to sunshine coming through the window. She wasn't in her bedroom at the inn. Sitting up, she glanced around the space and slowly began to remember.

She was in the guest room at the Silver R Ranch. In an old iron-framed bed covered in a wedding ring quilt, and wearing one of Holt's white T-shirts. The panicked look on Corey's face had prevented her from leaving last night, not even for the short time it would have taken to get some clean clothes. At least she'd called her family and told them about the situation.

Leah pushed back the covers and got up. She retrieved her jeans from the chair in the corner, pulled them on, along with her blouse and stepped into her boots.

After brushing her hair Leah walked down the hall of the big, old ranch house. Obviously the place had been neglected for years, but there was beauty hidden under the faded wallpaper and worn carpet. The hallway led into four bedrooms, and a bathroom and the master suite at the far end.

At the top of the curved staircase, she held on to the oak banister and started down the wide steps covered in a dark brown runner. At the landing, halfway down she faced the entry at the front of the house and the solid oak door that had weathered over the years. She descended the remaining steps, thinking this place would make a wonderful home.

She headed for the kitchen in search of the new owner. In the doorway she stopped to see Holt Rawlins standing at the old stove, a towel tucked in the waist of his faded jeans. He wore a chambray shirt and scuffed boots.

She smiled. If only she had her camera.

A sullen Corey was busy setting the table and neither one were talking. Disappointed, she'd hoped that some sort of bonding would take place between the two. Obviously that was going to take a little more time. So as not to disturb them she was about to return to the bedroom when Corey looked in her direction.

"Leah," the boy called. "You're awake."

Upbeat, she walked into the kitchen. "I sure am. I smelled breakfast and couldn't wait to eat." She looked at Holt. "What do you need me to do?"

"Nothing," Holt said. "I have everything under control. There's coffee in the pot."

Even in his own home, he was a man of few

words, she conceded. She went to the coffeemaker. Once she doctored her brew, she took a long sip. "It's good."

Holt continued cracking eggs into the skillet. "How can you tell? You add so much cream and sugar."

"Not so much. It's just most men make it so strong."

He gave her a sideways glance. "I'm not most men."

True, she'd never met anyone like him. Someone who was so stubborn, brooding…handsome.

"How did you sleep?" he asked.

"Not too bad."

Their gazes locked, and Leah's heart began to race. She doubted it had anything to do with the caffeine. "So, how long have you been up?" she asked.

"Since five-thirty."

"You should have got me up. I could have helped with the chores."

"We finished them fast," Holt assured her.

"You and Zach?"

"And Corey."

The boy walked to the cupboard and took down plates. "Holt woke me up to help feed the horses."

She set her mug on the counter. "Well, on a ranch there are chores that have to be done. Animals have to be cared for."

"That's what Zach said," Corey told her as he carried the plates to the table. "Do you know that Lulu is going to have a foal in a few weeks?"

"I remember Lulu," Leah said, recalling John's favorite mare. "A pretty chestnut." A loaf of bread was on the counter. She took out four slices and dropped them in the toaster.

"Zach said that if I'm here I can watch the foal being born. He said it'll be Holt's first time, too, because he never lived on a ranch until four months ago. He came from New York." The boy took a breath and went to get the flatware. "Have you ever been to New York?"

Leah glanced at Holt and saw him in a whole new light. So the man was trying. "Yes, I have, Corey. It's a big place," she answered.

"I only lived in Texas and Colorado. My dad used to work in the mines until they shut down." The boy's expression grew sad. "He couldn't get a job after that and we had to move a lot."

Before Leah could comfort him the back door opened and Zach walked in. "Hey, looks like I'm right on time."

Corey went to him. "Breakfast is almost ready, Zach. After we eat can I go with you and Holt to feed the herd?"

The older man frowned. "That all depends. We still have to finish some chores around here."

"I can help, too." The boy's eyes lit up. "I'm a

good worker. I made my bed and cleaned up the bathroom like Holt asked."

"That's good, because everyone around here has to carry their weight." Zach poked the boy in the stomach and made him laugh. "First, we need to eat so you can put some meat on your skinny bones."

"Breakfast is ready," Holt called as he carried a platter of eggs and bacon to the table.

Leah buttered the toast, then took her contribution and set the plate down next to a jar of jelly. After the food was distributed, Corey asked if she was going to come with them.

"I need to go into town this morning." She caught a sad look from Corey. "Just to pick up some clothes. Don't worry, I'll be back in a few hours. In fact, I'll fix dinner tonight."

"Promise?" the boy asked.

The panic on Corey's face caused her pain. If she could help it, she'd never break another promise to a child again.

"That poor boy," Claire Keenan said as she sat across from Leah at the inn's kitchen. It was probably the first time her mother had been off her feet in hours.

"So I didn't feel I had a choice. I have to stay at the ranch."

"First thing this morning, I called Esther Perkins at the church. She's rounding up some clothes for the boy."

"Thanks, Mom. I'm also going to stop by the trading post and get him some underwear and socks—and a pair of shoes. He has a pair of old tennis shoes that I don't think even fit him." She thought about Corey's former foster family and got angry all over again.

"I know you've wanted to help this child, Leah, but I'm concerned about you, too. You've gotten so involved in the situation… Are you going to be all right when he goes to a foster home?"

Leah wasn't ready to talk about her own demons. She only knew that she couldn't walk away from this boy… Not like she had before with another child in another place, another time.

"It's Holt Rawlins who's taken the responsibility for Corey. I'm just helping him out."

"You've moved out to the ranch. I'd say you were helping quite a bit."

"Mom, how can you talk when years ago you and Dad took us in."

Claire Keenan smiled, tiny lines crinkling around her beautiful eyes. "Outside of marrying your father, it was the best day of my life. And from the moment we saw you, we fell in love with you, Morgan and Paige."

Leah grasped her mother's hand across the table. "And I love you and Dad. But please try to understand that since I'm the one who found Corey I do feel responsible." She blinked back tears. "It sounds crazy, but it's as if I were meant to help him."

"And he's lucky to have you," her mother continued. "I'm just concerned about what happens when you have to leave for your next photography assignment."

Leah didn't want to think about that. "I'd never hurt Corey intentionally."

"I know, but a lot of people deserted him in the past."

She groaned. "I have six weeks off. Maybe he'll be in a good foster home by then."

"Or maybe Holt Rawlins will keep the boy with him."

Leah frowned. "Well, they were getting along better this morning." But Holt as a foster parent? That was too much to expect. "I assume Holt will be going back to New York."

"That's not what I heard."

They both turned as Morgan walked into the kitchen.

Dressed in a far too long and loose fitting dress, her sister seemed determined to play down her beauty. She came to the table. "Mr. Rawlins has taken the Silver R Ranch off the market," she told them.

"Holt Rawlins is going to stay and run the ranch?"

Morgan shrugged. "That's what Susan Horan told me this morning. She's the real estate agent who was handling the property."

Leah had thought that Holt's plan was to go back to New York…and his life there. She wondered if there was someone special in his life. Her thoughts took her back to what happened at the waterfall yesterday. How could there be another woman when Holt had kissed her like he had?

"So tell me, little sister, you're home less than a week and you've already managed to move in with the best-looking man in town."

She frowned. "Morgan, you know why I stayed at the ranch last night. Because a frightened little boy needed me."

"I know." She raised her hand. "But you have to admit Holt Rawlins is a good-looking cowboy."

"Cowboy? Holt Rawlins is from the East."

Morgan's eyebrows rose. "Then let's agree he's got a lot of his father in him. The man could be on a billboard. Just ask any woman in town."

No one had to tell that to Leah. She could still see his smile, feel his touch and taste his kiss.

"Of course the town council was hoping to get a section of the Rawlins property," Morgan said.

"Why?"

"We're interested in promoting more tourism for revenue. A new ski area and hiking trails are at the top of the list. The Silver R's property cuts off access to what we have. I approached John about it, but we never really got down to the details before he passed away." She smiled at Leah. "Since you know Holt better than anyone else in town, I thought maybe you could talk to him."

"Oh, no." Leah jumped up. "The man barely tolerates me. And I don't know him that well"

"Sure. That's why he asked you to move in and help him with a runaway boy?"

"No, because Sheriff Larkin was threatening to take Corey to a group home." Leah paced. The one thing she did know about Holt was he was leery of people, especially of his father's friends. "Give me a few days to see how things go with Corey. Then I'll introduce you to Holt and you can ask him." She checked her watch. "I need to go shopping for a young man."

Leah spotted the apple pies cooling on the counter. "Hey, Mom, you wouldn't have any extra, would you?"

"Oh, I think your father can get by with one pie."

Pie in hand, Leah kissed her mother and sister goodbye and took off to do her errands. The first stop was the trading post to pick out clothes for Corey. She couldn't help but wonder how long it had been since the boy had anything but hand-me-downs. Well, a new pair of jeans and a shirt was a must. She walked by the shoe section and spotted a pair of buckskin boots.

She smiled. Every cowboy needs his own pair of boots.

* * *

Leah arrived back at the Silver R Ranch about two o'clock in the afternoon. When she found the house deserted, she went down to the barn. No one was there, either. It wasn't until she heard voices that she wandered outside to the corral where Corey sat on top of Daisy and was being led by Zach around the arena.

Holt sat on the fence as Corey took instructions on riding. Leah took the time to watch the man on the railing. As much as he tried to act indifferent, she could see he was intensely interested in the boy's progress.

Why did Holt hold himself so apart? What had happened between John and Holt to keep a father away from his son? She had a dozen questions that she knew she wouldn't get answered anytime soon. So she focused on the happy looking boy on the horse. Maybe Corey would be the one who broke through the man's tough shell.

One could always hope.

Suddenly Holt's face went through a transformation. His mouth twitched and curved into a hint of a smile.

The sound of Corey's laughter made her turn to the small rider on the horse. Zach had let go of the bridle so the boy handled the reins on his own. The youngster beamed as he sat high in the saddle and directed the horse around the corral.

"You're doing great, son," Zach called.

Leah watched as Corey glanced toward Holt. Even she could see that the boy wanted his approval.

She strolled to the fence, climbed onto the railing and sat down next to Holt. "Corey's doing great."

"Zach's been working with him." Holt turned to her. "Did you bring your things?"

"Yes," she told him. "Enough for a few days. I also picked up some clothes for Corey."

"The sheriff stopped by about an hour ago. He dropped off what the boy had at the foster home. Just some old clothes and another pair of worn tennis shoes, barely enough to fit into a grocery sack. I almost tossed it in the trash. But Corey grabbed the bag and took it into his bedroom as if it were some sort of treasure." He sighed and tipped his hat back.

"Oh, Holt. That's so sad."

"Yeah, and it doesn't get any better. Seems Corey's dad is in prison, and he isn't eligible for parole for a long time."

Her heart ached. "So he's been in foster homes for a while."

He nodded. "Speaking of which, Reed also said we'd be getting a visit from Social Services. Probably tomorrow." His gaze met hers. "I want you there with me."

Leah felt the heat from his look, trying to tell

herself this was only for the boy's sake. "Of course. And I want to thank you for doing this for Corey."

"It's temporary, Leah. I can't offer the boy any more."

She wanted to argue the point, but saw the pain in Holt's eyes. There were so many things she wanted to know about this man. But she knew he wasn't willing to share. Maybe he never would.

It was after seven o'clock. Leah had just finished cleaning the kitchen after supper. Zach retired to his small house out beyond the barn to watch television. Holt had disappeared into the den to do some paperwork. What did she expect from the man, to keep her company?

Corey came barreling into the kitchen dressed in his new blue Western shirt, dark denim jeans and a pair of buckskin boots. "Leah, how do they look?"

She smiled at his excitement. "You look great. How do the boots fit?" She knelt down on one knee for a closer look.

"I put on two pair of socks like you said." He nodded. "So they're okay."

She stood. Corey had eagerly accepted everything her mother had collected from the church. "Well, you'll probably outgrow them in a few months."

"I can wear the other pair of boots you brought when I help Zach tomorrow."

"Good idea. They're already broken in." The

ladies at the church had been generous in sending clothes along with a pair of kid's boots.

Just then Holt walked in. He glanced at Corey then continued to the coffeemaker. After pouring himself a cup he turned around and leaned against the counter. He eyed the boy more closely. "You need to break those in."

"I will," Corey said and glanced at Leah. "Maybe I should wear old jeans to work in and save these for good."

"If that's what you want," she said.

Holt gestured toward the clock. "It's not too late if you want to watch some television before turning in."

Corey nodded, then paused before leaving to look back at the two. "Good night, Leah. Thank you for the clothes."

"You're welcome. And good night, Corey."

The two males exchanged a nod and Corey disappeared from the kitchen.

Leah turned back to Holt. He was watching her. "Coffee?"

"No, thank you." She had enough things to keep her awake without the help of caffeine. "I think I'll say good-night, too."

Holt didn't want Leah to go yet. He'd spent too many nights alone in this house. He was beginning to doubt his decision to stay. "Wait," he called to her. "We need to talk about tomorrow."

She raised an eyebrow. "What's up tomorrow?"

"The social worker. She's coming out to see if I'm providing a suitable temporary home for Corey."

"Well, are you?" she challenged.

"You seemed to think so about twenty-four hours ago. Are you having second thoughts?"

"No. It's just that I'm worried about Corey. He seems a little jumpy around you."

"I've hardly said anything to the kid." He put down his cup and came to her. "And he avoids me about as much as you do."

Her eyes widened. "I told you I had errands to run and clothes to pick up."

"So you're going to be around tomorrow?"

"Of course. I want Corey to stay here—at least until they find a good permanent home for him."

Most likely that wasn't going to happen. Not many people wanted to adopt an eight-year-old boy. "That'll be a problem for the future. But if Corey is to live here for the time being, we need to play the happy couple…for the social worker."

"We didn't tell Reed we were a…couple."

Holt shrugged, enjoying her discomfort. "I'm not sure what we need, but when Social Services shows up we should at least act like we know each other."

"I guess you're right." She turned those velvet-brown eyes on him. "So, give me a rundown on yourself in twenty-five words or less."

That made him smile. She made him smile. "So,

don't you want to know more?" He cocked an eyebrow. "What if I have a sordid past?"

"What if I do?" she returned. "I mean, I've been out of the country for the past three years."

His eyes roamed over her petite frame that he'd come to appreciate more and more. Leah Keenan looked like the all-American girl. Just the type you took home to the family—the type you married. Definitely not his type.

"Were you ever in prison? Have you taken illegal drugs? Robbed a bank?"

"Of course not. You can contact the magazine I work for in New York. They'll vouch for me."

He fought to hold back a grin. "I was kidding. You've got small-town girl written all over your face"

"Unlike the city slicker from New York."

Holt had no doubt that she'd heard about his childhood when he'd lived here. "You already know John Rawlins was my father. When my parents divorced, my mother took me back to her family. I stayed there until college, and afterward I worked as a financial adviser for a Wall Street firm. I'm not married, not engaged, there isn't even anyone in my life…at the moment."

She drew a breath. "I lived here in Destiny since I was four months old. Since the day my mother brought her three daughters to the Keenan Inn and left us."

"Whoa…" He frowned. "How did that happen? How could she…?"

She shrugged. "I'm not sure how she could have done it. According to my adoptive mother, our biological mother didn't have a choice. Claire and Tim Keenan adopted us as soon as legally possible. So you see that was the reason I couldn't leave Corey to fend for himself."

Holt was surprised by her story, but Leah lived in a fantasy world. "There may not be a damn thing we can do to help Corey."

CHAPTER FIVE

IT WAS nerve-racking for Leah.

They were all gathered around the kitchen table as the social worker from Durango, Lillian Gerard, wrote in her notebook. She'd talked with Corey earlier, getting his personal account of his life in the last foster home.

"I'm not going back," Corey told her. "You can't make me."

The middle-aged woman stopped what she was doing and turned her attention to the boy. "We're not going to make you go back, Corey. We've discovered things about the…situation that make the house you were in unsuitable. The question now is, finding you another place to live."

"I want to stay here."

Mrs. Gerard looked at Holt. "That's what Mr. Rawlins and I have to discuss."

Holt straightened in his chair. "Corey, why don't you take Lulu an apple," he said.

Leah knew the boy loved to feed the mare. But he hesitated before he got up, grabbed the fruit from the bowl on the counter and headed out the door.

"Okay, Mrs. Gerard, let's cut to the chase," Holt began. "Do you have a home for Corey?"

She sighed. "Honestly, no. There's nothing available at the moment. He'll have to go into a group home."

"No, he can't," Leah said angrily. "He's only eight years old, and in the last two years, he's been in four homes. He's run away from every one of them."

The social worker looked sympathetic. "I know, but there just aren't enough good foster homes available."

"Isn't there's a relative who can take him?" Leah inquired, hoping they'd searched for someone who would care. She turned to Holt for support, but he sat stone-faced.

Mrs. Gerard looked over the file once again. "There is a distant cousin but she's in poor health. And since Corey's been labeled hard to handle, the available foster parents passed on him."

"Well, look how he's had to live," Leah said defensively.

"There's another option," Mrs. Gerard said. "He could stay here…temporarily."

Holt raised an eyebrow. "I qualify as a foster parent?"

"Since your home meets all the requirements, I

can give you emergency status, thanks to Sheriff Larkin's recommendation of you and Miss Keenan…and I know Leah's mother." She smiled. "And of course, we had to do background checks on you both. But most importantly, I've seen how Corey is when he's around you." She sighed. "So the question is, Mr. Rawlins, are you willing to keep the child here in your home?"

This time Holt's gaze connected with Leah's. Even though he'd been gruff to her, he'd been fair to the boy. He would be the perfect guardian for Corey.

"I'm a bachelor, Mrs. Gerard, I'm not sure I know how to parent…."

"None of us know how to be a parent in the beginning, Mr. Rawlins. We more or less learn as we go. I've seen you interact with the boy. He respects you. That's a big step."

Holt turned to Leah. "Are you going to hang around?"

She found she'd been holding her breath. "If you need me to, I'll be here." Was she crazy? How could she cohabit with this man?

"All right, Mrs. Gerard, I'm willing to keep Corey here…until a suitable home is found for him."

Over the next twenty minutes Holt filled out paperwork and they finally said goodbye to the social worker and watched her drive away.

Holt looked at Leah. "What have you gotten me into?"

"Me? I was willing to take Corey to my parents' home. You stepped in and said he could stay here with you."

His mouth quirked. "Well, you're in this with me." He stepped closer. "So pack your bags, darlin', because you're moving in. Looks like we're going to be one big happy family."

Later that afternoon, Holt adjusted his hat as he walked to the barn. He'd been crazy to let Leah talk him into this. But he'd let her talk him into a lot of things. The fact of the matter was, he'd let her get to him. New York had been full of beautiful, sophisticated women who knew the score. He'd been able to pick and choose and pretty much call the shots. But the one time he'd tried to have a long-term relationship, he'd failed miserably.

Now, it seemed the tables had been turned. Sassy Leah Keenan was calling the shots and suddenly he was responsible for an eight-year-old boy.

How could he give guidance to a child when he'd lacked positive male influences in his own life? Hell, his own father hadn't been in his life for years. Even his maternal grandfather hadn't been attentive to him as a child, or as an adult. His chest tightened as he recalled the familiar rejection. No matter what he'd achieved in sports, academics, in his career, Holt never could live up to his grandfather, Mackenzie Pershing's, expectations. And he'd never been given the chance to live up to John Rawlins's.

Holt entered the barn and found Zach cleaning a stall.

"So how did it go?" the old man asked.

"Looks like the kid will be around for a while," Holt told him. "I'm going to take out Rusty."

The old man beamed. "That's a good idea. Why don't you ask the youngin' to go along?"

Holt headed to the tack room. "Not now, I need some time alone. Besides, he and Leah are deciding how to fix up his room." He took the saddle off the sawhorse and carried it to the stall.

Zach followed after him. "You want to know what I think?"

"Not really." Holt soothed the gelding and slipped the bridle on.

The foreman ignored him. "Since you arrived here, you've kept to yourself too much. There's some good folks around here. Being a little neighborly wouldn't hurt."

"I'm a New Yorker. We're not known for being overly friendly."

Zach removed his worn hat and scratched his nearly bald head. "Just like your father. For years after your mother took you away, John pretty much stayed here, avoiding people." The old man smiled. "Until little Leah showed up. She was in high school back then, and cute as a button. All legs, and

with braces on her teeth. She was going to be a photographer and she wanted to take pictures of Hidden
Falls. Said it was for a school project. John wasn't
too keen on it at first, but she was a pesky thing and
finally he gave in. That boyfriend of hers kept
bringing her out here…"

"Her boyfriend?"

"Yeah, some big football player. I think they call
them jocks now. Whoever he was, he followed her
around, doing her bidding."

Holt didn't want to hear about Leah's old boy-
friends. "I know the feeling," he murmured as he
spread the blanket over the horse's back.

"You say something?" Zach asked.

"No." He lifted the saddle onto Rusty's back and
began to tighten the cinch.

"Well, like I was sayin', Leah was a frequent
visitor out here. John got so he looked forward to
seeing her."

Holt was tired of hearing about Leah's happy
times with John Rawlins. "I'm going to check the
herd. I'll probably finish repairing the pasture fence
and be back in a few hours." He slipped on his
gloves with the hope that some physical work
would help kill his awareness of Leah.

"You know, Holt, you're turning into quite the
rancher. You haven't shied away from any of the
hard work. Your father would be proud."

"Too bad it took so long for me to get back here."

The old man rubbed his jaw. "Maybe there were things John couldn't control. I wish you could have known him."

Holt stiffened. "And that's my fault? The man knew where I lived. He chose not to see me."

Holt led Rusty out of the stall hoping to find some peace. He sure wasn't going to get much with a full house.

That next afternoon, Leah went looking for the absent Holt. With directions from Zach, she rode Daisy along the fence into the grassy valley. Since Mrs. Gerard left yesterday she hadn't had a chance to talk with Holt. Alone. She had a suspicion he was avoiding her. Well, he wasn't going to ignore her any longer.

She spotted Rusty tied to a tree and not far away was the man she'd been looking for. She rode closer and discovered that he'd removed his shirt, leaving him in an undershirt, revealing his muscular shoulders and arms. Sweat beaded against his skin as he worked to stretch barbed wire along the newly placed post.

Holt looked up as she approached. He didn't seem happy to see her. "Is there a problem?"

"No, Corey's fine," she said as she climbed off her mount. "He's with Zach."

Holt went back to stretching the wire. "Then why did you track me down?"

"Maybe if you didn't just disappear all the time, I wouldn't have to. We need to talk."

He finished hammering the horseshoe nail into the wood, then turned to her. "Okay, tell me what's so important that it couldn't wait until I got back?"

"I wanted to talk to you…" She was suddenly distracted by the sweat glistening on his shoulders. "I mean about…how we handle Corey. Since it's summertime he doesn't have school. And he has a lot of time on his hands."

"Well, I don't," Holt told her. "I have a ranch to run. Next week is roundup. Tomorrow we're bringing the herd here."

"That's what I meant, if you would have taken the time to tell me…"

Anger flashed in his eyes as he dropped his hammer. Pulling off his gloves, he walked toward her. "And why would I feel the need to do that?" Under the shade of the trees, he removed his hat and stopped in front of her. "You're my pretend wife, Leah, not my real one."

"Nor would I want to be," she retorted.

His gaze roamed over her body making her feel exposed. Then he smiled. "Don't knock it, if you haven't tried it." He reached out and touched her cheek. "Maybe we should practice at being loving parents."

Leah pushed his hand away. "Stop it." She stepped back. "What is wrong with you? I thought you were okay with having Corey live at your house."

"I am. He's not a bad kid. It's you I'm having trouble dealing with."

She was hurt. "Me? But you asked me to move in. In fact you insisted on it."

Holt shut his eyes momentarily. He had insisted, but he didn't realize the toll her living in his house would take on him, on his sanity. "Yes, but all day every day. You're everywhere." If she wasn't in the kitchen, cooking, he could hear her laughter throughout the house. Even when he walked by the bathroom, he could catch the scent of her soap. His gaze locked with hers. "You're too tempting, Leah."

Her face reddened. "I'm not trying to be."

"But it's the reality."

"But for Corey's sake, it wouldn't be a good idea to act on those thoughts."

"So it's for the kid's sake that you rode all this way?"

He watched her breathing grow rapid. She gave him a weak nod.

"You're a liar, Leah" he accused. "You could have waited until I got back. Maybe you're feeling it, too. This thing between us."

Against his better judgment, he took a step closer.

She couldn't get away because Daisy was behind her.

"I should get back."

He knew she was right. He knew that he should just send her away, but ever since that day at the falls when he'd kissed her, he'd wanted to kiss her again.

"You should have just left me alone, Leah. A man can only take so much." He never realized how overwhelming just knowing she was sleeping down the hall from him… She was the first person he saw in the morning and the last person at night…

If he let her, she could become an obsession. "You want me to say that I want you? All right, I do."

His mouth lowered to hers, his lips caressed hers, then he pulled back to see her blink her big eyes at him. He was barely holding on to his control. "Tell me to stop, Leah, and I will."

She just stared at him, then parted her lips as he dipped his head toward hers. When his mouth closed over hers, she whimpered and placed her arms around his neck and let her lips part so he could deepen the kiss. He did. He tasted her and it was intoxicating. He wanted more. Much more. His arms wrapped around her and pulled her against his aching body. He was drowning in her, and never wanted to come up for air.

Finally his common sense prevailed, and he broke off the kiss. He gasped for a breath and stepped back. Was he crazy?

"Go back to the house, Leah," he demanded as he turned away.

Leah stood there frozen to the spot. She'd been crazy to let Holt kiss her. Crazy to get involved with this man. She had to stay focused on a more important problem. "Holt."

"I said leave, Leah."

"You can't keep ignoring Corey."

He turned around and nodded in agreement. "I'm not that big a bastard. I know I shouldn't ignore him. It's just that some of us aren't the best role models."

"It's not as hard as you think, Holt. Just give him some of your time, a little attention. The boy hangs on to your every word. I've already seen him emulate your mannerisms."

"I don't want him to," he told her. "His stay isn't meant to be permanent. Corey will be leaving."

"Well, while he's here, he's chosen you to be his hero."

The following evening, Holt drove into town and parked the truck in front of the Keenan Inn. Leah's parents had invited all of them to dinner. It was great for Corey and Leah, but he wasn't sure he was ready to socialize, to play out their situation in public. And he'd learned that Tim Keenan had been a good friend of John Rawlins.

"Wow! Your house is so big," Corey said from the back seat of the truck.

"Remember I told you that we only live on the third floor. The rest of the house is for guests," Leah explained. "Come on, Mom and Dad are waiting."

Corey eagerly climbed out of the truck's back door. He was wearing the new clothes that Leah had bought him. His hair, although still long, was neatly combed off his forehead. For all his excitement, the boy moved behind Leah when her parents come out on the porch.

Holt knew the feeling. He found himself putting his hand on the boy's shoulder as Leah hurried up the steps to embrace her family.

"It's okay, Corey. The Keenans are nice people."

The boy still looked frightened. "What if they don't like me?"

Holt couldn't help but smile as he pulled off his Stetson. It was funny how quickly boots and cowboy hats had become his uniform. "Just be polite and remember what we talked about."

"I know, mind your manners."

It was Mrs. Keenan who came down the steps and smiled at the boy. "My, what a handsome, young man. You must be Corey."

"Yes, ma'am," he said. "It's nice to meet you, Mrs. Keenan." With a nudge from Holt, he reached out his hand.

She shook it. "It's nice to meet you, Corey. And all the kids call me Mrs. K." She raised her gaze to Holt. "You must be Holt Rawlins. It's so nice to finally meet you."

"Yes, ma'am." He shook her hand as Leah's father showed up.

"Hello, Holt. It's nice to see you again." The older man smiled.

"Thank you for inviting us, Mr. Keenan," Holt said.

"It's Tim and Claire. And lately, it's the only way we can see our daughter," Tim joked. "But what she's doing is more important. Right, lad?"

The boy nodded. "Nice to meet you, Mr. K."

A younger woman arrived on the porch. She was a good four inches taller than Leah and had long auburn hair. Holt recognized her as Destiny's mayor. "Corey and Holt, this is our oldest daughter, Morgan," Mrs. Keenan said.

"You're the mayor," Corey said.

The pretty woman smiled. "Yes, I am. You can call me Morgan."

"And it's great to have two more guys to even the odds at the dinner table," Tim said. "Maybe we can talk sports for a change. How do you feel about the Denver Broncos?"

Holt had been a New York Giant fan all his life. "I'm looking forward to the upcoming season," he told his host as they went into the house.

As they walked through the house into the warm, aromatic kitchen, Tim Keenan said, "You both are in for a treat. My Claire is the best cook around."

Holt smiled. "I've been looking forward to sampling it all day."

Leah watched as Corey stayed close to Holt. Seeing his protective hand on the boy's shoulder something tightened around her heart. Since her trip out to the pasture, Holt had spent more time with the boy. At first it was awkward, but the two were making strides. At least they'd fared better than she at trying to forget Holt's kiss.

"Everything is ready," her mother called. "Holt, Corey and Leah, sit over there." The big table was set for six. A large pot roast, bowls of vegetables and a basket of homemade rolls were placed in the center.

When they were all seated, the blessing was said and food passed out. The conversation was lively while eating the scrumptious supper. By the time they'd finished dessert, everyone was relaxed. Her father took Corey up to the attic to search for some toys and games to take back to the ranch.

They were finishing coffee when Morgan directed her attention to Holt. "From what I hear, you've settled into ranch life."

"I have to admit it's a lot of work, but yes, thanks to Zach Shaw, I'm getting the hang of ranching." He smiled. "Of course, I might change my mind after the roundup next week."

Morgan turned to her sister. "Didn't you help John with the roundup a few times?"

Leah glanced at Holt. "A long time ago. I was just a kid."

"Don't let her fool you, Holt. She was quite the cowgirl back then."

Holt studied Leah. "Oh, really. You never stop amazing me."

"Well, don't expect much. I pretty much followed John's and Zach's lead." She glared at her sister.

"Do you have other men to help out, Holt?" her mother asked.

"Zach has lined up some of the neighbors, Jim Bakersfield and Bart Young."

"Good, men," Claire said. "It's nice that you're going to meet some of the townspeople...since you're going to be living here."

The mayor raised an eyebrow. "Isn't it mighty peculiar you being a New Yorker that you've decided you want to live here?"

"I was born here," he said. "It wasn't my choice to leave." He glanced around the room. "I'm sure everyone in town knows about my parents' marriage. At the moment, I'm where I want to be— here in Colorado."

Morgan smiled. "And we're glad to have you."

Tim appeared in the kitchen doorway. "And your father would be happy that you're running the Silver R. It was something he'd planned since the day you were born."

Holt stiffened, trying to hold on to his reserve. He'd never known what his father wanted...only that he hadn't wanted him.

CHAPTER SIX

MUCH later that night, unable to sleep, Leah sat at the kitchen table. She had her laptop open and decided she needed to go over the series of pictures she'd taken on her last assignment. Her editor had e-mailed a list of the pictures they wanted to use for the magazine's next issue.

If there was any consolation to her job it was that a lot of readers would see the famine and destruction in the already war-torn area. She wanted her photos to help the cause, the children especially. Another picture appeared on the screen and Leah stopped breathing.

Soraya. She was a beautiful little girl. At the age of six, she'd already experienced too much heartbreak in her short life. She had lost her entire family in the earthquake and had been living in a tent camp, begging for food from anyone who would throw her some scraps. When Leah found the child she was starved and close to death.

Leah clicked the mouse and another picture appeared. Soraya's big brown eyes looked back at her. Leah clicked on another, and another as tears rolled down her cheeks.

"What are you still doing up?"

Leah recognized Holt's voice. She swiped the tears from her cheeks and looked up to see the bare-chested man standing in the doorway, dressed in only a pair of low-riding jeans. She swallowed hard. "I couldn't sleep so I decided to do some work. Sorry, I didn't mean to disturb you."

He shrugged. "I heard you come downstairs, but when you didn't return, I wanted to see if you were okay."

"Just a little keyed up." She didn't want to talk about herself. "Corey had a good time tonight."

"Yeah, he did." Holt walked to the table. "What about you? You look like someone stole your puppy."

She forced a smile. "I was just concentrating on work."

Holt knew it was a lie. She'd been crying, and he hated the fact that it bothered him. That he felt the need to comfort her. "What have you got there?"

"Some of the pictures I took on my last overseas shoot."

"Mind if I have a look?" He didn't wait for her permission and looked over her shoulder.

She hesitated. "I…I guess not. This group is from my most recent assignment. I was shooting the thousands of people who are still displaced by the earthquake." She began to scroll through the pictures.

"Man, these are something." He studied each picture and was amazed at how Leah had captured the defeat and despair on their faces. Next were the children with their hopeful smiles as they posed for her. It was hard to look at their emaciated bodies, realizing they were caused by starvation. A beautiful dark-haired girl appeared on the screen whose big dark eyes tugged at his heart.

"They needed so little, but yet, so much," Leah said, tears in her voice. "And with all the other tragedies in the world, there just isn't enough money, enough help. No child should have to live this way." Along with the sadness came an angry tone. "It's all so cruel...so tragic."

Holt pulled up a chair, sat down and placed an arm around her. "I know, but you can't save them all."

Leah covered her face with her hands. "But why couldn't I have saved one?" she asked. "Just one little girl, Soraya." A sob racked her body. "Oh, Holt, she was doing so well... I found her a shelter, and I promised to come back to see her. I was going to bring her home to the States so she could live with me."

She shook her head as tears flooded her eyes. "I couldn't save her. She died."

Holt drew her into his arms and held her close

as she cried. He wanted to absorb some of her pain, her agony. How long had she carried this with her? "It's not your fault, Leah. It was a natural disaster in a country devastated by years of war."

She raised her head and looked at him. "But I promised her I'd help her…to keep her safe."

Now her obsession with Corey became clear to him. "Leah…you did the best you could do. You were probably the only one who took the time for Soraya. For a short time, you were able to give her love…and hope."

That seemed to make her pause. "You think so?"

Emotions tore at him as he nodded.

As if she all at once became aware of their closeness, she sat up straight. "My editor needs me to go back."

Seeing the pictures, Holt suddenly realized how dangerous her job could be. The last thing he wanted was for her to go back.

"I thought you had at least a month."

"I do. But they never really want you to take that much time. I'm staying until after Mom and Dad's anniversary."

He found he didn't want her to leave at all. "I'm not an expert, but I think you could use some time off."

"But the more pictures I take, the more the world will see what's going on there…with the children."

"So, single-handedly you're going to try to save them all?"

"No, but I need to do something."

"And your pictures do that. People will see these children in the magazine." An idea hit him. "Do these photos go to your editor?"

"They've already bought the ones they want. These others are mine."

Mesmerized, he studied the photos again. "I hope you know, Leah, you're an incredible photographer." Her pictures should be displayed in a gallery, or at the very least put into a book, he thought.

Leah gave him a trembling smile. "Thank you."

"I'm just speaking the truth," he told her, thinking about his friend, Jason Mitchell, back in New York. He owned a gallery on Fifth Avenue and specialized in new talent.

Although he would be getting more deeply involved in her life, he couldn't seem to stop himself. Suddenly he realized he'd do about anything to keep her safe…and here. And it had nothing to do with the deal they made about Corey.

The next morning, Holt got up at dawn, but there weren't any sounds from Leah's room as he passed by. Corey was already in the kitchen and starting breakfast. Holt had to admit that the boy was a hard worker.

"Mornin', Holt. Zach said you and him are going to move the herd today. I was wondering, since I cleaned my room, if I could go with you?

Holt knew how hard the boy had worked the past week to learn to ride. And he'd done pretty well. Holt also remembered all the times he'd wanted to go places with his grandfather, but the man seldom had time for him. Zach was right, a boy needed to prove himself.

"It's going to be a long morning. You sure you're up for it?"

Corey's eyes widened in expectation. The freckles across his nose and cheeks seemed to become more prominent. "Zach said I can handle it. He's been teaching me to rope and cut a calf from his mama."

"I guess there's no better teacher than Zach. He's been doing it for a long time. He even taught me."

"I know." Corey took a pitcher of orange juice from the refrigerator. "Zach said you turned out to be a pretty good cowboy, too—for a city boy."

"He did, did he? That's high praise. Well, if he thinks you're ready, then I suppose you are."

Those blue eyes rounded. "Really? I can go?"

Holt nodded.

The boy let out a loud whoop. But before Holt could quiet him down, Leah appeared in the doorway, her hair mussed, her dark bedroom eyes still heavy from sleep. Dressed in a conservative pink cotton robe, with a print gown underneath, she exposed just enough of her leg to cause his blood to race.

"What's going on in here?" she asked.

"Sorry, we didn't mean to wake you," Holt said.

Corey went running to her. "Leah, Holt says I can go to help move the herd today."

"That's great," she said, then looked at Holt and smiled. "Guess that makes you an official ranch hand then."

"I've got to get my boots and my hat." The boy ran out of the room.

Leah smiled tentatively at Holt. She'd tried to stay in bed until he had left the house. She was still vulnerable from their middle of the night encounter. He'd learned more about her than her own family. What amazed her was he just let her talk and cry it out. And the sexy cowboy hadn't taken advantage of the situation. He was so not the man she once thought he was. Why did he try so hard to hide this side of himself?

Leah marched across the room and stood in front of him. "Looks like you're playing hero again."

"It's not my intention," he said uncomfortably. "But it's not going to hurt Corey to come along."

"Well, whatever, you've made a little boy pretty happy. And thank you for helping me out last night, too." She rose up on her toes, wrapped her arms around his neck and pulled his head down to meet hers.

The minute their lips met Leah knew she was in trouble. She quickly discovered she wasn't in control of anything, least of all her heart.

* * *

The woman made him crazy.

Holt looked across the herd of Herefords to see Leah riding along with Zach. The old man was right. She knew how to handle a horse. And Corey had wanted her to come with them, too.

Ordinarily he wouldn't mind having her ride with them, until she'd planted that kiss on him this morning. A kiss so explosive he nearly lost all coherent thoughts. Then she ended it and walked out the door as easy as you please.

Well, he wasn't going to get involved. She had nice girl written all over her. A woman who didn't play games. She was the worse kind, a woman who wanted a permanent relationship. But he hadn't been willing to do a lot of things until Leah Keenan came barreling into his life.

Zach walked his horse up beside him. "How you holdin' up?"

"I'm fine. Why?"

"You keep looking in my direction." A lazy grin spread across his weathered face. "Of course maybe it wasn't me you've been lookin' at. Could it be Leah?"

Did the old man have radar? "It's my land, I can look anywhere I please."

"If it helps ease your pain, she's been stealing glances at you, too. The boy and her make a nice pair."

Holt sighed. "You're the only pain I have. Now, why don't you help me get this herd into the pen?"

Zach rode off, his laughter ringing in Holt's ears. Damn. The last thing he needed was to think about Leah all the time. He had enough on his plate with the ranch, and Corey. He didn't want to fall for a woman who was going to be headed off to God knew what country.

He'd always been the one to walk away first. That way it didn't hurt so much. Who was he kidding? He'd had a lot of hurt in his life. It hurt that his own mother couldn't see past the hatred she had for his father and love her son. He hated that his own father couldn't love him enough to come and see him.

He looked up as Leah kicked Daisy's flanks, sending the horse into a gallop as she went after a stray. Her hair was flying in the wind, her body moved in unison with the animal. They moved as one, and he thought he'd never seen anything more graceful. Corey cheered her on as she chased down the calf and directed it back into the herd. Suddenly Leah's attention turned to Holt and she smiled.

Or anyone more beautiful.

"This was the best day ever," Corey said as they returned to the barn.

Zach walked by carrying his saddle. "You may not say that later when your backside is aching."

"My backside doesn't hurt."

"Just give it time," Leah said, starting to feel the effects of four hours in the saddle. "But you're right,

Corey, it was fun. It's been a long time since I've ridden like that."

"It was so cool when you went off to get the calf."

"Well, when you're older, you can do the same thing. I've had a lot of practice. Maybe…" She paused not knowing how long he'd be here. "Maybe Zach can teach you."

"Or Holt can," the foreman said. "He can handle a cow pony pretty good. I'd say he was a fast learner."

The boy's eyes rounded. "Really?"

"Well, I already knew how to ride before I came to Colorado," Holt said. "I just had to adjust to a Western saddle."

Zach closed the stall gate. "Yeah, Holt used to wear those fancy breeches and hat, and use a funny looking saddle."

"That's because it was an English saddle." He frowned at the foreman. "We don't chase a lot of cows back in New York."

Zach's eyes twinkled. "Just a funny wooden ball."

"Polo. You played polo?" Leah asked. She couldn't hide her surprise as her gaze roamed over the ultimate looking cowboy.

Holt glared at Zach. "I did for a few years. My grandfather belonged to a polo club. It was a tradition. Do you have a problem with that?"

Leah shook her head. This man never ceased to

amaze her. Even knowing it was dangerous to her heart, she found she wanted to know more about him.

"Holt, will you teach me to play polo?" Corey asked.

"I think we're a little busy now," Holt told him.

"Maybe you have some pictures?"

"Not that I brought with me." He turned away. "Maybe we should think about finishing the morning's chores."

"Maybe we should have lunch first," Leah suggested. "It's after twelve."

"Okay, I'm getting pretty hungry," Zach said. "What do ya say, Corey, that we head up to the house and put together some sandwiches?"

"I'm hungry, too," the boy said.

"I'll heat up the soup my mother sent out yesterday," Leah called after the two as they headed toward the barn door. "Give me a few minutes."

Leah finished with Daisy and walked out of the stall. She was about to take the saddle and bridle back to the tack room when Holt stopped her.

"I'll get it," he told her. "You go on to the house."

"Are you coming?"

"I have things to do," he said. "I'll be by later."

She'd seen him withdraw when he'd started discussing his life back east. "You know," she began, "there are a lot of things in our past we'd all like to forget. Things we can't change. My big concern right now is making a life for a little boy. And he needs you to help him."

"I've given him a roof over his head."

"And that's wonderful. But you of all people should know that's not the only thing that's important. He needs you."

His eyes met hers. She saw stubbornness in the green depths, but also a vulnerability that reminded her of Corey.

"If you want some sort of family man, you better look somewhere else. That's something I can't give him."

She wanted to pound some sense into this man, but at the same time she wanted to pull him in her arms and let him know someone cared about him.

"You might be surprised, and in the meantime you might just find what you've been looking for, too." She turned and walked away so she wouldn't do something stupid again.

Like kiss some sense into him.

That night, Holt rolled over in bed and glanced at the clock. It was nearly midnight. He cursed as he threw back the sheet and sat up. It had been nearly a week since he'd been able to sleep. Hell, he hadn't had a decent night's sleep since Leah Keenan stormed into his life.

He couldn't stop thinking about her, the kisses

they'd shared, her softness…the feel of her body against his. The ache he'd felt whenever she was close.

Damn. He raked a hand through his hair. He was slowly going crazy. He got up and went to the window, opening it wider in search of the mountain breeze. Anything to cool off his heated skin. He got some relief, but not enough. Nothing could drive Leah from his thoughts…from his already complicated life. The strange thing was, he didn't want her to leave the ranch. She'd filled the old house with energy and laughter. Even as he'd tried to stay in the background, she'd pulled him in, including him in a family she'd help create with Corey.

Holt shut his eyes. As a kid, he'd wanted to belong, but every time he'd reached out to his grandfather, he'd been rejected. And he never had a chance with his father…

The stillness was suddenly interrupted by a soft cry. He immediately recognized Leah's voice coming from her room next door. He grabbed his jeans off the chair, pulled them on and went out into the hall. He listened at her door and heard the pain-filled sound again. After a moment's hesitation he let himself into the dark room. With the aid of the moonlight through the window, he saw her slender body thrashing around on the bed and went to her.

"Leah. Leah, wake up." He sat down on the mattress and gripped her shoulders. "Leah, wake up."

She finally gasped and jerked upright. "Holt?"

"You were having a nightmare."

Leah brushed the hair from her face and drew in a deep breath. "I'm sorry. I didn't mean to wake you."

"You didn't. I'm more concerned about you. Are you all right?"

She nodded, but the moonlight revealed the fear in her eyes.

"Do you have nightmares often?" he asked.

"Sometimes," she said, her gaze avoiding his. "Really, Holt, I'm okay."

He knew she wasn't. "Maybe you should talk to someone…professionally."

"I'm fine. It's just, sometimes the memories…"

"You're not fine, Leah," he said. "You've spent a lot of time in war-torn counties. You were probably dodging bullets in your dreams." That thought made him shiver. "At the very least, talk to your family."

"It's not that bad. I just need to get some rest. I'll be fine by the time I go back."

He tensed. She was leaving. "So you're continuing your quest to save the world."

"I have to. I made a promise…" A sob shook her slight frame.

He wrapped his arms around her. "Shh, it's all right," he whispered. "I'm here." He brushed a kiss against her hair as he held her. "Oh, Leah. What am I going to do with you?"

She burrowed into his embrace. "Just…don't leave me."

Never, he promised silently. "I won't." Impulsively he bent down and placed a kiss on her mouth before pulling away. "Just let me check on Corey." He hurried down the hall to the boy's room and found him sleeping soundly. After covering Corey with a light blanket, he returned to Leah. Holt closed the door behind him and went to the bed. Her wide-eyed gaze showed her sudden apprehension.

"Holt…maybe it would be better if you go back to your room."

He sat down and picked up her trembling hand. "Do you really want me to?"

She hesitated, then shook her head.

"Then go to sleep, Leah." He stretched out on top of the blanket beside her, and pulled her close. "I'm right here…if you need me."

"Thank you," she whispered as she curled against him, her hand resting on his chest. Within seconds she was sound asleep. It took Holt a lot longer, but having Leah close was worth a sleepless night. For the first time in a long time, he didn't feel alone.

The next evening, Leah was anxious to see her sister, the mayor, in action at the town council meeting. She had also managed to convince Holt to attend. Since he was staying in Destiny, he should get to know the town's residents.

That had been all she'd managed to talk to him about during the past day. Even though they'd shared a bed most of the previous night, he hadn't said a word about it.

That morning, she woke up when she felt him brush a tender kiss against her forehead before he left her bed at dawn.

Maybe it was best they hadn't discussed sharing the moment together. They had already gone too far beyond the reason for them being together.

Corey.

The small community of Destiny was already talking about their situation. Maybe it was time Leah thought about moving back to her parents? Corey would understand.

"Are you sure there are going to be other kids here tonight?" Corey asked as Holt pulled his truck into the parking space.

"There usually are during the summer," Leah told him. "My parents and Morgan will be there. And there's always cake and cookies."

They climbed out of the truck and walked together toward the old hall. The structure held maybe three hundred people and served many of the town's functions. On a warm night like tonight, it was bound to be filled. Everyone was gearing up for Destiny's Founder's Day celebration. And Leah suspected that they wanted to meet their newest citizens, Holt Rawlins and Corey Haynes.

At the door, her father waited. "Hi, Dad."

"Leah." Tim Keenan greeted her with a kiss. "Corey, good to see you."

The boy smiled as her father ruffled his hair. "Hi, Mr. K."

Tim Keenan looked at Holt. "Holt, nice to see you could make it."

The two shook hands. "Your daughter can be pretty persuasive."

Tim winked. "She gets that from her mother."

Claire Keenan appeared. "I heard that." She offered her daughter a kiss and one for Corey. She surprised Holt and hugged him. "Holt, it's nice you're here."

He glanced around. "It looks like a big turnout."

"It is," her mother said. "And a perfect opportunity for Tim to introduce you around." She nudged her husband and the two men walked off together. "And, Corey, there's someone I want you to meet." Claire glanced around then motioned at someone. Suddenly a dark-haired boy about eight years old appeared.

"Corey, this is Mason Langston. Mason, Corey Haynes. Mason, Corey is staying at the Rawlins Ranch. He hasn't had much of a chance to meet anyone. Do you think you could show him around?"

"Sure, Mrs. K." He looked at Corey. "Hey, do you like chocolate chip cookies?"

Corey shrugged. "Yeah."

The boy motioned to follow him. "Come on, before Kenny Dorsey eats them all."

Leah watched the two boys run off.

"Not to worry, they'll be fine," Claire told her.

"I know, but Corey's very vulnerable. He's been through a lot."

"And Mason is a good boy. He'll be nice to Corey." Her mother turned her attention to her husband and Holt as they made their way around the hall. "The two older boys seem to be getting along nicely, too."

Leah was glad that Holt was meeting people. "Holt should know his neighbors," Leah said. "He's going to live here."

"He seems to be attracting the ladies, too."

As much as Leah tried to ignore that comment, she noticed that Kaley Jenkins Sims was standing very close to him. "Kaley hasn't changed since high school. She goes after any good-looking male. I heard she's divorced now."

"About a year ago," her mother said. "She has a sweet little girl."

Leah found she didn't like seeing Holt and Kaley together. "Well, it looks like she's on the hunt for number two."

"Maybe you should stake your claim," her mother suggested.

That got Leah's attention. "What? I'm not going to stake any claim. I'm committed to my job. Besides, the man has a lot of baggage. The last thing Holt wants is a woman in his life."

Claire Keenan smiled. "You can always change your career. And all men claim to be loners before they realize they can't live without us. From what I can see Holt Rawlins is interested in you."

Leah couldn't consider that possibility. She had a feeling, whether intentionally or not, the man could hurt her.

Holt looked up from the conversation and glanced across the hall at Leah. He knew she was enjoying this. He'd met so many people tonight he'd never be able to remember their names.

"I hear that you were a financial advisor in New York."

He turned to the blond woman named Kaley something. She was attractive in a too-made-up sort of way. Her jeans were a little too tight as was her tank top that carried one of those sayings that he didn't dare attempt to read.

Luckily the mayor was walking their way. He reached for her arm and pulled her into the circle. "Hello, Morgan."

"Holt, it's nice that you could make it," she told him with a smile that reminded him of Leah.

"Your sister thought it was time I met a few people."

"I, for one, am glad he came," Kaley said as she moved in a little closer.

"So am I," Morgan said. "Holt, if you have a

minute, I need to speak with you." She glanced at Kaley. "If you'll excuse us for a moment…"

Kaley frowned, but finally managed a tight smile. "I guess I can let Holt go…for a while. Maybe later we can share some refreshments."

"Maybe," Holt said as he took Morgan's arm. "What do I owe you?" he said when they found a deserted area.

"Sorry, Kaley is a little…overeager."

"You're too nice. If you hadn't shown up she'd be naming our children."

Morgan laughed. "Well, she's used to men giving her attention. But I only want to discuss a little business." She took a breath. "First, I want to say that, speaking for the town, we're glad you've decided to stay in Destiny."

"Thank you. I'm glad I'm staying, too."

"And secondly, I want to talk to you about a section of your property. Maybe Leah has already mentioned it to you."

He shook his head. "No, she hasn't said anything. So what's this about my land?"

"I'm been looking for a way to bring revenue into town, and it seems logical that we build a ski resort. The town owns an ideal parcel of land, but we just need access from the highway before we can develop the area."

"Where is this land?"

"It's Silver Wolf Pass."

Holt knew the location. It would cut right by Hidden Falls. "You want to build a road through my property?"

Morgan raised an eyebrow. "It's not as drastic as it sounds. Maybe you should come by my office so you can see the plans."

Holt didn't like being blindsided like this. Was Leah supposed to butter him up so he'd be more agreeable when approached? "Did you ever talk about this with my…with John?"

"I did, in fact."

"And what did he say to your idea?"

"I'm afraid we didn't have much time to discuss it, but he did promise to think about it."

"Well, I'm not going to think about it, because I don't want anyone building a highway across my land. Now if you'll excuse me, I need to find Corey." Holt knew he was being rude, but at this point he wasn't sure he could contain his anger. Had Leah planned to get him to agree to this?

Before he could reach her, Leah was cornered by another group of people just as the meeting was called to order.

He forced himself to take a seat, but he wasn't finished with this. He would just have to wait until he got Leah back to the ranch, then he'd set her straight.

Set everyone straight.

CHAPTER SEVEN

LATER that evening, Leah was in the ranch's kitchen when Holt finally came in from checking on Lulu. Her foal was due anytime and he'd been watching her closely.

"How's the mother-to-be doing?"

He walked to the coffeepot and poured a cup. "She's getting close. Zach's going to call when it's time."

Leah was excited. "Could I go down, too? It's been a long time since I've watched a birth."

He shrugged. "I don't have a problem with that."

He sure knew how to make a girl feel welcome. "I promised Corey he could go, too, I should wake him." He started to leave the kitchen when Leah stopped him.

"Holt, is there something wrong?"

He looked at her with that unreadable hooded gaze of his. "Why should there be something wrong?"

"Maybe because you haven't said more than a

few words to me since last night when you came into my room. I thought that…"

"You thought what?"

"I thought we could now at least talk to each other if something was bothering one of us."

He frowned and crossed the room to her. "Okay, maybe we should talk. When were you planning on telling me about the town wanting me to sell land for an access road?"

She swallowed hard. "I'd forgotten all about it."

"Were you elected to sweet-talk me into agreeing to give the town access?"

Leah was starting to get angry over his constant mistrust. "Well, whatever the plan, it seems that I've failed miserably."

"I don't like being used."

"And I don't like you thinking I would use a friend like that. Besides, all Morgan wanted me to do was present the idea to you. You have the choice to look over the plans and tell them yes or no." She threw up her hands in defeat. "Word was people in town thought you came here to sell the ranch, then head back to New York."

"Well, I'm staying," he said.

"Then prove it. Stop closing yourself away from everyone and get to know your neighbors."

He opened his mouth to protest and she stopped him. "And don't say they're just curious because you're John's son, or I'll clobber you. You are John

Rawlins's son. If you're not proud of that, there's something wrong."

Raw emotion flashed across his face. "I am tired of being compared to the man. He wasn't in my life. This ranch, this land, is all I ever had of him."

"I'm sorry about that, Holt." She stepped closer and placed her hand on his arm. "I know you never had the chance to know John, and I wish so much you had." She felt him start to pull away and she tightened her grip. "No, please listen to me. The man I knew would have loved his child—his son. There had to be something that happened between your parents to keep him away."

"Well, whatever it was, it worked. I never saw him after I left here." Holt broke free and walked out the door. As much as Leah wanted to stop him, Holt Rawlins wasn't going to listen to anything she had to say.

"Wow, look, Holt." Corey gasped. "She's getting up."

"I see," Holt said as he leaned back on the railing in the birthing pen. He was exhausted, but even more amazed at the Silver R's newest equine resident.

"That's what a foal is supposed to do," Zach said. "They got to stand up to see if everything works, that she'll be able to reach her mama to eat."

Holt watched the still-wobbly golden-chestnut filly check out her new surroundings. He wiped his hand on a towel and glanced across the gate at Leah.

"Congratulations, Dad," she told him.

Almost against his will, he found himself smiling. "Thanks. Am I supposed to hand out cigars?" He couldn't believe how a new foal could bring him such joy. Maybe it wasn't the recent birth as much as the shared experience with Corey. And Leah.

"I guess someone needs to come up with a name," Zach said. "You have any ideas, Corey?"

"You want me to name her?"

Zach exchanged a glance with Holt. "Sure."

"Her coat is all golden," Corey said.

"How about we call her *Golden Girl*?" Zach suggested.

"Goldie, for short," Corey said.

"I like that." Holt nodded. "Goldie it is."

When Corey yawned, Zach suggested they all turn in. He'd keep an eye on the filly.

Once Corey was settled in bed, Holt followed Leah into the hall, but he stopped her before she retired to her room. When she looked at him with those big eyes, he nearly forgot what he wanted to say. But he couldn't lose his nerve now.

"Leah, about earlier… I guess I jumped to conclusions before I knew the whole story."

She didn't say anything.

"You were right, I'll go and talk to your sister in a few days."

She sighed. "That's all Morgan wanted you to do in the first place. You've got to start trusting people." Leah started to turn away, but Holt stopped her.

"I wish I could change that."

Leah wanted to believe him. She wanted a lot of things. She wanted to know the man behind the armor. The same man who held her one night when she was afraid to be alone. "There's nothing wrong with admitting we need someone." Unable to stop herself, she leaned into him and rested her head against his chest. She loved the sound of his pounding heart. "Just so you know. I'm here if you need a friend."

Holt pulled back and his intense gaze locked on her. The heat between them quickly became electrifying. "Friends? Friendship is not exactly what I'm feeling for you right now."

His head lowered and his mouth covered hers. The kiss started out slow and tantalizing, then began to feed on their hunger for one another. He wrapped his arms around her waist and drew her closer, pressing his body against hers as his mouth magically caressed hers. With a moan, she parted her lips, allowing him inside.

Suddenly Holt broke off the kiss, leaving her dazed and confused. His eyes narrowed as he fought to slow his breathing. "Oh, Leah. I think we both want more than just friendship. A lot more."

The following weekend was the Silver R roundup.

It wasn't a large herd, but Holt needed help to bring the cattle in for branding. More men than

Holt had expected showed up at dawn. All Zach had told him was that he had contacted enough neighbors to get the job done. The foreman had said nothing about the men bringing their families.

By midmorning, the mamas and bawling calves had been separated into the holding pens. Up at the house another crowd had gathered, then Leah and Claire Keenan ushered the bevy of women into the house.

"Relax," Zach told Holt. "This is how we do things in Colorado. Neighbors help out neighbors."

"There are so many people. How are we going to feed all these…neighbors?"

Zach nodded toward the women, and Holt saw the answer in the parade of dishes being carried into the house. "I don't think you have to worry on that score, either. Leah and Claire have things in hand. Now, let me show you how to brand a calf."

After the next few hours Holt decided he had never been so dirty, or so tired. Since he wasn't an experienced roper, he ended up being the one who held down the calves to brand. It seemed like an easy job, but that changed after he'd gotten kicked in nearly every part of his body. Dust filled his eyes and nose, and the stench of burning fur and flesh hung in the air.

"Hey, Holt," a neighbor, Bart Young, announced. "The ladies are calling us to eat."

Holt turned to find that a number of tables had

been set up under the trees on one side of the house. One table was covered with food and some men were already in line to eat.

His stomach growled. "Then I guess we better go eat."

As the men washed under the water spigot next to the house, Holt looked around for Leah and found her with Corey. The boy had been a little help earlier, but now he was off to play with his friend, Mason.

Leah glanced over her shoulder and smiled at Holt. Sudden warmth spread through his veins clear down to his toes. The memory of their kiss the other night flashed into his mind. How he wanted to replay it again…and again. He quickly shook away the thoughts that would only get him in trouble.

"Well, look at you, Mr. Big City Boy," Leah greeted him.

"I guess I am pretty dirty."

"Ranching is a dirty business." She gave him a slow once-over. "It seems to suit you, though. How are you handling it?"

He shrugged. "Not bad, but I'll probably be black and blue by tomorrow."

"One good thing, you'll be so sore that you probably won't even notice the bruises."

They both laughed.

"You should get some food," she said.

He glanced at the heaping platters of fried

chicken, and the overflowing bowls of salads. "Zach says I have you to thank for organizing this." He took off his hat and ran a hand through his hair. "I guess I never thought about food for today."

"I figured," she said. "And since there isn't any pizza delivery out here, I called Mom and she got the women together to arrange this."

"I'm indebted to her, too."

Leah frowned. Would she ever get through to this man? "These people don't want you to feel indebted. They're doing this because John was a friend and neighbor. And I have no doubt that you'll be just as willing to help them, too. Now, you better eat. You still have work to do this afternoon."

"Only if you join me."

She hesitated. The whole town was watching their every move anyway, so why not? "Sure. I'll fix you a plate while you clean up.

"Great. Just make sure you get me some of whatever your mother made." Grinning, he started walking as he popped the snaps on his shirt.

She managed a quick glance as his broad chest came into view. Then all too soon, Holt turned away and she started for the buffet to discover the other wives smiling at her.

She ignored them. What was the big deal? So Holt had kissed her a few times. Okay, so they'd been mind-blowing kisses. There wasn't any law against that.

Leah picked up a plate, scooped up her mother's potato salad, a few deviled eggs, two pieces of chicken and a roll. She then went to find two empty chairs at the table. Going back, she got her own food, but when she returned she found another visitor had arrived at the ranch.

Kaley Sims was dressed in a hot-pink tank top and jeans. She had taken Leah's seat, but as close as she was to Holt, she might as well have been sitting in his lap.

Looking guilty, Holt stood when Leah arrived at the table. "Leah, you're back." He pulled out the chair on his other side. "Look who's here," he said as he nodded at Kaley.

"Hi, Leah," Kaley said, but her attention was on Holt.

"Kaley, what a surprise." Leah forced a smile. "Since when do you come to roundups?" She doubted the woman ever wore her boots for anything besides dancing.

With an innocent smile, Kaley leaned in closer to Holt, nearly spilling out of her tank top. "I heard that Holt was having his first roundup, and I had to bring by a pie."

"That was thoughtful of you," Holt said as he tried to concentrate on his food. "This chicken is good, Leah."

"I made it," she admitted, pretty sure that Kaley had purchased her pie at the bakery.

Kaley sighed. "Oh, Leah, you and your sisters are all such good cooks. The kitchen just isn't the room I'm the best in."

Leah choked on her food.

"Are you okay?" Holt asked.

She nodded. "Some food just went down the wrong way." She turned to the woman. "Well, if you want to help, you could stay and wash dishes."

Kaley glared at her. "I'm sorry to say I can't. I need to pick up my daughter." She stood and placed her hand on Holt's shoulder and bent her head toward him. "Maybe another time. Holt, I'm in town and in the book."

Leah clenched her fists under the table.

"Thanks for stopping by," Holt called as she walked away.

Never looking at Leah, he returned to eating. "All that work this morning makes a person hungry," he said.

Too bad Leah had lost her appetite. "It's a shame Kaley couldn't stay." She stabbed at her food. "She's so…attentive."

Holt stopped eating, a faint trace of a grin starting. "I didn't notice."

She stood. "You would have to be dead not to notice Kaley Sims."

Holt stopped her. "Will you sit down? I'm not interested in Kaley."

"I couldn't care less either way," she fibbed. "But

fair warning, Kaley always gets what she goes after…and she's coming after you."

Leah turned and marched off toward the house, hating that she'd let herself care. But she did care, darn it. Especially when she knew that Holt had a life here, and she wasn't going to be staying.

Not even her feelings for the man could change what she had to do.

By late afternoon, the last of the calves were branded and back in the pen. The men walked toward the house for a cold drink and to relax. Thanks to Leah and the other women, they had leftovers waiting along with iced tubs of soft drinks and beer.

The party began.

It wasn't by any means a wild party, everyone just sat around enjoying the quiet evening with friends and family. Holt looked for Leah and Corey and found the kid playing with his new friends. Leah talking with a group of the women.

He couldn't help but watch her. She had such an easy way with people. Everyone liked her, himself included. His gut tightened with need. Not just the physical need she'd awakened in him, but a different need he'd never experienced before. The need to see her smile…to hear her laughter…or just for the scent of her hair when she walked past him.

"Leah's grown into a pretty woman," Bart said as he appeared next to him.

"Since I didn't know her as a kid, I couldn't say. But yes, Leah is pretty."

The fiftysomething rancher handed him a longneck bottle of beer. "She was cute as a button."

The last thing Holt wanted to do was talk about his relationship with Leah. "Bart, I want to thank you for all your help today," he said, changing the subject.

"Glad to do it." The man pushed back his hat. "I guess we were all a little curious to see how you would handle your first roundup." His grin caused tiny lines to crinkle around his eyes. "Guess we can't call you a big city boy anymore. I'd be proud if you'd come and help me out at the end of the month."

His neighbor's acceptance meant a lot to Holt. "I'd be happy to," he told him. "Just tell me the time and place."

"Will do. Can you sweet talk Leah into bringing some of her fried chicken?"

Holt laughed. In the past few weeks Leah had become such a part of his life. He found he was eager to return to the house each night, knowing she would be there.

"I'll see what I can do," he told his neighbor.

Bart just winked and together they strolled back to the group that gravitated around the open pit. With the cool of the evening ahead, Zach had started a fire.

It was an opportunity to talk to everyone. "I want to thank you all for coming here today. I couldn't have done this without your help. I hope I can return the favor." He raised his bottle and smiled. "And to the lovely ladies who prepared all the delicious food. Thank you. I haven't eaten this well in years." He patted his flat stomach. "And it's a good thing."

That brought a laugh from his neighbors, and he searched the group for Leah. She was standing in the back. He found he wanted her with him.

"Does this mean that you're going to hang around?" The question came from one of the ladies.

"I think so," he said honestly. "I know I have a lot to learn, but I'm beginning to feel like I belong."

"You're John Rawlins's son. Of course you belong here."

Holt's smile froze, but he willed himself to relax. He wasn't going to let his father spoil another evening. Suddenly everyone's attention went to one of the men who pulled out a harmonica, and began to play. More leftovers were eaten and the kids roasted marshmallows.

Holt glanced at Leah, realizing with her here, this was about as perfect as it could get.

Leah went into the barn to escape. She felt like there was a spotlight on her whenever Holt looked at her. Her mother was even singing the man's praises. Leah didn't need anyone telling her what kind of man Holt Rawlins was. She already knew, and she already had feelings for him.

She walked down the center aisle to Lulu and Goldie's stall. The mare greeted her with a neigh and came to the gate.

"Hello, girl." Leah stroked Lulu's muzzle "How's it going?" She glanced down at the filly at her side. "Hi, Goldie." but the two-week-old foal skittered away when she reached out her hand. "A little shy after all the visitors today, huh?" Corey had been showing off the new addition to the ranch.

Although the filly didn't want attention, Lulu did. Leah felt comforted by petting the mare. It relaxed her, too. Today had been busy, but she loved all the work. She'd gotten to visit with people who'd been such a big part of her life.

Her life. Leah sighed. At one time, she thought she'd had it all planned out. From an early age, she'd known what she'd wanted. A career and travel first. Not until she was thirty would she even think about settling down. Now suddenly she was playing house with one sexy cowboy, and a surrogate mother to an eight-year-old boy. And she was crazy about both of them.

"So, this is where you've been hiding out," Holt said.

Leah jerked around to find him leaning against an empty stall across the aisle. Even dressed in dirty jeans and shirt from the day's branding, he looked handsome…sexy…mouthwatering.

She finally found her voice. "I was just checking on the filly."

"I think Goldie's been checked on by nearly half the town today." His smile was slow and easy and it took her breath away.

He pushed away from the stall and walked to her. "I had a feeling that you are avoiding me."

She continued to stroke the horse, but Lulu changed allegiance and went to Holt. Fickle female. The mare nudged against his hands, begging for attention and Holt began stroking her nose.

"She just can't get enough attention," he said.

Leah met his heated gaze, then recalled an earlier event that day. Several women had been immune to his charms, especially one shapely blonde. "Reminds me of someone else."

"If you're talking about Kaley, I'm not interested. She's definitely not my type."

"Who says I care?" she told him, trying to sound convincing.

Holt clutched his hand to his heart. "Oh, that hurts."

Leah worked hard not to smile. "Go cry on Kaley's shoulder." She turned serious. "Encouraged or not, the woman goes after what she wants. And she wants you."

Holt took a step closer and reached for Leah. "I don't want her."

Leah suddenly felt hot. "It's none of my business."

He leaned toward her. "Yes, it is." He brushed back a loose strand of her hair. His grazing touch caused her to shiver. "Because, Leah, you're the one who keeps me awake at night, the one who makes me ache until I think I can stand it any longer." His head descended to hers.

"Holt…this isn't a good idea…you kissing me…" Her resistance was weak; even she didn't believe her words.

Holt searched her face, the blatant desire in his green eyes caused her heart to pound in her ears. His warm breath caressed her face, making her shiver. "That's why you're going to kiss me," he whispered. "So you'll have no regrets."

Leah swallowed hard. "I still don't think this is wise…to start anything." Even she didn't believe what she was saying.

Holt touched her cheek with the back of his hand. "Don't think, Leah." His low, husky tone was slowly mesmerizing her. "Just feel…" he breathed and she lost the battle. With a tiny whimper she surrendered, went into his arms and her lips touched his.

This one time wouldn't hurt.

Now if only she believed that.

CHAPTER EIGHT

THE next day, standing on the inn's porch, preparing to snap a picture, Leah was still reliving Holt's kisses. She didn't want to think about them at all. But as hard as she tried she couldn't stop the feelings.

None of that mattered. She was heading off in a few weeks for her next assignment. That meant leaving her family and friends behind. And worse, this time it would mean leaving Holt and Corey. Although she was crazy to feel that way. She'd be a fool to expect a commitment from Holt, and Corey would probably go into a foster home soon, and there was nothing she would do about it. She sighed, feeling her eyes burn. Too bad because he and Holt were great together and needed each other badly.

"Leah, are you going to take the picture today?" Morgan called.

Leah shook away her thoughts, realizing her sister and parents were on the inn's porch waiting for her.

"Sorry, I was checking for the best light," she fibbed. "Okay, now smile." Her parents obliged and she took the picture. "That's it."

Morgan came down the steps. "Where else do you want to go?"

Leah smiled at her sister's excitement and she was glad she'd volunteered to take pictures for the town's new brochure and Web site. "How about if we call it a day? I'm losing the light and I need to get Corey back to the ranch for dinner."

Just then Corey and his new best friend, Mason, came running from the backyard. They were both wet and dirty, proof they'd been playing in the creek.

"Looks like you both have been busy," Leah said, not caring that the boy was a mess. He was smiling.

"We caught some crawdads, but put them back," Corey said.

"I, for one, am glad to hear that. We should get back to the ranch."

Just then Mason's mother, Judy Langston, pulled up. She waved and Leah went to the car. "Sorry about the condition of your son."

Judy laughed. "Don't worry, I'm used to it." She waved to her boy. "Come on, Mason. It's time to go."

"Ah, Mom, I want to play with Corey. Can he come to our house?"

Judy looked at Leah. "We'd love to have Corey spend the night." The boys began to cheer.

When Leah was unable to reach Holt by phone, she gave permission for the sleepover. After cleaning up the excited Corey, she sent him off to the Langstons's house. Then she gathered her camera and headed back to the ranch, trying not to think that she would be staying with Holt Rawlins. Alone.

By the time she reached the ranch, a tired-looking Holt was walking up from the barn.

"Where's Corey?"

"He's sleeping over at Mason's tonight," she began, then hurried on to say. "I tried to call you, but you must have been out. Mom knows the family, and Mason's mother, Judy, is very nice. She said she'd drive Corey home in the morning."

He raised a hand. "It's okay, Leah. I don't mind that you let him go." His mouth gave away a hint of a smile. "That means we get the night off. What do you say we make the most of it, and go out?"

Leah felt her heart race. A date? In public? Would that be wise? "Thank you, but I have a lot of work to do. I want to go over the pictures I took today."

"I could help you after we get back." He walked up to her. "So why don't you go and get ready?"

She knew it was a bad idea to spend any more time alone with this man, but all her logic seemed to disappear. She wanted to spend the evening with him. "What should I wear?"

"Whatever you decide will be fine." His smile widened. "But you better hurry…you've got thirty minutes."

Leah used all of the time allotted her to get ready for her date with Holt.

She managed to shower and change into an Indian-print broomstick skirt and cotton turquoise blouse, and to slip on a pair of low-heeled sandals.

With one last glance in the mirror, she checked her makeup and hair. Unable to do anything with her wayward curls, she used clips to pull the long strands away from her face. Then she drew another long breath, released it and walked to the door.

This was crazy. Why was she so nervous? She was only going out for dinner. One would think that she'd never had a date before. This was different. They'd already had an intense relationship, just living in the same house. Not to mention the fact she couldn't resist the man's kisses.

Well, starting tonight she was just going to try harder. With renewed determination, she made her way down the steps to the landing and stopped when she saw Holt in the entry. Her pulse shot up.

In a pair of dark trousers and a wine-colored shirt, he looked nothing like the rancher she'd been living with the past weeks.

He looked up at her, gave her an appreciative once-over and smiled. She felt her knees go weak.

This was bad. She managed the stairs as he came to meet her at the bottom.

He took her hand. "You are well worth the wait. You look beautiful."

She felt herself blush. "Thank you. You're not so bad yourself. You seem to have lost the rancher look."

"Do you mind?"

She inhaled his woodsy scent and felt light-headed. "No, not at all."

His smile widened. "Good." He checked his watch. "We should get going. I made reservations at Francisco's Cantina in Durango."

"Oh, I haven't been there in years," she told him as he tucked her hand under his arm and walked her out the front door.

"So I made a good choice?" he asked as he opened the door to his truck.

"A very good choice," she told him.

He leaned forward. "Good. I want tonight to be…memorable."

Holt sat across from Leah at the corner table. It was a weekday and the restaurant wasn't busy. That made him happy since he wanted some quiet time with Leah.

"Do you miss being a financial advisor?" she asked.

"Surprisingly, no. Of course, I was able to keep a few of my clients."

"Is that because you aren't sure that ranching will work out?" There was a hint of a smile.

"I have to admit when I discovered John left me the ranch, I wasn't sure what I would do." He leaned forward at the table, mesmerized by Leah framed in the soft candlelight. "I was curious more than anything."

She smiled. "I'd say you seemed to have taken over the position as rancher as if you were born to it. You handled the roundup like a pro."

"Thank you." Her praise meant a lot to him. "You should have seen me a few months ago. The three times a week in the gym didn't compare to tossing bails of hay. Zach was a big help. Never once has he given up on me, but he never let up on me, either." He smiled, realizing how much he was enjoying being with Leah. "Enough about me. Tell me about you, and your job. Have you always wanted to travel the world?"

She grew serious as she shook her head. "I've always wanted to be a photographer. And after college, I more or less fell into the job at *Our World* magazine." She frowned and took a sip of her wine. "It's hard to pass up the opportunity."

"You've made a name for yourself, you could go and work anywhere…even for yourself," he said, wishing she wasn't going to be leaving so soon.

"Maybe I will…someday."

He nodded. "You can't blame me for wanting you to stay around."

"Maybe you'll be the one who doesn't stay around. For someone who's lived in New York for so long, I'd think you'd missed the nightlife…the people.

"Sometimes," he admitted. "I enjoyed being able to go to fine restaurants and seeing a Broadway show. As for the people, I was involved in a relationship, but before I left we ended it." His gaze feasted on her. "I'm beginning to discover that Colorado has what I really want."

She smiled as her slender fingers toyed with the stem of her wineglass. "As I said before, you definitely fit in at the ranch."

Unable to resist any longer from touching her, he reached out and placed his hand over hers. "If things had been different, maybe I would have," he said. Not wanting to ruin tonight's mood, he pushed aside the old bitterness and leaned closer. "No doubt you and I would have met a lot sooner."

Leah wrinkled her nose. "And you would have run the other way. I was all braces, skinny and a tomboy."

"Oh, I would have noticed you." He threaded his fingers though hers. It felt good, and so right.

"I would have noticed you, too," she whispered.

His breath caught in his chest. "I think it's safe to say that we've definitely noticed each other now. Isn't that what counts?"

She nodded. "Too bad there isn't much time…"

He touched a finger to her lips, stopping her words. "Let's not think about what's going to happen later on. Right now is all that matters."

Nearly two hours later, Leah's heart was pounding hard as Holt parked the truck at the back door. It was only eleven, but their time together was almost over. Sadly, she realized that her time with everyone she cared about was about to come to an end, and soon.

Silently Holt climbed out, walked around the truck and opened the door. He took her hand to help her down. All at once, she lost her footing on the running board, and began to fall. She gasped as he caught her body against his and helped her to solid ground, but then he didn't release her. He held her close, so close she could feel his rapid heartbeat. Her own pulse was racing. She knew she should step away, but when his hands moved up and cradled the back of her head, she shivered.

Slowly she looked up. "We should go inside," she whispered, feeling his breath against her cheek.

"It is getting late," he agreed, his gaze never leaving hers, weakening her resolve to keep her distance—to not get involved with this man.

Leah finally lost the battle. Her hands slid up his chest and circled his neck. "Very late." It was already too late for her… She was falling in love with Holt Rawlins.

"Then maybe I should say a proper good-night."

His head lowered and his mouth covered hers in a searing kiss. She trembled at the sudden rush of desire, but quickly became a willing participant. She combed her fingers in his hair and clung to him. With a groan, he parted her lips and delved inside to taste her, but it didn't seem to be enough for either of them.

No man had ever made Leah feel like this. She'd never had the time, never found a man she wanted like this.

Holt tore his mouth away. "This is crazy," he breathed, resting his forehead against hers. "You make me crazy," he confessed, before he cupped her face and returned for another kiss.

Leah was out of her mind, too. She shouldn't allow this to happen, but she couldn't seem to stop herself.

He finally broke away. "I better get you inside."

Leah wasn't able to speak as Holt led her into the house and up the stairs. Once in front of her bedroom, he stopped and pinned her against the door for another kiss.

"If I don't stop, I won't be able to leave you." His mouth found hers again and again, finally he eased back and looked down at her. She saw her desire and need mirrored in his eyes.

Leah's grip tightened. "Don't leave me, Holt. Please."

His intense gaze searched hers. "Are you sure, Leah?"

She wasn't sure of anything but her need for

this man. She couldn't let him walk away. "Yes," she breathed and opened her bedroom door. Together they went inside and walked to the bed, illuminated by soft moonlight. Not a word was spoken as Holt began to remove her clothes, layer by layer. None was needed as his hands and lips caressed her.

Leah was in love with Holt and she wanted to show him…if only for tonight.

Dawn came too soon, Holt thought as he rolled over and looked at Leah. Her beautiful face was relaxed in sleep. They'd been up most of the night, sharing an incredible experience. Fresh feelings stirred in his gut and the sudden need for her hit him like a bolt of lightning. He hadn't seen it coming, but it got him just the same.

Just like Leah had gotten to him.

Holt suddenly smiled. Resisting the urge to kiss her awake and begin their lovemaking all over again, he slipped out of bed. Gathering up his clothes, he headed to his bedroom to shower. There was still a ranch to run and Corey would be home soon. Holt found himself grinning again. He was looking forward to the routine.

Leah released the air from her lungs, and opened her eyes the second the door clicked shut. Holt was finally gone. She didn't want to face him just yet, nor did she want to analyze her feelings. She hadn't the right to give herself to a man, knowing there couldn't be any future for them as a couple.

"But you love him," she whispered in the silent room. She closed her eyes and began reliving last night. His touch, his caresses…his mind-blowing kisses. He pleased her in every way.

That didn't change the fact that she had to leave him.

An hour later, Leah finally came downstairs to find Holt in the kitchen fixing breakfast. He glanced over his shoulder and saw her. With a smile, he crossed the room and kissed her.

"Good morning," he said.

"Good morning," she returned, and stepped out of his arms. "You shouldn't have let me sleep in."

"There wasn't any reason for you to get up. I did the chores. I would have come up to your room if you hadn't come downstairs soon." He pulled her back into his arms, and kissed her.

Leah couldn't resist him, but as much as she wanted to give this relationship a chance, she knew she couldn't. She finally moved away. "Holt, about last night…"

"It was incredible," he finished for her.

"Yes, it was." She was dying inside. "But we have to think about Corey."

Holt could see Leah's uneasiness, and he didn't

like it. "So we need to set a good example for the kid, huh?"

She nodded. "We jumped in pretty fast and… what happened last night can't happen again. I'm leaving soon…"

Her words were interrupted when the phone rang.

Holt wanted to ignore the call, but it could be about Corey. He went to answer it. "Hello,"

"Hello, this is Joy Bryant, the editor for *Our World* magazine. I'm looking for Leah Keenan. Her mother gave me this number."

Holt's gut tightened. He wanted to say he'd never heard of Leah Keenan, but knew that wouldn't stop what was about to happen.

"One moment." He held out the receiver. "It's your editor."

The look on Leah's face showed her surprise. "I need to take this," she said, and carried the cordless phone out of the kitchen and into the office.

Holt went to the stove and turned off the flame. Breakfast was the last thing he wanted, not when his life was suddenly on hold.

Within minutes, Leah came back in and hung up the phone. "My editor wants me to go next week. There's been an uprising."

He waved off her words. "Isn't there always an uprising? Somewhere? Surely you told them you can't go now."

She shook her head. "This is my job, Holt. How could I tell her that? Besides it's only for a few weeks."

"What are you going to do? Drop in between assignments?" He glared at her. "Don't you deserve some time off to be with your family—to be with Corey." He left out himself as the familiar feelings of rejection nearly overwhelmed him. How could he have been foolish enough to let himself care again? "I guess he doesn't matter."

She blinked, not able to hide the hurt. "How can you say that? Of course I care, but you knew I was going back. How important this is to me."

"There are other people who need you, Leah. What about Corey?" Holt refused to let her know how much he'd gotten accustomed to having her here every day. Needing her to be here. For him.

"Corey has you and Zach."

"So that's your excuse for copping out on us."

"I have a few days before I need to leave. By then Corey will be used to the idea."

Holt doubted it. "Maybe you shouldn't stay here until then. Just cut the cord now."

Holt watched her as she swallowed hard. "If that's what you want. I can be packed and gone in an hour." She blinked. "If you don't mind, I'd like to see Corey and tell him about my new assignment."

"You can pick him up from his sleepover."

Leah nodded and turned to leave, but paused. "I know you won't believe this, Holt, but I'll never

forget you. Both you and Corey mean a lot to me."
With that she hurried out of the room.

"Just not enough," he whispered to the empty
room. Even busying himself with fixing breakfast,
he could still hear her moving around upstairs.

A few minutes later, he heard her come downstairs, then the front door closed. He had to stop
himself from going after her. What good would it
do? She'd still leave. Carrying his food to the table,
he sat down. A car door slammed and the engine
started. Then there was only the sound of her
driving away.

It was over. Leah was gone. Now, if he could just
get rid of her memory. He closed his eyes and immediately saw her smile…heard her laughter. She'd
touched every corner in this house…and in his
heart.

Now it was all empty.

"But I don't want you to leave," Corey said, tears
in his voice.

Leah turned away from the highway and looked
at the boy in passenger seat. "It's my job, Corey. I
have to go. I'll get back as soon as I can." His sad
face broke her heart. "You'll have Holt and Zach
here for you." She prayed she wasn't lying. "They
aren't leaving you. And we can e-mail and write
letters to each other."

The boy looked panicked and she couldn't blame

him. His life was about to be turned upside down…once again. How could he believe anyone?

"Are you really coming back?"

She hoped this assignment was only three weeks as her editor promised, but she knew there were no guarantees. "Really. I told my editor that I can't miss my parents' anniversary party." Steering the car off the highway and into ranch property. Time was running out and she needed to tell Corey the rest of it. "And since I'm leaving so soon, I've moved back with my parents at the inn."

She saw the panic on his face. "But why can't you stay here with us?"

Because she couldn't deal with Holt—seeing his caring turn to hatred. She wished things could be so different. If he loved her…if she hadn't made a promise she couldn't break. "It's just that I haven't spent much time with my parents and sister. I'll be seeing you, too."

"You promise?"

She parked at the back door, and turned in her seat. "I promise, Corey." She reached for him and pulled him into a big hug. She couldn't believe how much this little boy had come to mean to her. "I won't forget you."

He pulled back. "I won't forget you, either," he said. "I just wish you and Holt could stay with me…forever and ever," he cried. Embarrassed, he swiped the tears off his cheeks and slowly climbed out of the car.

She watched him take off toward the barn where Holt appeared in the doorway. He greeted the child with a quick hug, but never took his gaze off her. For a spilt second, Leah wanted to be the one running to him. Instead she backed up the car and drove away before she changed her mind.

The next day, Holt's mood only worsened. Corey spent the evening asking him questions he couldn't answer. He almost drove into town to face Leah himself, but what good would it do? She'd made her decision, and he wasn't a part of her future.

Zach walked in the back door. "What's for lunch?"

"Whatever you intend to fix. I'm not hungry."

The foreman went to the sink and started washing his hands. "I see you're still grumpy as an old grizzly."

"Sorry. Just for you, I'll try to sweeten my mood."

Zach grabbed the towel and dried his hands. "Look, none of us are happy about Leah leavin'. She means a lot to all of us, but at least we should make an effort for the boy. He wants to spend the afternoon with Mason. Since you've been in such a great mood, I told him he could go."

Holt nodded. "That's probably a good idea."

"Maybe a little time to yourself will help you get

your priorities straight. I could be wrong, but I thought you had feelings for Leah." The old man arched an eyebrow, waiting for an answer.

Holt didn't have one, nor had he a chance to analyze his feelings for Leah. He knew one thing— he couldn't put the boy in the middle of this. Holt had to put his personal feelings aside, and make his first concern Corey, and how this affected him.

Before he could respond there was a knock at the back door. Holt went to answer it and found the social worker, Lillian Gerard, standing on the porch.

"Hello, Mrs. Gerard," he said as he opened the screen door and allowed her to step inside.

"Mr. Rawlins," she greeted him. "I apologize for not calling before coming out, but I was in the area and decided to take the chance you would be here."

What did she need to visit him for? "I'm usually around or close by." He escorted her into the kitchen. "You remember my foreman, Zach Shaw."

"Hello, ma'am." Zach nodded, but stayed across the room.

"Nice to see you again, Zach."

They all stood there in an uneasy silence until Holt finally asked, "May I offer you some coffee?"

She shook her head. "No, thanks, I really don't have the time. I have another appointment to go to." She sighed. "I just wanted to tell you in person that a foster home has come available for Corey."

Holt's heart jump into his throat. They were taking Corey away from him, too. "Really. It happened pretty fast. Who is this family? Where is this home located?"

"It's a nice family in Durango. They have a boy about Corey's age. Their last foster child was recently returned to his family. I think this is a good solution, Mr. Rawlins." Her warm hazel eyes met his. "Unless…you can think of something else."

Holt wanted to demand to keep Corey with him, but deep down he knew it wasn't what was best for the boy. He couldn't give him…a family. "No. My only concern is that Corey be happy."

"I understand." There was another long pause. "How about I stop by tomorrow and we'll talk about it with him?"

Tomorrow was too soon. "Okay." After walking her to the door Holt stood there until the social worker drove away, feeling more alone than ever.

Zach just stared at him, then finally he asked. "You're just gonna let them take the boy?"

Holt tried to act unconcerned. "There isn't a choice here, Corey has to go."

"Says who?" Zach argued. "You could keep him yourself."

It had surprised Holt how many times over the past few weeks he'd thought the same thing. "That's a crazy idea. I have no idea how to be a father." All his own insecurities rushed to the surface, and he couldn't push them aside. "It isn't as if I had much of an example."

Anger flashed in the older man's face. "You know, since you've come here all you've done is bad-mouth your father."

Holt only stared at Zach.

"That's right, John Rawlins was your father. The best man I ever knew—ever could know. I truly thought when you decided to stay here and listened to stories about him, you'd feel differently. John was a good man. But he was also a sad, devastated man because he'd lost what mattered more to him than anything else. You."

Holt didn't want to hear this. "Too bad I never knew that man," he told him sarcastically.

"It goes both ways, son. Did you ever wonder why he never saw you?"

More years than he wanted to count, he said silently.

"So as an adult, why didn't you confront John— ask him why he never came to see you?"

"What was the use? He didn't want me."

Zach released a long sigh. "You know, it's about time you got to meet the man you despise so much." The foreman motioned for Holt to follow as he walked out of the kitchen, through the house and upstairs, all the way to the door that led to the attic. The old man turned on a light, and climbed another series of steps.

Curious, Holt followed, brushing away cobwebs as he kept up with the old guy. Zach maneuvered around old furniture and arrived at a stack of boxes against the wall. Surprised, Holt saw his name printed on the side of one of them.

"Here it is," Zach said as he slid out a crate, reached inside and took out a shoe box, then handed it to Holt. "Go ahead, open it. I dare you to find out who John Rawlins really was." The old man turned and left Holt alone.

Holt realized his hands were shaking as he pulled off the lid. Inside he found dozens of letters tied in bundles. All were addressed to him at his mother's home, and all were stamped Return To Sender.

They were unopened.

CHAPTER NINE

HOLT hadn't gotten any of them.

Not one.

For a long time, he just stared at the letters. Unopened. Then he decided he had to know the truth about his father once and for all. He pulled one of the oldest postmarked letters from when he'd been five.

His hands shook as he unfolded the aged paper. The first letter was printed in big block letters.

Dear Holt,

I miss you a lot. I hope you like your first year at school. I hope you can come and visit me this summer. Zach and Buddy miss you, too.

Love, Dad

Buddy. The golden retriever puppy his father brought home to him one day. A dozen other long buried memories flashed into his head, of other happy times with John Rawlins.

Holt searched through dozens of letters, checking each date. His father had written him a letter a week. Holt went through the entire box. Never failing, John's letters went out on schedule at the end of every week…for the first few years, then they slowed to about once a month.

Holt spent the next two hours going over years of letters. Each year one that had been dated September, his father asked about his school. Every May he discussed plans for Holt to come and spend the summer with him.

"Why didn't I?" Holt whispered in the musty attic. "Why didn't I get to visit my father?"

Through box after box Holt continued his search for the truth. He found more personal things. The divorce decree, along with another legal paper. "A restraining order," he read aloud. "John Rawlins is restrained to within fifty yards of Elizabeth Rawlins, or their minor son, Holt Rawlins."

Holt struggled to relax, to breathe. Either this paper was phony or his mother had lied to him for years. There was one other possibility—his father had been abusive to his mother…and to him.

Holt had only vague memories of his father. His mother had refused to talk about him. She never wanted her ex-husband's name mentioned in front of Grandfather Pershing.

Holt thought back to his grandfather and how many times he'd spoken about his close friend, Judge Harold Clayton. Surely his grandfather wouldn't… Holt tore through the document to the back page and scanned down to the signature, Harold J. Clayton.

The pain he felt was overwhelming. He went to the one small dormer window and struggled with the aged sash. It finally opened, and he gulped in much needed air.

Until his grandfather's death a few years ago, everything had always revolved around Mackenzie Pershing and his wishes. His only daughter had never crossed him, except maybe once…when she married John Rawlins.

How hard had Elizabeth Pershing Rawlins tried to make up to her father for that mistake?

Holt took another gulp of air as Zach climbed the steps and poked his head into the attic. "You okay, son?" he asked.

"Why didn't you tell me about these before?"

"John asked me not to."

Holt could barely control the rush of emotions. "But all those years…all that time I could have known him, spent time with him." Tears blurred his vision and he turned away.

Zach went to him. "John did come to see you. Many times. He parked across the street from your grandparents' house and waited for a glimpse of you. He'd come back here and talk about you for days. How much you'd grown…how much you looked like your namesake, Grandfather Holt."

"But what about after I was an adult? Why didn't he come to me? Tell me he wanted to get to know me…"

The foreman sighed. "He was there the day you graduated from that fancy school, but he ran into your mother. She was furious, and told him it was too late to try to start up a father/son relationship. That you hated him."

Was it true? For years, he had hated his father. But he never knew… "All these years, I thought he didn't want me."

Zach searched Holt's face. "John had a powerful love for you. After that day at your graduation, he thought he couldn't be a part of your life…ever. He finally gave up the hope of having you back." The older man shook his head. "I was so worried about him. Then one day Leah Keenan showed up here." Zach smiled as if he were remembering. "She could never replace you as his child, but she brought sunshine into his life. Just like she's brought it into yours."

Leah had been trying to pack for her trip all morning, but her heart wasn't in it. For the past twenty-four hours all she could think about was Holt.

And their night together…

They both knew they'd shared something so special. And yet, Holt couldn't understand why she had to leave. That was why she hadn't wanted to get involved with him. Why she hadn't wanted to care…

There was a knock on the door and her mother peered inside. The look on her face showed she wasn't happy her daughter was leaving, either. "How are you coming with the packing?"

"Fine. I can only take a duffel bag and my camera bag. So I just need to make sure I have plenty of clean socks and underwear."

"Just what a mother wants to hear." Claire sat down on the edge of the bed. "I wish you didn't have to go. I feel I haven't had much time with you."

Leah felt the same. "We've talked about this, Mom. I have to go. It's my job." She stuffed two more bundled pairs of socks into the duffel's pocket.

"I would usually agree with you, if I felt your heart was in it," Claire Keenan said. Her knowing gaze locked on her daughter's. "Can you say it is, Leah?"

Leah closed her eyes. No, her heart wasn't in it. "I made a promise," she whispered. "I have to help the children."

At the knock on the door, they both turned to find her father, holding the cordless phone. "There's a call for you. It's Jason Mitchell, he's from the Mitchell Gallery in New York."

Leah frowned. She didn't have any idea who this man was. She took the phone. "This is Leah Keenan."

"Hello, Ms. Keenan, my name is Jason Mitchell. I hope I didn't call at a bad time."

"Actually this isn't really a good time, I'm just about to leave for my next assignment."

"Then I apologize for disturbing you," he said. "If I may have the name of your agent, I will contact him or her directly."

"My agent?" she asked.

"Yes. Holt neglected to give me the name when he sent me your photos."

"Holt? He sent you my photos?"

"Yes. I'm sure you've heard this before, but you have an incredible talent, Ms. Keenan. Those photos of the children were both beautiful and heart-wrenching."

Holt had sent her photos to a gallery in New York? She shook her head. "You're interested in my photos?"

"Very much so," Mr. Mitchell said. "And if you have any others I could see, I would love to look at them. The reason I called was, I do a show featuring debut artists every September. If it's possible I'd like you to participate."

This was a dream come true. "Could I get back to you on this, Mr. Mitchell?" Her mother handed her a pen and paper to jot down the gallery owner's private number before she hung up.

"The Mitchell Gallery in New York wants my photos in their next fall show," she told her parents.

"Oh, Leah, that's wonderful," her mother said and hugged her.

Next her father gave her a big bear hug. "We're so proud of you."

"Holt sent him my photos," she said, still amazed at the fact.

"Sounds like Holt is pretty proud of you, too." Tim exchanged a look with his wife. "I'll be downstairs if you need me," he said and left the two women alone.

Leah couldn't think about Holt, or how much she cared about him. "Oh, Mom, what am I going to do?" she sobbed. "I have to go back, but…"

"Sweetheart," Claire said. "You have no idea how much your pictures have helped tell the world about those children's struggles."

"But I lost Soraya."

Her mother's gaze searched hers. "It wasn't your failure. It was the cruelty of nature. You did everything you could to save her."

Leah sank back on the bed. "I wanted to give her so much."

"And you were able to…for a short time anyway. Some times these things happen for a reason." Claire took her daughter's hand. "Do you ever wonder why you were the one who found Corey…and Holt that day?"

Leah thought back to the first time she'd seen Holt. How angry and distant he'd been. And Corey…he'd been so afraid to let anyone close. "They need each other."

"They need you, too," her mother told her, tears filling her eyes also.

Leah knew her mother had to be thinking about when she took in three little girls. "Like Morgan, Paige and I needed you and Dad."

Claire nodded. "Sometimes…things happen for a reason." She squeezed her daughter's hand. "There was a reason you girls were brought to us. And there's a reason you came into Soraya's life and Corey's…and yes, Holt's."

Leah couldn't speak.

"If you'd do a show with your photos, the money you make could be used to help children."

For the first time in a long time, Leah felt hopeful.

Claire raised an eyebrow. "It's not a sin, Leah, to put your heart over your head. What do you want to do?"

Leah wanted Holt to love her. "To stay here and help Corey. But I'm afraid that isn't possible. Holt doesn't want me…"

Her mother sighed. "Holt has had a lot of rejection in his life. It's hard for him to show his feelings."

Her mother's warm gaze met hers. "But it seems to me the man has already shown his heart to you. Don't you think you should offer yours to him?"

"What if it's too late?"

"What if it isn't?" her mother challenged. "You don't have anything to lose. And there's a big chance you might gain everything you want."

Her parents had that kind of love. "I want what you and Dad have."

Claire stood. "Then it doesn't matter who is right or wrong. Holt isn't going to care who makes the first move. Only that you loved him enough to go to him."

Her mother was right. She did love Holt and she wasn't going to let him give up on them. Not without a fight.

Leah arrived at the ranch in less than twenty minutes, still afraid that she might talk herself out of it. She'd rehearsed everything she wanted to say to Holt, but by the time she went into the kitchen, she'd forgotten it all.

Expecting to see Holt, she was surprised to find Zach fixing some coffee.

"Leah, you came back," he said with a smile.

She hoped she had. To stay. "Is Holt here?"

Zach nodded. "I was just going to take him some coffee. I bet he'd rather you did it." He held out the mug to her.

She took it. "Is he in the office?"

"No, in the attic. He's going over some old letters." Kind hazel eyes held hers. "I think it's safe to say that he could use a friend right now."

Leah wasn't sure that Holt would consider her a friend right now, but she took Zach's direction and went to find him. Outside the attic door, she hesitated, released a long breath before making her way up the last section of steps. At the top, she found Holt sitting on the floor, with stacks of papers around him.

"Hey, Zach, did you know that John had boxed in the Navy?" Holt said. When he didn't get an answer, he turned around. "Leah…" He got to his feet.

Leah wanted to run, but forced herself to walk to him. "Hi."

"This really isn't a good time," he told her.

Seeing the sadness in his eyes, she wouldn't let him push her away. "Zach sent up some coffee." She handed Holt the mug and glanced around at the scattered papers on the floor. "What are you digging through?"

He shrugged. "Just some old letters."

Leah knelt down, picked one up and read the name. It was addressed to Holt. Her gaze went to the corner of the envelope. They were from John Rawlins. There were dozen more of them strewn around the floor, all were stamped, Return To Sender.

"These are from your father…" she whispered

and looked up at Holt. His jaw was rigid, his body tense, but his eyes told her of a boy's years of loneliness, a boy who had needed a father, who had wished for his father every day of his life…

"Oh, Holt." She rose and went to him, but he raised a hand to stop her from getting too close.

"Funny isn't it," he began. "All these years I've worked up a good hate for the man…" His voice quivered and he turned away momentarily. "And now, I find out that all he wanted was…his son."

Leah swallowed hard to keep her own emotions in check.

Suddenly anger slashed across his face. "I hope to God it was my grandfather sending back the letters…" He shook his head. "I don't want to think my own mother kept me from my father, but…it really doesn't matter now. Dammit! It's too late."

"It does matter, Holt," Leah insisted. "It matters that you know your father tried to stay in touch with you. That he loved you."

"And thanks to my grandfather's money and power, he managed to stop him."

She wanted to absorb his pain. "Oh, Holt, I'm so sorry—for you, for John and what you both lost. A parent should never be kept from his child." She stepped into his arms.

Like an anchor, Holt wrapped his arms around Leah. She felt so good. And she'd come back. "At least I now know the truth."

She looked up at him. "Now, you have to let go of your anger, Holt. Don't let it consume your life. That's the last thing that John would want for you."

Holt couldn't think right now, he only knew that he didn't want to lose Leah again. "It's hard for me…"

He was so torn up inside, and didn't know if he'd ever recover. "You've always said that John was a good man. I've learned that he'd come to see me every summer. He'd park across the street from my house for a chance to see me, and he even was at my graduation."

"Sounds like he loved you a lot."

His grip tightened. "If only I'd known, if only I had the chance—"

Leah placed her finger against his lips. "Holt, it wasn't your fault. It was your grandfather who kept you from your father. John knew that. And he'd be the last person who would want you to blame yourself."

"But things could have been so different." His voice was rough. "I could have known my father."

"You have these letters, Holt. Years and years of letters to learn about him. How wonderful is that?"

He worked hard to smile. "You've been his champion from the beginning."

"John was easy to love. I cared a lot about him."

"He cared for you, too." Holt leaned closer. "You're hard to resist." His gaze searched her lovely face and he reached out and touched her cheek. "And I haven't been able to," he said breathlessly.

"You haven't?"

He shook his head. "I never should have let you walk away." His head dipped and his lips touched hers. "I should have understood how much your job meant to you. I'm sorry."

"My, it seems as if you've acquired a lot of insight in the short span of twenty-four hours," she said.

"In the past few hours, I've learned more about my father and myself than I ever have before." Holt hurried to get the rest of the words out. "I've never been good at relationships, Leah. In fact I've been pretty good at running from them. I've always ended things first, so not to get hurt." He paused. "Until you, now you're going to leave, too."

Leah could barely speak, she could barely breathe as she waited for Holt to say what she longed to hear. "I wasn't leaving you, Holt, I was…"

He stopped her words when his mouth captured hers, and she forgot everything except this man and how much she cared about him.

She broke away. "Holt, I can't think when you're kissing me, and we need to talk."

"I think we need to do more of this." He kissed her cheek and made his way down her neck. "We've already wasted too much time…"

It wasn't her resistance that finally stopped him, but the footsteps on the stairs. They turned to find Zach's apologetic look. "I hate to disturb you, but I can't find Corey."

Holt stood, pulling Leah to her feet. "He went to Mason's house."

"No, he didn't. Mason's mother just phoned. Seems Corey called his friend a few hours ago and said he had a stomachache."

"Have you checked the barn? Lulu and Goldie's stall?" Holt asked.

Zach nodded. "I've searched inside and out and all the usual places."

"When was the last time you saw him?" Leah asked.

"Right before lunch," Zach said. "I was coming to the house. Corey was, too, just as soon as he finished straightening up the tack room. Remember? That was when Mrs. Gerard showed up."

Holt cursed. "Damn. He must have overheard her."

"What?" Leah asked. "Why was Lillian Gerard here?"

The two men exchanged a glance. "They found a foster home for Corey."

Leah's temper flared. "You were going to let Corey go into a foster home?"

"I didn't want to, but…you were leaving." Holt rubbed his hand over his jaw. "I thought it was the best for him. A family."

"Are you so dense that you don't know how much that boy cares for you?" She threw up her arms. "Of course, you don't, you don't even realize how much you care about him." She sighed. "Men!"

She started down the stairs, and Holt and Zach following her.

"Wait, we need to find him," Holt called.

Leah kept going until she reached the kitchen. "Yes, we do, but this time I'm calling the sheriff for help." When Holt didn't stop her, she picked up the phone. After talking to Reed Larkin, she looked at the two men. "Reed's on his way."

Holt and Zach headed for the back door. "We're going to saddle the horses," Holt said over his shoulder.

"I'm going, too," she called after him.

Holt stopped, and their gazes met. "I wouldn't leave without you, Leah. We're in this together."

Her heart suddenly started pounding. "I'm not going anywhere, either."

"You're sure?" he asked.

She couldn't trust her voice, but managed a nod.

Holt closed the distance between them and pulled her into his arms, holding her close. "We'll find him, Leah, then we need to sit down and talk…about our future."

CHAPTER TEN

HALF the town showed up at the ranch, wanting to help in the search. Neighbors came by on horseback and rode along the foothills. Some had four-wheel drive vehicles covering the ground through the pastures.

Sheriff Larkin had organized the groups of trackers. "Look, we're going to be losing daylight in about three hours, and the last thing we want is for anyone else to get lost. So keep checking in."

The word came back to the house that the abandoned mines were clear and there was no sign of the boy. There weren't any sightings of Corey. Anywhere.

Holt knew that the boy hadn't taken much in the way of food and clothes, and soon, he'd be cold when the temperature dropped. Although it was early summer, the mountains were downright chilly at night.

He had to find the boy. He had to tell Corey that he wasn't going to be abandoned ever again.

"We'll find him, Holt," Leah assured him. "The one good thing is Corey knows how to take care of himself."

"But I let him down," Holt told her, knowing he'd blamed his own father for the same thing. "He thinks I don't care. And all I wanted was for him to have a chance at a family."

"You can tell him that when we find him," Leah said, wishing that Holt had included her in the commitment.

Standing on the back porch, he raked his fingers through his hair and set his hat back on his head. "I can't just stay here, I've got to go search for him."

Leah followed Holt. She was just as frustrated, and scared. "Then I'm going with you."

After telling the sheriff of their plans, she followed Holt to their mounts, Rusty and Daisy, tied next to the barn. They'd been out earlier searching close to the house hoping to catch a break on Corey's whereabouts, but found nothing. This time they were expanding their search.

During the silent ride, Leah glanced over at Holt and saw his pain. She felt it, too. She loved Corey. She remembered the first day she'd seen the dirty eight-year-old trying to wash at the waterfall—

"Hidden Falls! Holt, I think that's where Corey went. To the falls!"

Holt glanced at her, then reached for his radio,

and relayed the message back to the sheriff. Then he turned to her. "Let's go have a look."

Ten minutes later, Holt tied the horses to a tree. He took Leah's hand and together they walked toward the falls. Holt heard the rushing sound of water, and as they passed the trees, he caught sight of the glistening water pouring over the cliff's ledge. His grip on Leah's hand tightened as they made their way across several of the large boulders and came up to the pond.

"Do you see him anywhere?" he asked Leah as they scanned the area.

"No, but he's here, Holt," Leah insisted. "I can feel it. That little stinker probably planned for us to come after him. Oh, I don't care. I just want him safe."

Holt's gaze searched her face. "You love him, too, don't you?"

"Yes," she said. "I should never have even thought about leaving him. Now, I just want another chance to tell him."

Suddenly a small figure caught his eye, and hope returned. Holt leaned down and pulled Leah close. "It seems you were right…Corey did come here."

"Really?" Leah gasped, but Holt refused to release her.

"He's hiding behind a rock just over your right shoulder."

Leah tried to slow her breathing. "What should we do?" she asked, afraid that he would run off again.

"I'm going to try not to spook him," he said as he helped her sit down on the boulder.

"You can't let him run off again."

Holt glanced over her shoulder. "I can see him, but before I call him out, I need to be able to offer him stability. A permanent home." His gaze lowered to her. "Did you mean what you said about wanting another chance with Corey?"

"Of course I did."

"What about me?" he asked. "Will you give me a second chance?"

Her eyes darkened and she swallowed hard. "Do you want another chance?"

"I want as many as it takes to convince you." He lowered his head, brushed a kiss against her mouth.

Leah wanted, and needed his words. "So you want me to stay here? Just to help you with Corey."

"That's not all I want," he said in a husky voice. "I want us as close as two people can get…I love you, Leah…"

"Oh, Holt. I love you, too." She wrapped her arms around his neck and kissed him.

With a groan, he released her. "I'd like nothing more than to show you how much I want you, but there are things we need to talk about first."

She nodded.

He stole a look toward the boulder making sure Corey was still there. "I want you to stay here, but I had no right to expect you to give up your job.

You're an incredible talent, Leah. I'll support you all the way."

"Is that why you sent my photos to Jason Mitchell?"

He was busted. "I was trying to show you other options to help the children. So Jason called you, huh?"

"This morning. He wants me to do a show in the fall."

"I knew he would love your photos." He paused a moment. "So are you thinking about it?"

"It could be a good way to raise money for a good cause."

Holt cupped her face in his hands, looking into her golden-brown eyes, hoping he'd have the privilege for the next sixty years. "You're not going overseas?"

"I haven't had a chance to talk to my boss, but I'm staying in Destiny. My very wise mother helped me understand that there is a child right here who needs me."

"Us," he corrected, not as sure of his words. "You and me, together. I need you, too, Leah."

"Together."

"Sounds good," he said, but his happiness quickly turned to worry. "Now, we just have to convince one little boy that we want him to be part of our family."

"Just talk to him, Holt. He thinks of you as his father already."

"Then I should act like one and tell him how I feel."

He kissed her nose and stood. "Corey, we know you're back there," he called out loud over the sound of the waterfall. "You might as well show your face and talk to us. We're not going away."

Holt held his breath praying he'd said the right things.

"Just go away," the boy called back. "You don't want me anymore, and I'm not going back to another foster home."

"I'm not leaving you," Holt told him. "I admit I made a mistake, thinking I was giving you what you needed. For a while I thought I couldn't be a good dad to you." His throat tightened as Leah stood beside him and took his hand, giving him courage and support. "Then I realized that I can give you a good home, myself and…love."

The seconds ticked by and finally Corey climbed on top of the boulder. "You really want to give me all that?"

"Yes, I do."

The boy straightened. "What if you get mad at me?"

"Of course I'll get angry at you, just like you'll get angry at me. That's what happens in families. I didn't have a real family myself, not until you and Leah came into my life." He stared at the boy in dirty jeans and a shirt. No doubt, he'd been in a cave. "Nothing can stop how I feel about you, Corey. I love you, son."

He watched as the boy swiped at his check, but still he didn't move off the rock. "My dad isn't going to get out of jail for a long, long time."

"Then you'll stay with me for a long, long time. I'd like it to be permanent."

"Really?" Corey asked, the sound of hope in his voice.

"I want nothing more than for you to live with me."

"What about Leah?" he asked. "Does she want a family, too?"

The kid was a born negotiator. "I want her to be part of our family, too." Holt bit back a smile as he glanced down at Leah's loving gaze.

"You better ask her," Corey said.

Holt nodded, unable to take his eyes off her lovely face. "I love you, Leah," he whispered so only the two of them could hear. He brought her hand to his lips and kissed it. "I think I have since that day I found you here. I know I can be stubborn and moody, but one thing will never change, my love for you. Will you marry me? Will you be my wife?" he asked, then quickly added. "Just so you know…Corey and I are a package deal."

Leah never knew she could ever feel this way. She leaned into Holt's solid body and pressed her palm against his fast beating heart. "I happen to think that's a good deal. Yes, I'll marry you, Holt Rawlins, and I want nothing more than to be Corey's mother."

Holt kissed her hard and fast, then grinned as he looked at Corey. "She said yes," he called.

Corey pumped his fist in the air, and cheered. That's all Holt saw because he was concentrating on his bride-to-be. He lowered his head and his mouth covered hers as he tried to relay his feelings to her.

They broke apart just as Corey made his way to them. Leah watched as Holt scooped the boy up in his arms and hugged him close.

"Don't you ever run away again." He set the boy on his feet. "You scared us."

Corey pulled back. "I'm sorry. I won't do it again."

Leah hugged him, too. "They're going to have to fight us both, because we aren't letting you go. We're a family now."

All three of them turned around just as the sheriff's four-wheel drive vehicle pulled up and Reed Larkin, Leah's parents and Lillian Gerard climbed out. A few of the neighbors rode up on horseback.

Corey stiffened. "Uh-oh, are we in trouble?"

"No, son, you're not in trouble."

The first person to greet them was Mrs. Gerard. "Hello, Corey." She looked over his soiled clothes. "Looks like you had quite an adventure."

"Hi, Mrs. G." He stood close to Holt. "I'm sorry I made everybody worry, but it's okay 'cause Holt and Leah want to be my parents."

"I'm glad that everyone is safe." The social worker turned to Holt. "Am I to take it that you've changed your mind about being foster parents?"

"Yes, Leah and I want to keep Corey with us. But we want to change his status to permanent."

"Do you agree?" The social worker smiled when Leah nodded. "I'll start on the paperwork as soon as I get back to my office."

Leah felt Holt's arm around her shoulders as he spoke to the crowd. "I want to thank everyone for helping us find our boy, and to invite everyone to our wedding."

"Yeah, we're all getting married," Corey cheered.

The groups cheered and rancher Bart Young stepped forward and shook his hand. "Congratulations, Holt. I'm glad everything worked out with the boy." The rancher paused. "John would be proud of you."

"Thanks. I'm pretty proud to be his son, too."

Leah saw the emotion flash over Holt's face. She knew more than anyone how much that meant to him. She also knew how much family meant to him.

CHAPTER ELEVEN

Two weeks later on a perfect June evening, Holt stood on the ranch porch looking at the San Juan Mountains. In another hour the engagement party would start. Leah and the other Keenan women were inside finishing the last of the details. He decided it was best to stay out of the way and came outside.

In the past fourteen days, Holt had done a lot of soul searching. Not about his feelings for Leah. They were crystal clear. He loved her more than life. He'd been getting to know himself, and he'd done that by getting to know John Rawlins. He'd read every letter from his father. Every single one that he'd never received over the last eighteen years. He'd shared them with Leah, and together they'd laughed, and cried over what he'd missed with his father.

The hardest part had been when Holt confronted his mother. At first, she'd tried to deny what happened, then in a tearful confession she'd implicated her father, saying that he'd threatened to send both her and Holt away if John Rawlins was ever involved in their lives. She'd admitted that the restraining order involved a drummed up charge and was issued by a judge who'd been a friend of his grandfather. Holt refused to allow his mother to blame Mackenzie Pershing entirely. She had the ability to change the situation, to let Holt see his father.

Elizabeth Rawlins begged her son to forgive her and return to New York. Holt refused to return. Ever. He hadn't mentioned Leah or Corey. He wasn't willing to share that information with her. Maybe someday, but not yet.

Holt had also spent the past two weeks trying to legally adopt Corey. It hadn't been easy. First, he needed permission from the boy's biological father, Roy Haynes. Holt had gone to see him in prison and assured him that this was best for his son.

Surprisingly Mr. Haynes had agreed.

Holt then hired a lawyer, and once the paperwork was completed and the waiting period was over, Corey would be Holt and Leah's son. That was amazing for someone who'd once prided himself on being a loner.

Holt studied the same mountain range that his father had looked at over his lifetime. He felt John's presence here. A peace came over Holt. This was where he belonged. This was his home.

It was still rough. He'd always regret that as a kid he hadn't known his father, but knew he wasn't alone any longer. He had Leah, and soon, they'd be married. He took a small velvet box from his pocket. They weren't officially engaged yet…not until she got a ring.

"So this is where you've been hiding."

Hearing Leah's voice, he smiled. He slipped the box back into his pocket and turned to face his future bride. "I'm not hiding. I just needed a few quiet minutes before all the guests arrive."

As usual Leah looked beautiful. Tonight she wore a pale pink dress that fitted her petite frame perfectly, allowing layers of soft lace to float from her tiny waist to midcalf. Her shiny hair was pulled up and curls framed her face.

She frowned. "It's only a party, Holt. These people are friends and neighbors and they want to celebrate with us."

"I know, but I've always hated being the center of attention."

"Oh, you foolish man." She smiled. "Don't you know? All the attention is on the bride-to-be."

"As it should be. You look spectacular."

"It must be because I'm so happy." She moved into his arms. "I love you, Holt Rawlins."

He kissed her. "I love you, too, soon-to-be Leah Rawlins."

Despite his words Leah sensed that something

was bothering Holt. Maybe he was having second thoughts. Her chest tightened at the thought.

"Holt, if this is happening too fast… I mean it's only been a little over a month since we met. We could postpone—"

Holt's mouth came down on hers, his hunger an absolute denial of her suggestion. He finally broke off the kiss, but he didn't release her. "You and Corey are the two things that have kept me sane." His green eyes held hers. "It's been your love and patience that's helped me through this rough time. I won't survive if I have to wait much longer. I dream about you, every day walking around the house, going to bed with you every night, and us waking up every morning…together."

Leah touched his face. "I'm glad you're as anxious as I am. I've been miserable living in town. All I think about is curling up next to you…making love to you."

"Stop reminding me." He groaned, and held her close. "No regrets about your career?"

She shook her head. "How could I? I'm doing a show in September, and starting up Soraya's Foundation is more than I ever hoped for." Her eyes filled. "But my most exciting career is going to be the role of your wife, and Corey's mother."

"I'm glad." He grew serious. "But with every-thing happening so fast, I seem to have forgotten one important detail." He reached into his pocket and drew out a velvet box.

"Oh, Holt," Leah gasped. "You didn't have to get me a ring."

"I want you and the whole world to know how much I love you," he told her. "You've given me something I never thought I'd find. Not just your love, but your acceptance and a sense of family. Because of that, I want to give you this." He opened the box, and a gorgeous round-cut diamond in an old-fashioned yellow-gold setting was nestled inside.

"Holt…" Leah gasped. "This is…breathtaking.

"It belonged to my grandmother. After she died my father had it put aside to give to me…for my wife one day." Holt gave Leah a half smile. "Dad would be happy that I'm marrying you. Zach told me how much he loved you, Leah. How much he loved your visits."

Leah realized how emotional this moment was for Holt. She couldn't speak as she blinked back tears.

"If you don't like it, I can get you something else."

"Don't you dare," she threatened. "This is the one I want. No other ring could mean so much. It's precious."

"No, you're the one who's precious," Holt told her as he removed the ring from the box and surprised her by going down on one knee. "Leah, I love you and can't imagine living my life without you. Will you marry me?"

"Oh, yes," she breathed and allowed him to slip the ring on her finger.

He stood and drew her into his arms. His head lowered and he placed a kiss on her mouth, but the tenderness soon grew intense. When he finally broke off, they were both fighting for air.

"You're not playing fair," she accused.

"Oh, but it feels so good." He brushed another kiss against her jaw and began working his way downward to her neck. "How about we forget the party and find someplace to be alone?" Holt asked, whispering other intentions against her ear.

Leah shivered. "Oh, Holt, I'd like nothing better," she said. "But we have family and guests arriving soon."

The sound of approaching footsteps alerted them that they weren't going to be alone for long. Her mother and father walked out onto the porch. "So this is where you are," Claire said.

With a grin, Holt stood behind Leah, gathering her against him. "Yes, and I've been trying to convince your daughter to run off with me."

"Be patient, son," Tim said. "Soon the party and wedding will be over and you can have Leah all to yourself." With a wicked grin, he pulled his wife into his arms and kissed her cheek.

The love between them warmed Leah's heart. There had never been any doubt that Tim and Claire Keenan loved each other.

Corey and Morgan came though the door. "Is anyone here, yet?" the boy asked his new parents.

"Not yet," Leah said.

Corey looked so handsome dressed in inky-black jeans and new boots. He had on a blue Western shirt and a bolo tie.

His earnest blue eyes looked from Leah to Holt. "Then can I talk to you first? It's important."

"Sure," Leah said as her parents and Morgan discreetly walked down the steps and toward the end of the driveway.

Corey appeared so serious. "Is it for sure that you're getting married?"

"Yes, it's for sure," Holt said, taking Leah's hand.

"And you really want me to live with you? Forever?"

Holt bit back a grin. "I think it's reasonable to say that you will live here until college, son. And the Silver R will always be your home." Holt crouched down to be on the same level with the boy. "What is it, Corey? You know you can ask us anything."

Corey glanced back and forth between the two of them. "I was just wondering if…since you're adopting me…if it would be all right to call you Dad and Mom right now, or do I have to wait until the judge says so?"

Leah's fingers tightened on Holt's shoulder. "No, you don't have to wait. We'd like that very much, son."

Holt hugged the boy. "We love you, Corey, and we'll always be here for you no matter what."

Leah ruffled her new son's hair. "I always wanted a little boy like you."

Corey stood back and struggled to hide the tears in the corners of his eyes. "And I'm going to be the best kid ever."

Leah and Holt laughed. "We just want you to be Corey."

"Okay," he said and ran down the driveway. "Grandma Claire, Grandpa Tim, they said yes." Leah's parents hugged the boy.

Holt sighed as he drew Leah into his arms. "What have we got ourselves into?"

She gazed up at the man she loved with all her heart. "I think we got ourselves a family. A loving family."

Holt's green eyes met hers. "Best day of my life was when I found you."

"I think the best day was when you decided to come to Destiny. When you decided to come home."

"We're both home." Holt's head lowered and covered Leah's mouth in another searing kiss.

There were more footsteps on the porch. "I hear there's going to be a wedding."

Leah broke away from her man and saw her sister Paige smiling at her.

"Paige," Leah called and ran into her arms. "You're home."

"Of course, I am. I wouldn't miss your special day."

Morgan joined them, and the three Keenan sisters hugged each other.

Like old times, they were together again.

THE SHERIFF'S
PREGNANT WIFE

BY
PATRICIA THAYER

To Becky,
I was the new kid in town, and you gave me a hand and guided me through. You were there whenever I called for help…no matter what the hour. Thanks, friend.

CHAPTER ONE

PAIGE KEENAN needed to make a career change. And soon.

She could no longer live in Denver, not with a chance of running into…her past. Pushing aside the bad thoughts, she peered in the window of the empty brick storefront with the For Rent sign.

Although the light was dim, she could see hardwood floors, and ornate door moldings and trim that was characteristic of a 1916 building.

Intrigued, she tried the large brass knob. Surprisingly it turned and she pushed open the solid oak door.

"Hello," she called and her voice echoed back. "Is anyone here?" Stepping into the long, narrow room, she looked around. All at once she could picture the space as hers. A reception area adorned with oriental rugs and ferns and farther back a divider, separating the space for her private office.

Her excitement increased as she continued her search. It had always been her dream to one day have her own practice, but she'd gotten sidetracked with the excitement of working for the D.A. Suddenly her vision seemed to be more of a possibility—no, a necessity for survival.

Could moving back to Destiny be the answer to her situation?

In the back of the space, Paige found a storage room and another door. She tugged on the brass knob and it opened to a staircase. When she flipped the switch, a single light went on overhead, and she climbed creaking steps to a large musty-smelling room. Scarred hardwood covered the floors, and a tiny kitchen was tucked in the corner. Chipped cabinets hung open, displaying leftover canned goods from the last tenant. She was drawn to a bank of windows and a long, built-in bench beneath them. On the opposite wall another door led to a bedroom and small bathroom. Everything needed a good cleaning, and some paint.

She returned to the main room. It would take a lot of work, but she could make this livable. A shadow fell over the already dim room and through the windows she noticed dark clouds blocking the sun from the small Colorado mountain town. The wind picked up and it began to rain. Lightning flashed across the sky and seconds later the crash of thunder followed.

Paige turned to leave and noticed a man standing in the shadows of the staircase. She let out a gasp and her heart pounded in her chest. Another flash across the sky illuminated the gun he was holding.

"Sheriff," he announced. "Stay where you are."

Paige felt the blood drain from her face as he stepped

into the light wearing a khaki shirt and a silver badge. Then a familiar face came into view.

"Reed…" she whispered weakly. She tried to smile, but suddenly everything went spinning and her body began to crumple.

Reed Larkin holstered his gun and rushed to the woman just in time to catch her in his arms.

Not just any woman, but Paige Keenan.

Gently he lowered her to the floor, cradling her in his arms. Her silky brown hair fell away from her flawless, but pale face. He placed his fingers against her neck to find her racing pulse.

"Great job, man, you nearly scared her to death. Paige…" He cupped her cheek. The softness of her skin was nearly his undoing. He knew under her lids were those whiskey-colored eyes that had haunted his dreams for years. His gaze moved to her oval face—the straight nose lightly dusted with freckles, the tiny cleft in her chin. A beautiful package. His attention rested on her full mouth as he recalled how she had tasted…

It had been nearly ten years since he'd last seen her, but he'd never been able to shake the feelings she evoked in him. His pulse went into overdrive, his palms began to sweat. Damn, it was like high school all over again.

"Paige, wake up. Come on, honey. Let me see those big beautiful eyes."

Finally she shifted, making a soft moaning sound, and murmured the words, "My baby." Her hand moved across her stomach.

Paige was pregnant? Reed glanced at her ringless finger. She wasn't married. Before he had the chance to react to the news, her eyelids fluttered open.

"Reed…"

"Hi, Paige," he managed to say. "I've always dreamed of women falling for me, but not like this." He smiled, but quickly grew serious. "How do you feel? Should I call the paramedics?"

"No! I'm feeling better." She sat up slowly, avoiding his gaze. "I just forgot to eat…and you scared me to death pointing a gun at me."

"You are trespassing."

"The building is for rent and, I might add, the door was unlocked. I only came inside to look around."

"We've had some kids vandalizing." He frowned. Was Paige moving back to Destiny? "Are you looking for office space?"

She climbed to her feet and brushed her hand on her nicely fitting jeans. "Maybe. Any problems with that?"

He shrugged. Problems? *Only about a dozen.* "Just surprised that a big-time Denver attorney wants to open an office in a small town. I thought you outgrew Destiny, Colorado."

Paige straightened slowly, testing her steadiness. What business was it of his now? At one time they'd been friends—more than friends. That was a long time ago.

"I could say the same thing about you. A hotshot FBI agent returns home and becomes a small town sheriff."

Paige gave him a bold once-over. Reed Larkin was

definitely more filled out at thirty than he'd been at seventeen. She examined his developed chest and broad shoulders. One thing hadn't changed, he still had deep set bedroom eyes, a strong jaw and black wavy hair. He looked pretty good in uniform, too. But then he'd always looked good to her.

His voice broke into her thoughts. "I had my reasons for returning."

Years ago, Reed swore he'd never come back to Destiny. Never listen to another bad word about his family. Now Paige remembered why he'd returned.

"I heard about your mother's stroke. I'm sorry. How is she doing?" Sally Larkin had once worked at the Keenan Inn. That had been how Reed and Paige's friendship began.

"She has her good days, and her bad ones."

"Is she allowed visitors?"

He nodded. "Your mother goes out all the time."

"Is it all right if I visit her?"

"She'd like to see you." He studied her. "So are you going to be hanging around a while?"

"At least until Leah's wedding."

He nodded. "Holt's a nice guy. They seem happy."

Too bad Reed didn't seem happy to see her. That bothered her. Over the years, she'd missed their closeness. The way they had always been able to share things. That ended when she'd made a decision…to push him out of her life.

If she decided to come back to Destiny, she would see Reed…all the time. That shouldn't bother her, but it did.

Right now, she needed her entire focus on one thing. Her baby. Everything else she would deal with later, including Reed Larkin. So she had to ignore the feelings he stirred in her, blaming it on her already jumbled emotions.

"I should get going," she said. "I'm meeting with Morgan."

Reed raised an eyebrow. "You mean, the honorable mayor?"

"And your boss."

"Oh, I'm shaking in my boots."

His attitude was back and suddenly she was remembering too much…the skinny little boy she befriended when some third-grade kids were picking on him on the playground. But later she hadn't been able to protect him against the sadness over his father's desertion.

"I really should go," she told him, not wanting to return to the bad memories. She turned to leave.

"Paige…"

She stopped at the top of the steps. "What?"

"Have you told your family about…" His gaze went to her flat stomach. "Your condition?"

Paige tensed. How did he know? "I don't know what you're talking about," she denied.

"You murmured the words, my baby," he told her.

She started to deny it, but he would learn the truth soon enough. Everyone would. "I don't want to talk about this now."

He studied her for a few heartbeats. "There was a time we shared…a lot."

She didn't want to discuss her private business with a man who hadn't been a part of her life for years. "No, I haven't discussed it with anyone…yet."

"What about the father?"

Now, she was angry. "And I'm not having this conversation with you, Reed." She waved her hand. "Would you please forget that you even saw me today?"

She swung around to make her grand exit when another wave of dizziness overtook her, causing her to sway.

Reed rushed to her. "Whoa, I've got you." His strong arms went around her back and he guided her down on the top step. "I'm going to take you to the clinic."

She was very aware of the brush of his arm in the narrow space. It seemed to add to her instability. "No, I'm fine."

He cursed. "Like hell you are." He got up and went to the sink and pulled a white handkerchief from his pocket. He wet it under the faucet, then returned to her. He placed it against the back of her neck.

For the past two years and four months, Paige had worked tirelessly for the Denver D.A.'s office where she'd tried numerous criminal cases. But returning home to Destiny had her more nervous than prosecuting a high-profile drug dealer. And Reed Larkin was one of the main reasons. The other was telling her family about her pregnancy.

"I bet you didn't have much breakfast, either."

"My stomach is just a little queasy to eat much, but I was going to have lunch with Morgan," she fibbed, holding the cool cloth against her skin. It felt good.

"I'll call her," Reed suggested.

"No! I'm fine, and I can make it across town square to City Hall. So you can stop playing hero."

He stiffened. "Someone has to rescue you from yourself." He stood and headed for the door.

Just like ten years ago, Reed Larkin was walking away from her once again. The pain of his leaving this time, surprisingly affected her a lot. She felt just as alone. But just as before, she had to let him go…

Reed berated himself all the way back to the office. He should have just helped Paige out and not asked any questions, and he wouldn't have learned she was pregnant with another man's child.

Most guys had that special girl in high school, the one that was out of their league. Paige Keenan had been that girl to him. Pretty, smart and nice to everyone, but she'd dated the popular boys in school, and he was far from popular. Yet, she had been his friend.

The poor kid from the wrong side of town was off-limits. The boy whose father was the impractical dreamer, always looking for the pot of gold. Michael Larkin used to work the mine, had even partnered in one of his own, "Mick's Dream." Then one day the man walked out on his wife, Sally, a son, Reed, and daughter, Jodi, and never returned.

And no one had seen or heard from Mick in over seventeen years.

Sally Larkin had to take two jobs just to support her children. Later, Reed helped with part-time jobs, but his mother insisted he stay in high school. After graduation, he'd been offered a scholarship back east. His biggest supporter for going on to higher education had been Paige. He resisted a lot, but it hadn't been until she admitted that she'd outgrown their relationship that he had been hell-bent on leaving her and the town. After college, he went to work for the FBI, mainly so he could search for Mick.

Reed had always suspected that his father's partner, Billy Hutchinson, had something to do with his disappearance. But who was to question the richest man in town. Even with the technology available at the Bureau, Reed still hadn't found any answers, or his father.

Reed had finally put it to rest after a series of things changed his life. The first had been when his partner was killed in the line of duty. He, too, had been wounded, and after his recovery he had gone back to work for the Bureau, but it was never the same.

Then when his mother had a stroke twenty months ago it was the deciding factor. He returned to Destiny. She'd had to go into a convalescent home, and he made the choice to stay in town. For good.

He took a job as deputy, then just last year when the sheriff retired the small community voted him into the position. He had an area to protect, and just two deputies and a daytime dispatcher.

He was making a life here in Destiny. Even though his sister, Jodi, lived in Durango with her son, Nicolas, she was able to come on weekends. He visited his mother nearly every day.

Yes, he was dealing with things…and now, Paige had shown up. For years, he'd managed to keep her out of his thoughts. He now knew as soon as he'd set eyes on her again, it would be impossible to keep her out of his heart.

"Reed Larkin pointed his gun at you?" Morgan gasped as she sank into her chair.

Paige swallowed a bite of her sandwich. She was hungry and the food was actually helping her queasy stomach. "In all fairness to him, I was trespassing."

Her older sister brushed back her long auburn curls. "And what were you doing in the old Merlin building?"

Paige had arrived home last night, just in time to attend her younger sister's, Leah's, engagement party. She had been grateful that all the attention had been on the happy couple, and she hadn't had to answer a lot of questions. Questions about her career, her future.

She wasn't sure that she wanted everyone to know about her plans…yet. "Can you keep a secret?"

Her sister's green eyes sparkled. "Do you want to pinky swear, or would my word as mayor be good enough?"

Paige laughed. She had missed the interaction with her sisters so much. "Your word is good enough. I'm taking a leave of absence from my job. I'm rethinking my career goals."

Morgan brought her sandwich to her mouth and paused. "Does that mean you're thinking about coming home?"

Paige's thoughts turned to Reed. She'd be living in the same town with a man who's welcome had been on the chilly side. So what! This wasn't high school. He would just have to deal with it.

"Yes, but please, don't say anything to Mom and Dad just yet. I have to consider if I can make a living here." She couldn't seem to come out with the words, *I'm thirteen weeks pregnant.*

Morgan still looked skeptical. "What about your work with the D.A.?"

Paige sighed. "I need a change." And preferably to be far away from her baby's father. Drew McCarran had made it clear that he wanted no part of her in his life. She should be happy about that since all he'd said since they met had been lies.

She forced a smile. "Maybe I'll open my own law practice. What do you think?"

"It's a great idea." Morgan jumped out of her chair and came around the desk to pull Paige into her arms.

"Oh, Paige, this is wonderful. First, Leah returns home and finds the love of her life. Now, you're back to open your own practice. Leah will be so excited."

The phone rang and Morgan reached to answer it. Paige went to the large window overlooking the town square. There was a comfort seeing the three-tiered fountain where birds fluttered around cascading water. A white lattice-covered gazebo brought memories of band concerts on warm summer nights.

As one of the Keenans' three adopted daughters, Paige and her sisters, Morgan and Leah, had been blessed with charmed lives. Everyone in town had embraced the two toddlers and one infant who'd been left with Tim and Claire Keenan twenty-seven years ago.

Destiny's citizens would be thrilled that Paige was returning home. But what would they think of her when they discovered she'd made mistakes, and now, she had to deal with the consequences.

Morgan walked up beside her. "Sorry about that."

"Well, you are the mayor."

They both broke into laughter.

It was Paige who sobered and said, "Why don't we keep this between you and me? With the wedding in two weeks, I don't want any attention taken from the bride." And the news of the baby definitely would do that. "No matter what I decide, I have a month's leave to investigate my options."

Morgan nodded. "You're right. We need to concentrate on Leah's wedding."

Two weeks. Paige had a two-week reprieve. Her thoughts turned to Reed. Could he put his feelings aside, and keep her secret that long?

Later that evening, the Inn's kitchen was buzzing with activity while Claire Keenan prepared the family meal.

Paige's mouth watered when her mother pulled the large rump roast trimmed with red potatoes and carrots from the oven. Claire was easily the best cook in town, and Morgan ran a close second. Even Leah had learned a few things, but Paige was a lost cause in the culinary department. But since her appetite had recently increased with her pregnancy, she'd decided she better learn how to feed herself.

"Would you mind setting the table?" her mother asked as she added flour to the old cast-iron skillet to begin making brown gravy.

Paige's stomach growled. "Sure. Anything to hurry things along. I'm starved."

Her mother raised an eyebrow. "Good. You need to eat. You're too thin."

Not for long, Paige thought. How would her mother take the news about the baby? She walked back to the cabinets, knowing she had to tell the family and soon. She released a breath. Just not tonight.

Her mother looked away from her task, her gray-blue eyes full of concern. "Are you all right, Paige?"

Paige carried the stack of plates to the large, round table. "I'm fine, Mom. Maybe a little tired. I've just finished a difficult case," she told her. She wasn't exactly lying. She had finished a big drug case. And she ended her relationship with her baby's father.

"Well, your father and I are glad you finally took some time off." Claire smiled. "And we plan to spoil you while you're home."

Her mother's words brought tears to Paige's eyes. She worked swiftly to set the big, round maple table, then looked out through the large kitchen window to the setting sun. Large pine trees lined the back of the property, where a half dozen cabins had been built along a rocky creek.

Paige had loved growing up here. Any kid would. She didn't remember much before she and her sisters had become part of the Keenan family, but she knew she couldn't have had a better childhood, or more loving parents.

Now, with her baby on the way, Paige had questions about her own birth. About where she'd come from. Why had her biological mother left her three daughters on a stranger's doorstep? Maybe it was time to get some answers.

Paige's father walked into the kitchen. "It smells great in here," he said with a big grin and his dark eyes twinkled. But then she'd never known the big, burly Irishman not to be ready with a smile, a hug and a kiss.

"You say that every time you smell food," Claire said.

Tim Keenan came up behind his wife of nearly forty years, wrapped his arms around her and murmured in her ear. Claire blushed, and looked up at him with such unbridled love that Paige had to glance away.

The two had always acted like this. Paige had taken their relationship for granted. Now, she realized how special it was. Paige envied them. She'd worked harder on her career as a lawyer than on a personal life. Then she'd met Drew. Life had been perfect for a time, then everything came crashing down around her. When she needed him the most he wanted her gone from his life.

The pain Drew had caused her would never compare to the heartache she'd experienced when Reed left all those years ago.

It was an all-too-familiar story.

Back then she and Reed Larkin were friends and it had developed into a crush by the time they'd reached high school. All the girls had been attracted to the rough around the edges guy. Paige knew his tough act had been a shield.

Since Reed's mother had worked at the Inn, Paige had developed a friendship with him. That was until gradua-tion day and they'd both had decisions to make. Paige had always been college bound and then on to law school.

Reed had opportunity for college, too. To leave Destiny and the stigma of his father behind him. But he was willing to turn down a full scholarship to go with her. Not that she hadn't cared for him, just the opposite, but she'd wanted him to have a chance. In the process of con-vincing him to go away to school, she had to lie, causing her to lose the man she loved…and her best friend.

The familiar ache tightened in her chest as the memories flooded her head. She quickly pushed them away and continued to lay out the flatware. She had to stop reminiscing about the past. The future was what was important now. All her focus should be on her baby.

Men were off-limits.

Reed lived in Destiny, but that didn't mean they had to keep running into each other. It wasn't as if they moved in the same social circles. Her only concern was that he keep her secret for now.

The sound of voices caused Paige to turn around. Her sisters, Morgan and Leah, came through the door. Her baby sister's brown eyes were brimming with happiness, and why not? Leah was engaged to a great guy. She and Holt would be married soon, and they were adopting an eight-year-old boy, Corey. A complete family.

"Sorry, we're late," Leah said. "But we were busy trying to finish up some wedding plans." She took both her sisters' hands. "I need a maid of honor, and I couldn't choose between the two of you."

"It's okay, Leah…" Paige began to say Morgan could have the honor when her sister's grip tightened.

"Just hear me out," she said. "Holt and I talked it over. The only fair thing to do was draw a name. I mean, we'll all be getting married someday, anyway. So we can all take turns. The name I picked was yours, Paige."

Tears flooded Paige's eyes. "Oh, Leah, I wouldn't have been hurt if you chose Morgan…"

"Stop it, Paige." Leah smiled through her own tears. "Remember you don't want to upset the bride-to-be. So just say yes."

She glanced at Morgan. She smiled and nodded. "I'd be honored to be your maid of honor, Leah."

A tall, good-looking rancher, Holt Rawlins, walked to his bride-to-be and hugged her. His sandy colored hair had been recently cut, leaving a soft wave over his forehead. He had an easy smile and green eyes that sparkled with mischief.

"Boy, am I glad that's over," he said. "I'm also glad that I didn't have so much trouble choosing my best man."

"Who's doing the honors?" Paige asked.

"Holt asked me."

Everyone turned to see Reed Larkin standing in the doorway. He was dressed in jeans and a pale blue, Western-cut shirt, and looked devilishly handsome.

"Isn't it great?" Leah gushed. "Reed is going to be escorting you down the aisle, and you two get to toast us at the reception."

"Yes, that's great," Paige agreed as she caught the smile on Reed's face.

So much for not running into each other.

CHAPTER TWO

AFTER dinner, Paige made her way out to the porch. With all the wedding talk it was getting a little stifling inside the kitchen. She also hated the fact that she was keeping a secret from her family. An important, life-changing secret. Even though she'd come home several times since moving to Denver, tonight seemed different. Soon a lot of things were going to be different.

Leah was getting married in a matter of days. Paige was going to have a baby. The Keenan family was growing. In a few months the clan would have added three new members.

She pressed her hand against her stomach protec-tively, a habit she'd acquired since learning of her preg-nancy. This wasn't the way her mother and father had expected to welcome their grandchild. It hadn't been how Paige planned, either. She'd planned to bring her special guy home this summer to meet her parents.

How could she've been so wrong about a person?

She'd believed him when he said he was divorced—that he hated his wife, Sandy.

The day Paige had learned about her pregnancy, Drew announced that he was going back to his wife. In truth they'd only been separated for the past year, and Drew finally admitted that he wanted a second chance at his marriage. What she hadn't expected was his anger and his threat not to get in the way of his reconciliation. Then he stormed out of her condo and her life.

Paige wiped a tear from her cheek, refusing to cry over the man, or the past any longer. It was all about the future. The Keenans were going to be her baby's family. She and her child didn't need any man, especially a man who didn't want them.

"Would you mind some company?"

Paige tensed and glanced over her shoulder to see Reed. She shrugged. "It's a free world."

"Thanks," he told her, nodding toward the back door. "There's way too much talk about Gerber daisies and banana cream or strawberry filling for the wedding cake going on inside."

She raised an eyebrow. "Can't take it? And you're supposed to be the stronger sex."

He cocked a thumb toward the kitchen. "If you think I'm in bad shape, you should see how blurry-eyed Holt is."

That made Paige smile. Although she didn't know the groom well, she liked him. "Losing testosterone, huh?"

"Be careful, I'm feeling the urge to spit and find a belching contest." Reed walked to the railing, sat down.

"I'd appreciate it if you'd resist."

"I'll try." He leaned against the post and looked out at the rows of moonlit pines. "This is nice."

Paige wanted to ignore the fact that his nearness bothered her. What was wrong with her? She'd left those feelings back in high school. "I know. I've missed this place."

Reed turned to Paige. He could see that she'd been crying. He knew from his sister's pregnancy that women got emotional. Paige coming home to tell her family about her baby had to be rough. "Your family is going to be happy about the baby."

She glared at him. "I don't want to talk about this. And you promised that you weren't going to say anything…"

He raised a hand. "Hey, you have to know I wouldn't break a promise to you. I'm just trying to be a friend, Paige."

She remained silent.

He changed the subject. "Have you seen a doctor?"

She nodded. "Just to verify that I'm pregnant and to start my vitamins."

"You need a doctor here?"

She hugged herself. "I want an obstetrician."

"My sister had a good doctor. She's in Durango."

She nodded, but looked sad.

"Are you sure that you don't want to contact the father…?"

"That's the last thing I want," Paige whispered as she stared out into the night. Reed felt the familiar ache of wanting to take her in his arms and tell her he was here for her.

Damn, he hated that she could still turn him inside out. She'd come back to town and all he wanted was to be with her.

"I'm sorry…that things didn't work out for you, Paige." As much as he wished it, he couldn't make this right for her. Reed looked over at her and instantly wanted her. He always had, but it wouldn't work for either of them. They were both carrying too much baggage.

He stood up. "I should be going. I work tonight." He started to walk away, then stopped. "If you need to get a hold of me for anything, just call the station. If I'm not there, leave a message on my voice mail."

Paige turned around. "Reed, this isn't a good idea…I need to stand on my own. I have a lot to figure out."

He smiled as he reached out and tucked a strand of hair behind her ear, grazing her incredibly soft cheek. "I know, I was just thinking that if you needed a friend."

Her lower lip quivered. "We tried that once."

"Yeah, we did. Maybe this time we can handle it better."

He turned and walked away, knowing he was lying through his teeth. When it came to Paige Keenan, friendship wasn't all he had in mind.

The next morning, Paige woke up about eight o'clock, and made it into the bathroom before she got sick to her stomach. Luckily the family had gone downstairs and she was alone. How would she explain puking her guts out?

Paige showered and dressed in a pair of worn jeans, but had to leave the top button undone. While she put on a pale pink blouse she was unable to stop thinking about Reed. It would be such a bad idea to get involved with him, especially in her condition.

She was vulnerable, and could so easily lean on Reed. And that wouldn't be fair to either of them, even though he had suggested they could be friends again.

Paige smiled. In grammar school she could be friends with him, but now, the man was too good-looking and sexy not to stir her hormones. Any woman's hormones. No, she needed to stay as clear of Sheriff Reed Larkin as possible. Of course until the wedding was over, that wouldn't be easy.

She arrived in the kitchen to find her mother.

"Good morning," Claire said and kissed her daughter on the cheek. "How about some breakfast?"

No way. "Maybe some toast and juice."

Her mother put a cup of coffee in front of her. Of course Paige couldn't have caffeine during her pregnancy. "I think I'll pass on the coffee. I'm trying to cut back."

"Good. Your job is so stressful that you don't need it."

Paige took her place at the table and her mother brought the toast over and sat across from her. "So what are your plans for today?" Claire asked.

"Nothing until this afternoon when we go shopping for our bridesmaids' dresses. Until then I could help you here at the Inn."

Her mother patted her hand. "You're not here to work. You need this vacation."

"I don't mind," Paige said, needing something to fill her time.

"I have an idea," her mother said. "I'm going out to the nursing home to see Sally. You could come along."

Visit Reed's mother? That wasn't a way to stay uninvolved. "Sure." Paige finished with her toast and cleared away the dishes.

The Shady Haven Convalescent Home was about twenty minutes outside of Destiny. It was a fairly new facility with manicured grounds and the mountains as a backdrop. With its brick trim and red cedar singles the two-story building didn't look like a nursing home, but more like a retreat.

Paige doubted that Sally Larkin could afford this place on her own. Reed had to be paying a lot of the bill.

Claire and Paige walked though the double doors and notice the inside was just as impressive as the outside. A reception area was arranged around a fireplace, and gleaming hardwood floors. In an adjoining room, Paige could see several patients in wheelchairs, sitting at tables, playing cards and other board games.

Her mother approached the front desk. "We're here to see Sally Larkin."

An older woman with short gray hair smiled. "It's good to see you, Mrs. Keenan. Sally looks forward to your visits." She turned to Paige. "Is this one of your daughters?"

Claire nodded. "Yes, this is Paige. She's visiting for a few weeks."

"Hello, Paige. I'm Karen. I guess you could call me the social director around here."

"It's nice to meet you," Paige told her. "You have a lovely facility."

"Thank you. Our first concern is our residents." She stood and came around the desk, then motioned for them to follow her down a wide corridor. "Sally finished her physical therapy about an hour ago. She's doing very well. And she doesn't have anything scheduled until after lunch, so this is a perfect time for a visit."

They passed several rooms on the main floor. Most doors were open, revealing accommodations that looked more like mini apartments than hospital rooms. There was nothing generic about this nursing home.

At the end of the hall, Karen knocked on a door, then opened it. "Sally, you have some visitors," Karen said as she opened the door wider to reveal a small woman sitting in a wheelchair.

Sally Larkin wasn't as old as Claire Keenan, but the hard years, and a debilitating stroke had taken a toll. When she saw Claire and Paige, Sally's eyes lit up bringing back memories of the last time Paige seen Sally. Hers and Reed's graduation day.

Paige touched her hand. "You remember me, Sally?"

"Y…yes…" Tears formed in Sally's eyes.

"I hope you don't mind me just showing up."

The woman squeezed Paige's hand. "Wel…come." She struggled with the word. "P…Paige."

"Thank you, Sally. It's so good to see you." She hugged the frail woman, then looked into those eyes that reminded her so much of her son's. "I'm glad you're feeling better."

Claire joined the conversation. "Sally has improved a lot in the past year. She's talking again." Her mother smiled. "I'm glad my friend is back and we can share things. We're hoping she'll be able to come to Leah's wedding."

Due to the stroke, Sally's smile was crooked, but she was obviously pleased. "Doc…doctor said o…okay."

"That's great news," Claire said and looked at her daughter. "The facility has special vans and attendants that can take her where she wants to go."

"Who's taking who where?"

All three women turned to the door and found Reed. He was dressed in a pair of faded jeans and a burgundy polo shirt.

"Hi, Reed," Claire said and went to him. "The doctor said your mother can come to Leah's wedding. Isn't that great?"

He grinned. "Yes, it's great." He crossed the room and kissed his mother's cheek. "Maybe we should get you a new dress."

Sally frowned and shook her head.

"Oh, Sally, you shouldn't turn him down," Paige said.

Her eyes locked with Reed's, and once again, she was transported back in time to when they were sixteen.

He'd driven her to Durango to look for a dress for the prom. She was going with another boy. That had been when he confessed about his feelings for her. He wanted more than friendship.

"We should go," Claire said, breaking through her reverie. "We need to meet Leah for wedding shopping."

Paige patted Sally's hand. "It was good to see you again, Sally."

"C…come back."

"I will." Paige smiled, then looked at Reed to see he was pleased she'd come, too. She walked out of the room and he followed her.

"Paige, thank you for coming by today. Mom loved it. I appreciated it, too."

"It was no trouble at all."

His gaze refused to release its hold. "How are you feeling?"

Her mother had already reached the reception area and was out of earshot. "Better. This morning was a little rough. But I'm good now," Paige said.

He stuffed his hands into his jeans' pockets. "You look terrific."

A shiver went through her. She didn't want to analyze her reaction to the compliment. "I should go."

"Oh, I got the name of the doctor." He pulled a card out of his pocket. "Kimberly York. Jodi said she's the best."

Paige glanced down the hall again to make sure her mother was out of earshot. The business card actually belonged to Reed with his private phone number. The doctor's number was written on the back. "Thank you," she said. "I'll call and make an appointment."

"If you need someone to drive you let me know."

His offer was so thoughtful she suddenly had the urge to cry. She had to leave. "Thank you, again. I better go."

When she made her way to the reception area, she found her mother talking with a thin man seated in a wheelchair. He was bent over, with sparse white hair that stood out around his head. His face was weathered and lined with age. She blinked and studied the man closely. It had to be…old Billy Hutchinson.

Memories came flooding back to her. All the trouble he'd caused the Larkin family. And worse. Billy's manipulation had change the course of her and Reed's life. It was wrong, no matter if the cause had been a good one. But most of all, she'd always regret the lie…and losing Reed.

She approached them. "Mother…"

Claire turned and smiled. "There you are. Billy, you remember my middle daughter, Paige. She works in Denver now. She's a lawyer."

Paige swallowed her nervousness. It had been a long time since she'd seen or talked to this man. She wasn't eager to now. "Hello, Mr. Hutchinson."

"Bah, lawyers…they're all crooks. Give 'em a chance, they steal ya blind." He peered at her. "Why, you're that gal who hung around with that Larkin boy."

Paige's heart pounded. "That was a long time ago."

"Everything was a long time ago." He waved a crippled

finger at her. "You should stay away from those Larkins. They're no good."

After all this time Paige didn't want to rehash this, especially not with Reed just down the hall.

"You shouldn't upset yourself, Billy," her mother said. "That's all in the past."

Abruptly the man's agitation turned to sadness. "No, we can't change the past." His hazel eyes filled with tears. "Can't change a dang thing…what's done is done." He slumped deeper into his chair. "I didn't mean to…" He looked pleadingly at Paige. "It was an accident."

"What accident?" Paige asked.

He choked on the next word. "Mick…"

The lawyer in her couldn't stop asking more. "What about Mick?"

It was as if a curtain fell as she watched Billy's expression go blank. He stared off into space, not hearing them any longer.

Her mother stroked the old man's arm. "Billy has Alzheimer's. He's been here for the last year. There are days when he talks, then there are days when he just sits here." Claire sighed. "Billy has talked more with you today than he has in a very long time."

The attendant arrived and took charge of Billy, pushing his wheelchair down the hall. Paige stared after them recalling the old man's words. "Mom, what did Billy mean about an accident?"

"I'm not sure," her mother answered as they walked

toward the door. "Billy rambles a lot. It could have been something that happened years ago, or recently."

Paige knew that Billy Hutchinson had an interest in several silver mines in the area. And it was a fact that he hadn't always been fair about his business dealings.

"Not only had the Hutchinson family founded Destiny, but they've been pretty forceful in their efforts to control it," Claire said. "Maybe in Billy's advanced years, he wants to atone for his sins."

Paige wasn't the optimist her mother was; she knew the man was a schemer, because she had gotten talked into one of them. For ten years no one had ever known Paige's connection to Billy. And she wanted to keep it that way. She couldn't see the man again.

But all the way home old Billy's words bothered her. Was there more to his ramblings? The word "accident" kept nagging at her brain. Could Reed's suspicions be truth? Could Billy Hutchinson know more about what really happened the night Mick Larkin disappeared than he previously admitted?

Five hours later, the four exhausted Keenan women, Claire, Morgan, Paige and Leah, collapsed into the chairs at Francisco's Cantina in Durango. Numerous bags pushed under the table were the result of their shopping labors.

Leah smiled brightly. "Did I tell you this is where Holt brought me on our first date?"

"Yes," the other three women said in unison.

Leah pouted and her mother patted her hand. "It's okay, honey, we're just teasing you. We love hearing about it all. You've found a wonderful man and you're going to be married soon. You should be beaming with happiness."

Tears filled Leah's eyes. "Oh, Mom, it's just that I'm so happy. I love Holt so much."

Paige had to turn away. She was glad for her sister, but another side of her envied Leah's happiness. It was something she would never have with her baby's father.

Paige released a long breath as she picked up the menu and scanned it. That didn't mean she couldn't make a good life for her and her child. She didn't need a man to make a living. She was determined to give her baby enough love to make up for his or her father's absence. And it was time she started.

Paige closed the menu and placed it on the table. "I have an announcement, too," she said, drawing the three women's eager attention. "I've decided not to return to my job in Denver. I want to open a law office here…in Destiny."

"Oh, Paige…that's wonderful." Leah jumped up, pulled Paige to her feet and hugged her. "We'll all be living here."

Paige caught Morgan's smile, too. "We're glad to have you back home. So you're going to take the store-front in the town square?"

Morgan and Claire exchanged a look. "You knew about this?" she asked.

Paige held up a hand. "When I talked with Morgan yesterday I hadn't decided yet." She turned to Leah. "I kept quiet because I didn't want anything to overshadow your wedding."

"Oh, Paige. I don't care. I'm just so happy you're moving back."

Paige felt relieved to have shared at least part of her news. "I know. I've missed the family so much." *And I'm going to need all of you when the baby comes, she cried silently.*

"We've all missed you," her mother said as she squeezed Paige's hand. "Your father is going to be so happy."

"What am I going to be happy about?"

They all turned to see Tim Keenan approaching the table. The big man was dressed in a dark blue sport shirt and taupe colored trousers.

Claire slipped her arm around her husband's waist. "Tim, Paige has some wonderful news."

Holt walked up behind Tim and went to his excited bride-to-be then hugged her. "What news?" he echoed.

Paige felt herself blush at the attention. She hated that she hadn't told her family the entire story. Before she could say anything, another man approached the table. Reed Larkin. He was wearing a wine-colored shirt with dark trousers. She'd had no idea he was going to be here, but she was suddenly glad.

Paige gave him a pleading look. He seemed to read her thoughts and went to her side of the table.

"Don't keep us in suspense." Reed smiled.

"It's not that big a deal," she began. "I've decided to try private practice…here in Destiny."

"Oh, lass," her father cried and came around the table to hug her. "I'm so happy. Now, I have all my girls home."

"I love you, Daddy." She hadn't called him that since she was a little girl. Tim Keenan had always made her feel so loved…and so special. The last thing she ever wanted to do was disappoint him.

"It looks like we have a lot to celebrate tonight," he said as he sat down beside his wife.

"Let's just focus on the wedding for now," Paige said. "I took a month's leave from my job so I could think about my decision. I have plenty of time to help Leah with the preparations for her day."

Reed sat down in the only available seat right next to hers. Paige couldn't help but wonder if her sisters had arranged for that to happen. She hoped not.

Reed didn't need to be involved with her and all her baggage. Besides, she'd given up all chances with him many years ago. She stole a glance at him. He was definitely more handsome as a man than he'd been as a boy. Darn her hormones for making her notice, for making her feel something. She didn't need another complication right now.

But more came when the waiter arrived to take their drink orders. Paige ordered a ginger ale with lime, hoping no one questioned her passing on alcohol. No one did, especially when Reed ordered the same, saying he was on duty later that night.

After the waiter left, her father asked, "Have you decided where you want your office?"

"Yesterday I looked at the vacant storefront next to the real estate office. That's where I ran into Reed. He thought I was a vandal."

Everyone turned to Reed. "You can't be too careful."

Holt chuckled. "Yeah, we're overrun with crime in Destiny."

Before Reed could comment, Tim asked, "Doesn't Lyle Hutchinson own that building?"

Paige wasn't surprised. The Hutchinson family owned a lot of property in town square. It was well-known that Billy Hutchinson's son, Lyle, wasn't the best landlord.

"If you want any work done on the building," Morgan said, "you'd better plan to do it yourself."

"The place isn't so bad," Paige said. "It's a perfect space for what I have in mind, and there's even an apartment upstairs." She shrugged. "I don't mind the work. And I have a lot of family to help paint." She glanced at Holt. "And a brand-new brother-in-law."

Holt groaned. "Leah already has me working on the ranch house." He glanced at his friend. "Reed's the expert on remodeling. You should see how he's redone his mother's house."

Reed noticed Paige tense at Holt's suggestion. He didn't take it personally. What with a new career and…a baby on the way, her life was complicated enough. But he couldn't help but feel protective of her, wanting nothing more than to get a hold of the jerk that had deserted her. He'd like to teach him a lesson or two.

"Hey," he said. "If you find you need help, I can paint walls and sand floors."

She looked at him. "Thank you, Reed. First I have to discuss the rental agreement with Lyle. I might not be able to afford the place."

Her mother laughed. "If you handle Lyle like you did Billy this morning, he'll probably agree to your terms without argument."

Reed frowned. "You talked with Billy Hutchinson?"

"Only for a few minutes," Paige said, suddenly feeling guilty. "My mother saw him in the lounge when we left Sally's room. I just stopped by to say hello."

"Billy recognized Paige right away," Claire said. "And he just began chattering away. It was more than I've heard him say in a long time."

A familiar sinking feeling overcame Reed as he leaned toward Paige. "We need to talk…later."

The waiter arrived to take their order. Paige didn't look pleased, but Reed couldn't let this go. His only link to his father's disappearance was Billy Hutchinson. Reed was almost afraid to hope, but this was the best news he'd had in a long time.

Now, if he could just get Paige to help him.

CHAPTER THREE

BY THE end of the evening, Paige was positive that the members of her family were playing matchmakers. Her mother practically insisted Paige ride back from Durango with Reed, and she didn't protest.

In the passenger seat of Reed's late model truck, she planned ways on how she'd set her family straight. There was no future for her and Reed. What if she just came out and told them she was pregnant with another man's baby?

With a sigh, she leaned back against the headrest and closed her eyes, happy that Reed also seemed to enjoy the quiet, too. Drowsiness took over and she let the soothing vibration of the road lull her. All Paige's problems were temporarily erased from her mind as she recalled the pleasant evening with her family...and Reed.

Paige thought back to the shy, thin boy. How he'd walk her home from school and they would sit at the Keenan kitchen table and do homework while his mother cleaned the guest rooms upstairs. Sometimes they'd go outside and look for toads along the creek. They'd talked sometimes, about how it hurt him when people said things about his father. A lot of people in town had decided Mick Larkin was a thief and had run out on his family.

Besides her sisters, Reed Larkin had been Paige's best friend. But things changed when they went into high school. Girls started noticing tall, good-looking Reed, and other boys had shown interest in Paige.

Reed didn't like it and he'd told her so. Then he kissed her for the first time. She'd been surprised by the strong feelings he invoked in her.

No one could kiss like Reed Larkin.

"Paige…"

She heard Reed's husky voice calling to her. She blinked and finally opened her eyes to be met by Reed's dark gaze as he leaned toward her. She quickly realized her dream had definitely become a reality. And she couldn't resist him.

"Reed…" She reached for him.

Then she felt the soft caress against her lips. A too-brief touch of his mouth on hers, but it was enough to send her heart racing. Unable to stop, Paige turned her head toward him and the kiss deepened…grew bolder. She felt the tip of his tongue against her lips. With a whimper she opened and let him slip inside to taste her.

Wanting more, Paige slid her arms around his neck and combed her fingers into his thick hair. She opened to his caresses and returned his fervor as she stroked her

tongue against his. It had never been like this before…
she'd never wanted anyone like this. She struggled to
get closer.

Abruptly he pulled back, looking pleased with
himself. "I have to say your kissing skills have improved
since high school."

She shoved at him to see they were parked in the
Inn's parking lot. "Get away from me. You took advantage of the situation. I was half asleep," she lied.

"You whispered my name. What's a guy to think?"

Embarrassed, she worked at straightening her
clothes. "You're supposed to be a gentleman."

She heard his sigh. "You're right. I apologize."

He stared out the windshield. "Let's just say we
were both curious as to what it would be like after all
these years."

"Reed, I'm pregnant," she said, barely holding it
together. The last thing she wanted to do was fall apart.
"I can't afford the luxury to be curious…" Tears clogged
her throat, but she swallowed them. "My baby is all I
can think about."

"I'm sorry, Paige." He paused. "So the baby's father
isn't going to be a part of your life?"

"No. I realized too late, he was never really in my
life," she admitted. "It's better this way. Look, I've got
to go in." She went for the door handle when he reached
for her and stopped her. Somehow she ended up back
against him.

Reed had never felt anything as natural as having

Paige in his arms. "I'm sorry, Paige. Not because the guy's gone from your life, but because he treated you so badly. You don't deserve that." His hand moved soothingly over her back. "It's going to be all right, honey. Just let me hold you. Nothing more. No pressure…just lean on a friend."

She finally released a trembling sigh and buried her face against his shirt. Her tough act broke his heart. No matter what had happened to end their relationship, it didn't change the fact that he still cared about her.

"You're better off without the guy…and so is the baby. How can I help?"

She pulled back and gave him a little smile. "Some things I have to do on my own, Reed."

"And sometimes you have to rely on a friend."

She looked unconvinced. "That kiss—"

"Won't happen again—not unless you want it, too," he told her. He straightened. "Look, Paige, I'm content with my job. I came back here to make a life, but that doesn't mean it's easy for me to deal with the past." He saw her surprised look. "And yes, I'm still searching for clues about my father's disappearance."

"Reed, it was so long ago."

"I can't give up, Paige." He studied her for a long time. "I need your help. You talked with Billy today."

She nodded. "But…but he didn't say much."

Reed rested his arm on the steering wheel. "Look, Paige, Billy Hutchinson was the last person to see my father the night he disappeared. He also accused Mick of stealing from him. So whatever comes out of his mouth might have meant something."

Paige nodded, then began to repeat everything she remembered Billy had said to her—that he'd thought all lawyers were crooks, and to stay away from all Larkins.

Even with his FBI training, it was hard for Reed to stay objective. "What else?"

Paige frowned. "Billy looked sad and said, 'We can't change the past. Can't change a dang thing…what's done is done.'" Paige studied Reed's face. "His final words were, 'I didn't mean to. It was an accident.'"

"What was an accident?" Reed demanded.

"I asked him the same thing, and Billy just mumbled, 'Mick.' Then he just stared into space."

"Damn, don't you see Paige? Billy had something to do with Dad's disappearance."

During the following week, Paige was busy helping with wedding plans, but she had time to think about Reed, and their kiss.

It was a waste of time. She needed to think about her move…her career…her future. That was why she'd made an appointment with the Realtor about the storefront property.

Paige was doing another walk-through of the space, and she was growing more excited about starting up her own law practice.

"So the floors will be refinished and the walls painted by the end of next week," Paige clarified in her best lawyer tone. "It's imperative that I move in by the first of the month."

"There shouldn't be a problem, Paige." Kaley Sims jotted down notes on her pad. "Lyle is anxious to have this property rented. He'll agree to your requests."

Paige remembered the pretty blonde from high school. Kaley had been in Leah's class. Paige had heard that she was divorced and had a little girl.

"We can have it added into your contract."

Paige raised an eyebrow. "Good. If these upgrades aren't finished in time, Mr. Hutchinson will have to forfeit my security deposit. And I'll have the work done myself, or find another property that is suitable."

Kaley's eyes widened. "Listen to you. A lawyer now and opening an office right here in Destiny. It's going to be so wonderful. Are you going be taking on all kinds of cases?"

Paige nodded. "A general practice, but I specialized in criminal law since school, but now it's Door Law. Anything that comes through the door."

Kaley looked interested. "Do you go after ex-husbands who don't pay child support?"

Paige tensed, thinking that it was hard for single mothers. "If that's what you need."

"When you hang up your sign, I'll be your first client."

Paige smiled, then glanced around the second-story apartment. "Then get these floors refinished so I can move in."

"Will do."

They went downstairs and walked toward the front door when Reed stepped inside the building. "Hi, Paige." He looked at the blonde and nodded. "Kaley."

"Hey, good-lookin'," Kaley said. "I haven't seen you in a while."

"I've been around, mostly working," Reed said, looking uncomfortable.

Paige watched the quick exchange. Did these two have a past? Was Reed dating her? Paige quickly pushed the thought away. It was none of her business.

"Well, you know what they say," Kaley said. "All work and no play makes you a dull boy…" She gave him a bold once-over. "Haven't seen you at the Silver Bullet in a while."

"Like I said, I've been working."

This time Kaley looked uncomfortable. "Well, I better get back to work." She turned to Paige. "I'll have a crew out here tomorrow." She nodded to Reed and walked out the door.

"So you decided to take the place," Reed said as he glanced around the neglected building.

"There isn't much choice of office space in Destiny." She shrugged. "I took a two-year lease, in exchange for Lyle getting the repairs done and cheaper rent." Paige couldn't resist a chance to tease him. "But after the way you rebuffed Kaley, I'm not sure they'll get done now."

He glared at her. "There's nothing between us. All that happened was one night I ran into her at a bar and bought her a drink."

Paige tried hard to smile. Why did she care so much? "Did I ask?"

He strolled across the room to her. "You wanted to know, though."

"In your dreams, Larkin."

He leaned closer. "Oh, brown-eyes, don't you know, you've been there for years."

Paige sucked in a breath. "How can that be?"

He shrugged. "Do we ever forget the first?"

"Surely you've had other relationships…"

"You want to know if I lived as a monk for the past ten years. Hell, no!" His dark gaze blazed. "But if you want to know if I ever stopped wondering why you pushed me out of your life. Why you suddenly dumped our plans for the future? The answer is, *yes*."

Paige closed her eyes. "I can't give you the answer you want, Reed," she almost begged. "I can't."

He leaned closer. "I'm not buying it, Paige. We meant something to each other. I didn't believe it then and I'm not now." With that he turned and walked out.

Reed called himself every kind of fool as he walked into his office at the sheriff's station. Why had he said anything to Paige? Hell, until that minute he hadn't even realized how much he'd thought about her over the years.

But it was true. He had thought about her. Often. No matter that she'd ripped his heart out. He still couldn't get her out of his head, or his heart. Now, Paige Keenan was back…in his town and his life. And he couldn't seem to stay out of hers.

He picked up his phone messages and carried them back to his office and shut the door. He needed quiet to clear his head of Paige. But he didn't think that was possible.

Hell, she'd been there as long as he could remember.

Even when she was pregnant with another man's baby, he couldn't resist her, resist helping her…kissing her. But he doubted she would take any kind of assistance. She was the most stubborn, independent woman he'd ever met.

Now, other memories fought to surface. His partner in the FBI, Trish Davidson. If he'd ever had feelings for another woman it had been Trish. They'd shared a lot on assignments. There'd been times when they'd been asked to take on the role of husband and wife. Times when the acting as a couple seemed so natural. Familiar pain constricted his chest, making it hard to breathe. It had all fallen apart the day he couldn't save her.

Reed dropped in the chair behind his desk. He had no business trying to play anyone's hero. The past had proved he was lousy at it.

He needed to stop thinking about women and concentrate on what had brought him back to Destiny. His own family and finding out what happened to Mick. He glanced at the picture on the wall. It was the last one of his father and himself taken at the silver mine, Mick's Dream.

After hearing what Billy said to Paige, Reed was sure the man knew what happened to Mick.

Reed clenched his jaw. "Beware, Billy Hutchinson, I haven't given up, and I'm coming after you."

"Everything looks perfect, Paige," Dr. York said as she walked into her office, carrying a file with the test results. "The fetus is healthy and as far as I can tell, so are you."

Paige let out a sigh, not realizing she'd been holding her breath. "That's good."

"Just continue to eat right and no caffeine or alcohol. I also suggest that you exercise to alleviate the stress, especially if you're planning to work during your pregnancy?"

"Yes. I'm opening a private practice in Destiny to be closer to my family."

"So the baby's father isn't going to be involved?"

Paige looked down at her hands. How many more times did she have to answer that question? "No. We're not together. It was his decision."

Dr. York sighed. "Then it's probably better for both you and the child." She looked over the file again. "It states here that Reed Larkin referred you." She smiled. "He's a nice guy. He helped his sister during her pregnancy when her husband was deployed overseas."

Paige nodded. "He's a friend of the family."

"Can't have too many friends. And they make great baby-sitters, too."

Paige thought about her family. She would need all their help to raise this child. "I have sisters."

"Good. Sounds like you have a great support group."

The doctor stood. "If you have any questions just call the office, and I'll see you next month."

After they shook hands, Paige walked out and through the busy waiting room. She couldn't help but place her hand over her stomach protectively. There wasn't any movement yet, but there would be soon. She smiled. For the first time she allowed herself to rejoice over the fact that she had a life growing inside of her. A baby.

Suddenly she longed to share the news with someone. With that decision in mind, she headed to her car and back to Destiny. To her family.

"You're pregnant…" Morgan breathed.

Paige nodded from across her sister's desk. She had given her sister a brief synopsis of her situation, before the news. "It's not something I planned. I thought we had a serious relationship." Her voice grew soft. "He didn't feel the same."

"Oh, Paige…"

"I would have told you, and Mom and Dad right away, but I didn't want to take anything away from Leah's wedding. But after my doctor's visit, I'm about to burst with the news."

"So you just handled this all on your own. You went to the doctor alone…" Morgan came around the desk and pulled Paige into her arms. "I hate that you've had to go through this by yourself."

"Well…not entirely. Reed discovered the news right

away. He helped me." Tears flooded Paige's eyes. "He gave me the name of his sister's doctor." She smiled but it didn't stop the waterworks and Morgan was there to hold her. "I'm okay, really, it's just these darn hormones…I cry at everything."

"You can cry all you want," Morgan said. "I'm here. What do you need me to do, outside of putting a hit on one Denver detective?"

Paige pulled away. "He's not worth it," she said. "It's just that I feel like such a fool for falling for his lies."

"You loved him."

Maybe once, Paige thought, but whatever she'd felt for Drew had died with his lies and deceit. "I'll get over it. This baby is my only concern right now. That's why I'm moving back home. It's important my child has family around."

"This is so wonderful. A baby." Her older sister's green eyes lit up. "I'm going to be an aunt." She gasped. "Mom and Dad are going to be grandparents."

Paige sank down in her chair. "How are they going to handle this news?"

"Like they have everything else, with open arms," Morgan assured her. "What they won't like is that you didn't go to them right away."

Paige knew she was right. "I'll tell them as soon as the wedding is over. I want Leah to have her special day."

"You're lucky that it's only two days away. All you have to get through is the rehearsal dinner and the day of the wedding."

Paige wasn't worried about the ceremony, but that she'd be spending that time with Reed.

Paige stood up at the head table and tapped her knife against her water glass to get the attention of about fifty guests in the Keenan Inn's dining room.

The murmurs died out as Paige glanced at Reed looking entirely too handsome in his black tux. He smiled his encouragement and she swallowed before she looked at Leah and her new husband, Holt Rawlins.

"I have to tell you I'm standing here because I won the coin flip." She smiled as chuckles filled the room. "As all of you know the Keenan sisters are close. And although we've been apart the past few years that closeness never wavered. Now, Leah has added a man into the mix." Her smile widened. "But all I have to do is see the way these two look at each other to know they're in love. And Leah isn't just getting a new husband…but a son, too. Holt and Corey, I think you both know how lucky you are to have Leah."

Paige raised her glass of sparkling cider. "To Holt and Leah…may their happiness and love grow through the years."

As she drank from her glass, she felt Reed come up behind her, pressing his hand against her back.

"Now, it's my turn," he said as he looked at the bride and groom.

"As you all know Holt has only lived here a short time. A New Yorker who was going to run a ranch and make a life here." The crowd laughed. "We thought he'd never work out. He proved us wrong. He had guts, and learned to ride and brand cattle with ease, but he had his hands full with Leah Keenan. The sparks began to fly from the get-go." He raised his glass and looked at the couple. "If I've ever seen two people who belong together, it's you two. Here's to love…and sparks." He took a sip from his glass.

There were more tapping sounds and calls for the bride and groom to kiss. They did.

Paige continued to smile when a sudden dizziness hit her. She swayed but felt Reed's hand grip her waist.

"I got you." His grip tightened at her waist as he led her through the door and into the hall. They smiled at guests, then continued walking until they got outside and the cooler air hit her. Paige sucked in a long breath as they walked the length of the wraparound porch toward the back of the Inn. He sat her down at one of the tables and pressed her head down to her knees.

"Take a deep breath," he told her, then left her momentarily. When he returned she felt a cool cloth against her neck. After a few minutes Paige raised her head, feeling somewhat better.

He looked concerned. "How do you feel?"

"Better, thanks."

He took off his jacket and wrapped it around her shoulders to ward off the cool evening temperature. He squatted down in front of her. If possible his shoulders looked wider in his pleated white shirt, even with the bow tie.

"I feel so silly."

"It's been a long day," he said. "You probably haven't been off your feet in hours."

"I have to go back inside."

His ebony gaze narrowed at her. "Says who?"

"I'm the maid of honor. I'm supposing to be attending to the bride."

"I think Holt is giving his bride enough attention." He tugged the jacket tighter around her. "It's you who needs a little TLC and I intend to do that."

Paige started to deny it when the sound of voices caused her to glance over his shoulder. "People are looking at us."

"So, they'll just think we're out here to be alone."

"Everyone will believe there's something between us."

He frowned. "Well, don't act like that's such a bad thing."

"I didn't mean it like that." She placed her hand on his arm. "It's just my…condition. People might think that you're…the father."

His gaze held hers; she couldn't pull away. "Like I said, would that be such a bad thing?"

Paige barely held back her gasp. She didn't want to analyze what Reed was telling her. It would be so easy to lean on him…get used to having him around.

Tears welled in her eyes. "Oh, Reed. You shouldn't say a thing like that.…"

"Why not? I want to tell you a lot of things, Paige. Like how beautiful you look today." He brushed a curl away from her face. "How beautiful you look every day."

"Wait until I get fat...."

"You're with child, Paige." His hands cupped her face. "You look more incredible...with each passing day." His dark gaze held hers so tenderly. "A lot of men, me included, think that's sexy—"

"Oh, Reed..." She touched his face.

"You're nurturing a new life inside you. That's a pretty special thing..."

Before Paige could speak, she heard her mother's voice. Paige glanced up to see her parents. "Are you all right?" her mother asked.

She stood. Reed wrapped his arm around her shoulders for support. "We were just getting some air."

Behind her parents, Morgan appeared along with Leah and Holt. "Paige, are you all right?" Leah asked.

Paige glanced at Morgan and her older sister whispered the words. "Tell them."

"Tell us what, honey?" her mother asked.

Tears pooled in Paige's eyes, and she felt Reed's hold tighten. "I wanted to wait until after the wedding...so not to spoil Leah's day, but I guess it's time."

She glanced back and forth between her mother and father. "I'm pregnant."

CHAPTER FOUR

REED stepped back as the Keenan family gathered Paige in a loving embrace. Tears flowed as they hugged and stroked their daughter and sister.

Holt came up beside him, and together they watched the fussing. "I take it you knew about this."

Reed couldn't deny it. "I only discovered it by accident. The day Paige arrived home she fainted, and I was there to catch her." He looked at his friend. "And the last thing Paige wanted to do was overshadow her sister's wedding."

Holt shook his head in disbelief. "Being an only child and from a dysfunctional family that didn't believe in showing any affection, I'm still having a little trouble adjusting to all this togetherness."

"Seems to me you're doing just fine…you already have the beginnings of a nice family."

Holt grinned and puffed out his chest. "Corey is a great kid and a pretty self-sufficient nine-year-old. A baby is a lot different," Holt said. "And a little scary."

Reed wasn't sure he felt that way. He looked at Paige, and an incredible longing came over him. Since high school he'd thought a hundred times about the two of them ending up together. But that seemed like ages ago. Things were different now.

"You'll make a great dad," he told Holt.

"I hope you're right, because Leah wants a baby right away. And after Paige's news, I doubt I can talk her into waiting a while."

A smiling Leah came to her new husband's side. "We should go back in to see to our guests."

Holt kissed her. "You sure? If you want to stay out here with your sister…"

"Oh, no, please," Paige said as she turned around. "I'm fine, really. This is your wedding day. Go!" She waved at the bride and groom.

"Why don't you all go inside," Reed told them. "I'll stay here with Paige." All eyes turned to him.

"Great idea," Paige agreed. "He'll make sure I'm fine."

Her mother hesitated, then said, "Reed would you make sure Paige goes upstairs so she can rest?"

"Sure, Mrs. K."

Paige watched her family walk off, then turned to Reed. "You don't have to baby-sit me. I can make it on my own."

"No go. I promised your mother, so don't make me carry you."

Although annoyed over Reed's bossiness, Paige decided not to test his words. To avoid any of the lingering guests, she followed the porch around and went in through the kitchen. The caterers were busy cleaning as she walked to the back staircase and Reed followed her. She had no doubt by tomorrow everyone would have them linked romantically.

On the third floor she headed down the long hall to the large room she'd shared with her sisters. She opened the door and walked into the pale pink room.

Three single beds lined the angled walls, each covered with a handmade quilt. On the other side, a small desk and three dressers were arranged under the dormer windows. There was a shelf filled with high school and college mementos.

She stood next to her bed. "Okay, I've made it. You can leave."

Reed ignored her as he looked around. "So this is the Keenan sisters' bedroom. Did you know how many guys wanted to end up here?" He grinned. "And look at me, I've made it into the inner sanctum. Wait until I tell Tommy Peterson."

"Knock it off, Larkin." Paige dropped to the bed and kicked off her high-heel shoes. Her wine colored bridesmaid dress dragged on the floor as she walked to the closet, pulled out a pair of sweats and marched into the connecting bath.

"If you need any help just yell," he called out as she slammed the door.

Paige tossed her clothes on the counter and reached behind her, only to realize she couldn't get hold of the zipper. "Damn."

She yanked open the door to find him standing right there. She turned her back at him. "You make any smart remarks and you'll be sorry."

She felt the zipper lower. "I meant what I said earlier, you looked beautiful today."

Paige felt bloated and her dress was too tight. "Thank you." Turning around, she found Reed staring at her.

"You always were, and even more so now." His gaze lowered to her overflowing cleavage.

"Don't say that…I can't deal…"

"It's the truth, Paige. You are beautiful." His hand touched her cheek.

"Oh, Reed." She was losing the battle to stay strong. Why did he always have to be around during her worst moments?

"I'm here, Paige." He pulled her close. "I'm here for you."

She laid her head against his shirt and began to cry. He wrapped her in his arms and held her. It felt so good…too good, and she didn't want to pull away. For a while she wanted to lean on someone. But Reed Larkin wasn't just anyone. He was someone she'd cared about for a lot of years.

And her body seemed to recognize those feelings. The difference was subtle, but his touch grew intense as he slowly stroked her back, causing her own awareness. She pulled back, but his dark gaze held her, refusing to let her break the connection.

His head lowered to hers, and she was eager to take

what he was offering her when the bedroom door swung open and Morgan walked in.

Paige quickly pulled out of Reed's embrace just in time to keep from making another mistake.

A week later, Reed sat in his office, reading his mail. One letter in particular interested him. It was from Lyle Hutchinson's lawyer. Since Billy Hutchinson went into Shady Haven, his only son had taken over all the business affairs. Lyle wanted to buy the Larkin family's share in the Mick's Dream mine. Why now? The mine had been closed since Mick Larkin's disappearance.

Years ago, his father's partner, Billy, had said the mine had been nearly stripped and would cost too much to keep the operation going. Mick had disagreed, and the night he'd disappeared he had confided in his son he'd found the big strike. Mick went out to celebrate that night and never returned home.

The next morning the sheriff had appeared at their door looking for Mick, saying he stole from Billy Hutchinson. Mick hadn't been able to defend himself because they'd never found him. Even during Reed's years in the FBI he'd never turned up anything. And it wasn't for lack of trying. It was as if the man had been abducted by aliens. Reed felt sure his father was dead. And someone had wanted to make sure Mick Larkin was never found.

A knock on his door brought Reed back to reality. His young deputy, Sam Collins, peered inside. He was just six months out of training, but he was enthusiastic. His other deputy, Gary Malvern, had a few more years experience.

"Hey, Reed," Sam greeted him. "You want me out on patrol, or working the desk?"

Checking his watch, Reed folded the paper and stuffed it in his pocket. He stood. "You handle the desk until Gary comes in at noon, then run patrol. I'm heading home. Call me if anything important comes up."

Reed was off-duty, and for the first time in a long time, he had places to go and people to see. First on his list was Paige Keenan, attorney at law.

Paige stood back and looked around at the boxes sitting on the newly stained floors in her office. She never realized how many law books she had accumulated over the years until she'd gotten them out of storage. And she needed every one of them and more if she was going to open her office.

Already two desks and several file cabinets had been delivered that morning. She wanted more furniture in the reception area, along with a rug, some plants and accessories. And when she could afford it, a receptionist.

Paige raised her gaze to the ceiling. Nothing had been done to the apartment upstairs. First, she needed to get her law practice going and make some money. She'd resigned from her job with the D.A. and she didn't want to deplete her entire savings account.

Her hand covered her slightly rounded stomach and

she smiled. Now that she'd explained the situation to her parents, they'd been nothing but understanding and loving. Their support was important to her.

Paige's thoughts turned to her childhood, and her biological mother. The mother who brought her and her sisters to Destiny and left them for the Keenans to raise. Had her life been so horrific that she couldn't keep her own children? Claire and Tim Keenan had told the girls that they'd tell them the story when they were old enough to understand. But they never had, and she and her sisters had never insisted. Maybe it was because Morgan, Paige and Leah were afraid to know the truth. Either way, the girls thought of Claire and Tim Keenan as their parents.

Paige couldn't think about that now. She had a practice to set up and went back to pulling books from boxes. As she carried them into the office, she wondered where the kids Morgan had promised to send to help her were.

Paige heard the front door open. Good, help had arrived. "All right, kids," she called. "You can start by bringing boxes back here."

She continued to fill the shelves, but glanced over her shoulder when she heard her help arrive. It wasn't a high school student. It was Reed.

He set a box down on the floor. "Are you paying minimum wage?"

"Of course." Paige smiled and eyed him closely. He looked too good in his worn jeans and blue polo shirt. She hadn't seen him since the night of the wedding and suddenly she realized she had missed him. "Are you applying for a job?"

"I'm off work, so I can give you a few hours."

"I can't ask you…"

"You're not asking, I'm offering. Besides, these boxes are too heavy for you…especially in your condition."

"Morgan's sending some kids by. Some of the football team."

He nodded. "Good. How are you feeling these days?"

"I'm fine. My mother is taking very good care of me. And the doctor said I'm healthy."

He walked to her desk. "So you like Dr. York?"

"She's nice. She also remembers you. Says you were good with Jodi."

He shrugged and sat down on the edge of the large desk. "I was just filling in for her husband." He shook his head. "It was quite an experience."

"Easy for you to say, you were just a bystander."

Reed couldn't help but stare at Paige. It had been a long week, and he'd missed not seeing her. That wasn't supposed to happen, especially now since her parents were available. But that hadn't stopped him from walking through town square, slowing at her office several times during the week, wondering how she was doing. Even his mother kept mentioning Paige during their visits.

Paige looked away. "I'd better get back to work."

"I'll help, but first, I need yours. I want to be your first client." He pulled out the letter and handed it to her.

After a few minutes, she looked at him. "Do you have any reason to want to keep the mine?"

"Not really."

"How does your mother feel about it?" She raised an eyebrow. "I take it you're handling her business affairs."

He nodded. "I don't want to talk to her about this just yet. I'm more concerned why Lyle suddenly wants the mine. It's been over fifteen years since Mick's Dream was closed. According to Billy, it's not worth anything. And you know as well as I do, the Hutchinsons don't waste their time and money on anything unless it's profitable."

Paige didn't want to get involved with this. But after speaking with Billy that day, she hadn't been able to forget the things he'd said. "Was there a partnership between your father and Billy? In writing?"

Reed shook his head. "Hutchinson says there's an agreement, but Dad always told us that he'd never give away any part of Mick's Dream. I think my father was tricked into giving up shares. Then the night he disappeared, he told me that he'd found a silver vein. Then he got a phone call from Billy and said he was going to meet with him. That was the last time I saw my father. The next morning the sheriff showed up, saying Billy had accused Mick of stealing from him."

Over the years, Paige had heard several versions of the stories. She and Reed had talked about what happened, but they never really knew the details.

"Back then did you tell the sheriff what your father told you about finding the silver vein?"

"Let's just say he wasn't interested in listening to Mick's kid. Not long after that day, Billy showed up and told Mom that he was closing the mine. He gave her a copy of the agreement Billy and Dad had. It's bogus. I had it tested when I worked for the Bureau. It's not my father's signature."

"Why haven't you gone to the authorities?"

He shrugged. "A lot of reasons. I couldn't drag my mother through this again. Anyway, Billy never pressed charges against my father."

"But you want to reopen it all now. Because Billy said some things to me."

Reed nodded. "And I need you to talk to him again. I know that man is behind Mick's disappearance." His gaze grew intense. "My father wouldn't run out on his family."

"Reed, no jury in the world is going to believe the ramblings of a man with Alzheimer's."

"It's not about pressing charges, Paige. I just want to know the truth. And after all these years, that isn't too much to ask." Those dark eyes bored into hers. "Now my question is, are you willing to take on this case?"

She studied his face for a moment, then said, "I can't, Reed, not if I'm going to help you."

Paige told herself for the hundredth time she had to be crazy. But she had agreed to talk to Billy Hutchinson, because she wanted to help Reed.

What she needed was to avoid the temptation of the

man, but she rode out to visit Sally Larkin with her son anyway.

They arrived at the convalescence home and Reed signed in, then they walked down the hall to Sally's room. Reed knocked and opened the door, then went to his mother sitting in the wheelchair.

"Hi, Mom."

Paige watched as mother and son exchanged a hug and a kiss. Then Sally looked in her direction and held out a hand.

Paige went to her. "Hello, Sally. How are you today?"

"Fine." She smiled and glanced at her son. Paige knew that the woman was thinking they were a couple again. And why shouldn't she. They'd been thrown together a lot the past two weeks.

"Good. I brought wedding pictures." Paige sat down beside Sally, and for the next ten minutes went through the reception that Sally hadn't been able to attend.

After a little while, Paige made an excuse to leave and waved her goodbye. She was nervous as she headed toward the lounge. She'd agreed to do this, but insisted Reed tell his mother about Lyle's offer to buy the mine.

Paige walked past Karen at her desk. With an innocent smile Paige waved at the busy director, and strolled into the sitting area. The room was nearly empty, then she spotted the old man in his wheelchair by the open French doors.

Billy.

He was by himself while his attendant stood across

the room talking with another employee. As if he recognized her, Billy motioned for her to come over.

Looking around the deserted room, Paige curled her shaky hands into fists and made her way to him.

"You looking for me, young lady?"

She was taken aback by his bluntness. "Sure. How are you, Billy?"

"I'm old and dyin'. Can't get much worst than that."

She forced a smile. "You've lived a long time. And you've accomplished a lot. Built a town, had a family, struck it rich in silver." She'd hoped that was all he remembered, and not their conversation years ago.

The old man's eyes lit up. "Yeah. Those were the good days. I had everything back then. Money…women… friends."

Paige had heard about Billy's prowess. He was shrewd in business and his reputation with women was legendary.

"Now, my son took it all away, and had me locked up in here."

Paige had no doubt that Billy needed to have assisted care. "You have to admit it's very nice here, Billy. And people can come to visit you."

He waved his crippled hand in the air. "Bah, my own boy only comes here so people won't talk. He has all my money and didn't even have to work for it. He's a lazy son of a gun," he growled.

Paige glanced around again, but no one was paying attention to them. She sat down in the chair next to him. "And you worked hard in the mines, didn't you, Billy?"

His eyes narrowed in concentration as if trying to recall. "Day and night. It's backbreaking work, but I finally struck it rich." He grinned. "A few times."

"You worked a lot of years. Weren't you a partner in Mick's Dream?"

The old man stared out into space, and Paige thought he wasn't going to speak. "I had to close it. There was a cave-in...and I lost... Oh, Mick..." He tensed and a panicked look distorted his lined face. "It wasn't my fault. He fought me... He wanted it all." His eyes were pleading as he gripped Paige's hand. "You believe me, don't you? It wasn't my fault."

"Who fought you, Billy?" she asked, trying not to be too insistent. But he didn't answer. His expression suddenly went blank. She'd lost him. Billy Hutchinson had escaped into his own world.

"Excuse me, ma'am."

Paige turned to see the large male attendant. "I need to take Billy back to his room for his nap."

She stood. "I'm sorry."

The young man smiled. "No, please, don't be. Billy doesn't get many visitors. It's nice that you stopped to talk to him."

She nodded.

The orderly turned the wheelchair toward the exit. "Maybe we'll see you again," he said.

Oh God. Paige's stomach turned over as she stood and headed for the exit. She needed some air. She walked through the door and sucked in a long breath.

Had Billy meant he'd accidentally killed Mick Larkin, or were they just the babblings of a sick man? What should she tell Reed?

"Are you all right?"

She jerked around to see Reed. His dark gaze showed his concern. "Get me out of here."

With a nod, Reed helped her into the truck, started the engine and pulled out onto the highway. He wasn't going to ask her now, but the look on Paige's face told him that she'd learned something from Billy. For years, he'd run into dead ends. Reed was sure that Billy Hutchinson was the only one who knew the truth.

He glanced at the exhausted woman beside him. He'd waited a long time for any news…a little while longer wasn't going to kill him.

Later that day, Paige couldn't believe she'd slept so long. She had no idea that being pregnant could make her so tired. Getting off her bed, she went into the bathroom and brushed her teeth, rehashing her visit with Billy this morning.

She had tried many cases in court, and knew what questions to ask, but she couldn't seem to interrogate an old man with Alzheimer's. But, in her gut, she knew that Billy had something to do with Mick Larkin's disappearance. And she had to tell Reed.

She ran a brush through her hair and applied some lipstick. She didn't want to keep the information to herself any longer. When he'd dropped her at the Inn, he told her he was off-duty and would be at home. So that was where she had to go.

The Larkin home had never been a showcase. A small run-down bungalow on an acre of land. Mick Larkin had spent all his extra time and money working in Mick's Dream. She pulled off the main street to be pleasantly surprised. The brick and wood structure had been refurbished with a new roof and paint. The lawn was manicured and rows of colorful plants lined the walkway.

Paige climbed the three new wooden steps to the porch. The solid oak door had been stained a dark color. It looked like Reed had been busy since returning to Destiny. She rang the bell and waited.

Finally the door opened, but to Paige's surprise it wasn't Reed, but a woman. A very pretty woman. Jealousy reared inside her as the dark-haired beauty smiled at her.

"I'm…I'm looking for Reed Larkin."

"And you found the right place." The woman's smile widened more. "This is Reed's house, but he's in the shower."

Paige backed away. So there was someone in his life. "I'll just come back at a more convenient time."

"No, you won't, Paige Keenan." The young woman reached for her. "You don't remember me, do you? I'm Jodi. Reed's kid sister."

Paige blinked. "Jodi? Little Jodi."

"I kind of grew up."

"You're beautiful."

"As compared to the little ragamuffin I used to be."

Jodi was a lot younger than Reed and Paige. Sally had put her in day care while working. "Oh, no. It's just when we went to college, you were so young. I didn't recognize you."

"You haven't changed at all," she told Paige. "Please come inside. Reed will be out of the shower soon."

Paige stepped inside the living room with the gleaming hardwood floors and snowy-white moldings. The walls were painted a taupe and the furniture looked new, except for some of the wooden pieces.

"The room looks great. Reed must have worked hard to redo the place."

"Yes, he did." Jodi motioned for her to follow her. "Come into the kitchen. That's my favorite room." A wall had been knocked out connecting the dining room to the kitchen where all new cherry wood cabinets lined the walls, and granite countertops glistened along with the stainless steel appliances.

"Pretty impressive, huh?"

"Reed did this?"

She nodded. "He wants it nice for Mom to come home to." The sound of a baby crying erupted in the silence. "And that's my man calling to me. Reed should be here in a minute. Coming, Nicky," Jodi called as she walked out.

Paige should go. She could call Reed and tell him what Billy had said. She walked around the counter, her hand traced the granite as she looked closely at the travertine backsplash. This place made her condo look downright tacky.

"Jodi, where are my clean clothes?" Reed's voice echoed into the room right before he appeared in the doorway. He looked just as startled to see her as she was to see him. "Paige?"

Paige swallowed hard as she stared at the wide shoulders and well-developed chest. Her pulse started to speed up as her gaze lowered to the towel that was the only thing that covered his magnificent body.

CHAPTER FIVE

AFTER Reed slipped on his jeans, he pulled a T-shirt over his head. He didn't mess with shoes as he headed back to the kitchen before Paige ran off. To say he'd been surprised that she'd come to the house was an understatement.

Reed walked into the kitchen and found Paige seated at the granite counter along with his sister and little Nicholas. It was like a punch in his gut to see Paige holding the baby. She looked so…natural.

Jodi was the first to notice his return. "I see you've managed to find some clothes," she said, with a sly smile.

"No thanks to you. If you'd leave my clothes alone, I'd know where to find them."

"You mean on the floor."

"I was sorting them for the wash."

Jodi grinned. "And that's your story and you're sticking to it."

"You got that right." Reed went to the refrigerator and pulled out a soda. "Paige, can I offer you something to drink?"

"No, thank you." She cooed at the baby. "I got my hands full."

Reed came to see little Nick. At six months old, the boy had grown like a weed. He gave his uncle a toothy grin and raised his arms up to be held. Reed put down his drink, and lifted him into his arms. He loved this little guy and had had the opportunity to be a stand-in dad. But when he'd come home today, he wasn't in the mood for company—not his sister's anyway.

"As you can see, Jodi invades my peace on the weekends. She tries to organize my things and my life."

"Only because you need organizing," Jodi told him.

"Can't wait until big Nick comes home so you'll leave me alone."

"Eight more weeks," Jodi breathed as she smiled at her brother. "And you're going to miss us."

He glanced at Paige and winked. "Maybe not so much. Besides, you're only as far away as Durango."

Jodi turned to Paige this time. "I try to visit Mom as much as possible. She loves seeing Nicolas."

"I bet she does," Paige said as she let Nicky grasp her finger. "I've gotten to visit Sally a few times. She seems to be doing well, and the home is such a nice place."

"Thanks to Reed. He makes sure Mom has the best of care."

"Jodi…" He didn't want to broadcast it.

"Well, you do." His sister stood and kissed him on the cheek. "You're the best brother a girl could have."

"I'm the only brother you got." Reed handed her the baby. "I think he needs a diaper change."

Jodi wrinkled her nose. "I should say so. Come on, big guy, your mama needs to change you." She glanced over her shoulder. "Paige, why don't you stay for dinner. Reed's barbecuing." Without waiting for an answer, she left them alone.

Paige looked at him. "Oh, I can't interrupt your family time…"

Reed shrugged. "Like I haven't been eating at your family's table a few times." Call him crazy, but he wanted her here…with him. "Besides, we have some things to discuss."

She nodded. "I'll call Mom so she won't worry." She reached into her purse for her cell phone.

Reed's hand covered hers. "Paige, I want you to know how much I appreciate what you're doing."

She nodded. "I just don't know if it'll help."

"You're helping by just coming here." That could be a lie. Paige was distracting him, but she always had.

"What are friends for?"

Jodi had been a little too obvious, going to bed just after eight o'clock. Maybe it was a good thing because Reed wasn't ready to let his sister in on what was going on. She had been just a kid when their dad had gone missing. He didn't want to drag her through anything yet, not until he had more facts.

Reed carried two glasses of lemonade out to the back

deck. The sun had gone down and the evening was cooling off. The sound of crickets filled the air along with the clean scent of the pines.

"Are you warm enough?" He handed Paige her glass.

"I'm fine," she said. "It's so peaceful here. I really missed this living in Denver."

Reed sat down in the teakwood chair next to Paige, realizing too late it was a mistake to sit so close. He was far too aware of the woman. Hell, he could be in the next room and he'd still be aware of her.

He stretched his legs out in front of him. "I finished the deck about a month ago. Mom bugged Dad for years to build one, but he never quite got around to it."

Paige took a sip. "It's easy to put things off."

He sighed. It was time to get down to business. "I've never stopped trying to find my dad, Paige. You, better than anyone, know the promise I made myself. All the years I had to see my mother's pain…"

"I know, Reed. And I want to help."

He turned toward her. "Then tell me what Billy said to you."

She continued to stare into the night. "He said no one comes to visit him, not even his son."

"So Lyle isn't the dutiful son." Reed took a sip of his drink. "Just when it comes to handling the money. Then doesn't it seem strange that Billy's son wants to buy out a worthless mine?" he murmured more to himself than to her.

"I asked Billy if he had any mines now. He said he had one, but he had to close it. Said there was a cave-in."

Reed didn't remembered a cave-in. Had something happened after his father's disappearance? "Billy never went back into the mine. No one did. He closed Mick's Dream immediately after he accused Dad of robbing him." The man was lying, or he was confused. "Sorry. What else did he say?"

"Like I said, he told me there was a cave-in." Paige looked at him. "Then Billy said, *I lost... Oh, Mick...* Billy shook his head and looked like he was in pain. *It wasn't my fault*, he cried. *He fought me... He wanted it all.*" Paige's gaze held his. "Those were his exact words."

"What wasn't his fault?" Reed asked.

Paige shook her head. "I'm not sure. Billy repeated it again, and kept asking if I believed him."

Reed took a drink from his glass. Had Billy killed his father? Where was the body? The mine had been searched.

"Reed, I'm a lawyer and I have to deal in facts. But I think Billy was trying to tell me something." She raised her hand. "I say this because Billy also told me that his son had him locked away." She paused.

"Don't stop now," Reed coaxed.

"Okay this is just speculation. But what if Billy told these things to Lyle? What if in his confused mind he confessed something to his son? Something about your father."

"You mean like what really happened that night?"

"What do you think happened that night, Reed?"

For years, he wanted to believe his father was alive, but as an adult, after years with the FBI, he dealt in facts, too. "I think Billy and Mick fought that night. And Dad…died."

Reed cursed and jumped up from his chair. He hated this. He wanted it all to end—to be finished for good.

Paige came up beside him. "Reed, you know as well as I do that you can't open an investigation based on the words of an Alzheimer's patient."

"Suddenly you're acting as my lawyer."

"No, as your friend."

"So Billy just gets away with it? Lyle gets to bury the secret when his dad dies. The Hutchinsons get to keep their good name, and the hell with the Larkins."

"No. But you still only have Billy's words. Reed, you've made a good name in this town. People respect you."

"I don't care about me. It's my mother and my father. She needs this to end. If I can't give her anything else, I want to give her some peace at this time in her life. Do you realize what she had to endure the last seventeen years? How hard she had to work? And I went off to college and left her."

Paige grabbed his arm and made him look at her. "Your mother wanted you to go to college more than anything. It was all she could give you. You would be surprised what a mother can give her child out of love." She blinked at the tears in her eyes. "And Sally Larkin loves her children. Your only way to better your circumstance was through college and she knew that. So don't ever think that you should have given that up. She wanted a better life for you and for Jodi."

"So did Dad. The night he disappeared, he told me he'd found the big silver vein." Reed's voice was tight with emotion. "He wanted to give his family things, too. A better life for his wife and kids. Dammit! And Billy Hutchinson, with his greed, put an end to a man's dreams."

"No matter how much we want to, Reed." She sighed. "We can't go back."

"It's funny, we've come right back…right back here to Destiny. Do you ever think about what would have happened between us if we hadn't broken up?"

Paige glanced away. "That was a long time ago, Reed. We were kids and college was the best thing for both of us."

"I know, we planned to go together," he reminded her. "Or I was going to follow you to Denver." He was going to work a year or so, then attend college. When a special scholarship came through for school back east, he hadn't wanted to take it—until Paige told him that it would be better if they went their separate ways.

"It worked out for the best."

He leaned toward her. The same feelings he'd felt for her then still stirred inside him now. Not a damn thing had changed for him when it came to Paige Keenan. Even after all this time, the questions still haunted him. And he needed an answer.

"Paige, you never did tell me what I did to make you stop loving me."

She immediately looked surprised at his direct question. "Reed, it was so long ago."

"Not that long ago. Not when we were so in love… we could barely keep our hands off each other." He had never taken things too far with Paige.

He still respected her now, but his hunger overtook his common sense. He reached for her. "It still is, Paige. When I look at you now all those years disappear." He bent his head and brushed a kiss across her mouth. She gasped and her eyes widened in desire. She could never hide that from him. He leaned down and captured her mouth in a hungry kiss.

She gave a tiny whimper and wrapped her arms around his neck and kissed him back. He brought her up against him, and reveled in her feel, her taste…

He decided then and there, he'd never gotten her out of his system…and most likely never would.

Over the next couple of weeks, Paige buried herself in organizing her new law office. She planned to officially open her doors in two weeks. Although the disarray hadn't seemed to matter to the six new clients who'd just walked in from the street in the last few days. As promised, Kaley Sims was there in line for her services.

Paige had also taken a job one day a week in family court in Durango. At least she'd be able to until the baby was born. She frowned. That had her thinking about the still bare apartment upstairs. She thought about her furniture still in Denver as she walked out of her office, and climbed the stairs.

The living quarters had greatly improved. All the walls were painted an eggshell. The kitchen cabinets had been repaired, and Paige had replaced the old knobs with brushed nickel, matching the new faucet and light fixture over the sink. It looked ready to move in.

That meant she had to go to Denver, and arrange for a moving van to put her things in storage. She'd decided to just rent her condo for now. In fact, one of her co-workers had needed a place to live.

Paige rubbed her temples. She wasn't looking forward to returning to Denver. Morgan had offered to go with her and help her pack up. How could she pack up nearly eight years of her life there, nearly five with the D.A.?

And what if she ran into Drew?

Paige knew she had to have contact with him one more time, then he would be out of her life and the baby's life for good. And she could move on. She didn't need a man in her life. She wasn't exactly high on trusting another man anytime soon.

Paige's thoughts turned to what Reed had said the other night. What if things had turned out differently? What if she hadn't broken up with him? Maybe they could have made it together. Back then she'd loved Reed enough. But he needed a chance at a future. And the only way she could guarantee that had been to break up with him, so he'd accept his scholarship.

Although they'd been determined to make it together, they were too young and the odds were against them. Paige shook away the thought. Nothing could change the past.

She wasn't going to think about regrets now. As awful as Drew had been about her pregnancy, Paige already loved this baby. They had each other…and that had to be enough for now.

Reed called out to Paige as he came through the office front door. When he didn't find her downstairs, he decided to try the apartment. He climbed the steps and saw her standing at the row of windows. She was dressed in a pair of black stretch pants and an oversize print blouse. Her hair was pulled back into a ponytail. She looked about eighteen.

"Paige," he breathed.

With a gasp, she swung around. "Reed! Why do you always have to startle me?"

"I wasn't trying to," he told her as he climbed the last few steps. "I called to you, but I guess you didn't hear me. Sorry."

She sighed. "I guess I was daydreaming."

He glanced around the empty room. "Was furniture involved?"

"I have furniture, I just need to get it here."

"You need some help?"

She stared at him. "You need a life, Larkin, if you want to spend your free time moving furniture."

Reed hadn't thought about his personal life in a long time. He'd been pretty busy between work and taking care of his mother, and the family home. But since Paige's return, he realized how empty his life was. How he'd come to the conclusion, especially after a series of earth-shattering kisses, he'd never stopped caring about her. "What I don't want is for you to move furniture."

"I'm not. I plan to store most of it, and buy some new. I still have to go to Denver."

"Sounds like you have everything under control."

Paige didn't have anything under control, especially when this man was around. So how could she think she'd loved one man a few months ago, then suddenly get feelings for another? This one she couldn't blame on hormones.

"It's how it's got to be for me." Somehow she had to keep Reed out of her life…her heart. "Is there a reason why you stopped by?"

"Yes. I wanted to apologize for last night." He crossed the empty room to her. "I overstepped, asking you to talk to Billy in the first place. It's just that sometimes, I need to grasp at any possibility."

She frowned. "Does that mean that you're giving up on this?"

He shook his head. "No, I'll just find another way. I've been putting it off, but it's time I went through my father's things. I had years ago, but maybe I missed something."

Reed knew he should leave, work was waiting back

in his office. But he'd always enjoyed being with Paige, talking with her. That hadn't changed. "Well, I should get going." He backed away, then turned around and headed for the stairs.

"Reed."

He stopped and looked over his shoulder.

"I could help you go over Mick's things if you want."

His day just got brighter. "I'd like that. I'll give you a call." He paused. "This means a lot to me, Paige."

"I want to help you find the truth."

Reed couldn't stop himself. He crossed the room and drew her into his arms. She was resistant at first, but her body yielded into his. Reveling in her softness, he tightened his arms around her back, drawing her closer, alerting him to the increased fullness of her breasts pressed against his chest, the slight mound of her stomach. He tried to relax, to ignore his desire for her.

He'd have to be dead to do that.

Two nights later, Paige returned to the Larkin home. This time was different since Jodi wouldn't be around to act as chaperone. They would be alone.

Not a big deal. Reed was a friend and she was only here to help him. And even if she admitted that she still cared about the man, he wouldn't want to get involved with a pregnant woman. She didn't need another complication right now, she kept chanting as she climbed the porch steps. What worried her more was that he'd learn the truth about why she broke up with him after high school. He'd never forgive her for lying. She still needed to help her friend.

Suddenly the front door opened and Reed appeared. Wearing low riding jeans and a black polo shirt, he looked sexy with his dark, bedroom eyes and black wavy hair falling over his forehead. He smiled and her heart lodged in her throat.

The man had complication written all over him.

"You're just in time," he said, took her hand and pulled her inside.

"In time for what?"

"Pizza." He led her to the dining room where there were two places set at the corner of the table. "It's just coming out of the oven." He disappeared into the kitchen.

"You don't have to feed me," she called to him, realizing she was hungry. "Did you make your home-made pizza?"

Reed returned with the round pie. "Is there any other kind?"

"It was all we had since there wasn't a pizzeria in town." His first attempts at making pizza hadn't been too successful. But they had had so much fun experimenting.

He ignored her as he cut her a slice and placed it on her plate. He nodded to her to sit. "Eat, it's got all the things you like."

"I hope your skills have improved over the years." Paige glanced at the golden-brown cheese topped with pepperoni, mushrooms and peppers. All her favorites.

"It does look good." Her stomach growled as she sank into the chair. "I guess I could eat something."

Grinning, he sat down. "Good. And we can work while we eat." He took a big bite of his piece and chewed as he reached for a file. "I went through Dad's papers today. I don't think there's much. But Mick had kept some notes in date books." Reed pulled out several. "They mostly just log his hours in the mine."

"Your father had another mining job during the day, didn't he?" Paige asked.

"Yes, he only worked Mick's Dream evenings and weekends. I remember because he wasn't home much." Reed opened one of the booklets. "In here, he only stated the tunnel he worked and if any silver ore was found."

Paige had finished her wedge of pizza and reached for another. "Did your father ever find any silver?"

"He had little strikes, but it wasn't much and he'd always put the money back into the mine." Reed stared off into space. "There were nights I could hear my parents fighting over the money and all the time Dad put in at the mine. Mom hated it." Reed studied her for a moment. "I hated the town gossip the most. Dad was hardworking, and the most honest man I'd ever known." He sighed. "I know he enjoyed talking about finding the motherlode, but he'd never steal from anyone."

Paige had heard the stories, too. She saw firsthand how they'd hurt Reed. "And you really think he found it."

His deep gaze locked on hers. "I'd bet my life on it. Dad told me himself. What I don't understand is why

Billy and Dad fought about it. If it were the big strike, wouldn't there be enough money for them both?"

"Maybe Mick found out about the forged partnership papers. Or he could have told Billy about the strike to say he was going to pay him back the loan, and maybe Billy wanted a bigger share." Stuffed, Paige pushed her plate away. "What's sad is that Hutchinson may be the only one who knows the truth."

Reed stared at her for a long time, then glanced down at the glass in his hand. "For years, I thought because of what people said about my father might have been the reason you broke up with me."

"Oh, no, Reed, never."

Reed wanted to believe her. But it still ate at him. Why suddenly had Paige's feelings for him changed? How had she given up on them?

"I guess as a guy, I've wondered all sorts of things." He looked at her beautiful face. The face that he couldn't get out of his head for years. "Why, Paige? What did I do to make you stop loving me?"

Paige blinked in surprise. "Oh, Reed, we were so young. I guess I got scared…but I never stopped…" She stood. "I need to go."

Reed wasn't about to let her go, not when he was so close. He took hold of her arm and turned her toward him. "Can't you at least be honest with me, Paige?"

"It was so long ago, Reed. Why should it matter now?"

He touched her cheek. "It does to me. You've mattered to me… Even now."

"This isn't a good idea," she pleaded, but she didn't move away.

"Why, because I'm stirring up feelings that have never gone away…for either of us?" He drew her into his arms. "Because you still care about me."

Reed lowered his head and captured her mouth in a kiss that he'd been aching for far too long. He groaned as she wrapped her arms around his back and held on. His pulse raced and his gut tightened when his tongue swept into her mouth tasting her sweetness, her hunger. He broke off the kiss, and opened his eyes to see the mirrored desire in her whiskey-colored gaze.

He cupped her face. "You can't tell me there still isn't something between us. The need…the excitement…"

She shook her head. "We're both vulnerable right now, Reed. We're both reaching out for…comfort."

"I don't think that's all. We were friends a long time, Paige. We could depend on each…trust each other."

She missed that the most when she lost Reed. Their friendship. "Then be my friend now, Reed, and I'll be yours. I have too much on my plate right now to take it past that…for now anyway."

He grinned. "Can friends still kiss?"

Paige couldn't help but laugh and it felt good. Before she could answer her cell phone rang. She dug into her purse and answered it. She walked away for the conversation.

Reed went to the windows and stared outside, frustrated with himself for nearly blowing it. The last thing

Paige needed was him acting like a randy teenager. She wasn't ready for him…for any man in that way. He'd give her time, but he wasn't going to let her always push him away forever.

Paige hung up. "I'd better go."

"Problems?" Reed asked.

"Morgan has a meeting tomorrow that she can't re-schedule. She was going with me in the morning to get my things in Denver. We'll have to postpone until later in the week."

"No, you won't. I'll drive you."

"I can't ask you to do that." She swung her purse over her shoulder.

"You didn't, I offered," he argued. "I have a truck with a large bed in back. And as you already know I can carry heavy boxes—which you cannot. So you better get a good night's sleep because we have an early start in the morning." He gave her a gentle nudge toward the door, but Paige dug in her heels.

"You can't just take the day off."

He folded his arms across his chest. "I happen to have tomorrow off." He didn't, but had no doubt that one of his deputies would cover for him. "Besides, moving is a big job." His gaze narrowed while he waited for her to argue.

"And you happen to have strong muscles."

"Do you have a problem with that?" When she didn't say anything, he announced, "I'll pick you up at 5:00 a.m. Unless that's too early."

She stared at him a few seconds. "Anyone ever tell you, Larkin, you're bossy?"

"Only when I have to be." He kissed the end of her nose. "Now, go home and get to bed."

She glared. "Oh, I'm going to work you so hard tomorrow and you'll be sorry you volunteered."

He smiled as he watched her march out of the house. Never. He got to spend the day with her.

And that was a start.

CHAPTER SIX

THE next morning, Paige slept off and on during the long drive to Denver. Even though Reed's truck was a crew cab, she felt his constant presence, and kept inhaling the clean scent that was so uniquely his. That seemed to arouse a strong desire within her. She had the urge to lay her head against his shoulder and let him take care of it all.

No, she couldn't do that. This was her life, her new start, and she couldn't depend on another man. She had to do it on her own.

Finally Reed pulled off the interstate and Paige directed him to her neighborhood. To the place she'd called home for the past four years.

Although she'd only been gone three weeks, it seemed a lot longer. There had been so many changes in her life, and there were more to come. A new home, a new career and a whole new life all waiting back in Destiny.

Reed pulled into her parking space and shut off the engine. "We made it."

She looked toward her two-story town house. She

loved this place. When she got her job with the D.A.'s office, it had marked her independence, and the beginnings of a successful career.

"It seems strange to be back here," she said.

"If you want, we can go have coffee and return later," Reed suggested.

As much as Paige wanted to run away, she knew it was just postponing the inevitable. "That's not going to help. We better get started."

They went up the walkway and Paige inserted the key, then opened the door. Inside was a small entry that led to a living room with a fireplace. A bar with two stools faced a galley-style kitchen with maple cabinets and biscuit-colored tiled countertops. She was suddenly flooded with memories of Drew and her sharing the crowded space as they prepared meals together.

Paige turned away. "If you'll bring in the boxes from the truck, I'll start cleaning out the bathroom cabinets."

When Reed returned, Paige had him pack up dishes in the kitchen and she moved into the bedroom and cleaned out the closets. They were quickly filling up boxes and Reed loaded them in the truck. What she didn't need for her new apartment, she boxed and put in the storage unit over her parking space.

Reed checked his watch. "I don't know about you but I'm running on empty. Are you hungry?"

Paige blinked. "You mean I have to feed you, too?"

He smiled. "I'd say that was pretty reasonable for free labor."

Once again Paige noticed how good-looking the man was when he smiled…or when he frowned…or when he just stood there. "I guess I don't mind paying for your muscle."

"So you've noticed." He flexed his arms.

She fought a blush and lost. She would have to be dead not to notice. "I had to make sure you could do the job."

He stepped closer. "How am I doing so far?"

"I'll let you know when the work is done."

"Okay, but we both need a break. I'll go and get us some food, and you can keep working if you want."

Paige gave him her order and while he was gone, she called to have her utilities shut off on Monday. Her new tenant had already arranged to have hers turned on before moving in.

Paige leaned back on the bar stool. Everything was just about finished. The truck was nearly packed. All the big pieces of furniture were staying in the condo. It was cheaper to buy new than pay for a moving van.

Maybe that was a good thing. Starting from scratch, with no memories of her life here. No chances of running into Drew.

Suddenly the phone rang and Paige jumped. She reached inside her purse thinking it was Reed and he'd gotten lost.

"So you can't find your way back," she said.

"Paige…"

She tensed, immediately recognizing the voice.

"Drew…" She swallowed to clear her throat. "We don't have anything left to say."

"Oh, I think we do," he argued. "I waited to call until your new…boyfriend left. You work fast, Paige."

She stiffened. How dare he? "What do you want, Drew?"

"I just want to know what you're doing back here. You said you weren't coming back."

Was the man watching her? Suddenly feeling exposed, she got up and moved away from the windows. "When you walked out of my life two months ago you lost all rights. I'm not your concern."

"The hell you're not. And if you're here to cause trouble— You still pregnant?"

She wanted so badly to lie. "I am."

He cursed. "I warned you not to cause any trouble with my marriage."

If she'd had any leftover love for this man, it had just died. "The only thing I want from you, Drew, is to sign over to me all rights to this child."

"Only if you stay the hell out of my life."

"Gladly." Angry tears threatened, blinding her, but in reality she'd never seen more clearly than right now. "I'll get back you as to the time and place."

"This kid probably isn't even mine."

Another stab at her. "Think whatever you want, but this is a two-way street. I want you out of my, and my baby's, life."

"Maybe I'll just keep an eye on you to make sure you uphold your part of the deal."

He was watching her condo. "You stay away from me—"

Suddenly the phone was grabbed away. She swung around to see Reed place the receiver next to his ear. "I take it this is Detective Drew McCarran of Denver PD."

Reed paused. "Where I get my info is my business. And I'm sure there is much more on you, McCarran. I worked for the FBI for many years, and still have a lot of friends at the Bureau. If Paige says to stay out of her life, all you ask is how far away."

Reed listened, then laughed sarcastically. "Believe me, Detective, I can make more trouble for you than you can for us. So my suggestion is you do exactly what Paige wants and we'll get along fine." He nodded. "Good, now that we understand each other, I'm going to end this conversation." He flipped the phone shut and dropped it on the counter along with the sacks of food.

Reed wanted to break something. Instead he paced the kitchen, trying to calm down. Talking to that jerk made him angrier than he'd been in a long time. But when it came to Paige, he would protect her at all costs.

"Do you really have people at the Bureau who could hurt Drew?"

He shrugged. "I still have friends. And as a rule scumbags like McCarran have things in their past they don't want to come out... I haven't dug that deep...yet."

"I don't want you to do anything. I just want him

gone from my life." She brushed a tear off her cheek. "I can't believe I was so naïve to get involved with him," she whispered. "Oh God, I'm so ashamed."

Reed was right there taking her into his arms. "Shh, Paige. It's not your fault the man lied to you. You trusted that he'd care about you."

"It's not that, it's me." She pulled away. "I'm ashamed that I don't feel anything for Drew. And he's the father of my child."

"No, he's the sperm donor. There's a difference. The man doesn't deserve to be a father, or he'd stand by you."

Reed made her look at him, hoping she saw how he felt about her. How he'd always felt about her.

"As for your falling for the guy, we've all needed someone to be there." His voice grew husky. "Sometimes it might not be the person we want it to be, but we want love so badly…want someone to love us just because we're so tired of being alone."

Paige swallowed, then whispered, "Was there someone special?"

Trish Davidson's face flashed in Reed's head as he nodded. "Trish was my partner at the Bureau. We worked together on a lot of assignments. It seemed natural, and in life-and-death situations, you grasp at the living part."

"Is…is she the reason you left the FBI?"

"Partly. Trish died," he said and she gasped.

Reed had to keep talking…he had to get the story out. "I second-guessed my actions that night, wondering if there was something I could have done to save her." He glanced down at the compassion in Paige's eyes. "So see we all carry around baggage, a lot of wrong choices and a lot of regrets."

"I'm sorry, Reed."

He nodded. "When Mom had her stroke I made the decision to come back to Destiny. It was time. Time to stop running away…to face things." He sighed. "But it's hard when the past has a hold on you."

She reached up and touched his jaw. "And you've been hurt, Reed. It's hard to let go. I'm not doing so well, either."

He might have moved on with his career, but his dad's disappearance still haunted him. "You will."

"It frightens me sometimes." She pulled away and stroked her stomach protectively. "Starting up a new law practice, and having a baby is a little frightening."

"I have no doubt you can do it. Besides, you have your family around to help you."

"They've been great." She gave him a hint of a smile. "And so have you."

This time Reed couldn't stop himself as he placed his hand over hers. "I've wanted to be there for you, too."

She smiled. "Be careful what you promise. I may just take you up on it."

His heart was beating so hard, he thought she could hear it. "I care about you, Paige, and your baby. Would it be so bad for you to depend on me a little?"

Paige swallowed. It would be so easy, but they had

too much in the past. Too much to keep them from having a future together. "If things were different maybe I would take you up on it."

Reed reached for her. "There's nothing I see that's stopping us," he said as he lowered his mouth to hers.

It was a gentle kiss, but it didn't lack impact as he slowly, pleasurably, persuaded her into a response. Coaxing her lips apart, he slipped inside to taste her. She whimpered as his sure hands roamed over her back, cradling her against his strong body, making her feel both protected and needy. By the time he finally released her, she wanted to cry in protest. "Oh, Reed…"

"I think I made my point," he told her, then winked. He directed her to a chair at the counter where the food was. "Now, you'd better eat. I want you at full strength when I get down to some serious convincing about us being together."

Paige decided not to protest now. Later, she would set Reed straight about them.

Just as soon as she figured out what that was.

A week later, the honeymoon couple returned home and invited everyone for a get-together at the Silver R Ranch. The late-summer evening was perfect for an outdoor barbecue.

Even though Paige was busy setting up her office, she was eager to see Leah, and she admitted to herself, Reed, too.

It hadn't taken much encouragement for her family

to include Reed in their gathering, especially after all the attention he'd shown Paige.

The memory of their trip to Denver, and Reed's kiss still had her reeling. But that had been the last one. He hadn't been by her office to check on her, or even at her parents' Inn. Over the past week she'd only caught glimpses of him in his patrol car around town. He'd tossed her a wave, but that was as close as she'd gotten. It was good that he'd got on with his life, and she could live hers.

Paige turned off the highway and the ranch house came into view. Seeing the familiar black truck, her pulse began to race. She told herself she was excited to see her sister, but she knew Reed had been the big draw.

She got out and reached in back to pull out a large Queen Elizabeth rosebush she'd bought as a house-warming present and headed for the deck out back. Hearing the laughter, she quickened her steps. Since moving out of her parents' a few days ago, she realized just how much she'd missed her family.

Paige turned the corner and saw Reed right off, drinking a tall glass of iced tea. He probably had to go on patrol later.

Leah and Holt were wrapped in a loving embrace. Their smiling nine-year-old son, Corey, standing close by. No doubt he was happy that his parents were back home.

"I heard the world traveler was back in town."

Leah broke away and ran to greet her. "Paige," she cried as she hugged her, ignoring the rosebush. "How are you feeling?"

Paige laughed. "I'm feeling good, but you're smashing your welcome home gift."

Leah released her, but her smile held fast. "Oh, it's beautiful. Is it guaranteed not to die?" Holt appeared at her side and slipped a protective arm around her. The couple exchanged a look that seemed to heat the air between them. Paige glanced toward the deck to find Reed watching her.

"Honey, look what Paige brought us."

Never taking his eyes from his wife, he said, "It's beautiful, Paige. Thank you."

Paige smiled. "You're welcome. I'd ask how the honeymoon went, but I can see you both had a wonderful time."

"Hawaii was incredible," Leah gushed. "We swam and snorkeled and we walked on the beach…caught every beautiful sunset…" Leah turned to Holt as a blush rose across her cheeks. "And sunrises…"

"For someone who had spent the last four years traveling the world," her new husband said, "you seemed pretty captivated by the Hawaiian Islands."

Leah looked up at Holt. "I guess it was the company, and your persuasive ways." She leaned closer and whispered something that Paige didn't want to hear.

"I think I'll go say hi to Mom and Dad." She walked toward the back of the deck and hugged her parents.

"So how was your first night in your place?" her father asked.

"Just fine. I still have boxes to unpack but it's turning into home."

"If you change your mind, you know you can come back home," her mother said. "We could remodel your old room and…"

"Mom," Paige said warningly. "We talked about this. I've been on my own since college. And when the baby comes it won't be as disturbing, especially to the guests."

"This baby is our grandchild. We don't care who he or she disturbs." Claire finally smiled. "But your father and I understand your need your privacy and your own life. But we better be on the top of the list for baby-sitters."

"Oh, you definitely will be." She glanced at her older sister. "Morgan is running a close second."

Morgan walked over. "And I can't wait," she said. "I'm going to spoil her to death."

"Her!" Paige was feeling her own excitement. "Do you know something I don't?"

Morgan shrugged. "I just have a feeling it's going to be a girl. They do run in our family."

"I want a boy," Corey said.

"Well, it's going to be one or the other." Reed joined the group. "Hi, Paige. How are you?"

She could feel everyone's eyes on them. "I'm fine." *I've missed you,* she said silently. Who wouldn't?

Dressed in his usual jeans, with a dark green Henley shirt, he had on cowboy boots, making him even taller than his six foot one in height.

"Nearly all moved in," she said.

"Good," he said as his dark gaze made her too aware of him as a man…of his heated kisses, his slow, burning touches. And Reed Larkin was the last person she needed to be thinking about.

Somehow her parents had wandered off, leaving them alone. "Did you just get off-duty?"

"I'm going in later. I took Jodi and Nick out to see Mom today. Jodi and Mom both said hi."

"I should go see your mom." In truth, Paige hadn't wanted to go back to Shady Haven, but it had nothing to do with Sally Larkin.

"I could take you tomorrow." He lowered his voice. "Maybe you could talk with Billy again."

Paige didn't want to discuss this. "Can we talk about this later?"

He nodded. "I'll follow you back to your place."

Paige agreed, but she knew Reed wouldn't be happy with what she had to tell him, or her decision not to talk with Billy again.

It was after ten when Reed followed Paige into the alley behind her building. He parked his truck at the real estate office next door.

It had been a week since he'd been alone with Paige. She asked for time and, although it had nearly killed him, he gave it to her.

He climbed out of the truck and walked over to help her out of the car and realized a light was out over the door. "You should call and have the light fixed. It's too dark out here."

"I guess I haven't noticed it." She slipped the key in the dead bolt and opened the door to the dimly lit hallway. Immediately she went to the alarm system and punched in the code.

"Good, you have an alarm."

"I'll have private files here." She smiled at him. "So if someone breaks in I can expect a fast response for law enforcement?"

He grinned, enjoying her easy mood. "I'm here to protect and serve."

"That's good to hear. Come on, I'll give you the nickel tour." She led him down the hall to the front of the building to the reception area. There was now a chocolate-brown sofa and two chairs, along with a glass-top coffee table arranged in the waiting area. A geometrical patterned rug covered the hardwood. On the other side was a desk.

"This is nice. Do you have a receptionist?"

"Just me until I build a client list." She then walked him into her office and turned on the light. The walls had been painted a slate-blue and floor-to-ceiling book-shelves were bright-white and the books were neatly or-ganized. A dark red carpet felt plush under his feet.

He let out a low whistle. "Impressive."

"Thank you. That's what I was going for."

Paige stood across the room. All night she'd been careful not to get too close. "Does the upstairs look this good?"

"It's still bare bones. Give me another week to finish unpacking and buy some more furniture."

"That won't bother me. I bet you have a coffee-maker." He took her by the arm. "Make me a cup and we'll talk."

Paige didn't like the way Reed took over, but she allowed him to escort her upstairs to where there was a rust print love seat and a maple table and four chairs from her parents' Inn. A new mahogany bedroom set had been delivered only yesterday. "I'm still unpacking all the stuff we brought back from Denver." She was nervous of what he thought of the place.

He walked around. "Seems you have all the essentials."

"Typical man. Women like a little more decor." She went to the windows that she'd come to love. Morgan had made her Roman shades for privacy, and she could still enjoy the sunlight. "I need to concentrate on buying baby furniture." She went in the kitchen area, reached for a stainless steel canister and began scooping coffee into the coffeemaker. "Mom has a lot of things left over from Leah, but I suspect my sister will want a baby soon. So I decided to buy new."

Reed glanced at her slightly protruding stomach. For the average person Paige didn't show, but he'd felt the baby growing inside her. He'd noticed subtle changes in her body. She had a beautiful glow. "You're in the second trimester."

She paused from her task and glanced over her shoulder. She nodded. "Sixteen weeks."

"I only know because I've lived through this with Jodi. I think she read every pregnancy book to me."

"It's nice that you could be there for her."

The realization of his need to be there for Paige tore at him. But first, she needed to clear her life of her past. He did, too. "I know you've been busy trying to get your practice going, but I need you to talk to Billy again."

Paige carried two mugs to the table. "I hope you don't mind decaf. It's all I have."

Reed crossed the room. "Paige, I don't care about the damn coffee, I need to know if you're going to talk to Billy again."

Paige sat down at the table. "No, Reed, I'm not."

CHAPTER SEVEN

REED got off work at 6:00 a.m. and headed out of town, driving a little faster than the speed limit. He needed to clear his head of everything, especially of the woman who'd been crowding into his thoughts 24/7.

His other constant distraction was Billy Hutchinson. The old man talking about his father's disappearance had Reed more determined than ever to find out the truth. Damn, he felt so close to some news about his father.

For too many years, he hadn't been able to clear his family's name. He'd kept running into dead ends. And now, he finally thought he had a slim chance with Billy, but Paige refused to help him.

Once again she'd let him down.

Reed reached the highway turnoff to the mine and started up the dirt road. Shifting into four-wheel drive, he started up the rough incline. Tall pines lined the winding route and huge chiseled boulders stood out along the foothills, marking the way toward his destination. Mick's Dream.

Memories of his dad bringing him here flooded his head. Happy memories. Ones he'd never forget. And more than ever, they'd never be tarnished by what other people thought or said.

Reed drove over the rise and pulled his truck into a flat area under the tall pines only to discover another truck already parked there. To be on the side of caution, he took his sidearm out of the glove compartment and climbed out. Strapping on his gun, he headed up the gravel-like grade toward the mine. Someone was trespassing on private property. His property.

Reed hadn't been here in years. Not since the day he'd left town for college. Then the place had been boarded up under Billy's orders, supposedly because it wasn't safe. With his father not around, his mother hadn't argued Hutchinson's decision. She'd only wanted the ugly rumors of her husband being a thief to die down.

Reed had been just a kid then, but old enough to know that the sheriff back then had done very little, if anything, to aid in the search for Mick. What could Reed expect? Sheriff Don McGriff was one of Billy's "good old boy" buddies. Well, he was the sheriff now, and this was still Larkin property.

Reed stopped about twenty feet from the entrance when he saw the fencing materials. Two men came out of the mine and were carrying tools. He had a feeling Lyle Hutchinson had a hand in this.

He rested his hand on his gun. "Stop where you are."

Both men froze.

Reed didn't give them a chance to speak. "You're trespassing on private property," he stated, resting his hand on his gun belt. "I'm Sheriff Larkin. State your business here."

"Hey, Sheriff," one of the middle-aged men spoke up. "We're just doing the job we were paid for."

"Like I said, this is private property."

"We got permission from the owner."

"Doubt that since I'm the owner. Who sent you?"

The two exchanged another confused look. "Lyle Hutchinson hired us to board up the mine…permanently. He wanted to make sure it was secure…make sure that kids wouldn't get inside. So we're fencing the area."

Reed couldn't argue that it would be the safest thing to do. Too many foolish people were killed in abandoned mines. But it seemed strange that, after all these years, Hutchinson had decided to do it now.

"Okay, finish the job you were hired for, just make sure you drop off a key to the gate at my office." With their nod, Reed turned and walked away. He was finished giving Hutchinsons all the control. And maybe it was time he let Lyle know that.

Two hours later Reed arrived at his house to find Paige's car in the driveway. She was waiting on the porch. He wasn't ready to face her now, but it didn't look like he had a choice.

He climbed out of the truck and walked toward the house. She stood up as he approached.

She looked tired and sad, still nothing took away from her appeal. And nothing would stop the ache he felt for her, or the need to pull her into his arms, and bury himself in her softness.

He fought his feelings. "You're up early."

Paige brushed back a strand of hair and took a deep breath, trying to relax. She hated the edgy nervous feeling Reed caused in her. "I didn't sleep very well." Her gaze searched his. "I couldn't stop thinking about you...."

He tensed, but gave her a careless shrug. "Why? You said it all last night." He brushed by her and opened his front door, then paused to look back at her. "Or did you? Is there something else, Paige?"

"Yes..."

He stood back and motioned for her to go inside. Paige knew that things were going to change drastically if she walked through that door. She had no choice. No matter what, she had to do what was right. She squeezed by him and went into the living room.

"I don't have any decaf," he said. "Jodi left some tea. Would you like a cup?"

She shook her head. "I just came to say, I'm sorry... and if you want me to talk with Billy, I will." She fought to keep the tremor from her voice. "Just let me know when you want to go. Goodbye, Reed." She made it to the door and pulled it open when she felt his hand on her arm.

"What made you change your mind?" he asked, so close to her she could feel his breath against her cheek.

Paige looked up at him and was caught by his mes-merizing gaze. Her pulse shot off. "It's the right thing to do. I know you might not believe me, but I've always wanted to help you."

"And I appreciate that, Paige."

She nodded and turned to business. "Now, I'm no expert, but whatever happened that night between the two men, I have a feeling Billy has remorse, is looking for some forgiveness. And you might be the person to get him to confess."

Reed remained silent as if contemplating her words, then said, "So you'll go with me?"

She nodded. "It still isn't a good idea." Paige was also worried about what else Billy would say about her part in getting Reed to leave town. "I should stay out of this."

Reed raised his hand to her cheek. His touch was warm, and stirred feelings she didn't want to analyze.

"I want you with me, Paige. I've always needed you." He leaned down and placed a soft kiss on her cheek, then moved to the other side and repeated the action.

"Oh, Reed… This isn't a good idea."

He kissed her eyelids. "You and me together is the best idea."

She had trouble breathing. She wanted so badly to believe him, to push aside the past. "It's not just you and me. My baby."

Reed pulled back slightly and stared down at her. "You think I don't care about your baby? He or she is part of you, Paige, how could I not care?" He placed a hand against her stomach and his mouth covered hers in a soft kiss. "Do you want me to show you?"

Paige wanted to give in. Suddenly she heard footsteps on the porch. They jumped back to find Lyle Hutchinson standing there, smiling. "Well, what do we have here?"

Lyle was in his mid-fifties. Tall, slender and still a nice-looking man with thick gray hair, he was dressed in a tailor-made dark suit. He came from the first family of Destiny and had always tried to use that to his advantage.

"What are you doing here, Hutchinson?" Reed asked, holding Paige close.

"Since you threatened my crew, Larkin, I think it's time we got together. Besides, you'll want to hear what I have to say." Lyle glanced at Paige. "And maybe it's a good idea if your…lawyer is present to witness this. Then maybe we can get out of each other's lives once and for all."

When Reed opened the door to allow the man inside, Paige had a feeling that this wasn't going to end things. It was just the beginning.

The meeting took place at the dining room table, but Reed wasn't offering any welcoming gestures. He wanted to just get down to business. Lyle came prepared as he opened his briefcase, pulled out a paper and pushed it across the highly polished wood.

"What's this?" Reed asked, hating to be caught off guard.

"It's an official offer to buy out your family's shares in Mick's Dream. It's a fair offer, Reed. Probably more than it's worth."

What was going on? Reed read over the agreement that stated the mine was going to be closed permanently. Of course, the Larkin family didn't have any money to start up a mining operation anyway.

"Why now, Lyle? Why do you suddenly want to buy me out?"

Hutchinson didn't give anything away in his expression. "I'm just trying to clean up some loose ends. You have to admit that this mine is like a dark cloud over all our lives. There are no good memories of the place." He nodded to the paper. "This money should help with your mother's care."

That infuriated Reed. The Hutchinsons had never cared about Sally Larkin. "Leave my mother out of this. If your family had cared about my family, Billy would have never spread lies about Mick."

Lyle stiffened. "My offer is more than generous, but read the fine print. The offer's not going to be on the table forever." He shut his briefcase. "Think about it, Larkin. For everyone's sake." He headed for the door and walked out.

Reed looked at Paige reading over the agreement.

She blew out a breath. "This is a lot of money."

He only stared at her, then asked, "Is this the lawyer talking or my…friend?"

Paige studied him a moment. "As a lawyer, I'd say

this would insure you and your family a lot of security, but I know you, Reed. You want to find out what happened to your father." Her eyes were pleading. "My concern is, what if that never happens?"

"I know it might backfire in my face, but I can't just walk away." His throat was suddenly thick with emotion. "I've got to try."

A half smile appeared on her pretty face. "That's what I expected you'd say," she said. "If you want I'll go with you to see Billy. But you know if Lyle gets wind of this, he'll do everything he can to keep you away from his father."

"I know I can't use anything Billy has to say in court. I guess at this point I just need to learn anything that will tell me what happened to my dad. If Billy can lead me in the right direction I've got to go there."

"Even if that direction doesn't have a good end?"

Reed wasn't foolish enough to think his father was still alive. "You mean finding my father dead."

Paige shook her head. "I mean, not being able to make the guilty pay."

It was two days before Reed had a chance to go to Shady Haven. Over the weekend Jodi had visited while he had to fill in the shifts of his sick deputy. Today he was off, and he'd come out early to spend time with his mother, and show her Lyle's offer to buy the mine.

Reed knew that Sally Larkin's stroke had taken a physical toll, but there was nothing wrong with her mental faculties. He handed her the paper assuming that she'd want him to take the money for their future and little Nicky.

Reed wasn't worried about his financial future. He'd been paid well at the Bureau, and he'd invested wisely over the years. Even managed to send some money home. So Lyle's offer wasn't of any interest to him. It only told him that Hutchinson was guilty of something. And he was going to find out what.

"A lot of…money," Sally told him.

"We don't need it. I can take care of you," he said. "And Jodi."

Sally's clear blue eyes were kind and loving. She shook her head. "Mick's Dream…is trouble."

"I know, Mother. But I need to know what happened that night. Billy has said things that lead me to believe he lied about Dad."

She touched his hand. "Yes. Mick d…did not steal."

"I know, Mom. I'm going to clear Dad's name. Paige is going to help me."

Sally Larkin's smile was slightly crooked from the stroke. "You and Paige. Nice…"

"That was a long time ago, Mom. It's different now."

"She still…cares."

Reed wanted to believe that, but he was afraid to hope.

"Paige is pregnant," he said.

His mother nodded. "Claire s…said." She studied him. "B…baby bother you?"

He could lie and say he didn't wish the child was his.

"It's part of Paige." He stood. It was strange he was talking to his mother about this. "I don't care for the jerk she was involved with."

His mother's eyes and smile told him she wanted the two of them to be together. He wanted the same, but he couldn't think about that now. He kissed her cheek. "I've got to go. I'll stop by tomorrow. Love ya, Mom."

"L…love you."

Reed walked out the door. He probably was a fool to get involved with Paige. He couldn't seem to help it. Who was to say that McCarran wouldn't call her and say he wanted Paige back. Worse, what if she went running?

Reed reached the sitting area at the home and looked around. As usual, he found Billy seated at the wide doors, but this day he wasn't alone. Lyle was with him. He quickly turned and headed out the door. The last thing he wanted was for either man to see him. But he wasn't going to let Billy off the hook. He would find out the truth, one way or the other.

"The baby, at week sixteen, is four to five inches long, and weighs a bit less than three ounces," Morgan recited as they walked quickly around the park. "He or she can make a fist." Paige's sister grinned but kept her arms pumping as they walked briskly around Town Square Park. "Isn't it wonderful?"

"She sure feels more than three ounces pressed

against my bladder." Paige had read all this herself, but Morgan was getting a kick out of being a source of information.

"We can stop if you have to go," Morgan said.

"No, I think I can make it back to the office." Her sister had decided that exercise was a good idea for the both of them. So she'd started walking in the afternoons if her schedule allowed it.

The fresh air and increased heart rate seemed to be helping with her stress levels and her increased appetite. She had a doctor's appointment in two weeks and didn't want the scale to become her enemy at this early stage.

When they turned and cut across the grassy playground, she saw Reed ahead, walking out of the sheriff's office. She allowed herself the luxury of giving the sexy lawman the once-over. He must do his own workout to stay in such good shape and look that great. The tailored uniform shirt tapered over his broad shoulders and narrow waist. Oh, boy. Her body heated up and she doubted it was from the brisk walk.

As if he sensed something, he suddenly looked in her direction. His mirrored sunglasses hid his expression as he raised a hand and gave them a friendly wave.

She waved back just as she felt her ankle buckle and give way on the uneven ground. She gasped as she collapsed and fell to her knees.

"Paige," Morgan cried and rushed to her aid. "Are you okay?"

Paige was embarrassed more than anything, but there was pain, too. "I twisted my ankle." She sat down on the grass just as Reed appeared at her side. Several other Destiny residents made an appearance.

"Don't move," he insisted. "Where do you hurt?"

"My ankle." She released her hold on the pained area and he took over the examination. His large, sure hands were gentle as he tested her injury.

"Really, I'm okay, I just stepped in a hole."

"Do you hurt anywhere else?" His concerned gaze met hers. "What about the baby?"

She shook her head. "I caught myself with my hands."

"You sure?"

Suddenly Paige realized how serious this could be and was angry she let herself get distracted. "Yes, but I feel stupid for not watching where I was going."

One corner of his mouth twitched. "It happens to the best of us."

She glanced around at the crowd. "Seems I'm drawing attention."

He stood. "Okay, everyone, Paige is fine. She just twisted her ankle."

As people moved on, Reed was back at her side.

"Boy, you're good at crowd control."

"I scored high on my Bureau test."

Morgan leaned over. "I think we should take you to the emergency room to have your ankle looked at."

Paige wasn't going to argue, not until Reed scooped her up unto his arms. "Wait," she gasped, but wrapped her arms around his neck when he started off across the park. It was like a scene out of a movie. Instead she was being carried off by a real-life hero. "Reed, this isn't necessary," she said weakly, too aware of the man holding her.

"It's the fastest way to get you to my car."

Morgan trailed behind them. "Just enjoy it, Paige. You're seeing Destiny's finest at work."

They made it to the patrol car, and Morgan hurried ahead to open the passenger door. "I'll get your purse and follow you there in my own car."

Paige grabbed her sister's arm. "Promise me you won't call Mom and Dad until we hear what the doctor has to say."

"I won't, but you have to call them, Paige," Morgan insisted.

She watched as Reed went around to the driver's side. "Okay, I will, after I see the doctor."

With that agreement Morgan took off and Reed climbed in the car. First, he radioed the office to let them know where he was going, then he started the engine.

Before he could pull away from the curb, Paige grabbed him by the arm. "You turn on your siren, Larkin, and you're dead meat."

He cocked an eyebrow, looking sexy and dangerous. "Oh, threatening an officer, that's a serious offence."

"I mean it."

"Okay, you got a reprieve." His mouth twitched. "Now, what have you got for me?"

She suddenly blushed as her thoughts only came up with things that were X-rated. "You get my undying gratitude."

Reed nodded slowly, the humor gone from his intense gaze. "Is that all you have to offer?"

The heat only intensified between them. "Take it or leave it."

"I'll take time with you anyway I can get it."

Two hours later, Paige had had her ankle X-rayed and wrapped after the doctor told her it was a sprain.

Something she already knew. Next came the call to her mother.

"No, Mom, I'm fine. And the baby is fine, too." Paige tried to convince her, but she still wanted to talk to Morgan.

With her crutch under her arm and the assurance she'd stay off her ankle for today, Paige made her way to the reception area where she found Reed waiting for her. Her heart soared as he leaned against the counter. His uniform was gone, replaced by a navy-blue polo shirt and jeans. He spotted her and came to help.

"Please, I can walk by myself," she said.

He frowned. "I take it everything is all right?"

"Yes, it is, and that includes the baby." She was relieved, too. "I do have to go see Dr. York tomorrow."

"I'll drive you."

She glared at him. She didn't want to keep leaning on him. She didn't want to get used to it and then lose him again. "I can do this, Reed. I can't keep taking you away from your job."

"I'm off tomorrow."

Morgan appeared at her side. "Mom said you were to come home for dinner." She smiled at Reed. "All of us, Sheriff."

"I don't want to intrude," Reed said.

"Mom's made pot roast and garlic mashed potatoes."

"Keep talking…"

"Banana cream pie."

He groaned. "How can I turn that down?" He backed away. "I'll bring the car around." He disappeared through the doors.

Morgan cleared her throat. "He was pretty worried when you fell."

Paige countered. "I don't want him to worry."

"Whether you do or not, he does." Morgan sighed. "Paige, just because you got tangled up with a jerk doesn't mean all guys are like him. Reed has proved to be one the good guys."

"I just don't have the energy to start a relationship right now. I have a child to think about."

Her sister nodded. "I have a feeling that Reed would wait as long as it took."

Paige wanted to believe that. How easy it would be to depend on a man like Reed. But he wasn't hers anymore. Although years had passed, would he understand why she had to break up with him back then? Would he believe it was for his own good?

* * *

"Mrs. K, dinner was delicious," Reed said as he pushed his pie plate away. "Thank you for inviting me."

"You're always welcome here. Anytime."

"Thank you," he said. Paige's mother had always treated him like family. "It's nice to have the company, too."

"And you don't always eat well when you're alone." Claire Keenan's gaze went to Paige. "It's hard to cook for one."

"Mother, I eat just fine," Paige said as she tried to stand.

Reed relieved her of her plate. "Don't even think about it. You were told to stay off your ankle. Morgan and I can handle a few dishes."

Reed didn't want Paige to do a thing. He'd been frightened out of ten years of his life today. He never wanted to go through that again. He knew from experience that pregnant women weren't that fragile, but he worried that Paige was trying to do too much.

Morgan was at the sink rinsing dishes to go in the dishwasher. "Thank you for the help—and for today, too."

"Anytime."

"I do have another favor to ask you," Morgan hedged. "I have this conference call tomorrow. And Paige has a doctor's appointment at one… She doesn't want Mom and Dad to know she's going—so they won't worry. She shouldn't drive herself…"

"I can take her." Reed knew that it would be a problem, but only for Paige.

"She'll argue with you about it," Morgan countered.

"And I'll just argue right back. If I have to I'll carry her there."

Morgan smiled. "I knew I could depend on you."

Reed looked across the room at the woman in question.

Paige's soft pink blouse hung loosely over her rounded belly. In just days she seemed to have blossomed with her pregnancy. His gaze moved to her face and their eyes locked. Just one look from her and his body stirred to life. He glanced away.

"I want Paige to know she can depend on me, too."

The next afternoon Paige was wearing a paper gown and covered by a paper blanket, sitting on a paper-protected exam table. But she didn't care. Although Dr. York believed that the baby had not been affected by her fall yesterday, she was going to do an ultrasound.

Paige hadn't expected to have the procedure done for another two weeks.

There was a knock on the door and Dr. York peered in. She smiled. "Okay, Paige." She walked to the table. "You ready to see your baby?"

Nodding, Paige felt the tears well in her eyes. She suddenly wished she'd told her mother and asked her to come with her. This was a time when she didn't want to be alone. She nodded. "I'm nervous. You're sure there isn't anything wrong with the baby?"

The pretty, dark-haired doctor raised an eyebrow. "As I told you in my office, Paige, this is only a precaution."

"Okay." She just didn't want to face this alone. "Is Reed still here?"

Without saying a word, Dr. York went to the door and stepped outside. In seconds, Reed appeared in the room. He walked to her side and took her hand. "Are you okay?"

She released a long breath, flashing back to years before, recalling that he'd been her friend. "Would you look at my baby with me?"

A slow grin spread across his handsome face. "I'd love to." He leaned down and placed a soft kiss on her mouth. "It's going to be okay, Paige. I promise. Just hang on to me."

The doctor returned. "Well, ready to go?"

Paige nodded.

Reed moved out of the way, but refused to release Paige's hand. He also found he was nervous when the doctor lowered the sheet, exposing Paige's slightly rounded stomach. Emotions clogged his throat and he had to work hard just to swallow. She looked so beautiful.

The doctor took a tube of lubricant and spread some on Paige's stomach. "Sorry, it's a little cold." She placed a probe on her belly, then did some adjusting on the machine. Soon a rhythmic sound filled the room. The doctor smiled. "I just love the sound of a healthy heartbeat."

"That's the baby's…?" Paige breathed.

"That's your baby's heartbeat. It's steady and strong." The doctor shifted the probe. "Now, let's try to get a look at this kid."

Seconds ticked by until finally the picture on the

screen began to come into focus. "There you are," Dr. York said as she pointed to the image. "See, there's the outline of the head, the spine…"

"I see it," Paige gasped. "Do you see her, Reed?"

He saw the tiny shadowed image. "I see her."

The doctor smiled. "So you think it's a girl?"

"My sister Morgan is convinced it is," Paige admitted.

"Well, it's a little early, but I might be able to learn the sex." The doctor continued to slide the probe over Paige's belly, then stopped. "Bingo." She turned to Paige. "Do you want to know?"

Paige glanced up at Reed. "Do we?"

Reed stared at her golden-whiskey colored gaze. He was so close to losing it, it wasn't funny. The intimacy between them at this moment was like nothing he'd ever felt with anyone.

"Of course you do. Whenever could you wait for anything?" he teased. But what he was sharing with this woman wasn't a joke. He was so crazy about her… and her baby. "At the very least, you'll know what color to paint the nursery."

Paige fought a smile. "More likely who I'm going to be sharing my room with."

Suddenly he envied this kid. He wanted to be her roommate…permanently. "Okay, Doctor, give us the news. Is it pink or blue?"

"It's a girl."

They grinned at each other. "Perfect."

CHAPTER EIGHT

IT'S a girl.

Paige was still smiling hours later when Reed drove her back to Destiny. She was having a little girl, and had the ultrasound pictures to prove it.

She'd been so happy over the news that her stumble in the park hadn't hurt the baby that nothing else mattered, until it finally hit her. She was going to be a mother.

Her joy had been so overwhelming she hadn't wanted to come down just yet. And Reed never questioned her when she'd asked to go to the mall where she'd spent the next few hours looking at cribs and baby clothes.

"I bet you're tired," Reed said. "It's been a long day for you and…Sweet Pea."

She looked across the cab at his handsome profile. "So you've already nicknamed her."

"Well, you have to admit, she isn't much bigger than a pea."

Paige liked it. "Oh, Reed, can you believe I'm having a girl?"

"The question is, is the world ready for a Paige Junior?"

"Can't handle a strong woman, huh, Larkin?"

"Strong I can deal with, but combined with stubborn, bullheaded and know-it-all types it's lethal."

"Oh, you poor baby," she cooed. She had no doubt that Reed Larkin could handle any woman, young or old. Over the years she'd fantasized about the boy she'd loved so desperately, and always hoped one day they'd somehow get back together. But she knew it could be too late for that.

Turning away, she studied the ultrasound printout. "I can't wait to show these pictures to Mom and Dad. I called home and Morgan said they went out to dinner with some friends."

"Did you tell your sister?"

Paige shook her head. "Just that everything went fine. I want to tell everyone together." She recalled how Reed had been there with her, holding her hand. "Reed…I want to thank you for coming with me today."

He gave her an easy smile, making her heart flutter. "I'm honored that you asked me." He turned off the highway and entered the town limits. "How about I drop you off at the apartment, then I'll pick up a pizza for dinner?"

Paige knew she shouldn't, but she didn't want this day to end, or her time with Reed. "You don't have anything better to do than hang around with a pregnant woman?"

He pulled up in front of her building. "There's nothing I'd rather do. So I'll call in a pizza and be back in about twenty minutes."

She nodded. "I'll leave the door unlocked."

Reed pulled out his cell phone and began to dial the number before Paige was out of the truck. There was nothing wrong with sharing a pizza with a friend, she told herself, especially when that friend had given up his day to help her out.

Once inside the office, Paige listened to her phone messages. Two clients needed to reschedule their appointments. After she'd made the calls, and spent time to calm another client, she started toward the apartment when she heard a knock on the door. She walked through the reception area to see the familiar brown mail delivery truck. She pulled open the door and the driver handed her an envelope.

"I need a signature, ma'am," he said.

After scribbling down her name, she said goodbye and closed the door. She glanced at the sender to see a law firm in Denver. A sudden dread washed over her when she realized it was from Drew. She walked down the long hall to the back and made her way up the stairs to her apartment.

Dropping the envelope on the table, she went to the windows. This was her new sanctuary, the new home for her and her child. She'd added more and more personal touches each day. The bench had been covered in a cranberry and white toile print cushion, courtesy of her big sister, as was the beautiful quilt covering her bed.

Paige glanced back at the envelope. Why today? Why did he have to ruin today for her?

Well, she wasn't going to let him. She marched to the table and tore open the folder. Inside, she found several papers clipped together. She recognized the form immediately as the agreement she had sent to Drew at the first of last week.

The man couldn't even take the time to think about this life-changing decision. Paige scanned the papers and found his signature scribbled on the bottom line, and notarized by his attorney. She let out a long breath. That was it. Drew McCarran was out of her life…and his daughter's.

A tear found its way down her cheek when she realized her child was now fatherless.

"Paige…"

She looked up to see Reed standing at the top of the stairs. She tried to smile, but it didn't work. She sank into the chair and covered her face with her hands.

Reed set down the pizza box and rushed to her. He took the papers from her and glanced over them to find the familiar name on the bottom. Hell, the man's timing stank.

"I'm sorry, Paige," he whispered, but only meant it halfheartedly. He didn't want McCarran anywhere in her life.

"It's going to be okay." He drew her into his arms. She trembled against him, but refused to cry. "Let it go, babe. I'm here."

She pulled back, her expression sad. "How could I have been such a fool?"

"It's him, Paige, not you."

"But my baby… He doesn't even care about her." Her lip trembled as another tear found its way down her cheek. "She isn't even born yet…and she doesn't have a father."

Seeing the woman he cared about in pain nearly broke his heart. He pulled her back into his arms. "Hey, Sweet Pea will have something more important. She'll have people who truly love her. Your parents, Morgan, Leah…Holt and Corey…and me."

Would she let him love her and her child? "Would you let me in your life, Paige? Let me prove to you that all men aren't jerks?"

She sniffed and looked up at him. Her eyes were red from crying and her makeup smeared. She was beautiful.

"How can you want that? All those years ago…I left you."

He stopped her words. "That was a long time ago. Things are different now. We're different. The only thing that's the same is how I feel about you, how I've always felt about you."

She stepped out of his embrace and turned to the windows. "Don't say that, Reed. I can't trust how I feel…not anymore."

This time he refused to let her put him off. He came up behind her. "I'm not McCarran. I'm not going to leave you." He placed his arms on her shoulders and turned her around to face him. "I care so much for you, Paige."

Her eyes widened. "Oh, Reed…"

"Don't try to come up with another argument. It

won't stop the fact that whatever we had years ago is still there between us. And I still want you." He lowered his head. He heard her breath quicken and ignored it as he captured her mouth.

Paige was weak. She couldn't resist her feelings any longer. Within the confines of his strong arms she forgot all the pain, her loneliness—everything except Reed. His tenderness reached deep inside her and nudged at her heart. His touch excited her body, making her crave him. The combination made her move closer against him.

"You make me crazy," he breathed, his voice husky with need.

She opened her eyes and looked at his face. A shiver rippled through her. Being with Reed seemed so natural and so intimate. Something she'd never shared with anyone else. She didn't want it to end.

"Good," she whispered, suddenly feeling brave as she rose up and touched her mouth to his. She may have initiated the kiss but he quickly took over. She parted for him, letting him excite her, pleasure her…love her.

His kisses were slow, and thorough, meant to drive her out of her mind. They teased her until she began to squirm. He moved his hands over her stomach, almost reverently, then continued the journey up over her rib cage and between her breasts. She soon tugged his shirt out of his jeans and slipped her hands underneath to touch his bare skin. He groaned. She whimpered as her breathing grew labored.

"Reed…"

"I want you, Paige."

"I want you, too," she confessed.

Their eyes met. His were questioning, as if to ask if she was sure.

When she nodded, he lifted her in his arms and carried her into the bedroom. The sunlight through the windows was fading, leaving the room in shadows.

Reed stood Paige beside the queen-size bed. He watched the passion flare in her eyes. He could also feel her tremble. As much as he wanted to bury himself inside her, he didn't want her to have regrets.

"Paige. We don't have to make love. I could hold you and be happy."

Her eyes widened. "You don't want me?"

He cupped her jaw. "I've wanted you since I was fifteen years old. You've been in my dreams, in my every waking thought." He pressed his forehead against hers. "God, Paige, I can't recall a time I didn't want you."

"I've always wanted you, too," she admitted, her voice so soft, her eyes searching. "I wish we hadn't waited back then… I wanted you to be my first."

Emotions clogged Reed's throat, making it impossible for him to speak. He lowered his head and took her mouth, wanting to relay how much her words meant to him. Suddenly their need grew as did the kiss, but it wasn't enough. He wanted to finally make her his.

Reed unbuttoned her blouse and slipped it off her shoulders, then flicked the front hook of her bra, helping it off. He tore his shirt over his head and tossed it aside, then drew her back into his arms and kissed her again. He never wanted to stop. He loved the feel of her, and the taste of her.

Reed lowered Paige to the bed and looked down at her. His hungry gaze skimmed over her perfect body, then rested on the slight mound of her stomach where she carried a precious child. "You are so beautiful…" The words seemed so inadequate to how he felt about her.

He'd wanted her forever…and he was going to make sure she knew how much.

Paige blinked at the bright sunlight streaming through the window. What time was it? She raised her head and glanced at the clock. Seven-fifteen.

Relieved she hadn't overslept, she sat up as memories from last night came flooding into her head. Reed had made love to her. Her body swiftly reacted to the tender recollection. How he'd held her, stroked her through the night. She glanced at the other side of the bed to find it empty. Her hand stroked the pillow. Maybe he had to work the early shift.

Disappointed, she tried to think about her day, and all the other reasons it was best he wasn't here. That was when she heard a noise, then Reed appeared in the doorway.

"Good morning," he said.

"Good morning," she answered back.

Reed was only wearing his jeans, leaving his magnificent chest bare. Paige recalled how her fingers traced every inch of skin, and her mouth…

"You'd better stop looking at me like that, or I'll climb back into that bed with you."

She felt the excitement as he crossed the room and sat down beside her on the bed. Her gaze went to his face as she tugged the sheet higher over her nakedness. "I don't think that would be wise. We both have to go to work. In fact I should probably be in the shower." But she wasn't going to parade around in front of him.

Reed touched her cheek so she would look at him. "Paige, don't pull away from me. I promise I'm not going to push you too fast. I'm not going to move in… but please…" She watched him swallow. "Don't regret what happened between us last night."

She could see he was feeling just as insecure as she was. Besides, there were things between them that hadn't been resolved, and she was afraid that it would change how he felt about her.

"Oh, Reed, I don't regret last night. I was in a bad space, and you were there for me…again. I was just thinking you have better things to do than to keep rescuing me."

Reed didn't like where she was going with this. "If that's how you want to explain it away, I guess I did it all wrong." He stood and grabbed his clothes from the floor. "Maybe it's time I leave." He walked out of the bedroom. While pulling on his shirt, she came after him tying her robe.

"Reed, don't leave. Please. That's not what I meant."

He slipped on his shirt. "Then explain to me what you did mean."

She just looked at him. Her hair was mussed, her makeup gone, but her brown eyes were riveted on him.

"I'm afraid, okay," she finally said. "What's happened between us has been all-consuming to say the least. And last night was so wonderful…so…"

"Incredible works for me," he coached, fighting a smile.

"That, too," she agreed. "I just don't want to confuse what I'm feeling for you with needing you."

"I don't have that problem, Paige. I know exactly what I was feeling last night."

"How can you know that? Maybe you're going on memories from ten years ago. You said yourself that I was in your dreams. Maybe you just fulfilled that fantasy."

"You're damn right I did," he told her. "But I'm not a teenager anymore. I'm a man, a man who's crazy about you." He took a step closer. "I was nuts to let you push me away before. We're meant to be together, Paige. Last night had to tell you that."

She moved into his embrace, her mouth only inches from his. "Make me believe that, Reed. Make me believe."

His mouth closed over hers as her robe separated and his hands slipped over her body. All else was forgotten.

It wasn't until evening that Paige could get her entire family together. She found she was nervous going alone. Reed had to work. Even if he were able to go with her, she knew there would be a lot of questions to answer. And she wasn't ready to do that.

She was falling back in love with him. As if she'd ever stopped. But she had a lot to deal with right now. This morning over breakfast with Reed, she'd promised to go with him to see Billy.

And that meant the truth was bound to come out. It had to. How could she move on with a relationship without telling Reed the entire story?

Paige pulled up in front of the Keenan Inn. And when she saw her parents, all problems flew out of her head. She climbed out of the car and went to greet them, along with Morgan and Leah. Holt and Corey were in the kitchen when they came inside.

"Is everything okay with the baby?" her mother asked.

"Yes, I went to the doctor yesterday to be checked out as a precaution." Paige opened her purse and pulled out her picture. "And everything is fine. I just thought you'd like to see the first picture of your granddaughter." She handed the printout to her mother.

With a unified gasp, everyone gathered around the picture.

"A girl," her mother whispered.

"I didn't know you were having an ultrasound," Morgan said.

"I didn't, either," Paige confessed. "It wasn't scheduled for two more weeks."

"How can they tell?" her father asked, squinting at the picture. "I can't see anything."

Paige went around to show them.

"Are you sure?" Corey asked. "Maybe it could be a boy."

Leah and Holt both laughed. "You know, son," Holt said. "There are advantages to being the only boy. One day you'll be happy to be surrounded by females."

"No way," the nine-year-old said.

"Well, my little girl is going to need her big cousin to look out for her."

The boy's chest puffed out. "I guess I could do that."

Paige smiled, feeling the excitement. She wished Reed was here with her. They'd spent the morning together, part of the time in bed. But then reality interrupted them and he had to go to work, with the promise to stop by later to check on her.

Morgan looked at Paige. "Where's Reed?"

Paige tried her best lawyer face. "He's probably working. Why?"

Morgan gave her a knowing look. "He just always seems to be around these days."

Paige wasn't going to be goaded by her sister. "Destiny isn't that big. Of course we're going to run into each other."

Her family were all looking at her, waiting for answers, but she didn't have any, at least, not yet.

Two days later, Reed and Paige drove out to Shady Haven. This was the first chance they both had the time off to do this. He had to get this over with—to finally put an end to the lies about his father. He couldn't move on with his life until that happened. Reed parked the truck and came around to help Paige out.

She still had her ankle wrapped, but only as a precaution. She didn't limp anymore, but Reed made sure that he slowed his pace.

They walked in and without going to the desk, he looked into the common room. There were about a dozen people, some watching television, others playing cards. He glanced toward the patio area where Billy sat in his wheelchair by the French doors. Bingo.

Reed glanced at the large male attendant, to see he was sitting off by himself. Close enough if needed, but far enough away not to hear a conversation.

"Let's do it," he told Paige.

She looked worried. "I better go first because I've visited him before."

Reed nodded, and Paige put on a smile and went to the old man. "Hello, Billy," she said.

When he looked up confused, Reed wondered if he wouldn't talk. He was wrong.

"You're that lady lawyer."

"That's right, Billy," she said. "I came to visit you before. You know my mother, Claire Keenan."

His eyes brightened. "Pretty lady. Lucky man, Tim Keenan."

"I'll tell my dad you said so." Paige grew serious. "I brought someone who wants to talk to you, Billy." She moved aside and Reed stepped forward.

"Hello, Billy. You remember me, Reed Larkin, Mick's son?"

The old man looked frightened. "No. I don't know you."

Reed didn't back off. "But you knew my father. You were his partner and helped him with Mick's Dream."

"That was a long time ago."

"Yes, it was," Reed agreed. "Almost seventeen years. That's when you said my father stole your money and disappeared, but that wasn't true, was it, Billy?"

Billy's worried gaze darted to Paige. "He wanted it all…"

"But Mick's Dream was his." Reed wasn't giving up. "You didn't like that. You wanted part of the big strike, didn't you?"

The man didn't say anything.

"What happened that night, Billy?" Reed insisted. "What happened to Mick?"

"It was an accident." Billy shook his head. "He got mad and started to fight me."

Reed's heart lurched, but he couldn't stop now. "Where's Mick, Billy?" He kept pushing. "Where is he? Tell me."

Paige touched his arm. "Calm down, Reed," she said, her voice low.

"Just tell me where Mick's body is."

"It was my fault. He just kept coming at me. I had to defend myself." Tears flooded the old man's eyes.

Reed clenched his fist. "Where is he, Billy?"

"In the mine…"

"Just what the hell are you doing?"

They both swung around to see Lyle Hutchinson.

"You have no right," Lyle argued.

"I have every right to learn the truth," Reed finished.

"There is no truth here, just ramblings of an old man."

"An old man who accused my father of stealing, and who also just admitted that Dad is buried inside Mick's Dream." He saw the worried look on Lyle's face. "This is just the beginning, Hutchinson. I'm going to find my father."

Reed started to leave and Lyle grabbed his arm.

"No court is going to take an Alzheimer's patient's word," he told Reed.

"I don't need to go to court. I'm going to search the mine."

"You can't, it isn't safe."

"Says who?" Reed asked. "Billy? I never saw a report."

"There was a cave-in," Lyle said.

Suddenly it dawned on him. "Who's to say the cave-in wasn't man-made?" Reed asked as he glanced down at Billy. He'd already escaped into his own world. "I believe that your father has already confessed to you."

"My father isn't responsible for anything," Lyle insisted. "Besides, you can't prove it."

"Oh, I'm going to prove it, all right. So get ready, Hutchinson, because I'm about to cause another cave-in in this town."

CHAPTER NINE

DURING the following week, Paige talked with the State of Colorado division of minerals and geology, representing the Larkin family. The past two days Reed had been out at Mick's Dream with a professional crew to dig out the tunnel that had caved in seventeen years ago.

Things had started moving so fast that once they'd started the process, there hadn't been time to rethink it. The most important thing Reed had done was talk it over with his mother and sister before starting the search. Without hesitation, Sally Larkin had told her son to go ahead.

Even Lyle Hutchinson's ranting hadn't stopped the reopening of the mine. This time his name and money had no pull. Paige made sure of that. No matter what else came out of this, she knew Reed needed to learn the truth about his father. Although she needed to prepare herself for any other truths that might come out. But she'd never be prepared to lose the man she loved again.

Tired after her long day, Paige steered her car off the

highway toward Reed's house. He'd called her earlier and asked to meet him there. On the phone he'd sounded tired and defeated. As much as she'd wanted to be with Reed, he'd refused to have her or Jodi anywhere near the mine.

Paige hadn't cared to be there, either, except to give him moral support. Like he'd always been there for her. At least Holt and her father went to provide support.

The past forty-eight hours Reed was at the mine had given Paige time to think about their relationship. How close they'd become over the past few weeks.

She pulled up in front of the house, wondering how long it would last. If she and Reed were to have a future together, she had to tell him her part in sending him away.

She walked to the door, but turned at the sound of another vehicle driving up. Reed. He climbed out of the truck, and walked to her. He looked dirty and tired, but mostly he looked sad.

Her heart sank. He had news. "Reed, what happened?"

He remained silent as he continued toward her, then pulled her into his arms and held her tight. "They found a body," he said, his voice rough. "They need to run the DNA, but I know it's Dad."

"Oh, Reed. I'm so sorry." Her arms tightened and she felt him trembling as she just held him. "Have you been able to tell your mother?"

"No, not yet. I want the test to verify it's Mick, first."

She eased back and looked up at him. "What can I do?"

His dark gaze searched her face. "You're here. That's all I need."

"I wouldn't be anywhere else." She took his hand. "Come on, you need a shower and some rest." She led him to the front door and unlocked it with the key he'd given her. "Then I'm going to feed you."

They walked into the living room. She put her purse down on the side table and continued on to the hallway that led to two small bedrooms. The first one Reed had converted into an office, the second was Jodi's bedroom. Continuing down the corridor, they arrived at the master bedroom.

It was masculine with honey-brown hardwood floors, beige walls and a navy comforter on the king-size bed. On the dresser was one picture. A young Mick and Sally Larkin.

This was the first time she'd been in Reed's bedroom since the nickel tour of the house. After the morning he'd made love to her, she'd made sure to avoid the temptation. They both still had a lot to work through without continuing the physical part of the relationship. Lately they'd been focused on what had happened to Reed's father.

The funny thing was she'd been able to fall back into that comfortable space at his side. But they weren't in high school any longer, and life was a lot more complicated now. There was a lot more to lose this time.

Paige only hoped that after this was all over, Reed would take the chance and choose her.

She went into the remodeled small bathroom with the eggshell colored subway tiled shower stall. She reached in and turned on the faucet, then grabbed a big white towel from the shelf and put it on the counter. She glanced up and saw Reed leaning against the doorjamb, a half smile on his unshaven face.

"I like this. You and me together." He came inside, and pulled her against him. "I need you, Paige." He sucked in a breath. "I thought this…search would be easier… It was…hard."

"And I'm here, Reed." *I'll always be here as long as you want me*, she said silently and wrapped her arms around his waist. "We'll get through this."

He leaned down and captured her mouth. The gentle kiss quickly intensified as she opened to him and he swept inside to taste her. Suddenly he pulled back. "What was that?"

"If I have to tell you…"

"No, I mean, I felt something." He glanced down at her rounded stomach. "The baby?"

Paige smiled as her hand touched her stomach. "I've been feeling her, too, at night mostly. You really felt her move?"

His palm pressed against her stomach. "It was faint, but it was definitely something."

The flutter happened again and his eyes widened. "It's amazing." His gaze locked with hers. "It's humbling. And in a strange way it's telling us that life goes on." Once again they were forced back into reality, and what still lay ahead.

Paige nodded as steam began to encircle them in the small bathroom. "You better get in the shower before you run out of hot water." She backed away, knowing how much he needed her, but hopping into bed right now wasn't the answer for either of them.

She walked out and closed the door. In the kitchen she punched in her mother's number.

"Keenan Inn," Claire answered.

"Mom, it's Paige. Reed needs our help."

The next day, Paige was with Reed at the sheriff's station when the news came in about his father. The skeleton they had recovered was Michael Larkin.

Reed seemed to take the news in stride, but Paige saw how much he hurt. She also saw the little boy who fought the town when everyone thought that Mick had run off. Reed never wavered over his father's innocence.

The hard part for Reed was to relay the news to his mother. Sally Larkin took the news better than expected, but both Reed and Jodi stayed close. She, too, had always believed in her husband's innocence, and though it was hard, it provided closure for her.

The day of the memorial service Paige stood outside the church with the rest of the Keenan family. She was waiting for Reed who was with his mother and sister. The van from Shady Haven arrived, followed by Reed with Jodi and little Nick.

Reed was dressed in a dark suit and tie and a snowy white shirt. He looked handsome, despite being so tired.

Paige went to him and hugged him. "Thanks for being here," he told her.

"What can I do?"

Reed Larkin had always been the strong one, always there for his family, for her…

He squeezed her hand. "Stay close by."

Paige nodded then went to Sally and hugged her. "Whatever you need, Sally, I'm here."

"Be with Reed…" Sally gripped her hand. "He loves you…"

Paige gave a nod, wanting nothing more.

Reed drew a deep breath and released it. He had to get his family through this today. He gripped the handles on his mother's wheelchair and started into the church's vestibule where his father's oak casket rested on the stand.

Reed was surprised when Tim and Holt appeared, along with his two deputies, Sam Collins and Gary Malvern. They filed to the sides of the casket to be pallbearers.

Reed was touched. Then the priest, Father John Reilly, appeared and greeted them. He began the service with prayers and burning of incense over the casket. Then the altar boys opened the double doors of the church. Suddenly music swelled in the full chapel as a choir began to sing. The men walked the casket up the aisle and Reed and his family followed, passing so many of Destiny's residents. Reed wondered where these people had been so many years ago when his mother needed their support.

He shook away the bitterness. Today was not meant

for that. Today was for his father, for what Mick Larkin stood for…for family. Reed was never more proud to be his son.

It had been a long day for Reed. After the blessing at the gravesite, people came back to a reception held at the Keenan Inn. Just an hour ago, Jodi had escorted their mother back to Shady Haven.

Since Nicky was asleep upstairs with Morgan watching over him, Reed let his sister have her way.

Reed sat on the back porch nursing a longneck bottle of beer. He was tired, but he couldn't sleep. He'd taken time off from work to recover, and to finish up the legal part of his dad's death. There still was the investigation over the cause of death, but most likely it had been accidental. That didn't get the Hutchinson family off the hook.

"Would you mind some company?"

At the sound of Paige's voice he turned and smiled. She'd been the one bright spot in all this. "I would if it were anyone else." He placed the beer down, reached for her hand and pulled her to his chair. She was still wearing her black dress, her stomach more noticeable, but she didn't seem to mind that people knew she was pregnant. "I've missed not being with you." He eased her down on his lap.

"We've both been a little busy." She wrapped her arms around his neck. "I'm hoping that's going to change soon."

He placed a soft kiss on her lips. "If I have anything

to say about it, I can guarantee it." He returned for another kiss, but this time there wasn't anything gentle about his need for her.

"I want you, Paige," he whispered. "It's been too long since I've been able to hold you, touch you…make love to you."

"Oh, Reed." She kissed him. "Then take me home."

His thoughts suddenly went to his sister. He groaned. "I can't, Jodi's staying at the house tonight. I have to drive her home."

Paige smiled. "No, you don't. Jodi's upstairs with Nick. My mother talked her into not waking him up so she's staying here tonight. I guess that means I have you all to myself, but let's go to my apartment, it's closer."

"I like the sound of that."

The next morning Reed stood in Paige's kitchen. Their night together had been incredible and he wanted many more to come.

Paige needed sleep, so Reed got up to fix breakfast. When he heard the shower turn on, he knew she wasn't going to rest. At least he could help her and Sweet Pea with some nourishment to get them through her heavy work schedule.

Well, things were going to change. Paige had to take better care of herself. He was going to be around to make sure of that. He planned to be around for a long time…permanently if she'd have him.

He suddenly sensed her and turned as she came into

the room. She had on black stretch pants and a white blouse. Her hair was pulled back into a ponytail and she wore no makeup. This was the way he loved her. Hell, he didn't care what she wore. He'd take her in a potato sack.

"Good morning," he greeted.

"Good morning to you, too." She walked over and slipped her arms around his waist.

Oh, yeah, he could get used to this.

"You should have wakened me," she said.

"You need your sleep. You worked hard putting together the service yesterday. Did I tell you how much I appreciated it, especially for my mother?"

"You're welcome, but Mom and Dad did most of the work. There were a lot of other people who wanted to help, too. Many of the townspeople always believed in your father's innocence."

"I discovered that yesterday. But thank you for letting me see it." He kissed the end of her nose and sat her down to eggs and bacon. "Now, you need to eat."

Paige didn't argue. She was too hungry. She'd been hungry a lot lately. "I'm going to weigh a ton by the time I deliver." She scooped up the last bite of her eggs.

Reed swallowed his bacon. "Don't worry, I'll still love you no matter how much you weigh."

Paige paused but before she could say anything, there was the sound of the bell downstairs. She ignored it but it kept up, getting more persistent. She got up from the table. "I better go see who it is. I'll be right back so we can talk."

She went down the steps and walked to the front door to find Lyle Hutchinson standing there. "The office doesn't open until nine. Come back."

He glared at her. "I need to see you now. Open the door."

Paige unlocked the door and he rushed inside. "Look, Lyle, yesterday was a busy day. Can't we reschedule?"

"Oh, yes, the funeral for the beloved Mick Larkin. Sorry, I couldn't attend."

"I don't think you would have been welcome."

"I want to know what Reed is going to do about my father."

"I have no idea what you're talking about," Paige told him.

"I don't want the Hutchinson name dragged through the mud."

"You mean like you've done to the Larkin name for the last seventeen years?"

They both looked toward the back of the office to see Reed come out.

"Surely, *you* aren't going to try to prosecute my father."

"No, but I could sue the estate for damages. Just think, the Hutchinsons could suddenly be as poor as the Larkins were."

"That's not fair," Lyle argued.

"Not fair? Billy didn't seem to care that he took a man away from his family. Nobody thought twice that my mother had to work two jobs to support us. So why should I?"

"That's not true—Billy cared. He helped your mother keep the house. Hell, he even arranged for you to go to college."

Reed stiffened. "The hell he did. I earned a scholarship for school."

Lyle grinned. "And I have the canceled checks to show that Billy paid for four years of tuition."

Paige wanted to stop the nightmare from unfolding, but she couldn't.

"If you don't believe me just ask your girlfriend. Paige knew about it."

Paige saw his eyes begging her to say it was all a lie. To deny it. But she couldn't.

"Paige…"

"Reed, let me explain. Your mother and I only…"

His jaw clenched. "Did you help Billy get me out of town?"

"No, I just helped give you a chance at an education."

He glanced back at Lyle. "Okay, so now that you've relayed the info, you can get the hell out."

"I will, but not before you tell me what this is going to cost me. I don't want you to take retribution for something my father did years ago."

Reed stared at Paige, then looked at Lyle. "I don't want anything from you or your family. As far as I'm concerned this fight is over."

CHAPTER TEN

PAIGE told herself she had a legitimate excuse to see Reed.

For the past two days he'd ignored her calls. She wished it was because he was angry at her, but she knew that it went deeper. It was the pain she'd seen in his eyes that day in her office that would be impossible to erase from her memory.

If only he'd given her a chance to explain, maybe she could get him to understand why she'd done it. It happened a long time ago, and they'd both been hurt.

Reed hadn't known what she'd done was out of love.

Paige pulled up in front of the house next to Reed's truck. She hadn't phoned ahead purposely, knowing he wouldn't take her call.

She took a breath, got out and started up the walk when she heard the sound of a power saw coming from the backyard. She stepped off the porch and went around the house to find a large stack of lumber in the center of the lawn. Reed was on the covered deck, leaning over a table, cutting long strips of wood. Not wanting to distract him, she waited until he finished before coming any closer.

He finally turned and pinned her with a hard gaze. "What are you doing here?"

She straightened, hiding her hurt. "I need to talk to you, and you haven't returned any of my calls."

"We said everything that has to be said." He marched down the steps and followed a wide walkway that led to a concrete slab in the middle of the yard.

Paige refused to let him ignore her this time. She went after him, her heels sinking in the soft soil. "This is about business, Reed." She stopped at the pile of lumber and set her briefcase on top. "The geologist's reports came back. They sent it to my office since I've been handling everything." She took out the papers, but when she looked at him, he was measuring another piece of wood and ignoring her…again.

That hurt. "Reed, give me two minutes and I'll be out of your hair."

He stood up. She saw the hard line of his jaw, his unshaven face, the dark circles under his eyes. She wanted to put her arms around him, to comfort him, but knew that he hated her for what she'd done.

"I tried to get you at the office but they said you took the week off." She eyed the concrete walkway that led to a hexagonal shaped foundation. "What are you building?"

"A gazebo. For Mom." His expression softened. "They're going to allow her to come home for day visits."

"That's wonderful. Sally will love this."

He didn't react to her enthusiasm. "Look, I'm kind of busy. You said you had some business."

Her chest tightened painfully. She nodded, trying to get her emotions under control. "Yes, it seems that Mick was right about the silver strike. The geologist found a large vein in the tunnel where your father was…buried."

Reed took the papers and without so much as a glance, he folded them and stuck them in his back pocket. He turned away and went back to work.

His aloofness was the last straw. "You don't even want to look at the survey?"

He stood and glanced at her. "Why should I?"

"Because… Because you have a lot to think about. You could reopen the mine, work it… It's worth a lot of money."

"And it's also the place where my father died."

"I know, Reed. But as you said, Mick gave his life for Mick's Dream. You can't dismiss that." She suddenly got brave. "You shouldn't dismiss a lot of things so quickly, at least until you have a chance to know…everything."

"Some things will never heal."

"Not if we don't talk about them," she told him. "Reed, if you'll let me explain—"

"What's to explain, Paige?" he asked, glaring at her. "You lied to me. You sent me away…as if I didn't matter to you at all."

"Reed, you did matter. More than you know." She took a step closer, but he backed away. "At the time I thought I was doing the right thing, for all of us."

"You just decided to leave me out of the equation. You never gave me the opportunity to choose. Do you know what it felt like to hear you say you didn't love me anymore?"

Paige did know, because she'd felt the same pain. "We were so young, Reed. If we had tried to make a go of it…tried to work and go to school…we more than likely would have destroyed everything."

"So you just decided not to try at all. Much cleaner that way, huh, Paige?" He paced, then came back to her. "I can almost understand that reasoning, but to get hooked up with Billy…after what he'd done to my father…"

"I thought Billy wanted to help your family."

"Billy wanted to help himself. He didn't want me around to dig up the truth."

She swiped at a tear. "I didn't know that then, Reed. I only knew that you had an opportunity for an education."

Reed could only stare at her. This wouldn't matter so much if he hadn't fallen in love with her all over again.

"At what cost, Paige? You were willing to throw us aside. I loved you. You were my friend, my only real friend, and I thought I'd lost everything."

"I'm sorry, Reed."

He couldn't let her do this again. "We're all sorry, Paige. But sometimes it isn't enough. I can't do this anymore. I'll contact another lawyer to handle any other legal matters."

She nodded, biting down on her trembling lip. "I know that it doesn't mean much now, but I'm sorry things turned out this way." She turned and walked away.

Reed felt the pain shoot through him as the familiar scene replayed before his eyes. Once again Paige was walking out of his life.

It was even worse the second time.

What Paige liked about having her own apartment was that she could be alone. Alone to reflect, alone to cry. But after a few days of being miserable she knew she couldn't live this way.

She had to make a life without Reed.

For a while Paige thought about moving back to Denver. With her connections, she could make a good life there, but both she and her child needed the support of her family. Besides, she loved having her sisters close by. She also enjoyed being her own boss, and the delicious home-cooked meals from her mother. Paige hadn't shared this much time with her sisters and parents in years.

She walked into the Inn's kitchen for the weekly family dinner to find she was the last to arrive. Leah and Holt were smiling. Why shouldn't they be happy? They were in love, and were making a life together.

"Good, you're finally here," Leah said. "We have some wonderful news." She glanced at her husband who nodded. "I'm pregnant."

Cheers filled the room as everyone hugged Leah, Paige included as her sister came to her.

Paige smiled. "That must have been some honeymoon," she teased.

"It was," Leah said with a big grin. "Just think, now our babies are going to be born just months apart."

Morgan came up to the twosome. "I'm going to be a busy aunt."

"Maybe you should think about finding yourself a man and enjoying motherhood, too," Leah suggested.

"I think playing favorite aunt is enough for me."

Paige saw a flash of something in her older sister's eyes. She knew Morgan hadn't been serious about a man since college.

"Hey, where is Reed?" Leah asked.

Paige tensed. "I have no idea. Why should he be here?"

Leah shrugged. "Well, he's been around a lot since you came back to town. I just thought that you two were together again."

"Well, we aren't. I was just helping Reed find his father." Paige fought the tears. "Whatever we had ended years ago."

Leah exchanged a glance with Morgan. "Come on, we need to talk." She tugged on Paige's arm until the three sisters were upstairs sitting on one of the beds in their old room.

"Okay, spill it," Leah insisted. "What happened? I know you two were getting close again."

Paige shook her head. "Nothing happened. Reed is concentrating on his life…and I'm working on mine." Paige found it hard to hide her feelings.

"So there hasn't been anything going on between you two? That's not the way it looked to me," Morgan stated. "I thought I saw Reed leaving your office early one morning."

"Really," Leah gasped. "Oh, I miss so much living in the country. Talk, Paige."

"Okay. Okay," Paige relented. "I thought that Reed and I could resurrect what we had years ago. It didn't work."

"We want details," Morgan said.

Paige went on to tell them about what happened ten years ago, and how Reed learned the news from Lyle.

"Doesn't Reed know how devastated you were, too?" Morgan asked. "I remember how you cried yourself to sleep. How you almost gave up your own college scholarship because you wanted to go after him."

Her older sister got up and paced. "Surely Reed can understand that you both were just kids."

"He hates the fact that I made a deal with Billy Hutchinson."

"You didn't have a choice," Leah argued. "I'll go and talk to him."

"No," Paige called. "You can't. My life is complicated enough. I'm having another man's baby. It was only a matter of time until Reed decided he couldn't handle that. Better now than later." She forced a smile through her tears. "But I love you both so much for wanting to help." She placed her hands on her stomach. "I think the best thing now is to concentrate on my baby. I don't seem to have such good luck with relationships."

Maybe that was because she couldn't stop loving one man. And she never would.

A knock on the door brought her out of her reverie. Her mother and father peered in. "We're sorry to disturb you girls but we need to talk to you."

"Please, come in," Morgan motioned.

Claire Keenan sent a concerned look at her husband. "Go ahead, Claire," Tim said.

"Your dad and I had planned to do this years ago, but we kept putting it off. Now that Paige and Leah are both pregnant we thought you'd be curious about your biological parents, especially for their health history."

Paige sat down on the bed between Leah and Morgan. Suddenly afraid to know any more, she reached for both her sisters' hands. "Mom, if this is too hard…"

Claire shook her head. "No. You deserve to know that your biological mother loved you very much." She looked at Morgan. "I don't know how much you remember since you were about three years old when she left you here."

Morgan shook her head. "Not much, only that she'd promised she'd come back for us one day."

"Oh, honey, I know she promised, but she couldn't come back." Claire took a breath. "Your mother's name was Eleanor Bradshaw, and she had no choice but to give you girls up. Your biological father's name was Kirk Bradshaw and he was abusive toward your mother. She tried several times to leave him but he always found her. I met Ellie when we were in college. We stayed in touch over the years. When I realized what her situation was, I told her to come here with you girls, but she was afraid he would only find her again.

"Then one day she did show up, and said Kirk had become more violent. She begged us to take you girls, saying she couldn't risk you all getting hurt. And what I gathered was that Kirk was threatening her if she didn't get rid of you children." Claire looked at Tim. "Of course we agreed, thinking Ellie would come back here, but then just about six months later we were contacted by a lawyer about adopting you. We already loved you three, so we jumped at the chance to make it official."

Leah spoke next. "Did he continue to hurt our… mother?"

"We're not sure," her mother said. "We were unable to stay in touch with Ellie. At first she'd call and ask about you girls, but it was always from a different part of the country. About eight months later their lawyer contacted us and told us that Ellie and Kirk died in an automobile accident."

Paige closed her eyes. She didn't want to hear this, but she needed to. "Who caused the accident?"

"Kirk was driving," Tim said. "Later during an autopsy it was learned that your father had a brain tumor. They believe that was what caused his erratic behavior."

Stunned by the news, the three sisters sat together grasping each other's hands, trying to give each other strength. It was Morgan who pulled her sisters up and together they went to embrace their parents. And once again Paige and her sisters felt the love and security of this family. She needed them now more than ever.

Reed wondered if he should go back to work just so he could rest. Over the past week, he'd finished the gazebo, painted it and surrounded it with colorful bedding plants. He also built wheelchair ramps for both the front and back steps.

It was ready for his mother's first visit home.

A vehicle pulled up in the driveway. It wasn't Shady Haven's van, but Holt Rawlins's truck. He watched his friend stroll across the yard, dressed in jeans and Western shirt. His lazy gait seemed odd for the one-time New Yorker, but Holt Rawlins had adapted to ranch life quickly.

"Hey, Holt," he called. "What brings you into town?"

They shook hands. "Can't a friend stop by and share some good news?"

"Sure. I could use some."

Holt grinned. "Leah's pregnant."

Reed's heart tightened in envy, but he masked it with a smile. "That's great news." He slapped his friend on the back. "Must have been some honeymoon."

"It is when you're with the right woman. I sure got lucky with Leah." Holt studied him. "I was thinking that maybe you and Paige were going to get together."

"Well, things didn't work out."

"Too bad. I thought you two seemed perfect together. Leah said you and her sister were an item in high school."

Reed didn't like where this was going. "If Paige sent you here to talk to…"

Holt raised a hand. "I think you know Paige better than that. She'd skin me alive if she knew I was even here. But you have to know her sisters are worried about her."

"Why? Is something wrong with Paige—the baby?"

Holt shook his head. "No, they're fine. I just learned a little bit about what happened between the two of you and I'm not here to judge—but as your friend."

"Then butt out."

"Can't do that. You were there for me when I was having trouble with Leah." He smiled. "Believe me, I know how those Keenan women can get to you, and turn you inside out. But they also know how to love…totally, deeply…forever."

Reed didn't need to hear anymore. He'd spent sleepless nights thinking of nothing else. "I know all that. I've known the Keenan girls a long time. I still remember my first encounter with Paige. It was in third grade. I was a skinny kid then and a perfect target for the school bullies. One in particular, Robbie Carson. He loved to go through my lunch to scavenge for any food he liked. Paige marched up and told big old Robbie to get lost or she'd report him to the principal. Then she shared her peanut butter sandwich with me. And every day after that. Finally I got some height and bulk so I could handle Robbie myself."

"She's the fighter," Holt agreed. "Leah is the adventurous one and Morgan is the mother hen of the group."

Reed didn't want to think back to those times. "That was a long time ago. Things are different now."

"Are they so different, Reed? You have an opportunity to have it all, and you're blowing it. And don't say you aren't crazy about Paige and the baby because I see it every time you look at her." Holt glared. "Sometimes pride isn't worth it. In fact, it makes for a downright lonely companion."

He checked his watch. "I've got to go. If you want to talk, I'm always around."

"Thanks, Holt."

"Just don't think about it too hard. That usually gets us in trouble. All you need to know is Paige loves you."

Reed watched Holt walk away. He wanted to believe everything that his friend had said. He wondered if he and Paige had been doomed from the start. They had so much baggage this time around, and so many secrets.

Minutes later the Shady Haven van pulled up, Jodi came out of the house and they welcomed Sally Larkin home.

Thanks to the van's lift, his mother's chair was placed on the driveway. Reed took over and wheeled her to the walkway and out back to the gazebo.

Jodi had prepared lunch outside. With Nick in his high chair, the four ate together for the first time in a long time.

"It's so good to have you home, Mom," Jodi said and turned to him. "You did such a great job on this gazebo. You should have a party out here."

"I'm not much of a party guy."

He looked at his mother. "Unless they're small family parties."

"We should invite the Keenans," Jodi said. "They were so wonderful helping with Dad's funeral arrangements."

Little Nick started to fuss so Reed didn't have to give his sister an answer.

"It's time for your nap." Jodi carried him into the house, leaving Reed alone with his mother.

"Talk," Sally said. "To P…Paige."

His mother always liked Paige. "There's nothing to talk about."

"You're a…angry." She struggled with her speech. "Not her fault. Mine."

"It's not anyone's fault, Mom."

"Y…yes. Mine." She closed her eyes, then opened them again. "I asked…Paige to help me…t…to send you to college."

Reed frowned. "What do you mean?"

"Billy…and me…"

"Billy talked to you about college?"

She nodded and tears filled her eyes. "Yes… And I w…went to Paige. She didn't want to do it. S…she loved you."

"You asked Paige to break up with me?"

His mother glanced away. "College was the only way…out."

Reed's mind was reeling. It hadn't been Paige and Billy, but Paige helping his mother.

Jodi returned with the newspaper. "Holt phoned

while I was inside and he wanted to make sure that you saw the article in the paper." She opened it to the second page, finding the letters to the editor.

"Reed, you aren't going to believe this. It's a letter from Lyle Hutchinson." She went on to read,

To the Larkin Family,

First, and foremost, the Hutchinson family wants to express our deepest condolences over the loss of your husband and father. I know that the secrets that my father, William Hutchinson, kept were the cause in the delay of discovering the accidental death of Michael.

My father has been in failing health for years, and it could have contributed to his falsely accusing Mick Larkin of stealing.

We also relinquish any and all claims to any assets from Mick's Dream. All ownership will be signed back to your family.

Again my heartfelt sympathy for your loss.

Sincerely,

Lyle William Hutchinson

Jodi smiled. "Can you believe it? The high and mighty Hutchinsons are taking responsibility for Dad's death." She handed Reed another envelope. "This was in the mailbox."

He saw Paige's letterhead and opened it. Inside were the papers to Mick's Dream. On the front was a note from her, saying, "It's finally back where it belongs." She'd gotten the mine for him.

He showed it to Jodi, then to his mother.

"It's over, Mom," Reed said. "Everyone now knows that Dad was innocent."

Sally nodded and looked at her son. "C…can you f…forgive me?"

Reed hadn't realized until then how much he'd been holding on to the past. "There's nothing to forgive."

She reached for his hand. "Go to Paige… No more past…"

There would always be a past, but Reed didn't want to think about a future, without Paige. "It may be too late."

"Are you too proud to grovel?" Jodi grinned. "Women love that, along with flowers and, of course, a commitment…"

Reed's spirits lifted. Did he dare hope? "You think it will work?"

Jodi hugged him. "You use the right words, and Paige will forgive you anything."

"I'm praying for that."

The next day, Reed chased Paige all around town but couldn't seem to catch up with her. He didn't blame her for not wanting to see him. He had treated her badly. He didn't deserve to have her in his life. If she'd let him, he was going to make it up to her.

Earlier, he'd learned from Holt that the weekly family dinner was tonight. With a bouquet of pink roses in hand and a ring in his pocket, he was about to crash it. When no one answered the door, he walked inside and back to the kitchen where the Keenans were all gathered around the table. He almost lost his nerve, especially when everyone turned toward him. The room grew silent as he just stood there staring at Paige.

He hadn't seen her in days, and until that moment he hadn't realized how much he missed her. How much he hungered for her. Her beautiful face, those whiskey eyes and honey-brown hair.

It was Mrs. Keenan who got up from the table to welcome him. "Reed, what a surprise." She smiled. "Would you care to join us? We have plenty."

He tore his gaze from Paige to look at Claire Keenan. "Thank you, Mrs. K but if it's not too much trouble, I need to speak to Paige."

Paige looked almost angry. "Reed, could we do this tomorrow…we're about to eat."

"No, Paige, I need to do it now. Alone, please."

Everyone turned to her. She continued to sit there feeling the heat rise into her cheeks. "This isn't a good time."

The family members all turned back to Reed. "I guess we could have our private discussion in front of everyone," he said.

Now, she was angry, Paige got up from the table. How dare he walk in here and start giving orders? "You have five minutes, Larkin."

She marched out the back door and stopped at the

porch railing. She heard him follow her, but she wouldn't look at him. She gazed out into the fading sunlight, hoping to find calm. "I thought we said all that needed to be said."

"I was wrong," he said in a husky voice.

"Well, get it over with." She didn't want him here. It hurt to keep rehashing all this.

"I'm sorry."

She swung around in time as he held the flowers out to her. "Fine, you're sorry. Now, leave. And I don't want your flowers."

"I don't blame you," he told her and tossed them down on the chair. "I wouldn't blame you if you never want to speak to me again. I said some pretty rotten things." His dark gaze met hers.

She tried to look away, but he had a pull on her, he always had.

"I was angry and hurt, Paige."

She folded her arms to try to stop their trembling. "I understand. And I told you I was sorry. So please, just leave me alone." She turned and blinked into the fading sunlight, praying that she wouldn't humiliate herself by crying.

Instead of hearing the door shut, she felt him behind her. "I can't, Paige," he whispered against her ear and she shivered at the tremor in his voice. "I've tried. I spent ten years away from you. I don't want to do it again."

She stopped breathing, afraid to hope, afraid that she would give him the power to hurt her again.

"I could never get you off my mind," he admitted as

he gently tugged on her shoulders and turned her around to face him. "And for years I tried. When I worked at the Bureau and was partnered with Trish. I tried to love her, but you were always between us. I was never able to return her feelings. She died deserving more than I could give her." There were tears in his eyes. "See, there are things we've all done that we're not proud of."

"I'm sorry…"

He placed a finger against her lips. "No more, Paige. My mother told me she was the one who talked you into convincing me to go to college."

"We both only wanted the best for you. Billy owed your family that and more."

"You were what was best for me." He kissed her gently. "You're all I ever wanted. But you were right about one thing. We were too young."

"It hurt me, too," she admitted. "I loved you, Reed. I didn't want you to go." Her eyes filled with tears. "I thought we'd find our way back together. I wrote you, but you never answered me."

Reed remembered the letters. He'd been so angry that he couldn't even look at them. "I never opened them. When we broke up and you said you wanted to be my friend, I thought that was all it was. Just a friendly letter. So I threw it away. What did they say?"

She shook her head. "It doesn't matter."

"Please, Paige. I don't want any more secrets between us."

"I told you how much I still loved you, that I was

sorry we broke up and I let you go away. I hoped we could get together during the summer."

He cursed and looked away, then back at her. "I was such a fool, then and now. Can you forgive me, Paige?"

"We all made mistakes, Reed. We can't hold a grudge. We'll be living in the same town, and I'd like to think we can be friends…"

"Friends? I want more than friendship from you, Paige. I want you, all of you." He reached and lifted her chin to make her look at him. She was so beautiful in the setting sunlight. "I want a life with you, Paige, with your baby. I love you."

Her eyes widened. "You love me, but…"

"I know I messed up, but if you'll give me a chance I'll make it up to you."

"Oh, Reed. I love you so much."

He had never heard sweeter words as he pulled her into his arms and kissed her. Gently, slowly, then it quickly turned to hungry and needy, wanting to relay to her how much she meant to him. Only that would take a lifetime to show her.

"I love you, Paige." He kissed her eyelids and worked his way down to her cheeks. "I never want be without you in my life."

"I don't, either."

Suddenly Reed realized that he hadn't asked her the most important question. He stepped back and pulled the small box from his jeans pocket, then dropped down to one knee.

Paige gasped.

He took the solitaire diamond from its slot and held it up to her. "Paige Keenan, I've loved you forever and that's going to continue for as long as we live. I've come to think of your child as our child. Will you marry me, let me adopt and help you raise Sweet Pea?"

"Oh, Reed. Yes." She let him slide the ring on, then tugged at him to stand and went into his arms. His mouth closed over hers, promising her all her dreams.

A roar of cheers broke out and they looked through the kitchen window to see the entire Keenan family peering out smiling.

Paige looked at Reed. "Are you sure you're ready for this?"

He grinned. "The family is the best part."

Her parents and sisters rushed out to congratulate them, exchanging hugs and slaps on the back. "How soon is the wedding?" Claire Keenan asked.

Paige glanced at Reed.

"Soon," he said. "I want you to be mine."

She smiled. "I've always been yours for now…and forever."

EPILOGUE

IT WAS a perfect day for a wedding in a gazebo.

Paige stood in front of the mirror in Reed's bedroom in her antique-white dress. The empire-style of silk chiffon draped softly over her slightly rounded figure, angling out as it brushed the floor. The bodice had tiny straps and was delicately embroidered with silver thread and crystal beads, as was the edge of the train. Her hair was pulled up and her veil attached under the mound of curls.

"Oh, Paige. You look absolutely beautiful," her mother said with tears in her eyes. Dressed in a teal-blue dress with a short beaded jacket, Claire Keenan looked beautiful, too.

"Not too bad for being almost six months pregnant." She didn't mind people knowing about her condition. Most everyone thought Reed was her baby's father, and he loved that.

Leah and Jodi appeared in the soft pink bridesmaids' dresses. "I'll second that," Leah said. "Wait until Reed sees you." Her sister hugged her. "I'm so happy that everything worked out."

Paige felt her own tears and blinked them away. "Stop or you'll make me cry and I'll ruin my makeup."

"It's the hormones," Leah said, blinking, too. "But it's worth it."

Paige had worried about a lot of things in the past months of her pregnancy, but now she could share things with Leah and her new sister-in-law, Jodi.

Morgan entered, wearing a long strapless dress. As the maid of honor, her gown was a brighter pink than the other girls.

"Everything is ready outside." She smiled at Paige. "And the groom is getting impatient."

"So am I." They'd waited a long time for this day. During the past two weeks Reed and Paige had talked and shared their years apart. To be given a second chance was like a miracle.

Her mother kissed her and left to be seated just as her father arrived in his dark tux. He looked so handsome.

"Oh, Paige, you are a vision." He kissed her cheek. "I don't know if I can let Reed steal you from me," he whispered.

"You'll never lose me, Dad," she whispered back. "I'll always be your little girl."

He glanced at his three daughters. "Your mother and I have thanked God every day since you've come into our lives. You all brought us such joy." He took Paige's hand. "Now it's my job to give you away."

"Reed will take good care of me."

The sisters and Jodi went out. The music swelled and her father walked her out of the house to the deck and the beautiful garden before her. The gazebo was laced with greenery and baskets of flowers hung around the frame. Wide satin ribbons were draped on either side of the rows of white chairs along the aisle, and rose petals adorned the walkway that led to her man. Reed wore a dove-gray morning coat and pin-striped trousers and his eyes were on her.

The music swelled and her father escorted her down the aisle. Then Tim Keenan kissed her cheek and gave her hand to Reed.

"I've been waiting forever for you." He smiled. "But seeing you now, it was worth it."

Paige felt the pain from their years apart disappear as the minister asked, "Who gives this woman to be wed in matrimony?"

"Isn't it time to leave, yet?" Reed asked again as he watched the people seated at the dozens of tables around the yard. Some were taking another trip back though the buffet line even though they'd already cut the cake.

He was tired of smiling and shaking hands. Wasn't it time for the honeymoon? He wanted his new bride to himself.

Paige smiled up at him. "It will be over soon. Although I might be more willing to hurry it up if you'd tell me where we're going on our honeymoon."

"Not a chance," he said, drawing her against him. "Of course, if you want to try to get it out of me, I wouldn't mind some of your special interrogation tactics."

He had wanted to take Paige somewhere exotic and private, like a deserted island, but with her pregnancy, he thought it more practical to stay closer to home and decided on Coronado Island in San Diego, California.

"Just bring your bikini."

She raised an eyebrow. "I don't think you want to see me in a bikini these days."

"Oh, yes, I do. You have no idea how beautiful and sexy you look to me, carrying our baby." He glanced down at the low cut dress and her full breasts… "Have I told you how gorgeous you look in that dress, or how much I can't wait to get you out of it?"

He watched her face flush as her throat worked nervously. "You better be ready to back up those words."

This time he was the one who was swallowing hard. They hadn't made love since the day of his dad's funeral when he thought he'd lost everything. Thank God he'd wised up enough to realize how important Paige was to him…had always been to him.

"Have I told you how much I love you and little Sweet Pea?"

She went into his arms and kissed him. "Maybe it is time to change and say goodbye to my family."

"Don't take forever," he warned.

Paige returned to Reed's bedroom where her sister

Morgan was talking on her cell phone. When she hung up, she looked panicked.

"What's wrong? The town in crisis just because you took the day off?"

"Worse. That was Justin Hilliard's secretary. He's coming to Destiny next month to look over property for a ski resort."

"Oh, Morgan, that's wonderful." Seeing the distressed look on her sister's face, she asked, "It is, isn't it?"

"No! Yes! Oh, I don't know. I never expect someone like Justin Hilliard to answer my letter, or to even think about a small investment in Destiny, but now he's coming here."

"And you're going to impress him and sell him on your idea," Paige said.

"How? I'm not used to giving presentations to the CEO of a Fortune 500 company."

"Don't worry, I'll help you prepare."

Morgan frowned. "You're going on your honeymoon, then having a baby."

"I can multitask." She grinned. "We can do this."

"You can do what?"

Paige glanced at her husband standing in the doorway. "Oh, Reed. It's wonderful. Morgan has lured a hotshot executive here who wants to invest in a ski resort."

"Hey, that's great news, Morgan."

Morgan still looked worried. "I think I'll go tell Mom and Dad."

Once the door closed, Reed pulled his new wife into

his arms. "I thought I'd never get you alone." His mouth closed over hers in a heated kiss. When he finally broke away, he whispered. "That's just a sample of what's in store for my new bride."

Paige looked up at her husband. She couldn't love him more if she tried. "Are we going to make it this time, Reed?"

His eyes told her of his love. "There are no more secrets, nothing between us but a cute little bundle of joy." He touched her stomach. "I have everything I could ever want. And all I ever wanted was you…forever."

* * * * *

A MOTHER FOR THE TYCOON'S CHILD

BY
PATRICIA THAYER

CHAPTER ONE

THERE was no sign of him.

Morgan Keenan stared out the bay window of her craft shop at the family Inn, willing the tardy Fortune 500 corporate CEO to appear. Not that she didn't realize what a long shot it was to get Justin Hilliard to even consider investing in her project.

She glanced up at the clouds gathering over the San Juan Mountains, knowing the forecast was for snow flurries later tonight. It was still early in the season, but it could be a blessing for the old mining town of Destiny, Colorado. Especially when she was trying to promote the perfect location to build a ski resort.

Since being elected mayor last year, Morgan had worked hard, pulling together a cost effective package and looking for investors. She'd received a few nibbles over the previous months, but it hadn't been until she heard from Justin Hilliard of Hilliard Industries, that she thought she just might have a chance to pull off this deal.

And today, the CEO was coming to see the town…and to meet her. Or was he?

With one last glance at the empty parking lot, Morgan walked to the back of the craft shop she ran in her parents' bed-and-breakfast, the Keenan Inn. A wooden quilting frame was set up in the turret-shaped alcove. She took her seat facing the windows so she could keep an eye out for her visitor while relieving tension by working on the wedding quilt.

Morgan picked up her needle and took a measured stitch, a skill her mother had taught her years ago. It had been her salvation too many times to count. Lately the resort deal had been heavy on her mind, but after today, if Mr. Hilliard decided he wanted to invest in the resort she could breathe easier.

Busy with her intricate work, it took a while for Morgan to realize she wasn't alone. She glanced up to see a small dark-haired girl standing in the doorway. Dressed in a pink nylon ski jacket and matching bib overalls, she was too cute.

Morgan smiled. "Hi."

The girl didn't answer.

Since the Inn's guests didn't usually have children, Morgan decided the girl belonged to a day tourist. She glanced toward the front of the shop but didn't see anyone around.

"I'm Morgan," she said. "What's your name?"

"Lauren," the child answered softly.

"Pretty name. Do you want to see what I'm making?"

Her gray-blue eyes widened, then to Morgan's

surprise, the little girl walked to the edge of the stretcher board.

Morgan ran her hand over the multiblue patterned fabrics already sewn into circles. "It's called a wedding-ring quilt. See the circles?" She outlined one with her finger. "They look like rings."

The girl didn't speak, but leaned in to look at the half-finished quilt.

"I like to use blue," Morgan continued. "It's my favorite color. What's yours?"

Those big eyes rose to hers. Morgan felt a tug at her heart. "Pink…" the girl whispered.

"You want to see if we can find pink in the quilt?"

Surprisingly the little girl raised her arms to Morgan. She didn't hesitate to lift the child. A soft powdery smell emanated from her as she was tucked perfectly onto Morgan's lap. Morgan took a moment to savor the rare gift, because this would be as close as she would ever get to having a little girl of her own.

Justin Hilliard stood at the Keenan Inn's front desk. He hated being late. Punctuality had been a discipline drilled into him throughout his life. Even if it couldn't be helped because the company jet had a minor mechanical problem, and Lauren had fallen asleep. He'd decided that she needed the rest more than he needed to be on time.

"Sorry for the delay, Mr. Hilliard." The middle-aged innkeeper had short gray hair and warm hazel eyes. "We put you in the suite on the second floor.

My husband is bringing in a rollaway to accommodate your daughter."

"Thank you, Mrs. Keenan. I apologize for not informing you ahead of time."

"It's not a problem at all." The older woman smiled. "We've all been looking forward to your visit but especially, my daughter, Morgan."

He checked his watch. He was ninety minutes late. "I was to meet with her today. I'm going to have to reschedule. I want to get Lauren settled." He looked behind him at the antique love seat, but his daughter wasn't there. He glanced around the large entry that served as a lobby for the three-story bed-and-breakfast.

He tried to stay calm. "Lauren?"

Mrs. Keenan came around the desk. "I'm sure she's probably close by, probably just wandered into the craft shop." The older woman led the way along a hallway and into a room that housed the usual touristy things, along with several quilts hanging on the walls. But there was no sign of his daughter.

Panic rose in his throat. Lauren stayed close by his side, especially since her mother's death. The innkeeper walked ahead, then she turned and smiled, motioning toward an alcove.

Justin froze as he spotted his daughter seated on a woman's lap. A protective hand rested on Lauren's, guiding her small fingers through the task of pushing the needle through the fabric. His chest tightened at the enchanting scene.

Then other dormant feelings raced through him as

he took in the woman's long auburn hair brushing her shoulders in soft curls and encircling her heart-shaped face. Her pert nose wrinkled when she smiled. She had a fresh-scrubbed look that he found appealing.

"It seems your daughter has found a friend," Mrs. Keenan said, breaking into his thoughts. Then she turned and walked away.

Just then Lauren became aware of his presence. The joy in her eyes faded as she climbed down and hurried to his side.

Justin knelt and wrapped his arms around his daughter. "Lauren, you shouldn't have run off. I was worried."

"Sorry," she whispered.

"Just tell me the next time. Okay?" He rose and turned to the woman who'd managed to gain his daughter's trust. "I'm Justin Hilliard." He held out his hand.

"Morgan Keenan." They shook hands. "And I apologize. I had no idea that Lauren was missing, or that she was your daughter."

"She usually doesn't wander off." Or talk to strangers, he thought.

"Well, she's welcome here anytime." Morgan looked at the child and smiled. "As long as she asks for permission first."

Ms. Keenan was even lovelier close up. Her eyes were a deep emerald-green and expressive. Who would have thought the all-business mayor he'd talked with would turn out to look so soft...so feminine? His throat suddenly went dry. "I don't see it as a problem."

"Good." Morgan brushed her hand against her long skirt. "I hope you and Lauren had a pleasant trip here."

"We had a few delays," he said, his hand on Lauren's shoulder. "I hope my tardiness hasn't caused problems for you."

Morgan shook her head, fighting her nervousness. Justin Hilliard was more handsome than in his magazine and newspaper pictures. Tall, with wide shoulders, he was dressed in jeans, boots and a coffee-colored, cable-knit sweater.

Her attention went to his steel-gray eyes. "I'd planned to spend the day with you… I mean I was scheduled to present the Silver Sky Canyon project."

He frowned. "I apologize. I need to reschedule our meeting." He raised a hand. "It will be at your convenience. Since I've brought Lauren along, I've decided to stay the week. I thought I would mix business with some pleasure time with her."

It was a good sign that a busy CEO like Justin Hilliard was going to be here all week. "That's wonderful. There is so much to see and do around here. I hope you brought some warm clothes. They're predicting snow this week. Probably just flurries, but it's still fun to watch." Why was she babbling? "But then you get snow in Denver." She finally shut her mouth when she saw his smile.

"I'm sorry, Mr. Hilliard. As you can tell I'm anxious to tell you about the project."

"There's no need to apologize and, please, call me Justin."

"And I'm Morgan." She was just happy he was here. She'd been afraid he'd changed his mind. "And yes, we definitely can reschedule our meeting." She glanced at the little girl. "And maybe after you rest Lauren, we can have a look around town."

With questioning eyes, Lauren glanced up at her father.

"I think we both would enjoy a trip around Destiny," he said.

At that moment, Claire Keenan rejoined the group. "Then, let's get you settled Mr. Hilliard. We can send sandwiches up to the suite."

"I don't want to be a bother."

She waved her hand in the air. "Oh, it's not a bother at all. We want you to feel welcome."

Justin looked back at Morgan Keenan. "I thought that was your job."

A delightful blush crossed her cheeks. "I'll do my part, but my mother's cooking is just one of the fringe benefits Destiny has to offer."

The look in his eyes sent a strange feeling coursing through Morgan's veins.

"I can hardly wait to discover the others," he told her.

Morgan walked into the big kitchen, the hub of the Inn and the center of the Keenan family activates. This had been where she and her sisters, Paige and Leah, grew up.

It was the heart of the home, where family problems were discussed and triumphs were cheered, tears shed and laughter shared.

Claire Keenan turned as her daughter entered. "Are they settled in?"

"They seem fine. Thank you, Mom, for handling things."

"It wasn't a problem…we had the suite available."

"I should have booked him there in the first place, but I thought he would fly in only for the day. That he'd fly home tonight." She frowned. "And bringing his daughter with him. That was a surprise."

Her mother smiled. "And she's so sweet. I wonder where her mother is?"

Finding information on Justin Hilliard hadn't been hard. Morgan had gone to her sister. Paige had lived in Denver for nearly ten years and knew all about Hilliard Industries' CEO, both professionally and personally. "He'd been divorced for over a year and has had custody of his daughter since his ex-wife was killed in an automobile accident six months ago."

"How sad," Claire Keenan said. "That poor little thing. So both of them are alone."

Morgan didn't like her mother's curious look. It could only mean trouble. Since Morgan had returned from college, she'd tried to fix her up with every eligible man who'd come to the Inn.

Just then her sisters, Paige and Leah, walked into the kitchen. "Is he here yet?" Leah asked.

Morgan knew who they were talking about. "Yes, he's here," she told them.

"Is he as handsome as his pictures?" Leah asked. The petite blonde couldn't hide the twinkle in her brown eyes as she held out a computer printout from the Hilliard Industries' Web site.

Morgan had to admit that she hadn't expected a hard-driving businessman to be so good-looking. That dark, wavy hair and those gray eyes were… She quickly pushed away the thought.

"His looks have nothing to do with the man building a ski resort here."

Leah frowned. "Now, I am worried. She doesn't even react to a gorgeous man."

"Why are you looking at other men anyway?" Morgan asked. "You two are married women." She glanced pointedly down at their rounded bellies. "And pregnant."

"We're not dead," Paige informed her. The brunette's hair was perfect as was her makeup even though she was eight months pregnant. "Besides, Reed knows I love only him."

"As does Holt," Leah added.

Their mother joined in. "I love your father very much but Justin Hilliard even made me take an appreciative look. And that little girl of his…"

The two sisters turned back to Morgan. "He brought his daughter?" Paige asked.

"That's impressive," Leah added. "How old is she?"

"She's about five and adorable," their mother informed them. "Her name is Lauren and she's already gotten attached to Morgan."

Morgan covered her ears. "Stop it. None if this has anything to do with me getting the man to invest in our town. I haven't even given my presentation."

"You'll ace it," Paige said confidently. "He was interested enough to come here. It's a good investment."

"I still have to convince him."

Morgan wasn't about to tell her family that the man brought it to the surface, causing feelings in her she hadn't felt in a long time. Since college, she'd managed to keep men at arm's length because she wasn't going to chance getting hurt again.

Justin Hilliard could make her change her mind. But for her own sanity, she refused to give that power to a man. Never again.

When they reached the suite, Lauren went right to sleep, which gave Justin time to catch up with correspondence from the office. He sat at the antique desk and worked on his laptop, although this wasn't exactly the atmosphere for business. In the corner of the room there was a huge fireplace with a love seat arranged in front of it, along with a plush rug. The bedroom had a huge canopy bed, and the bathroom a large claw-foot tub.

He hadn't originally planned on bringing Lauren along, since the business meeting wasn't supposed to take longer than a day. Lately he made sure he was home in the evenings to be there for his daughter. In the past, he hadn't been much of a part of Lauren's young life, but that was all about to change.

His daughter was going to come first from now on. They were going to be a real family. But first he had to concentrate on business, but he was having trouble.

The memory of Morgan Keenan's pretty face kept popping into his head. And he didn't like that. He'd always prided himself on being able to stay focused on the task at hand.

After pouring a cup of coffee, he went to the window and looked out at the magnificent mountain range encircling the small town of Destiny. The once silver-rich town was thriving no more. Not since the last large mine operation had shut down ten years ago. Now, the few thousand residents remaining had to rely on tourism.

Mayor Morgan Keenan was doing just that, trying to bring industry to her town. Justin was intrigued, both with the town and the woman. Not a good combination, mixing business with pleasure.

Years ago, when his marriage to Crystal failed he decided he was never going to get serious about another woman. He wasn't going to live a celibate life, and when time allowed, he'd been discreet about his female companions, and extra careful not to end up in the tabloids.

He'd had enough of the front page during his circus of a marriage and his ex-wife's many indiscretions. Even after the divorce, Crystal had kept the drama going in his and their daughter's life. But the loss of her mother had been devastating to Lauren.

His child had always been his number one concern. That was what brought him here. They needed to get away from the past, to start a new life…in a new place. Maybe Destiny could be a fresh start for the both of them.

There was a soft knock on the door and Justin went to answer and found Morgan Keenan standing at the threshold.

"I don't want to disturb you or Lauren but we thought you might be hungry." She stepped aside to reveal a cart with sandwiches and milk and coffee.

"Please, come in," he said and moved aside so she could wheel the food tray in.

Morgan placed it in front of the hearth. He watched as the slender woman bent over the table to arrange the meal. Her long skirt prevented him from telling if she had any curves but did catch a glimpse of her slim ankles.

When she started for the door, he blocked her path. "Please, stay and join me," he asked. "I hate to eat alone."

She hesitated, then looked toward the bedroom. "What about Lauren?"

"She's sound asleep." He carried the chair from the desk to the table. "Please, sit."

"You don't have to wait on me."

"A lady should always be seated before a man."

When she passed by him, he caught a whiff of her shampoo. It was some kind of soft, citrus scent. He took a seat opposite her.

"I guess I should have asked if you'd eaten."

She shook her head. "Milk or coffee?"

"Coffee, please." He watched as she poured him a cup, then one for herself. He nodded toward the plate of sandwiches and after she took one, he helped himself to the thin sliced roast beef. It was delicious.

"Would you mind if we went over some questions I have about the project?"

She blinked. "Not at all."

"I'm concerned about access leading to the Silver Sky Canyon. The map shows it's pretty far from the highway."

"That was a problem for a while. The private land owner is my brother-in-law Holt Rawlins. The original road was to cut across his ranch. In fact it's a very beautiful natural area with waterfalls and wonderful hiking trails."

"Sounds like a place I'd like to see."

"It can be arranged for tomorrow, if weather permits." Her gaze locked with his, but she quickly glanced away. "To get back to your question about access to the ski area, we found another way in. It's on the back side of Holt's ranch. It's less intrusive to the environment and there's less chance of disrupting the beauty of the area. Most importantly, Holt is willing to sell the property."

Justin tried to focus on her answers, but found he was more interested in watching her sip her coffee. The slender fingers that held the bone china cup were the same fingers that made the intricate stitches in the quilt downstairs. How would those delicate hands feel on him? He swiftly pushed aside the thought. He was way off track.

"It sounds like you've spent a lot of time working out every detail of this project."

"It's important to me. This town is important to me. I've lived here nearly all my life. And as mayor,

I promised to help bring in revenue. We can't survive without new business resources."

Justin smiled as he got up from the table and went to the window. "The view is breathtaking."

Morgan joined him at the large window overlooking the mountains. "You must have a view of the Rockies in Denver."

"Denver is beautiful, too. But there's something here. A certain peace…serenity that seems to surround the town." He gave her a sideways glance. "I have to say, Morgan, I'm more than intrigued with this area."

Her smile was breathtaking, and so unconsciously seductive that his pulse began to race. She must have felt the change, too.

"I should go." She backed away, but her long skirt caught on the edge of the table and she started to fall. Justin reached for her arm and pulled her upright, but the movement brought her body against his. He immediately responded to her warmth…her softness. Morgan Keenan definitely had curves. But when their gazes met, she began to tremble.

"Are you all right?" he asked.

She nodded, and quickly untangled herself from him. "I'm clumsy sometimes."

"It happens."

"I should help my mother with dinner." Morgan hurried toward the door. "She wanted me to extend an invitation to you and Lauren."

"I don't expect your family to entertain us."

"It's a pleasure. Dinner will be at six," she said,

her hand on the doorknob. "If there's anything you need just call down. Goodbye."

Then she was gone, leaving him to wonder what had happened. Why did she tremble at his touch? There were a great many questions he wanted answered, but the main one was, did he want to get involved with a woman who wouldn't be easy to forget?

He turned back to the scene outside the window. Well, Morgan Keenan would definitely be part of the picture if he decided to make Destiny his permanent home.

"Dinner was delicious, Mrs. Keenan," Justin said as he pushed his plate away with the remains of his second helping of succulent roast pork and potatoes.

"Thank you." She rose from her seat next to her husband at the head of the long table in the Inn's formal dining room. Morgan was seated across from him. She'd changed into a black sweater that accentuated her fair skin. Auburn hair lay in waves around her face. He flashed back to the way she'd felt in his arms.

Not a safe place to go.

He quickly glanced down at Lauren seated beside him. She had wanted to change into a pretty pink dress for tonight, and he done his best to comb her hair and fasten it back with barrettes. Not his best skill.

"I hope you saved room for dessert, Mr. Hilliard," Claire Keenan said. "Morgan made double Dutch apple pie."

"Please, call me Justin."

"And we're Claire and Tim," she said as she collected plates.

Morgan stood and looked at Lauren. "Since you finished all your food, I have a special treat for you." Her smile and emerald gaze moved to Justin. "Of course if it's all right with your father."

The impact was more than he wanted to admit. He turned his attention to his daughter. She'd eaten her food without being coaxed. "Sure."

Morgan held out her hand to the child. "Want to come with me and help?" she asked.

Lauren nodded excitedly as Justin lifted her down and the twosome walked out hand in hand.

"Daughters. They're hard to turn down," Tim Keenan said as the two left.

Justin turned to the big man with the warm smile. He'd caught the loving looks Tim had shared with his wife.

"Lauren's had a rough time. It's hard for me to deny her anything."

"Losing a parent is difficult," Tim agreed. "Our girls lost their biological parents early on. We were truly blessed when they came to us."

Before coming to Destiny, Justin had dug deep into the town's history along with the young mayor's background. He'd learned how close the Keenan family was, and how the town helped raise the girls when they first arrived to town. It was apparent the three sisters had a special bond.

"You must be proud of them."

The older man nodded. "That goes without saying. And it has nothing to do with their careers or what they've chosen in life. Morgan, Paige and Leah turned out to be good people. They're kind and caring, and most importantly, happy. There's nothing more a parent could ask for."

"I'd give anything to make that happen for Lauren."

Tim stared at him. "I'd say you're making a good start. You brought her with you. There's nothing better than spending time with your child."

"It isn't always that simple in my line of work." After seeing her reaction to Morgan and the rest of the Keenan family, he realized how hungry Lauren was for a stable life. He wasn't sure if he could give her that.

Tim leaned back in his chair. "It's only as complicated as you make it. Of course there are choices to make."

"Explain that to my father," Justin said. Marshall Justin Hilliard, Sr. believed in success at all costs. Marriage and family had always come second.

"Hilliard Industries is a large conglomerate, with interests all over the world. I expect it takes a lot of manpower to run, but you should be able to delegate some of the work." Tim arched an eyebrow. "In fact, you could have sent an assistant to oversee this project."

Justin took a drink of his wine, not sure how much he should reveal right now. In the past, honesty had always been his strength in his business dealings and it might be time to lay out his plan.

Morgan came into the room with Lauren. His

daughter was proudly carrying a small dish of ice cream with colorful sprinkles on top. He smiled and helped settle her back in her chair.

There was nothing like seeing Lauren's happiness. "There's a reason I didn't send my assistant."

That drew Morgan's attention from across the table. "It's because if I decide to open a resort here, it won't be a Hilliard Industries investment," Justin began. "It will be mine and Lauren's because…if this project turns out to be right for us, Destiny will also be our home."

CHAPTER TWO

THE next morning in the conference room at City Hall a familiar feeling crept into Morgan's stomach, but she pushed away the nervousness. She could do this. She had worked for years to regain control of her life. She'd earned her position as mayor and the community trusted her to bring in new revenue. She wasn't going to let them down now. She'd gone over her proposal so many times that she could sell the idea to anyone.

But Justin Hilliard wasn't just anyone. Having that good-looking man sitting across the table, studying her closely, was a little intimidating. She'd better get used to it, since he'd announced his plans to live here permanently.

Even without his company behind him, he was powerful in his own right. He could do so much for their small community. Building the resort alone, would mean hiring hundreds of laborers. She felt her own excitement growing and took a calming breath.

"As you can see from the chart, this area is perfect for an extreme ski resort. In fact, the established resorts are booked solid all season and have to turn people away. We're hoping to get the skiers who want a more challenging run."

She pointed to the huge graphics chart that Paige had helped her put together, along with Leah's slide show of the incredible photos she'd taken of the ski area.

"With a new area opening up," she continued, "along with five-star accommodations, we could handle the overflow."

"What about the environmentalists?" Justin asked.

Morgan allowed herself to smile. "We've been okayed for the Silver Sky Canyon area as long as we limit the number of skiers on the mountain. The canyon is perfect for what we have in mind."

"Extreme skiing," Justin said thoughtfully.

She nodded. "It's the big craze right now."

"Won't that drive up the insurance costs?"

Morgan knew she was being tested. Justin Hilliard wouldn't have wasted his time in Destiny if he hadn't checked this all out. She glanced down the table to the town controller/treasurer, Beverly Whiting. The middle-aged woman had been Morgan's biggest supporter since she'd been sworn into office.

"It's all in Beverly's report," Morgan said. "And remember the caliber of skier we'll be catering to. They won't hesitate to pay for the excitement, the adrenaline rush."

Morgan watched as he continued to study the report, then glanced at Paige who smiled encouragingly.

"If I do decide to invest in the resort," Justin Hilliard began, "and build a hotel here, it could cut into some of the businesses in town."

"But if you employ locals in construction it will help our economy immediately, and we'll eventually get revenue from the ski run." In the original deal the town continued to own the land, but they needed an investor to build the resort and run it.

Morgan flipped her chart to the last page to show the mock-up of a planned strip mall next to the hotel complex. "And if you agree, we'd like to add a row of stores available for leasing. No chain fast food places, only fine restaurants, and one-of-a-kind shops."

"Like your quilt shop?"

She shrugged. "We have a silversmith that could make jewelry for shops, and there are artists in the area who would love to sell locally."

"What if I bring in my own people to run things?"

Would he do that? Morgan calmed herself once again. "They will still have to live and shop in Destiny. And I think you know that working with the community is more cost efficient."

Justin Hilliard sat there with his elbows on the table and his fingers steepled together as if thinking of another question. Then he closed his booklet and stood.

"Thank you, Mayor." He shook her hand, then went down to the end of the table and did the same with Beverly and Paige. He came back to Morgan. "Your presentation was impressive."

"This project is close to all of us. Several people

were involved in the planning." She no sooner got the words out when the door opened and Lyle Hutchinson barged into the room.

"Did you think I wouldn't hear about this?" the graying man in his mid-fifties said as he marched up to Morgan. "Just because you're mayor doesn't mean you get to make all the decisions for the town."

This was the last thing Morgan needed today. Lyle Hutchinson, a descendant of one of Destiny's founding families, hated the fact that he didn't have a say-so in this, or a chance for any financial gain from the future ski resort.

"Lyle, you were there when we voted on the project at the last council meeting," Morgan said. "Maybe if you met Mr. Hilliard…"

The usually impeccably groomed banker looked frazzled as he shook a finger in her face. "You aren't going to get away with this. Mark my words I'll stop you if it's the last thing I do."

Justin wasn't going to stand back while this angry man threatened her. He moved around the table.

"I think you better step back from Ms. Keenan," he warned.

The older man glared at Justin. "This isn't your business."

"I'm making it mine." Justin straightened. "For the last time, move away from Ms. Keenan, or I'll move you myself. Your choice."

The man continued to glare at Morgan, but he finally did as Justin suggested. "This isn't over, Morgan. I will remove you from office if it's the last thing I do."

"Please, Lyle," she said. "This isn't the time."

The door opened and a tall man in uniform with a silver badge pinned to his chest came in. He walked right up to the intruder.

"Hutchinson, I don't remember being told you were invited to this meeting." It seemed like old Lyle wasn't popular with anyone.

"If it concerns this town, Sheriff, it concerns me."

"Not if you're disrupting things. You should leave," the sheriff said firmly.

The angry Hutchinson looked as if he was going to argue, but changed his mind. "This isn't the last you hear from me." He turned and stormed out, leaving an uneasy silence in his wake. The sheriff followed him outside.

"I'm so sorry for the disruption," Morgan said.

Justin waved off her apology. "The hell with him. Are you okay?" He studied Morgan's pale face. Although she tried to hide it under oversize clothes, she was delicately built.

"I'm fine, really," she told him. "I can't believe he barged in here like that."

A pregnant Paige Keenan-Larkin came around the table to her sister's side and looked at Justin.

"Mr. Hilliard, Lyle Hutchinson doesn't represent the majority of the citizens who live here. But for many years the Hutchinson family controlled most of what went on in this town." Paige nodded to her sister. "Morgan had the guts to run against him for mayor. Let's just say she sees a new direction for the town. One that didn't profit the Hutchinsons."

The sheriff came back into the room. "I should have known Lyle would show up today. But I just had a little talk with him. I reminded him that he won't get away with intimidation and threats." He looked at Justin. "I'm Reed Larkin, Paige's husband." He stuck out his hand.

"Nice to meet you, Reed. Justin Hilliard." He smiled. "And they say small towns are boring."

Reed grinned. "You just caught us on a good day."

Paige nudged her husband. "Stop it. It's never like this. Mr. Hilliard, Destiny is a quiet town, and most everyone gets along," she assured him. "They elected Morgan because of her ideas on new growth and bringing in revenue."

Justin directed his next question to Morgan. "I take it that Hutchinson is opposed to the ski resort."

She nodded. "He says it will take away from the quaintness of the town, that we'll be overrun with tourists. It's not true. The skiing will be limited, and the resort is five miles out of the town. Besides, the ski lifts will only be open in the winter months."

A hint of a smile appeared on her lovely face. "That's not to say that we're not hoping people return in the summer for hiking, and camping. We have to think about the jobs and the money it will bring into the community." There was passion in her green eyes that had Justin intrigued, not by Morgan as mayor… but as a woman.

Paige Keenan-Larkin spoke up. "As I said, the majority of the citizens like Morgan's fresh new ideas." Paige checked her watch and glanced at her sister. "Morgan, I'm sorry, I have a doctor's appoint-ment but...if you need me to stay."

"No! You go and take care of that niece of mine. She'll be here soon." Morgan hugged her sister. "Reed, you drive her."

"I planned on it." He put his arm around his wife's shoulders and guided her to the door.

Slowly the rest of the people in the room left. Only Justin and Morgan remained. "You have a nice, big family."

"Not that big, but when Paige's and Leah's babies arrive the count will be nine."

Justin envied their closeness. He'd grown up in a large house with servants, but no family to speak of. His father, Marshal Hilliard, had never been home, and his mother wasn't maternal. One day she'd just left, but neglected to take her ten-year-old son with her.

"That's big to those of us who only have two members, just myself and Lauren," he said.

"What about your parents?"

"Let's just say my father has never been much of a family man...and my mother is...has been on an extended vacation."

"I'm so sorry. I don't know what I'd do without my family. It may sound corny but this whole town is like family to me, too. I've lived here most of my life, and wouldn't want to be anywhere else."

"You never wanted to leave?"

"I did once. I went away to college for a few years, but..." A sad look spread across her face. "I missed everyone so much...I decided to come home."

"Did you ever get the chance to finish?"

She nodded. "A few years ago I graduated from Fort Lewis College in Durango."

"That's commendable." He wanted to know more about this woman. "Most people who leave college never go back for their degree."

"My mother wanted me to finish. She didn't exactly nag, but let's say she strongly encouraged me."

Her smile broadened and he found it contagious.

"Always the politician," he said.

"Dad said I was born for this job."

"Well, you certainly have me captivated."

Morgan hated the fact this man could get to her. Justin Hilliard was handsome, powerful and he was flirting with her. But strangely she didn't feel threatened by him.

"Is there anything else?" she asked in an effort to cool down the situation. "I can show you around town before we head out to the resort site."

He checked his watch. "Do we have time to stop by the Realtor's office?"

Morgan's heart rate picked up. "Does that mean you're seriously considering the investment?"

He studied her closely. "If I wasn't serious, I wouldn't be here."

Two hours later, they were headed out to the ranch. Morgan couldn't stop thinking about Justin's words. Was it really possible that this deal would come together?

She turned her car off the road toward the ranch,

then glanced at the man beside her. "The Silver R Ranch has been owned by the Rawlins family for three generations. Holt just recently took over the cattle operation this past year." She smiled. "He's done very well for a New York financial adviser."

"And he's married to your younger sister, Leah."

She gave him a sideways glance. "I take it my mother has been filling you in on the latest news."

He was busy taking in the scenery. "Among other things. She was very kind to offer to watch Lauren today." He drew a breath. "It's beautiful out here. Not a bad backyard."

"I don't think watching your daughter is a hardship." Morgan's gaze went to the vast mountain range she'd taken for granted. The different brown hues of rock blended in with the tall green pines, today all trimmed with a dusting of snow.

"This is nice, but a small town has its downside, too," Morgan said, wanting him to know everything up-front about small-town living. "We have a limited choice of restaurants, no movie theaters close by and everyone knows your business."

"If I do decide to move here and take on this project," he said, "the hotel will have great restaurants, and there's always cable TV. And with a five-year-old, my social life isn't exactly hopping." His face grew serious. "And when you and yours have been splashed all over the media, going out has less appeal. I don't care for myself, but my concern is Lauren. She deserves a chance at a normal life."

Morgan's chest tightened. He was a good dad. If

she could ever consider allowing a man in her life, she could easily fall for this one… A sudden sadness swept over her. She would never be able to have a normal relationship.

No man would want someone with so many emotional scars.

"Morgan…" Justin's voice broke into her thoughts.

"Sorry, I guess I was daydreaming."

"Easy to do here. I feel like I'm playing hooky myself."

"That's how we want everyone to feel when they come to Destiny."

Morgan parked at the back door of the two-story ranch house. It had been recently painted white with dark green trim. The once manicured lawn had the-coming-of-winter golden hue. From the shiny red barn, to the newly strung fencing, Holt had worked hard restoring the place.

"Impressive," Justin said.

"Holt has spent the past year making improvements."

Morgan opened the car door and stepped into the chilly air. She raised her eyes toward the gray sky, and saw threatening clouds overhead. Snow was forecast for later tonight. She hoped it would hold off until they finished the tour. She pulled her coat closer around her body as Justin came to her side. Together they walked up the steps as the back door swung open and Leah appeared.

Her baby sister was petite and cute as could be. Even pregnancy didn't take away from her appeal.

"Welcome," she said as she stepped aside and allowed them inside where it was warm. They passed through a mudroom into a big kitchen with natural wood cabinets and dark granite tops. The original hardwood floors had been refinished and polished to a honey color.

"Leah, this is Justin Hilliard. Justin, my sister Leah."

"It's nice to finally meet you, Mr. Hilliard."

Smiling, Justin took Leah's small hand in his. The Keenan girls were all different and all beauties. The baby sister was blond and adorable. He just happened to prefer the willowy redheaded sister.

"Please call me Justin," he said. "And thank you for letting me have a look around."

"We're excited to have you. I just wish you had a warmer day." Leah turned back to her sister. "I tried to reach you before you left town. There's a slight problem."

"Is it the baby?" Morgan asked anxiously.

"No, the baby's fine. But it's about another baby ready to be delivered. A foal. Shady Lady's in labor and having a rough time. Holt's been with her since early this morning."

Just then the door opened and a young boy rushed in. "Hey, Mom, Dad's going to call the vet. Hi, Aunt Morgan."

The thin blond-haired boy looked about eight or nine. He hugged Morgan.

"Hi, Corey," she said. "How's my favorite nephew?"

He grinned. "I'm fine. I got to help Dad with Lady."

"That's great. Corey, I'd like you to meet Mr. Hilliard. Justin this is my nephew, Corey Rawlins."

"Nice to meet you, sir." Corey nodded and stuck out his hand.

The boy had a firm handshake. "Nice to meet you, too, Corey."

A tall sandy-haired man, dressed in the usual rancher's clothing, jeans, boots and cowboy hat, walked in.

"Man, it's cold out there." He stripped off his sheepskin-lined jacket, hung it on the peg along with his hat and came across the room. "Hi, I'm Holt Rawlins, you must be Justin Hilliard."

"That's me," he said. "I hear from your wife that you're having a little trouble."

Holt went to his wife's side. "Yeah, my prize mare is having a rough time giving birth. I just came up to call the vet and tell Morgan I can't leave right now."

Morgan looked disappointed but hurried to reassure him. "Not a problem, Holt. If you'll loan us the Jeep, we can go on our own."

"Sure." Holt frowned. "Just don't wait too long. There's a storm moving in later this afternoon. I'm sorry, but I've got to call the vet," he said and walked off down the hall.

Justin looked at Morgan. "I guess if we're going, we better leave soon."

"Sure," Morgan said, and turned to her sister. "Sorry to run off."

"I'd go with you," Leah began as she rubbed her slightly rounded stomach, "but I don't think baby would appreciate a lot of jostling around." She picked a nylon basket up off the counter. "At least I can send something with you. It's just coffee and some snacks."

Justin took the basket. "Thank you, Leah, that was thoughtful." He raised an eyebrow. "We better get going, Morgan."

"Thanks, Leah."

"I just want to help with the project." She smiled at Justin. "You're going to fall in love with the site."

Holt returned and slipped on his coat. "Vet's on his way. I'll walk you down to the barn."

There was a long, lingering kiss between Leah and Holt that anyone who didn't have a special someone in their life would envy. Justin glanced at Morgan. Was there someone special for her?

"You ready?" Holt asked breaking into Justin's thoughts.

With a nod, he followed Morgan to the door and the three of them walked to the barn where an old Jeep was parked. With a wave, Holt hurried off to the barn.

"I guess we're on our own," Justin said.

"It's not a problem," Morgan said. "I've been up to this area a hundred times."

Morgan wasn't concerned about the drive as much as the weather. Snow was predicted. If Justin Hilliard didn't see the site today, he might lose interest. At the very least, it would slow the project that she hoped would start in the early spring.

"We better hurry since snow is predicted for later tonight. This looks like our window of opportunity."

Justin walked around to the passenger's side of

the Jeep. "Then let's do it now. I like seeing what I'm buying."

His words sent a fresh ripple of excitement through her. She was going to make this happen, even if it meant spending considerable time alone with a man. Something she'd avoided for a long time.

The ride was bumpy, but going up this side of the mountain was the best way to see the future ski run. Morgan hoped that Justin felt the same way she did when he saw Silver Sky Canyon.

She parked the Jeep along the crest of the canyon opposite the ranch. "Come on, I want to show you the ultimate selling point." She opened the door, climbed out and Justin followed.

She carefully made her way to the ledge. Ignoring the wind whipping her hair, she took out her stocking cap and covered her head as she peered down at the canyon. There was little snow to hide the incredible rock formations along with the huge pines lining either side of the natural slope. At the base, the land flattened out.

"You were right this view is unbelievable," Justin said. "One would almost hate to do anything to change it."

"We actually aren't going to have to change much," she began. "Remember this isn't going to have a bunny hill, the slope is too steep. This canyon is perfect for the *extreme* skier."

He continued to study the area. "I did research on

this new phenomenon, and it's catching on, big time."

"And just think of all the ski gear they wear. The pro shop in the hotel could do big business just on equipment alone. Also there would be a ski pro and tour guides… Anyone using this slope will have to complete a specific number of ski classes."

Justin watched the beginning of snow flurries dance around Morgan's face. It was hard to stay on task when he was being distracted by this woman. It was a good thing that he'd done most of his research before coming here.

"And you probably have locals to fill those jobs, too."

She nodded. "Why not hire the best? The ones who know the area, who have skied these mountains since they were kids."

She was good. "Is there access from the highway?" He moved closer to her as she pointed down to a road.

"This is the back side of Holt's ranch. He's willing to sell us the land needed to get to the ski area."

"How far is it from the highway?"

"Ten miles." She motioned to the area. "It's scenic all the way in. And the only stipulation Holt asked for is no large billboards to mar the countryside."

Morgan glanced at him and their gazes locked momentarily, but it was enough to send a surge of awareness through him. He swallowed the dryness in his throat. "I agree with Holt on that. I'm liking this idea more and more."

She smiled and stepped back, suddenly losing her balance. He grabbed her hand and pulled her upright.

"Be careful," he said, not releasing her. Instead he walked her away from the ledge. "Maybe we should talk back here."

Morgan pulled her hand away. "I lie, I am this clumsy." Suddenly there was a strong wind mixed with snow.

He glanced up at the sky. "Maybe we shouldn't stay any longer. The storm is coming in sooner than expected."

Morgan agreed, a little angry with her reaction to Justin. They walked back to the Jeep and got in. She started the engine, hoping that she could make it back to the ranch without any more mishaps. But when she peered out the windshield at the white haze, she knew it wasn't going to be easy.

She turned on the wipers. "Well, here comes the snow that was forecast."

Slowly she backed up on the crest, maneuvered the vehicle around and started down the steep grade.

"This has really picked up," Justin said as he stared out. "Are you all right driving?"

"I'm okay." She hit a rut and gripped the wheel tighter. She wasn't sure if she was shivering from the cold, or from nervousness. "I'm just taking it slow, because visibility is so bad."

"If you want I'll drive," he offered.

She didn't dare take her eyes off the road. "Really, I'm doing fine," she lied. Had she been crazy to bring him up here today? Would he think she was? At this point she didn't care. The Jeep went over a big rock and bounced hard. She knew the trail pretty well, but she'd never had to tackle it during a snowstorm.

"This is like an amusement park ride," he tried to joke.

"Can I get off?" she kidded back.

"I'm with you on that."

Just then the Jeep hit another rut, and this time went sideways. She turned the wheel back, but not in time to stop the Jeep from heading toward a group of rocks. There was a horrible scraping sound from underneath the vehicle and suddenly they jerked to a stop. She gasped as she was thrown forward. The old Jeep's seat belts were useless, and she bumped the windshield.

"Are you all right?" Justin asked, reaching for her.

She nodded. "What happened?" She glanced out to see the Jeep sitting at an angle.

"We went off the path. Sit tight, I'll go check," he said, grabbed the flashlight from the glove compartment and climbed out into the blinding snow.

It seemed to take forever but he finally returned to the cab. She could barely see what he was doing, and worried that he could fall and hurt himself. God. What a mess. What a mistake she'd made.

The door opened and a blast of cold air hit her as he climbed into the seat, snow covering his coat. "The boulder tore out the transfer case."

Morgan had no idea what that was. "Is it important?" That sounded so dumb. "Of course it's important."

"It is, if you want the Jeep to move forward, or in reverse. Besides, we'll need help to get off the rock."

"So we're stuck here." This wasn't good.

"We should call Holt. Is there any reception here?"

Lord, she hoped so. She took out her cell phone and saw the bars were nearly nonexistent. "Sometimes yes, and sometimes no." She punched in the ranch house.

"Hello," Leah answered. "Morgan, where are you?"

"It's a long story. We're stuck about halfway down the mountain. The Jeep is…disabled. Do you think Holt could come get us?"

Her brother-in-law came on the phone. "Morgan, I'll try but in this weather, it may take a while. Just in case, you need to take cover."

Morgan looked around. The snow blanketed everything, but she'd been on outings with her dad. He'd taught all his daughters how to survive in the mountains. Did she remember anything? "Can't we stay in the Jeep?"

"Not if the snow keeps up. Look, I'll call Reed and we'll try to get through the pass before it's blocked. You need to give me some landmarks."

She looked at Justin. "Holt needs landmarks."

Without hesitation, Justin stepped out of the cab and looked into the dim late-afternoon light. When he returned, he took the phone from her.

"Holt, we're about two miles down from the summit and there's a huge rock formation that looks like a church steeple." He paused and listened, then reached in his pocket and wrote something down. "Yes. Yes, I'll try to call you when we reach it. Thanks." He pocketed her phone. "Bundle up. We have a short hike to a cave. Holt said it's the one Corey stayed in."

"I know that place." It still didn't ease her fears.

His eyes met hers. "Then we need to get going." He grabbed the basket from the back and a blanket and flashlight off the rear seat. "Holt said the cave was about a quarter of a mile from here." He rummaged through the glove compartment, took out a lighter and stuffed it in his pocket. "We can wait out the storm there."

Morgan buttoned her coat and tugged on her gloves. She released a breath, oddly feeling a calm take over. With a nod, she took the blanket, opened her door and followed Justin down the mountain trail.

For the first time in a long time she was about to trust a man she barely knew.

CHAPTER THREE

LOSING daylight and with the wind against them, it wasn't easy to get to their destination. Justin was shielding her as much as he could from the bone-chilling cold. Finally they reached the familiar ledge and he gave her a boost onto the rock, handed her the basket, then he braced his arms and jumped up.

Gathering their things, Justin shone the flashlight onto the ground as they continued to search for the elusive cave opening…and warmth.

"It's around here somewhere," Morgan called out as Justin illuminated the side of the mountain. He stayed close to her as they walked among the rocks.

"Here," she called. "It's here." She picked up the pace and headed to the opening.

She allowed him to go first. He had to duck his head at the entrance, but once inside there was room to stand up in the dark cave.

"Stay here." He set down the basket, and began walking around, shining the flashlight along the walls.

Morgan could see that other humans had taken

shelter here. There was a rough log, and next to it a pit that once held a fire. "Good, it seems to have enough ventilation to warm up the place." He turned to her. "Best part we don't seem to have to share it with any animals."

Shivering, Morgan hugged herself. "So we'll be safe here?"

"A lot better than out there. But I better get some firewood before it gets too dark." He walked to the opening.

She started to follow him.

"You stay here where it's warmer."

"Why? I can gather wood," she said.

"Okay, but stay close." His expression was clouded in the dim light as he pulled out the cell phone and called Holt. The reception kept breaking up, but he was able to tell him that they'd made it safely to the cave.

"At least Leah won't worry," Morgan said.

"Holt can't risk coming out tonight. I'm glad your mother is staying with Lauren."

"I am grateful for that."

They didn't have to go far because there was a downed tree about twenty feet from the cave. Morgan gathered twigs while Justin broke off the bigger branches. Finally loaded down, they lugged their bounty back to the cave. All the time, she couldn't stop blaming herself for this mess, especially for him having to spend the night away from his daughter...

Plus, she would be spending it with a man who was practically a stranger.

With the aid of the flashlight, Justin placed the twigs and some pine needles in the fire ring and pulled a lighter from his pocket.

"Remind me to thank Holt for keeping this in the Jeep." He flicked the lighter and touched the flame to the combustible material. After a few seconds, it took off. He quickly added more twigs, until the fire was blazing, illumining their temporary quarters.

He sat down on the log. "Not bad for a city guy, huh?"

"It's nice and warm." She spread her hands closer to the flames. "A lot better than being out there." The wind whistled past the entrance. "I can't tell you how sorry I am that this happened."

He shrugged. "You can't take the blame for the weather." He turned to her with his silver-gray gaze.

She looked away. "How am I going to tell Holt that I tore out the underside of his Jeep?"

"I don't think that matters to him as much as your safety."

"He warned us about the storm."

"And if I hadn't delayed us by stopping by the Realtor's office, we would have gotten an earlier start. But let's stop with the what-if's. I'm just grateful that we're both safe."

Morgan looked away, but she couldn't help being drawn to his seductive voice, or his mesmerizing gaze. It had been a long time since a man had made her feel this way.

She felt his hand on her arm and jumped.

"Sorry, I didn't mean to startle you," he apologized, but he looked confused.

"I guess I'm still a little nervous."

He gave her a half smile. "I'd say this trip has been a little…adventurous."

"Adventurous?" She found herself laughing out loud.

Justin joined in. "You have a nice laugh," he said as he studied her. "And a pretty smile."

"Thank you." Not knowing how to deal with the compliment, Morgan busied herself by opening the nylon basket and pulling out the thermos. "Oh, good, Leah sent us some nourishment." She took off the lid and inhaled the rich coffee aroma. "This should help keep us warm."

Morgan handed him a cup, then searched through the basket, found another and filled it for herself.

As Justin held the warm plastic cup between his hands, he couldn't help but watch Morgan Keenan. She was easy to look at, maybe too easy. He was pleasantly surprised when she'd showed up today in jeans. They emphasized what he'd already suspected: long slender legs and a shapely bottom.

Everything about Morgan Keenan intrigued him. She was smart and brave. And made no complaints about her discomfort. Crystal would have been screaming her head off, demanding he took her back…

"Are you hungry?" she asked, breaking into his thoughts. "Leah packed sandwiches." She examined one. "Ham and cheese or turkey."

He put another log on the fire and brushed his hands

on his jeans as he glanced into the basket. "By the looks of things, she was expecting us to stop for a picnic."

"I for one am glad she did."

He nodded. "I'll take the ham and cheese, unless you want it."

She handed it to him. "No, I prefer turkey."

Justin opened the bag, pulled out one half of the sandwich and took a big bite. It was the best ham and cheese ever.

"Have you ever gotten stranded up here before?" he asked.

She shook her head. "It's been a while since I've been one-on-one with nature. I mean, I believe we need to protect the environment and all, but I haven't had much time for hiking and camping outdoors. I'm the bookworm of the family." She smiled nervously, knowing she was rambling. "Now Leah, she'd think this was a wonderful adventure. She's been traipsing around these mountains photographing everything since high school. That's how she met Holt. He caught her trespassing. And believe me, back then he wasn't too happy to find her on his land." She had to stop her chattering.

"That's hard to believe. The guy's crazy about her."

Morgan looked at him. "He is now."

He studied her for a moment. "I have no doubt that all the Keenan girls could be very convincing."

She didn't want this to turn personal. It was distracting enough being in a cave with the good-looking man.

"Did I tell you that my nephew, Corey, hid out in this cave for a while?" They had a long night ahead of them…together.

"He's just a kid."

"He was a runaway back then. That's how Leah and Reed connected. They teamed up and went out and searched for him. The boy ran away from a bad foster home, and Holt took him in."

Justin took another bite. "And now they all live happily ever after."

"It happens sometimes." Morgan concentrated on her sandwich. "What about you, Justin? You seemed pretty good at gathering wood and starting a fire."

"I did do a few years in the Boy Scouts. I liked camping and hiking, but my dad was too busy to come along. I got tired of making excuses for him not showing up and just dropped out." He stole a glance at Morgan and saw the compassion in her eyes.

"I'm sorry," she said.

Justin shrugged as if it hadn't bothered him, but Marshal Hilliard not having time for his only son had hurt. "It's not a big deal."

"It is a big deal," Morgan argued. "Parents should spend time with their kids." Suddenly she looked mortified. "I had no right to say that. No doubt your father was a busy man."

"Please, don't apologize. Marshal Hilliard was a driven man, but not by his family. By business." Justin finished his sandwich and put the empty wrapper in the basket. "I don't want that for Lauren.

That's the reason I'm considering buying into this project—to get away from the big corporate life."

"Being CEO of a major company is a big responsibility."

"It can consume your life, too." He thought back to his failed marriage. "I also have no privacy and everything I do is scrutinized. That's hard when you want a personal life, and have a child."

"Lauren is precious. I can see why you're so protective."

The glow of the fire illuminated Morgan's pretty face. She had removed her cap, and her auburn hair was lying in soft curls around her shoulders. It had been a long time since a woman distracted him.

"My daughter is the most important person in my life. She's had entirely too much pain in her short life." He stared down at the fire. "First the divorce, then there was her mother dying in the accident." He paused. "Lauren was in the car, too." He heard Morgan's gasp, but continued. "I blame myself for many of the problems in my marriage. For a long time I wasn't there for Crystal…or Lauren. It was only after she died that I learnt the true extent of my wife's alcohol and drug abuse."

"I'm sorry, Justin."

Tonight, Justin didn't want to be thinking about his past mistakes. "I don't want pity."

"It's not pity, but I am sad that you and your child had to go through all the pain. You didn't cause your wife's addictions. She did that on her own."

"Then why do I feel so guilty?"

"Because when someone you love lets you down, it hurts, and it's easy to think it was your fault."

Justin studied her, seeing the flash of pain in her eyes. "You sound like you've experienced it, too."

She glanced away. "It was a long time ago." She busied herself, looking into the basket, and pulled out a bag of cookies. "Want one?"

"Sure." He took the homemade peanut butter cookie. "Was this guy the reason you quit college?"

Her eyes widened. "That was part of it."

Morgan stood, pulled her coat together and walked to the entrance. She hoped Justin would figure out that she didn't want to talk about this. He didn't, feeling him coming up behind her.

"Did someone hurt you, Morgan?"

"We all get hurt." She closed her eyes, fighting off the dark memories. Even after all this time, the pain was still there. Her heart began to pound, her breathing quickened. She leaned outside to gather more oxygen into her tight chest.

"Was he your boyfriend?" Justin stayed close, his voice soothing and nonthreatening, but she couldn't share the dark time in her life. She never had and never would.

"It was so long ago…"

"We all remember our first experience of being in love."

If only she could forget. If only she could block out that awful night…. She drew a steady breath. "Maybe we should talk about something else."

When she started to walk away, he reached for her. She panicked and jerked away. "Don't touch me."

Justin immediately raised his arms in surrender. "It was never my intension to offend you. I just wanted to say that I'm sorry you were hurt."

She brushed her hair back. "No, I overreacted. It's being in this situation, being here."

"We're okay, we'll be out in the morning." He frowned. "But if I'm making you nervous, or uncomfortable, I apologize. I also assure you that you have nothing to worry about."

He walked away and sat down on the log.

"Justin, it's not you." She released a sigh when he turned to face her. "This is a crazy situation for both of us. And this project is so important to me that—"

"You're going to fight the attraction between us," he finished for her. "And you're wondering if it will mess up the business deal?"

She couldn't say anything to that.

"Well, let me assure you that I want the Silver Sky Ski Run as much as you do. But I have to be honest with you, Morgan. The minute I set eyes on you holding my daughter on your lap, I felt something." He paused. "I think you feel it, too."

Morgan didn't know what to say. She was afraid he would walk away, and she wasn't so sure it was only the business part she cared about. And that scared her to death.

"It wouldn't be a good idea," she told him. "Not if we're going to work together."

He took a step closer. "Don't you think I know that? I want this deal to go through, too. From everything I've learned about the town of Destiny, it sounds like a perfect place to raise my child, and start a new life. The last thing I expected to think about was getting involved. Then you appeared…"

Morgan was thrilled by his words, but at the same time terrified. "This is crazy. You've only been here two days. It's just the extraordinary circumstances…"

"That, too. But whenever I'm around you, there's this awareness between us. Yet, I feel that makes you nervous." His eyes were so kind and understanding. "I never want you to be afraid of me. And you are…"

She couldn't deny it.

"Morgan, just tell me is it me, or is it all men?"

Morgan had no intention of getting this personal with a virtual stranger. A man she'd barely known for forty-eight hours. Most important, he was a possible business partner.

"Look, Justin." She drew a breath. "If a relationship is connected with the finalizing of this deal, then you can turn around and go back to Denver." She held her breath, studying his clenched jaw, knowing she could have just blown this project.

"I apologize if I've made you feel uncomfortable. It was never my intention." His gray-eyed gaze locked with hers. "I won't lie to you, Morgan, there is an attraction, but I'd never use you to get the Silver Sky project."

Morgan didn't know if her shivering had to do with Justin's admission, or from the cold. She didn't want to think about it, either, or the fact that she'd felt the same pull he did. But there was no way there could ever be anything between them.

She wouldn't trust him or any man again.

"This is a business proposition." She paused. "It's the only way, Justin." Her own words didn't help her empty feeling, or the constant, lonely ache around her heart. For just an instant she thought about taking a chance. But she knew she wouldn't. Couldn't.

Justin could see the pain in Morgan's green eyes. He wanted nothing more than to take her in his arms and reassure her he would never hurt her, or let anyone hurt her again.

"Who hurt you, Morgan? Who was the man who stole your trust?"

She looked shocked, and then closed up completely. "I'm not going to discuss my private life with you." She moved past him and went back to sit on the log.

Justin couldn't let it go. "You're right. I have no business asking you personal questions." He hesitated, not taking his own advice. "But I've been there, Morgan. You can't keep running away... believe me I've tried."

Her head snapped up and her eyes narrowed. "You don't know enough about me to make assumptions."

"I think you've been hurt...badly. And you haven't let it go." He straddled the log, far enough away not to threaten her.

She tried to laugh, but it caught in her throat. "It has nothing to do with you." She blinked rapidly. "Our connection is business. Please remember that."

She was breaking his heart. "If I decide to take on this project, Morgan, I'll be around. We'll be working together. It's a little awkward if every time I get near you, you jump."

"I don't normally," she denied. "But you have to admit that these circumstances are a little unsettling." There was a hint of a smile as she hugged herself. "I've never conducted business dealings in a cave."

"I think this is a first for me, too," he said as he added another branch to the fire. The temperature had dropped, and the wind was still howling just outside.

"Why don't we set aside all business until tomorrow?" He stole another glance at her. "Maybe you could tell me about growing up in Destiny."

She smiled. "You might get a prejudiced account. I love this town. From the moment I arrived, I knew I didn't want to live anywhere else."

He frowned. "You weren't born here?"

She shook her head. "No, but I was only three, and my sisters were even younger, when we were left in the Keenans's care. Our mother said she was coming back but she never did. Circumstances beyond her control made that impossible. It was about a year later that the Keenans adopted us. So Destiny is really the only home we've had."

Justin watched as emotions played across her pretty face.

She came out of her daze. "I'm sorry," she breathed. "It's a pretty boring story."

Nothing about this woman could bore him. "It must have been nice to know most everyone in town."

"It was. The entire town sort of pulled together to help Mom and Dad raise us." She smiled again. "They even nicknamed us Destiny's Daughters."

"I bet Lyle Hutchinson wasn't so nice."

"That's not true. Both Lyle and his father, Billy Hutchinson, were very active in the goings-on in town. It's just that a lot has happened lately to the founding family that's threatened their status in Destiny. Billy's now in a nursing home with Alzheimer's, Lyle is having trouble with his father's illness and the progress in town."

"And you're all for progress."

She grew serious. "It's not like when the mines were open, and employing hundreds of workers. The town needs new revenue."

Justin liked to listen to her. She cared about the town and its people. That was what he liked the most about Destiny and its mayor. "That's where I come in."

"Hopefully. It's a very good investment, or you wouldn't be here."

"Whether it is or isn't, Lauren is my main focus." His gaze held hers. "She deserves to have a normal childhood. I don't want a housekeeper or nanny to raise her. I want to be there to pick her up from school. To help her with homework, share her meals."

"It's hard being a single parent, Justin," Morgan said. "But everyone needs help."

"Would you help, Morgan?"

She finally looked at him. "Help you with what?"

"I want Lauren to have a childhood like you and your sisters had. And that's the reason I've decided to take on the Silver Sky project."

CHAPTER FOUR

MORGAN shivered from the cold and burrowed closer to the source of heat. Slowly a soothing band of strength wrapped around her, drawing her in. She purred at the complete feeling of solace as she inhaled the earthy male scent that was so intoxicating.

All at once she realized a different feeling as a hand moved over her back in a circular motion. It wasn't long before her breathing changed and tightness erupted in her stomach as she tried to absorb the new feelings. Then she felt the touch, a soft caress against her cheek, which sent shivers down her spine. She tipped her head back, wanting…

"Morgan…"

Morgan heard her name through her sleepy fog, but the erotic feeling kept pulling her back. The pleasure was too great…too intense for her to want it to end.

"Morgan…wake up," the man's voice whispered.

The familiar voice jarred her and she blinked to find Justin Hilliard staring at her. Suddenly she realized that she was practically lying on top of him.

She jumped back. "Oh, my. I'm sorry."

He sat up, too. "It's okay, Morgan."

"It's not okay," she argued. She tried to move away, but she was lodged in between the log and him.

"We were only trying to stay warm." He had the nerve to smile. "And I didn't mind helping out."

She gasped, looking at his large chest, covered by soft flannel. "Was I like that…with you…all night."

Justin ran a hand through his hair. "No, just the last hour or so. The fire probably died out. We needed body heat for warmth."

"You should have woken me up."

His mouth twitched in amusement. "Having a beautiful woman in my arms wasn't exactly an unpleasant experience for me."

Morgan felt a sudden rush of heat through her body, realizing this had been the first man she'd let get this close in a long time. And it was wrong. They were going to be business associates.

She started to argue that point when she heard, "Morgan! Justin! Hey, help has arrived."

They both looked toward the entrance and saw Holt and Reed standing there.

"Seems you two managed to stay warm," Reed said.

Morgan climbed to her feet. "Holt! Reed! Are we happy to see you."

"Yes," Justin said as he got up, too. "We ran out of Leah's peanut butter cookies."

"She'll be so glad you're both all right that I'm sure she'll make you another batch."

Morgan drew Holt's attention. "Holt, I'm sorry about the Jeep. I'll pay for any damage."

"No, I'll pay," Justin said. "It was my fault we started so late."

"I should have known better," Morgan countered. "So it's my fault."

Justin turned to the two men. "Are all the Keenan women so stubborn?"

Holt and Reed exchanged a glance, then Holt said, "Only if they think they're right."

"It just so happens I am about this. I pay." Morgan gathered up their things. "Come on, I want to get out of here."

She needed to put some space between herself and Justin. That was the only way this project was going to work.

The trip down the mountain was easy, since the snow had nearly melted away by the sun. When they arrived at the ranch, Morgan saw that the entire family was waiting for them. Justin climbed out of the sheriff's four-wheel drive vehicle and hurried up on the porch to little Lauren.

"Daddy! Daddy!" she cried as she raised her arms for him to lift her up. He did, and swung her around in a circle as he kissed her cheeks.

All Morgan could do was stand back and watch. Watch as Leah hugged Holt, Paige reached for Reed, even her parents had each other.

She was the odd one out.

Her parents rushed to her and they exchanged hugs. "Oh, Morgan, we were so worried."

"Well, we were fine. We found shelter and built a fire." They'd always been there for her and she loved them for that.

The group stepped into the warm kitchen where Leah had breakfast nearly ready.

"Daddy, I helped Mrs. K. and Leah to make breakfast for you."

Corey ran up to Morgan. "I'm glad you're okay, Aunt Morgan."

"So am I." She hugged him. "And thanks to you for finding that cave. It sure came in handy last night."

"Did you build a fire?"

Justin set his daughter down. "Yes, thanks to the lighter I found in the Jeep."

Holt grinned. "Glad I could help. If you want to clean up before breakfast, there's a shower upstairs."

"Daddy, we packed some clothes for you," Lauren said. "I helped a lot."

"I bet you did." He turned to Claire. "I can't thank you enough for watching her."

The older woman smiled. "You're welcome. She was a joy to have around." She looked at Morgan. "I brought you some clean clothes, too."

Before Morgan could say she'd wait until she got home, her sister nudged her up toward the stairs.

"Use our bathroom," Leah insisted, then turned to Justin. "Justin, your bag is in the guest bedroom at the top of the steps, and the bathroom is right across from it." Then she sent them off each with a mug of coffee, telling them breakfast would be served in twenty minutes.

Morgan rushed on ahead, not wanting to be coupled with Justin any longer. Not this man who'd made her feel things...things she thought she'd never feel again.

Standing in the shower she let the warm water wash over her, but it did nothing to relieve the tension from her night with Justin, or the memory of waking up in his arms this morning.

After putting on clean underwear, a pair of jeans and a warm peach-colored sweater, Morgan pulled her hair up with a rubber band and headed back to the kitchen. She came down the hall toward the stairs when the bath room door opened and she collided with Justin. Her hands went to his bare chest as he grabbed her to steady her. That was when she realized that, except for a towel around his waist, he was naked. Her heart rate suddenly went crazy as his gaze leveled on her, then an apologetic smile appeared on his freshly shaven face.

"I'm sorry...I left my clothes in the bedroom," he told her.

"Well...then, I should let you get dressed." She pulled back, but couldn't help admiring his broad chest and trim waist. Thoughts of sleeping against his strength flooded her head and her entire body reacted with a jolt.

Her gaze went to his face. "They're probably holding breakfast for us."

"Probably." He didn't move. "Morgan, about last

night… Please believe what I said, I'd never take advantage of the situation. You have my word."

Justin wasn't the guilty party. She was. "I know. I'm the one who should apologize to you. I was the one stealing your warmth."

He smiled. "I think it's safe to say we had plenty of heat to keep each other warm."

Oh, boy, did he ever. "It was only out of necessity."

"Of course, necessity." He shook his head. "It's been an interesting forty-eight hours. I can't wait to see what's next."

Surprisingly Morgan was curious about the same thing. It both thrilled and frightened her.

Every chance he got, Justin stole a glance at Morgan across the kitchen table. They'd all finished a hearty breakfast, then sat back to enjoy another cup of coffee.

Nine-year-old Corey had taken Lauren into the den to watch a video with a promise to visit the new foal later.

"So where are you planning to live?" Holt asked.

Justin jerked his attention back to the conversation. "I'm not sure. Probably in town, and I'll commute to the site when we begin construction. I do want to be settled in a home right away. I don't want to be going back and forth to Denver. It's not good for Lauren."

Claire Keenan refilled the coffee mugs. "She was so worried last night when you didn't come home. I reassured her that you were safe from the cold in a cave with Morgan."

"What did she say to that?"

The older woman smiled. "She turned the tables on me and began reassuring me that her daddy would take care of Morgan. In Lauren's words. 'If Morgan gets scared Daddy can hold her real tight until all the monsters go away.'"

Every eye turned to Justin and he felt uncomfortable.

"That's so sweet," Leah said, then sent a questioning look to Morgan. "Were you scared?"

Morgan's gaze jerked to Justin's, then quickly looked away before he could read her thoughts. She turned to Leah. "Only when I hit the rock and tore out the underside of the Jeep."

Laughter filled the kitchen, along with a feeling of family that Justin had never experienced before. He glanced around the table to see love expressed in every look, every touch...in every word. This was something he'd been searching for his entire life.

"Have you talked with a real estate agent?" Morgan asked.

He nodded. "I'm scheduled to look at a home later today. The big colonial on Birch Street."

"The old Calloway place?"

"Yes. Is there a problem?" Justin asked.

"Only it's going to take time, and a lot of money to restore," Tim told him. "The place hasn't been lived in for years."

"That's Morgan's house," Paige jumped in. "The one she always wanted to live in. Remember?"

Justin caught Morgan's blush. "Your house?"

"I was ten years old when I said that," she replied glaring at her sister. "It's a great house, but Lyle Hutchinson owns it."

"Oh, the rude man I told to leave your office?"

"Don't worry, when it comes to money, Hutchinson doesn't hold a grudge," Morgan assured him.

"I hope so," Justin said. "I'd like the chance of restoring the place back to the original state."

"It's pretty run-down," Claire said. "It was once owned by a wealthy miner. After he went broke, he had to sell it." Her smile brightened. "Oh, it's nice that it's going to be a family home again. You should ask Morgan for help with the decorating. She's our history buff."

Destiny's mayor continued to amaze him. "Maybe you'd be willing to give me some pointers on things."

Morgan groaned inwardly. She didn't need to spend any more time with Justin Hilliard. "Aren't you getting ahead of yourself? Lyle hasn't even agreed to sell."

"I'm pretty good at convincing when I want to be."

Her breath grew rapid. "Maybe…you won't like the house once you've seen the inside."

"The structure looks solid, although the porch columns will probably have to be replaced, and I can't imagine not loving the architecture inside." His gaze met Morgan's. "I could use your help."

Morgan should be excited about all this, but there were her usual doubts…and fears. She knew how important it was to work with this man. She'd already agreed to that. So what would it hurt to look at the house? Nothing, as long as she remembered she was doing this for the town…and the citizens who'd always been there for her and her sisters.

"Why don't we finalize the ski lodge deal with the city council, then we can discuss it," Justin said.

"I don't foresee anything that we can't compromise on." Morgan was sure, too. She'd like to add that she could only see Justin during business hours. But she knew with him living at the Inn, they'd run into each other.

He made her feel needy and vulnerable and she didn't like that at all. Oh, yes, she needed to avoid Justin Hilliard at all costs.

Justin Hilliard had returned to Denver two days ago. Morgan hated to admit it, but she'd missed both the man…and his daughter. She'd kept busy finishing the proposal for the council meeting, but she'd still managed to reminisce about their time together.

It had been so long since she let a man interest her. Nearly ten years. Not since college…and Ryan.

She'd been so young, and eager to go away to school. Wide-eyed and naive, she'd fallen in love with the idea of being on her own. And in one short year, her idyllic life had been destroyed. Her innocence lost.

Worse, because of a man, she'd lost what was most important—herself.

"Mayor Keenan," George Pollen called to her.

She shook away the thoughts. "Excuse me, what did you ask?"

The owner of the Gold Mine Steak House pointed to the financial sheet. "You said that Mr. Hilliard has read over and signed the contract."

"Yes, he has." She held up the papers. "He overnighted the contracts to me and I received them this morning."

She'd remembered back to their lengthy phone conversation. It hadn't been all about business. Justin asked about other things, like family and their lives... He even talked about Lauren and his daughter's excitement about coming to live in Destiny.

Morgan felt that same excitement.

She glanced around the eight-person council. "Now, all that is left to do is vote on awarding the Silver Sky Canyon project to Justin Hilliard."

She eyed the panel again for any protest.

"When I call your name, please say yea, or nay." She began reading off names, knowing pretty much who would and wouldn't agree to this project. When she reached Lyle Hutchinson, she didn't even pause when he called out, nay.

After the roll call it was five to three in favor of the project. Hers was the deciding vote to get the two-thirds needed to pass.

"And I vote, yea. The majority has it. Justin Hilliard wins the bid to start the project in the spring." She raised her gavel and hit the block. "This meeting is adjourned."

Applause broke out as Lyle Hutchinson glared at her. "I hope you're not sorry for this," he said as he marched out the door.

Morgan hoped so, too.

"Daddy, is Morgan waiting for us at the Inn?" Lauren asked.

"I don't know, sweetie." Justin glanced around at his daughter strapped securely in the back seat of his SUV. "She might be at work."

"She said I could help her make her quilt when I came back."

"Well, Morgan might be busy." He hoped she could find some time to spend with him. That it wouldn't be only to discuss business.

"I know, Daddy. She is the boss of the whole town."

He bit back a grin. "She does have an important job."

"Corey says Aunt Morgan has to tell everybody what to do. Will she be the boss of you, too?"

Justin glanced in the rearview mirror and saw those big blue eyes that had stolen his heart over and over again since the day she was born.

"Let's just say, we'll be working together. And Morgan isn't the boss of the town. She just makes sure everything runs smoothly."

"Oh." Lauren's attention went to the window as they approached the outskirts of Destiny. "Can we go see our new house?"

"Our house isn't exactly new, sweetie. Remember I told you that it needs some work before we move in."

A dozen times in the past seventy-two hours, he'd wondered if he'd done the right thing packing up and moving them both to a new town, away from everything that was familiar to Lauren.

Justin wasn't happy that he'd left Denver without resolving things with his father. Of course it hadn't been the first time that Marshall Hilliard was disappointed in his son. In two years Justin would turn thirty-five. At that point he was supposed to take over the CEO position at Hilliard Industries. It had been something his father wanted, never him.

Not to say he hadn't tried his father's way, but now, after a failed marriage, and with a daughter to raise, he had to decide what was important. What he wanted out of life.

"I'm glad we're staying at the Inn," Lauren said, breaking into his thoughts.

"So you like it here in Destiny?"

Her head bobbed up and down. "Mrs. K. lets me help her. She said we can make a pie this time. Mr. K. tells me stories about princes."

Justin felt guilty that his daughter never had grandparents who could give her that special love and attention. But the Keenans were good surrogates.

"I'm glad we both like it," he told her.

"Do you like Morgan, too?" she asked.

"Yes, I do." He had to admit the small-town mayor had been disturbing his thoughts far too much over the last four days. He kept telling himself that he didn't want to get involved in a relationship, especially with someone he'd be working with, and someone who had permanence written all over her.

He thought back to the nightly phone calls. When the business was concluded, their conversations had not. Over the phone, Morgan had been relaxed, easier with talking about herself. Maybe it was the fact that there had been some three hundred and eighty miles between them.

That was what stumped him. She wasn't shy, unless he got personal, then she pulled away.

"Daddy, we're here," Lauren called out. "Mr. K. is on the porch."

Justin pulled into a parking space and climbed out of the car. "Hello, Tim."

"Hi, Justin," Mr. Keenan called as he came down the steps. "Glad you made it back safe and sound." He immediately went to the rear of the car and opened the door for Lauren.

"Welcome back, Princess Lauren." He bowed. "May I help you out of your carriage?"

Justin watched as his daughter cupped her hands over her mouth and giggled.

Tim sent him a wink. "I used to play this game with my girls." He grew serious. "While you were out in the storm, the pretending helped to distract her."

As Tim reached in the back seat, Justin looked toward the porch. Morgan came out the door and his own excitement caught him off guard.

She had on a long skirt and a blouse with a green sweater hanging over her hips. Her glorious red hair glistened in the sunlight, lying in curls against her shoulders. He doubted she had any idea how beautiful she looked standing there. She glowed with a natural beauty that made him ache.

Justin followed Tim and Lauren along the walk and up the steps to the porch. His throat was suddenly dry.

"Hello, Morgan," he managed to say as their hands touched, sending a heated current through him.

"Justin." She nodded. "How was your trip?"

He reluctantly let her hand slip from his. "The weather cooperated." He lowered his voice. "So did my daughter."

Morgan smiled, then turned to his daughter. "Welcome back, Lauren." She clasped the child's mitten-covered hands. "I should say, welcome home."

Lauren's eyes lit up. "My daddy and me are going to live in a big house, for ever and ever."

"How about that." Morgan glanced back at Justin and their gazes locked. "But you're going to stay here with us for a while—aren't you?"

"I know, it's gonna be fun," Lauren said excitedly. "I get to go to school." Suddenly a panicked look changed her expression. "But I don't know any kids."

Tim Keenan came to the rescue. "I forgot to tell you, princess, there's going to be a tea party tomorrow. Seems there are some little girls who want to meet you."

"Really?" Lauren wiped her eyes.

Justin watched as the burly man gently soothed his daughter's fears and a smile reappeared on her face.

"Daddy, we're going to have a party 'cause all the little girls want to meet me."

"That's wonderful, sweetie." He looked at Tim and mouthed a "thank you."

Tim pulled him aside. "Don't thank me. It was Morgan's idea." Then Mr. K. took Lauren's hand and walked her through the door. "Come on, Mrs. K. has lunch ready for all of us."

"Claire, you didn't need to go to any trouble," Justin said.

"When you get to know my wife, you'll realize that she loves to cook," Tim told him. "And that family and friends eat in the kitchen. So you'll join us?"

"Thank you. We'd love to," he said.

Tim walked off with Lauren, and Justin stayed back with Morgan.

"We should join them," she said.

"First, I want to talk with you."

Morgan found herself staring. He looked just as good as she'd remembered, dressed causally in his new attire of jeans and a sweater. He pulled off his navy peacoat and hung it on a hook.

Morgan was glad he was back. She had missed them both.

Justin reached for her hand but she resisted, pulling away. "I've missed you," he told her. "It surprised me...but I found myself thinking about you far too much."

She was thrilled and frightened at the same time.

He took a step closer. "I know this could complicate things, but I want to spend time with you, Morgan."

She tried to act calm. "I don't think it's a good idea…"

When her mother called to them, Morgan said, "We should go to lunch."

He frowned. "Okay, I'll let this go for now. Would you at least go with me this afternoon to meet the contractor at the house?"

She hesitated, torn between really wanting to see the old house and keeping away from Justin. She finally gave in. "Okay."

"Good." This time he took her hand. "And maybe later we can discuss why you keep running away from me."

She started to argue, but his grip tightened and all arguments were forgotten.

"At least tell me, are you glad I'm back?"

This time she didn't hesitate. "Yes, I'm glad you're back."

CHAPTER FIVE

Two hours later, with Lauren under the watchful eye of the Keenans back at the Inn, Justin and Morgan drove to Calloway Manor. They entered through huge double oak doors with an oval cut-glass pane.

Morgan hadn't seen the dirt and grime from years of neglect as she walked across the marble floor of the massive entry.

"It's beautiful," she said, wandering around in amazement. The arched staircase that circled the room was missing some of the railing, but that could be easily replaced. A crystal chandelier, laced with cobwebs, hung over a scarred pedestal table that had been left behind.

The walls were dingy, and the detailed woodwork incredible, but dull from lack of attention. She walked into the sitting room. The focal point was a set of bay windows that looked out onto the large yard and to the street. She walked to shredded sheer curtains, recalling her own lost dreams from her childhood.

I'm going to live in that big house, she'd told seven-year-old Paige. *I'm going to marry a handsome man, and have lots of babies. I'll be the best mom in the world. And I'm never, never going to leave my children.*

"Morgan…"

She jerked around. "Sorry. Did you say something?"

He came to her with a smile on his face. "I asked, how do you like the place?"

"I've always liked it." She glanced into the dining room with its detailed wainscoting and hardwood floors. The marble fireplace had a carved oak mantel. "That's a lie. I've always *loved* this house."

Justin glanced around. "I'm beginning to conjure up some serious feelings myself," he said. "It's a shame no one has lived here in so long."

"It's been close to ten years," she told him. "When I was about seven the Jarrell family moved here. He was an executive of the Sunny Haven Mine. They entertained a lot. Fancy parties, as we used to call them as kids."

"Did your family ever attend any of the parties?"

She wrinkled her nose. "Not hardly. The closest we got was when Paige and I sneaked out one night and hid in the bushes. I watched ladies in beautiful ball gowns get out of fancy cars. I couldn't wait until I would be old enough to go to my own ball."

She turned to him and saw he was smiling at her. "Sorry, I got carried away." Justin Hilliard had probably been to dozens of formal dances.

"Please, don't apologize." He sighed. "It's great to remember when life was so simple."

"Yeah, it ends so fast," Morgan said as the dark memory clouded her enthusiasm. She fought her sadness of the lost innocence.

His gray eyes met hers, concern laced with interest. "What happened, Morgan?" he prompted, his tone soft. "What happened to take your dreams away?"

Morgan tried to look away, but his gaze held her captive. "I grew up," she insisted. She wanted to get away, but she couldn't. Justin drew her. He made her feel things she hadn't let herself feel in a long time.

"But you can't stop dreaming," he said. "Nor living."

Before she got the chance to argue, his cell phone rang. She used the distraction to go into the kitchen.

Once again she was taken back in time. Although cabinet doors hung open and counters were nearly destroyed, the charm was still there. She walked to the breakfast nook and the windows that overlooked the backyard. Everything was barren outside, but she could picture it in the spring with colorful roses draped over the arbor, fragrant flowers in rows and freshly mown grass.

She felt Justin come up behind her. "That was the contractor. He got held up on another job so he won't be able to make it until tomorrow."

"Ben Harper is the best, so it's worth the delay."

"I missed you, Morgan. All week in Denver I kept telling myself that I should stay away from you…"

"Maybe you should," she whispered, feeling an ache for this man like nothing she'd ever felt before. "I can't get involved with you, Justin." But she didn't move away.

"Our lives can't always be about business."

"It's safer…" She didn't mean to say that. "Then no one gets hurt."

"The last thing I want is to hurt you, Morgan." He leaned in closer. "It's just that when I'm with you… there's this pull…this feeling…" Slowly he turned her around to face him, then brushed his mouth across hers.

Morgan sucked in a breath. Her pulse began pounding in an erratic rhythm as a sensation she'd never known made her heart dive into her stomach. Another feeling of warmth and awareness dismissed her fears…momentarily.

His lips moved over hers, caressing, tasting her, making her want more…and more. His tongue slipped inside and she found her own need surfacing. Her hands moved over his chest to around his neck and returned his fervor.

With a groan, Justin wrapped his arms around her and drew her closer, trapping her against him. Suddenly the familiar nightmare engulfed her like a stranglehold. She couldn't breathe.

She moaned and struggled to break free. "Please, don't."

"I apologize." He raised his hands in surrender. "I didn't mean…"

"No, I'm sorry." Her hands were trembling. "I told you I'm not any good at this."

He watched her for several heartbeats. "It's more than that, Morgan. What happened?"

"Nothing," she denied. "I want to leave."

Justin couldn't ignore her obvious terror, or reaction to him. "I can't forget it. The past four days, we've been talking over the phone. I thought…I thought there was something happening between us."

He started to reach for her, but seeing her fear, he dropped his arms. "Morgan, tell me…who hurt you so badly that you can't trust anyone else?"

Her eyes widened, then came the quick answer, "No one."

"Then why are you shaking? What have I done to make you fear me?" He started toward her. "And it's not because you don't want my touch… I've seen the desire in your eyes."

She shook her head. "We can't. We'll be working together."

"How can we work together if you're terrified of me?"

Tears pooled in her emerald eyes as she raised her chin in defiance. "If you'd rather have someone else handle…"

"No, I want you." He realized at that moment he wanted more than business from her…so much more. "I want to help you, Morgan." He lowered his voice. "I don't want to hurt you, but someone has… Please, tell me."

Morgan was so tired… All these years she'd fought the ghosts…the nightmares. The guilt. When she looked at Justin…she wanted so badly to go into his arms and let him hold her. "I can't."

"You can tell me anything. Pretend you're talking on the phone, and telling me about your childhood."

When she didn't say anything, he started using his own imagination. "Was it a guy? Some guy who treated you badly." He paced back and forth. "Tell me who…and I'll go after him and make him sorry he ever touched you."

She shook her head emphatically. "No, Justin. It's over… It happened a long time ago." A lone tear rolled down her cheek and she couldn't stop it. All the pain and anguish that churned up inside her, suddenly spilled out of her. "I…was raped."

Justin clenched his fists as her words echoed in his head. He wanted to hit something. Hard. Then he saw the look on Morgan's face, full of pain and anguish, and it made his heart ache. He fought to keep in control. His own anger wouldn't help. That wouldn't help her.

"I'm sorry, Morgan."

"Don't say that." She held up her hand. "I don't want your pity."

"You're not getting it. But no woman deserves to go through something that brutal. Just tell me the bastard is rotting in jail."

"Oh God, I can't believe I told you," Morgan whispered as she wiped the tears from her face and turned away. "We should go back to the Inn."

"They never caught him?"

She paused. "I…I never pressed charges."

He cursed under his breath. "You knew him?"

She didn't say anything, just walked to the window seat and sat down. "Like I said, it was a long time ago…in college. I'm fine now."

He went to her, aching to hold her. "You're not fine. Not when you tense up every time a man touches you."

"It was never a problem before…" She stopped her words.

Justin was thrilled at her near confession. "So do I make you want more? Do I make you feel things again?"

He'd never met a woman who talked less. "You make me feel things, too. Things I haven't felt in a long time." *And never with Crystal,* he added silently.

Her eyes widened. "Please don't say that."

"Why not? It's true." He leaned against the window ledge, surprised at his own admission. "I came here to get away from never being able to live up to my father's expectations, and the guilt that I couldn't keep my wife happy. My only concerns were myself and my daughter. Then you appeared." His eyes searched her beautiful face. "It was like a sucker punch to the gut. I want to see where this…you and me…goes."

She straightened. "It isn't a good idea…not when we need to put all our energy into the project."

He saw a flicker of interest along with her denial. "I have faith we can do both." He smiled. "But from the first time I saw you, I knew I wanted something more with you." He raised a hand. "I'll go as slow as you need to go."

"I've tried this before, Justin." She swallowed hard. "I get so far and I can't…" She closed her eyes for a moment. "This is so embarrassing." She sighed. "I can't give you what you need."

"You've given me more than you realize. But I want to help you to trust again… You trusted me enough to curl up next to me in the cave."

"I was trying to keep warm."

He pushed some more. "If you were honest, you'd admit it was more than that. Your body was doing more than stealing my warmth."

A blush rose over her cheeks and his heart soared.

"Answer me this, Morgan. Did you enjoy the kiss we just shared?"

"Maybe… But that doesn't mean you should kiss me again."

He folded his arms over his chest. "And I'm not going to."

She looked doubtful at his words.

"Believe it, Morgan. The next time we kiss, you're going to be the one who initiates it."

A twitch of a smile crossed her lips. "Oh, really? You're pretty sure of yourself."

"I'm pretty sure of you and that you can't resist my charm." He grew serious. "And you're pretty irresistible, yourself."

"Gee, thanks," she said with mock irritation.

"I could show you how I really feel about you, but you'd be running for the hills."

He took her hand. Somehow she'd get used to his touch, because he didn't plan to stop anytime soon.

"Just give me a chance."

By the next afternoon Morgan was even more frustrated by Justin Hilliard. He had to be the most distracting man she'd ever met. She knew what he was trying to do, and darn it, it was working.

Seated at the desk in her office, Morgan watched him in the tailored slacks and blue dress shirt with the sleeves rolled up his forearms. Justin looked as good in a suit as he had in jeans.

One thing was for sure, since yesterday's trip to Justin's newly acquired house, he hadn't mentioned or even approached her about anything personal.

It had been business as usual.

For him maybe, but not her. She hadn't been able to sleep at all last night, reliving the kiss, his touch. Her gaze went to his mouth. He had a great mouth and knew how to use it. A sudden heat began churning deep inside her stomach.

"Morgan…"

She blinked and refocused. "Sorry. What did you say?"

A glimmer of a smile caught her eye just before he pointed to the written proposal on her desk. "I asked how well you knew the work of this contractor…R & G Construction. They've never worked on a project this large, but they're from Durango." Those silver-gray eyes searched hers. "And I know you'd like to hire local workers if possible."

She regained some of her composure. "Only if they're the best. Maybe this time we should rely on experience." Her gaze met his.

"Just because they aren't experienced doesn't mean they can't do good work. Maybe we should divide the work. R & G Construction could do the strip mall and a Denver based company handle the hotel. What do you think?"

She wished she could concentrate. "Sounds like a good idea."

"Do you have a problem with using my project manager, Marc Rhodes?" he asked.

"No. He's worked for you before."

"He's the best. He'll bring this project in on time and on budget."

"I like that. Looks like he's the person for the job. Could you get me Mr. Rhodes résumé before the next council meeting?"

Justin nodded as he jotted down some notes. "Looks like that's all for now." He checked his watch. "I wonder how Lauren's tea party is going."

Morgan was surprised and pleased that in the midst of business he thought of his child. She glanced down at their agenda, seeing they'd finished. "Probably fine, but if you want to run back to the Inn and see for yourself, go ahead."

"I don't want to intrude on her party." He raised an eyebrow. "I was told it's for *girls* only."

Morgan suddenly thought of a solution. "I know a way you can see how she's doing without her seeing you."

"You have some secret passage into the dining room?"

"I guess you'll have to wait and see." She stood and headed for the door. "Are you going to follow me?"

He tossed her a sexy smile. "Anywhere."

* * *

"And we're going to live in a big house at 300 Birch Street," Lauren told the cute blond girl across the miniature table set up for today's party. "We can't move in yet 'cause it needs to be fixed up. And I'm going to have my room painted pink and I get to have a sleepover."

Justin stood inside the converted closet that at one time provided access for the waiter. The roll door was raised a few inches, just enough to see the four five-year-old girls: Lauren, Delaney, Mary Elisabeth and Sarah.

He glanced at Morgan next to him. "I don't remember agreeing to a sleepover," he whispered.

"Lauren has to have a sleepover, if not, she'll be a social outcast."

Justin groaned. "You're kidding?"

Morgan shook her head and fought a smile as she glanced back through the slit in the window. "She's also the new kid in town, and trying to make friends."

Justin knew how hard all the changes had been on Lauren. Suddenly more girlish laughter broke out and his heart swelled at the sound. "Then she'll have the best sleepover ever…and you can help me."

"Me?" Morgan gasped as she straightened in the closet area.

It smelled slightly musty, but with a mixture of Morgan's familiar citrus scent. Who would think the combination would be so intoxicating?

"You're better equipped than me," he whispered. "You're a woman." *Yes, she definitely was that.*

Justin stood there, staring at her. After Morgan's

admission yesterday, he hadn't been able to sleep. His own anger had kept him tossing and turning most of the night.

So many times during the day he'd wanted to go to Morgan and comfort her, but knew she was a strong, independent woman. He also knew how much courage it took for her to tell him she'd been raped.

"Well, I should get back to City Hall," she said.

"Don't go yet," he blurted out.

She stopped. "Is there some more business we need to discuss?"

"No, I just want to spend time with you," he admitted, feeling as awkward as a teenager.

"Justin…"

"Have dinner with me tonight."

She glanced over her shoulder. "You don't need to take me out because you feel…"

"Please don't say it's because I feel sorry for you," he finished for her. "You think this is a pity date? Hardly. Spending time with you is for my *own* selfish reasons. I feel good being with you." His gaze moved to her full mouth. "And I want you to know how beautiful and desirable you really are." She looked surprised. "Maybe you aren't ready to hear it now, Morgan, but I'm going to be around." He tossed her a grin. "And I thought if we went out on a date it would be a good opportunity for you to kiss me."

"Excuse me…you thought I would kiss you?"

He nodded. "I know when a woman likes my kisses and you do."

"That is so arrogant."

"No. It's truthful. Have dinner with me so you can get to know me better."

She blew out a long breath. "I'm not sure that's wise."

"Come on, Morgan. It's just dinner. Nothing is going to happen unless you start it."

She was thinking about it. "People will talk, Justin. They'll label us a couple. There are people in town who would like to use that against me."

"You're allowed to have a private life."

She didn't answer for a while, then said, "What about Lauren?"

He opened his mouth when he heard, "Daddy, what are you and Morgan doing in the closet?"

He swung around to find four little girls standing in the doorway, giggling. Darn if he didn't feel like he'd been caught doing something wrong.

"Uh, Morgan and I were looking for something."

More giggles. He loved that sound. "Is your tea party over?"

Lauren nodded. "It was so fun, Daddy. Mrs. K. made little cakes and sandwiches, and we had real raspberry tea."

"I hope you thanked Mrs. K."

Her dark head bobbed up and down. "A lot of times. Daddy, these are my new friends, Sarah, Mary Elisabeth, and Delaney."

"It's very nice to meet you, girls."

They waved shyly at him.

"Daddy, Delaney's mommy invited all of us to a

sleepover tonight." She drew in a breath and cupped her small hands together. "Can I go, please? Please."

He glanced at Morgan. "I don't know her parents."

Morgan knew the pretty divorced blonde, and no doubt Justin would get the opportunity, too. She hated the fact that she cared. "Delaney's mother is Kaley Sims. She went to school with Paige."

"Does she work at the real estate office?"

Morgan nodded. "She moved back here last year."

The little blonde, Delaney, spoke up. "We live with Grandma cause my daddy and mommy aren't married anymore."

Justin knelt down. "Well, I'm sure your grandmother is happy you came to live with her."

"She watches me when Mommy works. She said I can have a sleepover 'cause Lauren is going to live here. So can she?"

"I think that's so sweet of your grandmother. And yes, Lauren can spend the night."

All the girls started jumping up and down cheering, then set off down the hall toward the stairs. Morgan saw the panicked look on Justin's face.

"I'll go help her pack her things," she said.

"I'd appreciate that," he said. "Then when you come down we'll discuss where to go for dinner."

"I haven't agreed…"

"But you want to, so tell me what kind of food you like?" He followed her to the staircase where he stopped as she corralled the girls and continued up.

"What's your favorite food?" he called after her, but she ignored him.

"It's Mexican."

He turned to find Claire Keenan standing in the hall.

"Oh, Mrs. Keenan, I want to thank you for all you've done for Lauren. She loved the party."

"It was our pleasure." She sighed, her soft eyes crinkled with a smile. "Sure brought back a lot of memories. Morgan was big on tea parties and playing princess. She was big on pretending." The older woman shook her head. "They grow up so fast."

He chuckled. "Sometimes I think Lauren just turned thirty overnight. It was good to hear her laugh."

"She's a beautiful child."

"And I can't thank you enough for all the help. I didn't realize how complicated raising a little girl can be."

"You seem to be doing just fine." Her smile grew. "And not so bad with the big girls, either. There's a great Mexican restaurant in Durango called Francisco's. It's Morgan's favorite."

"Thanks for the tip." He paused, wanting Morgan's family to know his plans. "Just so you know, tonight and this dinner has nothing to do with business. It's personal between me and Morgan."

CHAPTER SIX

THREE hours later, Lauren was at Delaney's house with all her new friends while Morgan sat with Justin in the corner booth of the candlelit restaurant, Francisco's.

Justin looked gorgeous dressed in his wine-colored sweater, emphasizing those broad shoulders of his.

And he kept looking at her, smiling.

"Have I told you how lovely you look?"

Morgan felt herself blush. "Yes, and thank you… again."

Paige should get all the credit for how she looked for her date. Once her sister had heard about her evening with Justin, she'd rushed over with an off-the-shoulder black angora sweater and a pair of slate-gray pleated slacks. The hairstyle was her idea, too. Morgan's long hair was pulled back from her face with clips. Paige then added makeup, eye shadow and lip liner. Too bad her sister couldn't do anything to cure her nervousness. Which was silly; it was only a dinner.

Justin watched Morgan. He'd tried everything to ease her tension, but nothing seemed to work.

"You know two people who spent a night in a cave, and an afternoon in a closet, shouldn't be acting like strangers."

She blinked. "We didn't spend an afternoon in a closet. It was only about twenty minutes."

"I apologize. Maybe it was just me wishing it were longer." He leaned closer. "You're very hard to resist, Morgan."

She took another sip of her wine.

"Don't get panicked, I'm only being honest, Morgan. I care about you, and I think you're attracted to me." When she started to argue, he raised his hand. "But since I'm making you feel uncomfortable maybe we should work on our friendship, discuss something else." He thought a moment. "Ben Harper came by the house this afternoon. He's agreed to take on the Hilliard Manor project."

"Oh, Justin, that's wonderful. How soon before he begins?"

"The end of the week. He's going to start restoring upstairs. Painting and some repair work to the master suite and two other bedrooms. One will be an office and the other Lauren's room. He says he needs two weeks to make the bedrooms and a bath livable."

"I bet Lauren is excited."

"She doesn't know, yet." His gaze raised to her green eyes. "You're the first person I've told." He realized Morgan was the one he wanted to tell. "I need your expertise, too. Would you help me choose some paint colors?"

"Shouldn't you hire a decorator?"

"I want the place to look like a home, not a museum. Your mother said you handled redecorating of the guest rooms. I especially like the colors in your shop and your quilt. Is blue your favorite color?"

She nodded.

"I have a fondness for blue, too." He reached for her slender hand, examining her long fingers. "Okay, maybe it's tall redheads who like blue." He took a chance and laced his fingers with hers.

"You can't paint your entire house blue," she whispered.

He leaned closer. "Maybe not. What would you paint the rooms?"

She gave a shuddering breath when his fingers stroked the back of her hand. "Yellow…for the kitchen. Maybe a pale yellow for Lauren's room… No, it should be pink."

Her gaze met his, and he rejoiced to see the spark of desire in those green depths.

"What about my bedroom, Morgan?"

Her full lips parted, and her breathing grew a little labored. "I…I haven't seen your bedroom."

Justin fought back a groan as he conjured up images of them together. "I guess I'll have to show it to you." Leaning toward her, he whispered, "We could stop by tonight on the way back to the Inn."

"It'll be late," she protested weakly.

It was already too late for him. "Ten minutes," he told her. "I promise all we'll do is just look at the room." He locked his gaze on her. "Unless…you have other ideas. You're in the driver's seat. I'm not going to make the first move on you, Morgan. That will be up to you."

During the drive back from dinner in Durango, Morgan let Justin Hilliard talk her into stopping at the house. Of course, since she hadn't gone upstairs the other day, she jumped at the chance now.

Well, she'd show him it was still going to be business between them, no matter how much the man distracted her.

And she was only giving him five minutes.

Justin unlocked the door and turned on the light in the entry. "A crew is coming by tomorrow to clean up the place and rope off part of the downstairs from Lauren while they're working." He took her hand and led her to the stairs. "It's going to be a while before they finish remodeling the kitchen. So it looks like we'll be cooking with a microwave for a few months."

"But it will be well worth it in the end," she told him.

At the top of the stairs, he flicked on another set of lights, illuminating the hallway that led them past four bedrooms. The one at the end of the corridor was the master suite. He reached inside the double doors and turned on the overhead light, a crystal teardrop chandelier.

Morgan's eyes adjusted to the sudden brightness and she took a step into the huge, empty room. Hardwood floors made an echoing sound as she walked to the marble fireplace framed with a dark wood stained mantel. A window seat made a cozy area overlooking the back of the house. She went into the dressing area, and the large walk-in closet.

"This is wonderful. So much room."

"Give you any ideas?"

She swung around to see him sitting on the window seat, his arms crossed over his chest. *He* gave her ideas all right. A shiver went through her. Surprised, she quickly shook away her wandering thoughts.

"What does your furniture look like?"

"I don't know. I'm going to furnish this house with everything new. You have any thoughts on what style of bed I should have?"

"Big. In this size room it needs it. And masculine…"

"Whoa…I don't want it too masculine. I'm hoping I'm not going to be living in here all by myself…"

Morgan couldn't look at him. Of course, he wanted a woman. A normal, healthy man like Justin would want a woman to share his bed. She just wasn't that woman. "I should get back to the Inn." She started out when he stopped her.

"Are you going to keep running from what you want?"

She paused at the door, and looked over her shoulder. "And what exactly do I want?"

Even from across the room, his heated gaze reached her. "A loving relationship with a man who cares about you. You want me."

She could only blink at his arrogance.

"Of course, no more than I want you."

"Look, Justin, just because you learned about my past…and you made a silly bet about a kiss, doesn't give you the right…"

"I think it gives me every right. I care about you, Morgan. I didn't plan to, but it happened and I want to see where it could go with us."

Suddenly she found she wanted to, too. But she was frightened. What if she never could be what he wanted…and needed? "I can't…"

"Yes, you can. I'm right here to help you."

"I did try when you kissed me, but I had to pull away when you tried to hold me…"

"Maybe you weren't ready for that much contact. And I held you too tight," he finished for her. "So you take charge, Morgan. You kiss me."

Morgan gripped the doorknob, feeling a rush of excitement. She wanted to. She wanted to be the woman he wanted…he needed.

He arched an eyebrow. "You run a town, you own a business and you're going to head a large development project, and you're telling me you can't give me one little kiss?"

She didn't answer.

"Just tell me this, Morgan. Do you want to kiss me?"

Her heartbeat shot off pounding. "Yes…"

"Show me," he challenged in a husky, rough voice. "I'll sit here. I won't even put a hand on you."

She tried not to be affected, but felt the pull.

"I dare you, Morgan. I dare you to kiss me."

She took the first step, then the second and realized she had to keep herself from going too fast. "This is crazy."

She stopped in front of him, telling herself that she was doing this just to shut him up. As if taking medicine, she braced herself for the worst. She placed her hands on his broad shoulders, feeling his strength. She leaned down, and placed her mouth against his. His lips were warm and firm. The slow awareness began to curl in her stomach as her mouth moved tentatively over his. She pulled away, her heart drumming in her chest as she looked into his pewter gaze.

"Again, Morgan," he breathed. "Kiss me again."

His husky words made her daring, or it was just the fact she couldn't seem to resist him. This time she grew bolder, hungrier as her hands moved to his hair, combing through the dark thickness as her mouth caressed and stroked his. She finally pulled back, but only inches, so she could study his incredible mouth.

"Again…" he breathed.

Justin Hilliard was quickly growing addictive. He made her feel things. Good things, but scary none-theless. Her mouth pressed to his, and this time, she felt his tongue running along the seam of her lips. On a soft moan, she opened to him, then heard him groan and delve deeper inside to taste her.

"That's it, green eyes. Let me taste you."

Quickly Morgan became lost in the pleasure he made her feel. She'd never, ever experienced any-thing like this…and she wanted more.

"Justin…" she breathed against his mouth. "I've never…never…"

"Excuse me," said a voice from the doorway.

Morgan swung around and saw her brother-in-law, Sheriff Reed Larkin.

"I'm sorry, Morgan…Justin." Reed looked as embarrassed as she felt. "We got a call that there was activity in the house." He rubbed his forehead. "It…means someone was inside. I had to check it out."

"It's okay, Sheriff," Justin said as he stood up, but kept Morgan close. "I was showing Morgan around upstairs."

Reed nodded. "Sorry for the intrusion, I'll be leaving. Have fun." He winked and disappeared.

Morgan was mortified. "This is so embarrassing."

"Why? So what if your brother-in-law caught us kissing? I'm sure he and Paige have done their share."

"You don't understand." She paced. "The entire family is going to find out."

"And that's bad because…"

"Because I told you, I'm not good at…this."

He raised an eyebrow at her. "The way you were kissing me, you could have fooled me."

Morgan gasped. "That's only because of the things you were saying."

He smiled. "You mean because I was encouraging you?"

She nodded.

"It worked because we both wanted to keep on kissing."

She got that strange feeling in her stomach again. She wanted it, too. "There will come a time when you want more."

He frowned. "Morgan, no one has a right to make you do anything that you don't want to do."

Justin fought to hide his anger at the man who'd done this to her. He took her hand and led her back to the window seat to sit down, and searched her face. "And I might not like it, but if you say no, that means no."

Her gaze stayed on their clasped hands for a long time, then she finally raised her head. Her chin trembled and tears welled in her eyes. "After what happened with Ryan…he said I'd been teasing him for too long…and it was bound to happen."

Justin cursed, wanting to find the person who'd done this to her. "He lied, Morgan. It wasn't your fault. No matter how he explained it, he took what you weren't willing to give him." He wanted to wrap his arms around her and just hold her…absorb her pain and the guilt she'd carried all these years.

"I'm not him, Morgan." Taking a chance, Justin raised his hand and touched her cheek. "You're too precious to me to ever hurt you like that. When we get together, I want you to want me as much as I want you."

Her eyes rounded. "But what if I can't…"

He smiled. "I'm willing to wait for that day."

The next morning, Morgan went down to breakfast at her usual time. With Justin as a guest here, she didn't have any choice but to face him.

I'm willing to wait for that day, he'd told her. She'd stayed awake most of the night, reliving his words and the kisses they'd shared. Although her experiences had been limited, she'd never before felt this close to a man. But it was different than when she was with Ryan. For one, she was older now. Although Ryan came from an affluent family, Justin had never thrown around his wealth. Never made her feel that they didn't fit together.

It would be so easy to fall in love with the man, but being the woman he needed was another story.

Hearing some commotion, she hurried down the back stairs that led into the kitchen where her parents, were seated at the table with Justin and Lauren.

Lauren spotted her first. "Morgan! You're here." The girl ran over to meet her, her dark ponytails swinging back and forth. "I'm going to kindergarten. It's my first day."

"That's right it is. Are you excited?"

The child nodded. Dressed in a pair of jeans and a pink blouse and matching sweater, she looked adorable.

"Delaney and Mary Elisabeth get to go on the bus, but I can't 'cause Daddy wants to take me."

Morgan stole a look at the terrible father who wanted the pleasure of taking his child to her first day of school. He was dressed in his uniform of late: jeans and a green crew-neck sweater. Her attention went to his freshly shaven face, and his mouth, and suddenly she recalled his heart-stopping kisses. His silver gaze locked with hers and he smiled.

She glanced away. "Well, looks like you have a problem." She hesitated a minute, then came up with a solution. "Your daddy just wants to make sure you're happy in your new school, and meet your teacher. So maybe it would be okay—just this once—if your daddy drives you. And so he can take pictures for your scrapbook, and then you can ride the bus home with your friends."

The five-year-old pursed her cute mouth. "I guess that's okay." She turned and walked to her father. "Daddy, you can take me to school today."

"Thank you, sweetie." He looked at Morgan and she had trouble catching her breath. "And thank you," he whispered as he walked by. "I'll see you later."

Morgan worked to regain her composure as she helped Lauren on with her backpack. Then she was rewarded with a hug from the child. "Bye, Morgan."

"Bye, Lauren. You have a good day in school."

The girl hugged both the Keenans, then father and daughter left. Morgan went to the coffeemaker and poured herself a cup. When she returned to the table, her parents were watching her.

"What?"

"I was just thinking what a sweet little girl Lauren is," her father said. "She reminds me a lot of you when you were that age. She knows exactly what she wants…and goes after it."

"And Justin is such a good father," her mother added.

Here it comes, Morgan thought as she drank her fresh coffee.

"And he's such a handsome man. It's a shame he's all alone." Her mother glanced at her. "How was your date last night, honey?"

She wanted to deny it wasn't really a date, but it was. "It was fine."

Her mother raised an eyebrow. "Just fine?"

Tim Keenan placed his hand over his wife's. "Claire…Morgan doesn't want to talk about it. I think we should respect that."

Morgan discovered she wanted to tell them all about how much fun she'd had being with Justin, how he made her feel. But at this point, she didn't trust her own feelings.

"Mother, we have to work together. Our first concern has to be the project. There isn't any time for much else."

"That's a shame because both you and Justin could use a life outside work. Of course, if there aren't any sparks between the two of you…" Her mother took a sip of her coffee. "By the way, Paige called earlier. She said Reed ran into you and Justin last night at the Holloway house." Claire Keenan smiled. "So…you're taking Justin up on helping him decorate his place."

Morgan groaned. This was exactly what she was afraid of. "I kind of got talked into it."

Later that morning, Morgan was in her office, but the work on her desk sat untouched. She hadn't been able to concentrate. There was a knock on the door and Justin peered in. "You got a minute?"

Morgan's stomach took a dip, quickly sending

her off balance, but she pulled herself together. Here was the reason why she couldn't focus. She gave him a nod as she came around the desk.

"Were we scheduled for a meeting?"

Justin closed the door behind him. "No, I just wanted to see you and thank you."

"Thank me…?" Why couldn't she form a sentence?

His smile brightened. "For this morning. Lauren was insistent about going on the bus until you convinced her otherwise."

Her attention went to his mouth. More memories of his gentle touches and soft kisses flashed through her mind, causing a shiver to go through her. She quickly pushed them away. "I…I hope you got a lot of pictures."

He nodded. "With her friends, teacher, even the class fish tank."

They both laughed. He sobered first. "I enjoyed being with you last night."

"So did I."

"Good. I hope we can do it again."

"I'm not so sure it's a good idea." Morgan walked back to her desk. Justin followed her.

"I see. Any particular reason that you've changed your mind since last night? I thought you were willing to give us a chance."

She remained silent.

Justin knew there was chemistry between them, more than he'd ever felt with any other woman he'd been with. He wasn't about to let her give up on them. "You're going to have to explain this to me."

She finally turned around. "It's not the kisses. I don't want to lead you on… What if I can't go any farther…than kissing."

Oh, he wanted more, all right. "I told you, you set the pace."

He took her hand and loved the fact that she didn't pull away when he touched her. "We're going to erase all those bad memories, Morgan. I meant what I said about helping you. It started last night when you kissed me…and kissed me."

She closed her eyes, and he noticed a change in her breathing. She wanted him, too.

"Intimacy between a man and a woman can be a beautiful thing, Morgan. And I want to be the one to show you." He sank down to sit on the edge of the desk. He tugged on her hand. "Now, I need you to kiss me."

"How can you be so sure about this?"

"About the kiss?" he tried to tease as he brought her hand to his pounding heart.

"No, about us being…together."

"About me making love to you?" he asked as he watched her eyes light up, and her cheeks flush pink. "Because I think you want it as much as I do." He rushed on. "Maybe not as soon as I do, but I'm going to wait until you do. I care about you, Morgan."

"I care about you, too." She frowned. "I'm just afraid that if I mess this up that it will affect us working together."

"We actually won't be working together much. Marc Rhodes will be the hands-on person for the resort. He's more than capable of handling the job. I meant what I said about having time for Lauren… and myself. I've spent a lot of years working eighty-hour weeks. No more." His grip on her hand tightened. "It's going to be all about family and enjoying life. But that won't stop us from spending time together."

Morgan was standing so close. It tormented him to have her that near and not be able to kiss her. If she knew his true feelings she'd run so fast…

"I'm afraid, for now, I'll be spending most of my time at the house," he told her. "Lauren needs her own space, and so do I."

"You're so good with her, Justin."

He grew serious. "I wasn't always. It's taken me a long time to get my priorities straight. It's time she has a real home."

"Do you still want my help?"

"Oh, yes. I'm headed there today and thought you could come along. You can start on the wall colors."

There was a knock on the door and she drew her hand from his and went to answer it. It was her secretary with some papers for Morgan to sign.

"I have a meeting in a few minutes for the upcoming Western Days in two weeks. But I could stop by in about an hour." She glanced at the clock. "When do you have to pick up Lauren?"

"Not until three. She's going to Delaney's house for the afternoon." He sighed. "I'm not used to Lauren being so independent."

"That's because she's thriving, and happy."

"And you and your family have to take credit for a lot of that."

"Her daddy should take some credit, too." She went to him, lifted up on her toes and planted a long, lingering kiss on his surprised mouth. She pulled back and smiled. "And you have a way with women."

CHAPTER SEVEN

ABOUT noon that day, Morgan arrived at the Hilliard house with lunch. Stepping up on the worn planked porch floor, she grew nervous in anticipation of seeing Justin. Somehow, in just a few short weeks, she'd let him get to her.

She'd become far too eager to share his enticing kisses. Not long ago the man was a stranger, but even then she'd ended up spending the night with him in a cave, sleeping in his arms. And every time she'd set foot in this house she managed to end up kissing him.

Instead of reaffirming her resolve to stay away, she felt a little thrill, wondering just how Justin would persuade her today.

Morgan opened the front door to the sound of a power saw coming from the second floor. She climbed the stairs and walked down the hall to the second bedroom. There was a man leaning over the makeshift worktable propped upon sawhorses. Justin. He was running his power saw over a sheet of plywood.

Faded jeans encased his narrow hips and a carpenter's tool belt hung even lower. A form-fitting black T-shirt stretched over his broad shoulders and back. His ebony hair was messy and sprinkled with sawdust. Sexy didn't begin to describe him.

When the saw stopped, he looked up and smiled.

He had her heart pounding without even saying a word.

"Well, hello." He put down his tool and came toward her.

"Hi…" She tried to steady her breathing. Impossible.

He took the bags of food from her and set them on the floor. "I know you can give a better greeting than that." He took a step closer.

Morgan swallowed. Seeing the desire in his eyes, she couldn't seem to stop herself. She leaned in and placed her mouth on his. She was about to pull away when he groaned and began to deepen the kiss. So much for willpower. Following his lead, she opened to his passion with her own. She pressed her hands against his chest to keep space between them, but instead slid them up over his hard chest and around his neck.

This time she whimpered as his tongue dipped into her mouth, teasing and tasting her. She boldly returned the favor as her fingers tangled in his hair and held him close. She was quickly getting lost in the pleasure when Justin broke off the kiss.

He rested his forehead against hers. "Wow. We'd better slow down a little."

"Oh…" Morgan took a step back when Justin reached for her hand.

"No…don't pull away, green eyes," he told her.

The last thing Justin wanted was to discourage Morgan's advances. "I love what you're doing. It just was a little…intense." He grimaced at her. "And I'm just a guy who wants you very much." He was a little disappointed when she didn't admit to anything.

She pointed to the bags. "I brought you lunch."

"Maybe it's a good idea if we concentrate on that." He picked up one of the sacks and looked inside. "Do I smell pastrami?" When she nodded, he said, "My favorite."

She finally relaxed. "Good, I wasn't sure what you liked."

"I'm pretty easy. There isn't much I don't like." He carried the food to the window seat and Morgan followed with the drinks.

She took out the foam cups of iced tea and sat down. "Are you working as a carpenter now?"

"No, I'm making the shelves for Lauren's doll collection." He took a big bite of his sandwich and chewed. "This is great!"

"Just so you know, we have an excellent deli here in town. One of the fringe benefits."

Justin stopped eating and stared at her. His pulse raced just with her close. "There are a lot of benefits in this town, starting with the beautiful mayor."

She glanced away. "Thank you."

The shame of it was, Morgan Keenan didn't think she was beautiful, and she did everything she could think of to keep other people from seeing it. "You don't have to thank me. It's the truth." He leaned toward her, aching to touch her. "Your skin is flawless, all creamy with just enough freckles across your nose. Oh, and your long, slender neck, that begs to be kissed. But it's those green eyes of yours that cause my heart to stop every time I look at you…"

"You shouldn't say…"

He cocked an eyebrow. "I shouldn't tell you the truth? Why not? You're a lovely woman, Morgan Keenan. And you make me feel things that I've never felt before…with any woman."

She hesitated. "But…you were married."

He refused to feel guilty about Crystal any longer. "Yes, I was married. And I won't speak badly of my ex-wife because she's gone." His gaze held hers. "Crystal and I weren't good together. That's the shame of it. We both needed different things out of our marriage. We'd been divorced for over a year before she died." He hated to spoil the mood, but he wanted Morgan to know about his past.

"Lauren suffered the worst." He smiled sadly. "That's the main reason I want to give her a good home life… I didn't have it growing up with my father, but Lauren will."

Morgan picked at the crust on her sandwich, hearing Justin tell her how much he wanted a family, a wife and children. She still wasn't sure if she could give him that. Yet, she found she wanted to try at having a relationship with a man. This man. He cared about her feelings, and he'd helped her with her fears. That gave her the courage to ask. "Justin, you know that meeting I had to go to this morning?"

He nodded and continued chewing his food.

"It was for our Western Days celebration in a few weeks. Friday night is Miss Kitty's Saloon Casino Night, and on Saturday there's a Sadie Hawkins dance."

"Sadie Hawkins, huh. Isn't that the dance where the woman asks the man?"

Morgan nodded this time.

"Are you trying to warn me that a lot of desperate single women are going to be pursuing me?"

"Could be." She laughed, then quickly sobered. "But it's this woman who is asking you. Justin, would you like to go to the dance with me?"

He raised an eyebrow. "So you're going to save me from all the others?"

She found it easy to play along. "Do you want to be saved?" she asked.

"Only by you."

She swallowed hard. "So you'll go with me?"

He nodded slowly. "But only if I get a kiss to seal the deal."

"You drive a hard bargain, Justin Hilliard." She placed her sandwich down on its wrapper and leaned toward him, finding she was eager to comply.

"Well, I have to take advantage of any opportunities."

"You're wrong, Mr. Hilliard." She slipped her hands around his neck and whispered, "This is my opportunity."

She brushed a kiss across his mouth and pulled away, then returned. This time she nibbled on his lower lip to hear him groan. She didn't wait for him to take the initiative, she teased his mouth with her tongue, then delved inside.

By the time she broke away he was breathing hard. His eyes met hers.

"You're just full of surprises, Mayor."

"Daddy, I like that pink the best," Lauren said as she pointed to one of the many sample colors on the bedroom wall. "Morgan said it's called Cotton Candy. It's my favorite. Delaney likes it, too."

The two five-year-olds nodded in agreement.

It had been over a week since the workmen had started on the house, and things were moving fast. After several samples had been applied to the wall, his daughter had finally decided on one. Justin smiled. It was the brightest pink from the many samples Morgan had chosen. "If you're really sure, then I'll have it painted tomorrow."

"Yes, Daddy, I'm really, really sure." Lauren cheered as both girls jumped up and down. "Then can I have a sleepover?"

He'd been afraid of this. "You don't even have a bed yet."

"Daddy, we can use sleeping bags." Those big blue eyes gave him a hopeful look. "Please…"

They were a week from even moving in. "We'll talk about it later."

"Okay, but don't forget," she reminded him. The

doorbell rang. "Delaney's mom is here." The two girls charged out of the room, their footsteps echoing down the hall.

Justin rubbed his forehead. Between the meetings about the resort, and trying to get the house livable, he wasn't sure what was going on. Of course, Lauren's room took priority over everything else.

Suddenly he heard voices and he looked toward the door. The girls had returned, bringing with them a petite, blue-eyed blonde about thirty years old. Delaney's mother.

The woman boldly eyed him from head to toe, then a slow smile appeared on her ruby-colored lips. "Hello. I'm Kaley Sims. You must be Justin Hilliard."

"Yes, I am." He came across the room to shake her hand. "It's so nice to finally meet you, Mrs. Sims. I need to thank you and your mother for having Lauren over so much these past weeks."

"We love having her," she said. "Delaney and Lauren have become such good friends." She began playing with her blond hair. "It's hard when you're a single parent. Thank goodness for my mother's help. She's one of the reasons I moved back to Destiny."

"This town is a great place to raise a child."

Her smile widened. "So I see you're sold on small-town living. I thought maybe you were here only for the duration of the project."

"That's what brought me here, but this will be Lauren's and my home."

"Good, then we'll be seeing you around. Do you know about the upcoming Western Days celebration?"

"I've heard about it."

Kaley opened her mouth just when the girls started making a commotion. He and Kaley turned to see that Morgan had arrived.

Why did he feel as if he'd just been saved? "Morgan," he called and went to greet her.

Morgan's smile slowly faded when she saw Kaley. "Hello, Justin. Kaley."

"Hello, Morgan," the blonde said.

"Kaley just stopped by to pick up Delaney."

They all studied the two girls playing. "The two have been inseparable since the tea party," Justin said.

"That's all Delaney talks about." Kaley glanced back at Justin. "Like I was saying, there's Western Days next weekend."

"Morgan has been telling me all about it. A Sadie Hawkins dance." Justin knew what Kaley was about to ask and wanted to make it clear he had feelings for a certain mayor. "I haven't been to one of those since high school." He smiled at Morgan. "And thanks to Mayor Keenan it looks like I'm going to another."

"You're going?" Kaley said, unable to hide her surprise.

"Yes," Morgan said. "Justin's agreed to go with me."

The blonde eyed the couple, then said, "Well, that's nice. I'm not sure I'll be going this year, but I will be working the casino night." She gave Justin a sly smile. "Stop by my table and try your luck." She gathered up her daughter and walked out. Lauren went off to her bedroom.

"If you'd rather go with Kaley… I…can…"

He turned to Morgan, not believing what he was hearing. "Have I given you any reason to think that I'd rather go with Kaley?"

She shook her head.

"Good, because you're the only woman I want to be with. And quit looking at me like that, Morgan, or I'll break my promise and kiss you right here and now to prove it to you."

It surprised him that Morgan didn't give him a panicked look. Instead she turned to him and sighed. "Then I guess I'd better go talk to my sisters, because Kaley Sims needs to find a guy…of her own." Then she stood on her toes and placed a kiss on his mouth, surprising him once again.

Morgan knew she was acting crazy. But since Justin Hilliard had come to town, she'd been doing so many things that weren't like her. Her mouth moved over his, savoring his taste, a flavor that she'd become addicted to.

She finally broke off the kiss, but didn't retreat. She boldly looked into his eyes. "You're the only man I want to be with."

"You're not playing fair, green eyes." He took a step back. "We better change the subject…for now."

She nodded, realizing she wasn't ready to commit to much more than dating and kissing. But when the time came, would she be willing? She didn't know. All she knew was if the time came she wanted that man to be Justin.

"Okay, what brings you by the house?"

"I've talked with Marc Rhodes by phone. He wants to set up a meeting. When are you available?"

"I've made myself available in the morning until Lauren gets out of school."

"That should give us enough time."

He leaned toward her and lowered his voice. "There's never enough time when I'm with you. How about tonight? We can take Lauren out to dinner."

Morgan was excited that Justin thought of them as a couple. She was working on that, too. "How about you and Lauren come to family dinner at the Keenans—but be warned, my sisters and their husbands will be there. You'll probably be drilled with questions, at least by my lawyer sister, Paige."

Justin folded his arms across his chest, looking thoughtful. She knew that since he'd been living at the Inn, he'd refused to intrude on the weekly family get-together.

"I can handle it, but what I don't want is for you to feel pressured or uncomfortable."

He was leaving this up to her, too. He'd been so considerate and patient with her when most men would have walked away. "I won't. Not with you."

An hour later, Justin followed Morgan and Lauren into the Keenan kitchen, which was already crowded with the family. Claire and Tim Keenan were the first to greet them, the sisters exchanged kisses and hugs. All the affection was something Justin still had trouble getting used to. But not Lauren. She took hugs from everyone.

"Glad you could join us," Tim said.

"Thanks for having us. I know it was short notice."

"You and Lauren are always welcome here."

Reed walked to him. "How's the house coming along?"

"Fine. They're painting tomorrow morning. And the bedroom furniture arrives in a few days."

"And then we get to move in," Lauren said. "My room is gonna be Cotton Candy Pink. Morgan helped pick it out and I get to have a sleepover as soon as we move in."

"Whoa, sweetie. I told you we'd talk about the sleepover…later."

"Daddy, Mary Elisabeth and Delaney and Sarah already said they want to come." Her lower lip quivered. "I promised 'em."

Paige Keenan Larkin looked at him. "Yeah, Daddy, she promised. What's the matter—can't handle all those females?"

He grimaced. "You're right. I'm a bit concerned about dealing with four little girls. More to the point is that parents aren't crazy about their young daughters spending the night without any adult female in the house."

Paige rubbed her rounded stomach. "Oh, my," she breathed. "I guess I didn't think about that."

"That's hard to explain to a five-year-old, especially since all her new friends have invited her to their houses. I owe everyone."

"There's got to be a solution," Paige said, looking thoughtful. "I have an idea. Just a second." She hurried off, grabbed Leah's and Morgan's hands on the way to their mother at the stove and began to talk quietly.

"That can't be good," Holt said, nodding at the group of Keenan women. "Whenever they do that they're cooking something up. And it's not food."

Reed and Tim joined the men. "What did you say to Paige?"

After Justin told them, Holt said, "I can see your dilemma. Now, I'm doubly glad I have a boy. Corey loves sleeping on the ground." He frowned. "Of course Leah could be carrying a girl."

"Girls may be complicated, but they're worth the effort," Justin assured them. "Even with all the bows, ruffles and dolls, I wouldn't change a thing about Lauren."

"I'm going to be in the same boat," Reed said, and smiled. Justin knew Paige's baby was a girl. "I'm going to spoil my daughter rotten."

"Not if Paige has anything to say about it," Tim said as he arrived at the group. "Men, you have to be strong. The women in this family already have too much power."

Just then all four Keenan women turned to them and smiled. "I knew it, they're cooking something up," Reed said. "Paige already knows I can't say no to her. And believe me, she uses it against me."

"It's probably not so bad," Holt said, looking lovingly back at his pregnant wife.

Justin didn't care, either. Not when Morgan smiled at him.

Finally the women returned and Mrs. Keenan spoke. "We have an idea that might solve your problem, Justin."

"What problem?"

"The problem with Lauren and her sleepover," Claire said. "How about if you had Lauren bring her friends here?"

Justin flashed a glance at Morgan. "Oh, Claire, I can't ask you to do that."

"You didn't ask, we offered. Since your house isn't…equipped for girls, why not bring the girls here and have the sleepover on the third floor in the girls' old bedroom?"

Justin couldn't even absorb the idea before Lauren rushed over. "Oh, Daddy, please. Please, can we?"

"I still don't have a chaperone."

"Yes, you do," Morgan said. "I'll spend the night with the girls."

He couldn't believe that Morgan was doing this. "You really want to stay up all night with four five-year-olds?"

"I doubt they'll make it all night, but yes, it'll be fun. Unless you have a problem with it."

"Only that you'll be doing all the work."

"Oh, no. You're paying for the pizza." Morgan reached down and tickled Lauren.

"Yeah, Daddy, you have to buy us lots of pizza… and ice cream…and candy."

"Whoa, whoa." He raised a hand. "I don't want everybody getting sick."

Lauren grew serious. "Okay, a little ice cream and a little candy."

"That's better." He looked at Morgan. "Can I talk to you for a moment?"

Morgan glanced around the crowded room, wondering if she'd overstepped this time. "Sure." She led the way though the kitchen to the door and into the entry. "I'm sorry, Justin, I didn't mean to let Lauren overhear before you got the chance to decide."

"I'm not angry, Morgan. I just wanted to ask if you're sure about this. When I mentioned you helping with a sleepover, I was only kidding."

"I know, but I want to do it. And Mom agreed because there aren't any guests in the Inn right now. It's also the best solution to your…problem. It's very important Lauren fit in, Justin. She's in a new home…a new place… She needs this."

Justin stared at her for a long time and it was beginning to make Morgan nervous. Finally he said, "I wish I'd never made you that promise…"

"The promise?"

"The one where I said I wouldn't kiss you, because I want to…badly."

His confession thrilled her, and she discovered she wanted him to kiss her, too. Mindful that her family was close by, she leaned forward. "Then maybe I should put you out of your misery. Kiss me, Justin."

His gray eyes were dark with desire, then he smiled. "Oh, I know your plan. You think since your family is so close, I won't."

She hesitated, then said, "No, I'm hoping you will. Kiss me, Justin," she repeated.

"You have no idea how long I've been waiting to hear you say those words," he said as he reached out and placed his hands against her waist. "You sure you're okay with this?"

"Yes." And she was. So much so she that she stepped closer into the embrace. He leaned his head into hers and brushed a kiss against her mouth. She sucked in a breath, feeling the excitement, along with a warm tingle at his touch. He pulled back a little, his gaze questioning.

"Kiss me again," she breathed.

This time his hands cupped her face. "There's nothing I want more," he said as his head lowered and he captured her mouth, brushing his tongue over the seam of her bottom lip. She opened to him. Soon, they were both lost in the passion when she heard a gasp.

"Daddy, you're kissin' Morgan." Then Lauren's footsteps retreated, then came the distant sound of, "My daddy's kissing Morgan."

"Seems we've been discovered," she said, looking at him.

"Do you have a problem with that?"

She shook her head. "None whatsoever."

"I'm glad." He brought her hand to his lips and kissed it. "Come on, it's time to face the music. Together."

CHAPTER EIGHT

"I WANT my toes painted next," Delaney said, perched on one of the double beds in the Keenan sisters' old bedroom. It was nearly ten o'clock and there were no signs of any of the four five-year-olds' energy fading.

"Just let me finish Mary Elisabeth's first." Their toenails were so cute. Morgan finally finished her task and stood back to examine her work. All the girls were in pajamas and their hair had been styled. She also was dressed in flannel pajamas and the girls had given her a new hairstyle, too.

"I want Pink Diamonds," Delaney said. "Please."

Morgan went through the colors she'd purchased for tonight and found the bottle. All the girls watched as she applied the polish to the last toe. Once finished, she said, "Okay, you all have to sit quietly on the bed until it dries." She went to the television and put in *The Little Mermaid*.

Morgan blew out a breath as she looked at the four little angels seated along the bed. Their faces made up and their toes painted. Earlier they'd played dress-up with clothes and jewelry from an old chest in the attic. Thank goodness her mother hadn't thrown anything away. Then Justin had brought pizza and soda.

She was sure they'd had a good time because she was getting tired. She glanced at the clock to see it was after ten o'clock. Who would have thought that four tiny girls could have so much energy? Seeing the droopy-eyed children, Morgan hoped they'd fall asleep soon.

A soft knocking sound drew Morgan's attention. With the girls engrossed in the movie, she went to the door and found Justin standing in the dimly lit hallway. Her parents' bedroom was two doors down and they'd retired for the night.

"Hi," she whispered, and stepped out, pulling the door nearly closed behind her.

"How's it going?" His voice was hushed as his amused gaze eyed her from head to toe. Morgan knew she looked ridiculous with her hair in four different ponytails and the heavily made up face.

"Hey, nice pj's."

She looked down at her oversize pink flannel.

"Sexy, huh?"

"Oh, green eyes, you have no idea." He tugged on one of her ponytails. "I particularly like your lipstick. In fact I need a taste…" He leaned down and covered her mouth with his. The kiss slowly turned heated and when Justin finally broke away, she was dizzy.

"I—I should get back to the girls," she managed to say.

He touched his forehead to hers. "I can't thank you enough for doing this for Lauren." He trailed kisses along her jaw to her neck. He was making a good start, she thought, wrapping her arms around him.

"It's been fun… But you should go, you're in 'no boys' territory." She pulled away again.

"How about a good-night kiss?" he asked.

She raised an eyebrow. "What were we doing?"

"What can I say? I can't get enough of you." He reached for her and she went willingly into his arms. Each kiss only increased her feelings for this man. He made her feel things she hadn't felt in a long time…if ever. Suddenly the sound of giggles broke through her haze.

She jumped back to see the four girls standing in the doorway. "You kissed Lauren's daddy," Delaney said and all the girls nodded in agreement.

Morgan blushed as Justin released her and crouched down to the girls. "That's because I'm the kissing monster… I come out at night looking for pretty girls to kiss." He winked up at Morgan, then turned back. "And it looks like I found some more pretty girls."

The girls screeched and ran back into the room.

Morgan couldn't help but laugh. "I think you better go."

"So, no more kisses, huh?"

"I think you've had enough."

He pulled her to him. "I don't think that's possible." He kissed her nose. "I'm looking forward to having some time with you myself."

"So am I," she admitted.

His eyes grew intense. "Will you come by the house tomorrow? The furniture is going to be delivered."

Morgan heard the giggling voices. "Okay. But I've got to go now."

"Thanks for trusting me, Morgan."

Her heart leaped. "Thank you for being patient."

"All good things are worth the wait—and that definitely includes you."

"I think it finally looks like we're where we want it to be," Justin said as he looked over the blueprints of the future resort on the new drafting table in his home office. The twice-revised model of the hotel was like a dream come true. His dream. His project without his father breathing over his shoulder, without the continual criticisms.

This was his success. His future.

"Well, they say the third time is the charm," Marc Rhodes said. The young project manager had always come through for Hilliard Industries. This time it wasn't any different.

"I can't wait for Morgan to see this."

"Can't wait for me to see what?"

Both men turned to the door as the woman in question walked in.

"Morgan…"

Justin was taken aback seeing her in a black

angora sweater tucked into fitted taupe slacks with a gold belt looped at her tiny waist. Her hair was pulled back into a bun and big hoop earrings adorned her ears. Damn. She looked good.

And Marc noticed her, too.

"Hello, I'm Morgan Keenan," she said as she walked across the room and held out her hand. "You must be Marc Rhodes."

He shook it. "Guilty. It's great to finally meet you, Morgan. After all our phone calls I feel like I know you." He smiled and looked her over appreciatively. "But you're still a surprise."

Justin wasn't happy. Okay, so Marc was a single thirty-one-year-old guy. And women might find him attractive with his sun-bleached hair and easy smile. He just didn't want Morgan to.

"Morgan, come here and see this."

Morgan walked to the desk, eager to take in the completed room. The rich Mediterranean-blue walls were a great contrast with the dark mahogany furniture, but the small model of the resort drew her to the table. The hotel was a rustic structure using logs and cedar shingles. Even though it was a five-story building it still looked as if it belonged in the mountains.

"Oh, Justin, it's perfect. Just what I'd pictured." She was also surprised to feel such deep emotions, but she'd been working on this project a long time.

"We think so, too," he said. "Now, just because the outside looks rustic, but the inside will be anything but… It's five-star all the way."

"I have no doubt it will be," Morgan said. "I can't wait until we get started."

"I also have to say that I'm looking forward to beginning, too," Marc said. "Since the weather has been so mild, we can get all the preliminary work done next week, and if we're lucky, break ground soon after that." He turned to Morgan. "How does that time frame work for you?"

"Fine. Great," she said. "After this weekend my schedule is clear until the first week in December."

"What's this weekend?" Marc asked.

"It's our Western Days celebration. We turn back the clock over a hundred years. There's Miss Kitty's Casino night Friday and on Saturday the Sadie Hawkins dance." Morgan glanced at the project manager's naked ring finger and she got an idea. "If you're going to be around, Marc, you should come. I mean, unless you have to go back to Denver to see your wife, or girlfriend…"

Marc frowned. "No, I don't have either. In fact, I'll need a place to rent here." He glanced at Justin. "I don't want to end up sleeping in the construction trailer."

"Really." This was just too easy, Morgan thought. "I happen to know someone who could help you with the search."

"That would be nice."

"Let me make a call." Morgan reached into her trouser pocket and took out her cell phone. Walking away from the men, she punched in the Realtor's number that was boldly painted on the storefront next to her sister's law office.

The phone was answered on the second ring. "Hutchinson Realty, Kaley Sims."

"Kaley. It's Morgan Keenan."

"Hi, Morgan."

"I need your help," she said. "Justin's project manager, Marc Rhodes, has just arrived in town and he needs a place to live for the next six months or so, and the company will also need office space. I told him you could help."

There was a long silence, then Kaley said, "Tell me he's good-looking and single—and there are no more Keenan sisters around."

Morgan laughed and turned away from the men in the room. "Yes, to all the above," she told her. "Who knows, this could be more than a commission for you."

"Then send him over."

"Will do. Bye." Morgan flipped the phone closed and went back to the men and gave Marc directions to the realty office. "Just ask for Kaley Sims. She'll be able to help you. I also told her you might be interested in office space, too."

"Good idea. We need to start hiring a crew. Thanks, Morgan," Marc said, then looked at Justin. "Do you need anything else from me today?"

"No. Just go and get settled."

Marc nodded. "Then I guess I'll see you around."

"If you're free, come by here for supper," Justin said. "We'll order pizza."

Marc's gaze went to Morgan. "I think you'll be busy."

Justin put his arm around Morgan's shoulders. "You never can tell, you might be, too."

Looking puzzled, the project manager left.

"So," Justin began. "When did you turn into the town matchmaker?"

"I'm the mayor. I was only trying to help out a new resident."

"And Kaley…"

Morgan shrugged. "I think Kaley and Marc just might hit it off."

"You may be right. I know Marc had been in a long relationship. The girl broke his heart. I think it would be good for him to meet someone new."

Smiling, Justin sat down on the edge of the desk and pulled her between his legs. "You know you didn't have to worry about Kaley."

She frowned. "I'm not worried."

"Good, because you're the only woman I want." He kissed her softly. "I did notice that Marc showed a little more than a passing interest in you." He trailed kisses along her jaw to her ear and whispered, "I thought I was going to have to punch him out."

He felt her smile. "He was just being friendly."

He pulled back. "You walked in here and looked like a million bucks." He looked down at her sweater, over the curve of her full breasts. "Damn, you look great," he whispered.

With a breathy gasp, she took a step closer and wrapped her arms around his neck. He hadn't expected such a soft giving away of control, and it sent a wave of pleasure through him as she touched her lips to his.

With a groan, he stood and slowly increased the assault on her mouth, delving deeper with long, lazy strokes. Her breathing rough, she pressed her body against his, causing a torturous friction between them.

Good Lord. This was crazy. He had to stop… before things got out of hand.

He broke off the kiss and looked down to see the desire in her eyes. "Morgan…you're not helping me here. I want you." He cupped her face. "But I don't think you're ready."

He took hold of her hand and smiled at her dazed look. "You can't say we don't throw off sparks." He grew serious. "It's going to happen between us, Morgan, but only when you're ready."

She blinked those big eyes at him. "I've never felt like this, Justin. I never wanted this so much… until you."

He sighed. "That's not helping me cool off, either. But I can't tell you how happy that makes me." He touched her face because he had to. "I've never wanted a woman like I want you."

"Oh, Justin…"

Morgan was having trouble handling the new feelings. The trembling she felt whenever he touched her, along with the deep ache in her stomach that she wanted him to ease.

"I think we should maybe step back from temptation." He stood. "How about I give you a tour of what's been done around the house."

Surprisingly Morgan wanted to pull him back. She wanted to stay in his arms…forever. To have him show her pleasure, have him tell her how she could please him. She felt the sudden heat touch her face, knowing how close they were getting to that next step.

"You're right. I want to see your bedroom…"

He grinned. "I think that could be arranged." He tugged on her arm and escorted her down the hall. Opening the double doors, he stood back.

"Oh, Justin… It's beautiful." Her gaze traveled around the large room. The walls had been painted a mocha color that offset the dark wood furniture. A huge king-size bed with four carved posts had a dark blue comforter covering it. An armoire stood directly across from it and a blue chenille-covered chaise sat next to the fireplace.

"I still need linens, and the drapes haven't arrived yet."

"It looks pretty good considering a few weeks ago the place was a mess. What about Lauren's room?"

"Come, you need to see this." He motioned for her to follow him to the room across the hall. Lauren's bedroom. Morgan peered in to find bright pink walls, softened by off-white furniture.

"Oh, it's so pretty. Lauren will love it." The double bed had a lace canopy and a dust ruffle. The mattress was bare, with new linens still in their packaging. She walked to the shelves that lined the opposite wall. Justin had finished them off with an intricate trim and painted them white.

"So how did I do?" he asked.

She turned to see he was waiting for her approval. "They're perfect. And Lauren will love them because you made them for her."

"You think so? I measured them to fit her doll collection." He crossed the room. "I hung them here so she could see them from her bed." His expression turned sad. "She and her mother had started collecting the dolls a few years ago. I wanted her to have some good memories of that time."

"It's a wonderful thing to do." She walked into his arms because it seemed so natural. So natural to be with this man, to feel his warmth. He'd been so willing to help her overcome her fears, that she never thought much about his problems.

His arms came around her. "I have a lot to make up for. I wasn't around much when Lauren was a baby." He paused. "The problems between her mother and me kept us at odds. It wasn't healthy. Then, when the divorce finally happened and Crystal couldn't cope… I let my in-laws take care of my daughter."

Morgan stepped back. "Justin, we all make mistakes. That doesn't mean you didn't love your daughter. We can't look back. It's now that's important…and the future. You've brought Lauren here, retired from an all-consuming job to put her first. She knows that." She smiled. "There's no doubt she loves you."

"You and your family have been a big help too," he told her.

"It hasn't exactly been a hardship on us." She laughed, but realized how important Lauren had become to the Keenans…all the Keenans. And Justin. How easily it would be to fall in love with father and daughter, then realized she was halfway there already.

The following Friday night, Morgan examined herself in the mirror in the hotel room. Western Days were in full swing and she, along with her family, were working Miss Kitty's Saloon Night.

Morgan had chosen the most modest dress from the 1880's wardrobe, if there was such a thing. An emerald-green satin that had an off-the-shoulder neckline, but the fitted bodice created cleavage she never knew she had. The skirt was gathered and hit her at the knees, revealing a lot of leg. High heels added to her height.

"Are you sure this looks all right?" she asked and when she didn't get an answer, she turned to her sisters.

"You look incredible," Paige said.

"Really?" Morgan couldn't stop thinking about how Justin would react to her outfit. "You sure it's not too much?"

"You're kidding, right?" Paige glanced down at her large belly. "I'm eight months pregnant and dressed as a saloon girl." She grinned. "And Reed will think I'm sexy as hell."

"Men think everything's sexy," Leah added, rubbing her smaller belly of five months.

This was probably the first time Morgan had truly envied her sisters. They were both having babies. A family of her own had always been Morgan's dream.

Maybe it had to do with their own parents' desertion. A strange yearning settled in her stomach at the thought of a little girl like Lauren…and having a man like Justin.

"I bet Justin is going to think you're sexy," Leah said. "I mean, the man can't keep his eyes off you as it is."

Morgan wanted to deny that there was anything between them, but since Lauren had broadcast their kiss, it was futile. The funny thing was, Morgan wanted them to be a couple. And she was a little frightened about how long he would wait for her to get over what happened years ago.

Her biggest fear was she might never be the woman Justin needed, and she would lose him.

Dressed in jeans, a Western shirt and boots, Justin walked around the saloon at the historic Grand Hotel. Ragtime music played on the piano as mixed sounds of winners and losers filled the crowded room.

He carried a stack of chips he'd bought for tonight's gaming, but he didn't care a lot about the gambling as he did about finding Morgan. He knew she had to work at one of the blackjack tables.

He walked past the roulette table to see Kaley Sims taking the bets, and an attentive Marc Rhodes playing the game of chance. He wished the project manager luck and walked on.

At the sound of more commotion, he glanced around and saw a noisy crowd at a table. He went over to find what he'd been looking for. Morgan

Keenan was dressed like he'd never imagined. Wrong. He had imagined it, but only in his dreams. Suddenly his hopes soared. His heart raced as his body stirred with desire.

She looked incredible. Her hair was swept up, exposing her delicate neck and shoulders. The low-cut green dress matched her eyes and showed off an enticing amount of cleavage. He swallowed the sudden dryness in his throat.

A player got up from the table and he moved in before anyone else had the chance. And there were plenty of guys lurking around. He looked at Morgan, but she seemed to be handling all the attention.

He finally caught her eyes.

"Well, hello, stranger." She gathered up the cards and began to shuffle, but her gaze never left his. "You must be new in town."

"Just got here, ma'am."

"So you're thinking about playing a game of chance?"

"I'll try my luck." He slid four chips along the felt table to his spot.

"Good luck," another gambler called. "She's cutthroat."

Justin gave a sideways glance at the guy next to him. "She doesn't look so tough."

"Trust me, son, she's tough when it comes to getting money for this town," the middle-aged man said. He held out his hand. "Hello, I'm Father John Reilly."

A priest. He shook it. "Hello, Father. Justin Hilliard."

"It's a good thing what you're doing for this town…and the people."

"Well, if things work out right, it's money all around."

The priest nodded. "I like that…spreading the wealth and the jobs. Bless you, son."

"Thank you, Father. I could use it."

As Morgan dealt out the first cards, Justin couldn't stop looking at her. The player to his right asked to be hit with another card, then went bust. The second player said he'd hold at seventeen, since the dealer was only showing a six of hearts.

"What about you, stranger?" Morgan smiled. "Looks like you have a decision to make."

Justin managed to steal a glance at his cards. An ace and a two of clubs. "Hit me."

Morgan turned up the six of hearts.

His mind wasn't counting anything as those emerald eyes mesmerized him. He tapped the table again, unable to see or think about anything but Morgan.

The table erupted in cheers. He glanced down to see the two of clubs. With a smile, he leaned back in his chair. "I think I'll stay."

Morgan moved on to the next person. The player stopped at nineteen, then came the dealer's turn. She flipped over her bottom card to reveal another six and the group began cheering for a face card. It must have worked, because she pulled out the Queen of Spades.

"Looks like I busted." Morgan smiled as she paid off the happy winners.

Justin sat for another thirty minutes when Claire Keenan arrived dressed in a black satin dress and a feather in her hair. "It's break time, Morgan."

The group grumbled until Claire took her place behind the table. "Okay, guys. Let's see if you can keep up with Claire." She winked at Justin as he got up to follow Morgan. He took her hand and together they walked through the casino to the buffet line.

He wanted a more private place to greet her, but he knew that she was the mayor tonight and had to be visible for the charity event. And he, too, should meet and greet.

"Are you having fun?" she asked.

"I am now," he whispered against her ear. "But I have this need to kiss this beautiful…sexy blackjack dealer."

Surprisingly Morgan tugged on his arm, and greeting Destiny's citizens along the way, managed to lead him to the other side of the hotel, up a staircase and along the hall to a door. They went inside to find it vacant except for all the extra costumes.

She turned to him and gave him a coy smile. "I usually don't do this sort of thing, mister, but since you're a stranger in town…and all." She stepped into his arms. "We want you to know what a friendly town Destiny is."

Her mouth met his in a searing kiss.

Justin groaned as he tried to let her keep the lead. It was killing him. He wanted her…more and more with each passing day. Her desire was evident, too.

She kissed him like she was drowning, and he was

her lifeline. Her body moved against his as her tongue slid along the length of his. Finally he raised his head to see her flushed face. He dipped down and took another taste of her, once again, then retreated half a step back.

Morgan's eyes fluttered open. "Oh, my."

He moved further away from temptation. "You are lethal, woman." His gaze roamed over her dress and down to her legs. He could imagine, those long, incredible legs wrapped… He quickly shook away the picture.

"We should get back." He headed to the door.

"Justin…is something wrong?"

He turned around to see the beautiful woman, looking half made love to, and he ached to finish what he started.

"God, no. You are…" He reached out to touch her, but pulled back. "It's not you, Morgan, it's me. I want you so much that, if I touch you again I might break my promise."

He watched her take a shuddering breath. "How about if I release you from that promise? What if I say I want you, too?"

CHAPTER NINE

AN HOUR later, they arrived at Justin's place. Morgan thought she'd be nervous, but she wasn't.

She was with this wonderful man.

Morgan had changed out of her costume into a pair of jeans and a light-blue sweater, but she hadn't taken the time to let her hair down or remove her makeup. After she'd seen Justin's smiling face waiting at the bottom of the hotel steps, she was glad.

Lauren was spending the night with Delaney, and Morgan had told her mother that she'd be going with Justin. She didn't offer any more explanation, nor had Claire Keenan asked for one.

Tonight was just for them.

Silently Justin escorted her through the door, where a soft glow from the light in the entry helped them find their way. Hand in hand, they walked up the sweeping staircase to the second floor, and down the hall. Her heart pounded hard as he opened the door to the master suite and flipped on the light, softly illuminating the room.

Morgan glanced around at the new touches he'd added since her last visit. Beige and blue pillows were scattered on the bed. A large beige and wine rug covered the spacious area in front of the fireplace. Justin reached for a remote on the mantel, pushed a button and flames appeared from the gas logs in the hearth.

"Instant atmosphere," Morgan said as she went to the window seat where a long cushion covered the top.

"It also warms up the room."

She didn't need any more heat. The man across from her was warmth enough.

"How about a drink?"

When she nodded, Justin went into the connecting room, then after a few minutes returned with two glasses and a bottle of wine. She took the crystal goblets from him.

"This may help us relax," he said.

"Do you think I need help…?"

He leaned down and placed a soft kiss against her lips. "Maybe not you, but I do." His mouth was inches from hers. "I want to make this special for you, Morgan. Making love isn't just about the act, it's about sharing, and pleasing the other person…" His gaze searched her face. "It's something you've never experienced. As far as I'm concerned, this will be your first time."

She released a long breath. "Oh, Justin…" There was no doubt she was in love with this guy. "I want to please you, too, but…"

He covered her mouth with another kiss, stopping her words. By the time he pulled back, she forgot what else she was going to say.

"This isn't a test, Morgan." He stood back and worked the cork on the already opened bottle, then poured some wine in each glass. "And we have all night."

He set the bottle down on the end table, then returned to her and held up his glass. "To us…"

"To us…"

Justin couldn't take his eyes off her. Morgan had put such trust in him and he prayed he wouldn't let her down.

She sat on the cushion on the window seat as she sipped her wine. "You've added a lot since I was here last."

"Do you like it?" He took the place next to her.

"Yes, I especially like the rug."

"It was delivered this morning. Thank you for directing me to the furniture store in Durango." Why were they talking decorating? He took her hand in his, kissed it and pressed it against his thigh. "I've liked all the ideas you've given me for the house."

"I'm glad I could help." She took another drink, then she looked at him. "This house is special. It's wonderful that you're restoring it this way." Her hand began moving against his leg. "I don't want to talk about the house all night."

"I don't, either." He took the wine from her and put it on the table, then cupped her face. "God, you're beautiful." He reached up and removed the pins from her hair and helped the fiery curls fall to her shoulders. Then he lowered his mouth to hers, and tasted her, mixed with the wine. Sweet. When her sigh escaped into his mouth, suddenly everything shifted speed. He wrapped his arm around her, and with his lips never leaving hers, he lowered her backward onto the seat. He deepened their pleasure when his tongue mated with hers.

When he released her he looked into her eyes, happy to see the desire there. "You okay?"

She nodded and reached up to caress his face. "I'm more than okay."

He groaned. No woman had even gotten inside him like this. He kissed her again...and again until her body arched wanting more. He moved his hand to her waist, slipped under her sweater and began stroking her bare skin.

She shifted under his touch. It was a small movement, but enough to encourage him. He raised his head and watched her as his hands moved upward to cover her breasts.

Morgan couldn't stay still with Justin touching her. She wanted more...so much more.

She boldly tugged at his shirt and, when it wouldn't budge, she popped the snaps on the Western style shirt.

Justin smiled. "So anxious?"

She felt her face redden. "Well, it only seems fair that I get to touch you, too."

"Then why don't I make it easier for you?" He stood and tugged the shirt from his jeans and stripped it off, leaving him bare from the waist up.

Her pulse raced and she sat up as Justin came back to her. He captured her mouth in another kiss, but it wasn't enough, wasn't helping the ache inside her.

She broke off, grabbed the hem of her sweater and yanked it over her head.

For a long time he just stared at her. Then he finally reached out and touched her, cupping her breasts in his hands. She released a sigh and pressed into his palms.

"Perfect… I knew you would be," he breathed as he lowered his head. Brushing kisses along the exposed fullness, he soon began to concentrate on her hardening nipples through the sheer lacy material of her bra. She gasped when he used his fingers to tease her further.

He raised his head. "You like that?"

Morgan could only nod, then with shaky hands she unfastened the front clasp, baring herself for his eyes. "More…please…" She held the back of his head, bringing his mouth to the sensitive tip.

Justin had waited so long for this…to be with Morgan, but he had to take it slow…and easy.

"Gladly." He closed his mouth over the pebbled nub, using his tongue to add to her pleasure. When she cried out and arched her body to bring him closer, he knew he'd succeeded.

He raised his head to find her emerald eyes dark with hunger. He glanced down at her beauty and he nearly shook from need. His hand moved to the snap on her jeans.

"I want you, green eyes. I want to make love to you…but only if you're ready."

She gave him a slow smile and touched his face. "I've wanted you, too. I've wanted this since we spent the night together in the cave."

"I think I've been waiting for you all my life." He took a long breath and released it, then stood and began to tug off her jeans, revealing her long slender legs.

He stood back and took in all her beauty, from her pretty feet, up her long legs, slender hips and delicate waist to her breasts. She was perfect.

Justin drew another breath and released it, telling himself again he needed to go slow. He placed a tender kiss on her lips and lifted her up in his arms.

"I'm going to make love to you, Morgan," he began as he crossed the room to the bed. "I'm going to tease you into a slow burn, then show you a pleasure you never knew could exist between a man and a woman."

He heard her quick intake of breath as he laid her on the cool sheets. With his gaze never leaving hers, he stripped off his jeans, then stood before her, waiting for her to make the final move, showing that she trusted him to not hurt her, trusted him enough to take her to paradise.

When she reached out her hands, he knew that this was a new beginning…for both of them. He climbed into bed beside her and pulled her into his arms.

This was home.

* * *

Morgan felt light on her face and opened her eyes to the rising sun. A smile creased her lips as she recalled last night, and Justin.

She rolled over and found the man in question beside her, sound asleep. He should be tired. They'd been up most of the night, touching…and loving each other…

She smiled, not the least bit ashamed or embarrassed. Why should she be? She was in love with Justin.

She recalled how patient he'd been with her. How he'd let her take the lead…set the pace. And he helped her discover things about her body. As promised, he showed her pleasure she never dreamed possible.

Morgan's thoughts turned to her sisters. No wonder Paige and Leah were always so happy. Now she knew and she could share in their secret.

She turned to the man who was helping to erase all her bad memories and replace them with good ones. His dark hair was mussed and his jaw already showed dark stubble. His lashes were black and long. She wanted to kiss every square inch of his handsome face.

He blinked and opened his eyes. "What's got you so happy this morning?"

She jumped. "Oh, I thought you were asleep."

He wrapped his arm around her waist, drawing her against him. "I think I still am. I have this beautiful naked woman in my bed. This has to be a dream."

She giggled. "No, I'm real."

His hand covered her breast. "I can tell." He smiled. "Good morning, green eyes."

"Good morning."

"You can do better than that." He leaned over her and captured her mouth with his. A slow, lazy kiss quickly turned heated and hungry. How could she want him again?

He tore his mouth away. "That's one powerful kiss."

"You did pretty good yourself."

He brushed the hair away from her face. "I wish we never had to leave here." He made a throaty sound. "I can't seem to get enough of you."

Morgan's heated gaze locked with his. "Oh, Justin…last night was unbelievable. I never thought… it's just that I never realized how beautiful it could be."

"It's not like this with everyone. It has to be the right person. And it has to be about more than just sex. It was definitely more than that for me last night." He kissed her fingertips.

The phone rang, breaking the mood.

He groaned. "I better get that. It might be about Lauren."

Justin turned toward his side of the bed. He was going to get rid of whoever was calling and fast. He grabbed the receiver. "Hello."

"Mr. Hilliard, this is Carlton Burke."

Burke was Marshal Hilliard's right hand man. What was his father up to? "So my father has you calling me now. What does he want this time?"

Justin didn't appreciate being disturbed on a Saturday morning. He glanced over his shoulder to see Morgan was up, had put on her bra and panties and was slipping into her jeans.

"I'm afraid there's bad news, Mr. Hilliard. Your father had a heart attack last night. He's in intensive care at University Hospital."

Justin's chest constricted as he sat up on the side of the bed. His father was never sick. With the receiver between his shoulder and ear, he grabbed his boxers off the floor and slipped them on. "What is his condition?"

"He's stabilized for now, but the doctors are running tests."

His father could die. "Arrange for the plane to fly to Durango. I'll be there in two hours."

Morgan glanced at him as he gave the order. "I'll see you later today," Justin said and hung up the phone.

"You're leaving?" she asked.

"My father had a heart attack last night. I have to go to Denver."

Morgan rushed around the bed and slipped her arms around him. She could see the pain and confusion in his eyes. "Justin, I'm so sorry. How is he?"

"He's stable for now, but I have to go there… today. Damn." He stopped. "I have to take Lauren, too. Darn she'll miss school."

"Justin, she's not going to care as long as she's with you." That's more than what Morgan had. "Do you want me to pack some of her clothes?"

"That would help me…"

Morgan started to walk away, but he pulled her back into his arms. "I don't want to leave you, either, Morgan. This wasn't how I planned today." He drew back and stared at her. "I want this to be just the beginning for us, but I have to be honest…I don't know what's going to happen. This can't be resolved in a few days."

"I know. And I'll be here, waiting." She hugged him, then went off to pack Lauren's clothes.

She would stay here, but she couldn't help but wonder if Justin would make it back to Destiny. He was returning to his old life in Denver. Whether it was his choice or not, he was still leaving her. Why did she feel she was being abandoned again?

The next day the family gathered in the Keenan kitchen for the Sunday meal. All the talk had been about the Sadie Hawkins dance the previous night.

Morgan hadn't attended the dance, not with Justin in Denver dealing with his father's situation. She wished so much that there was a way she could help him get through this. The trip back wouldn't be easy, considering the two had been estranged. Maybe this situation would help them get closer. Or would the long recovery enable his father to convince his son to stay in Denver?

Another part of Morgan wanted to be selfish. She wanted a chance to be with Justin. A chance at the life he'd hinted at yesterday morning. But would that happen now?

"Morgan," Leah called to her. "Have you heard any more news from Justin?"

She shook her head, telling herself that Justin had been too busy dealing with the crisis to phone her. "He said he would be at the hospital while his father went through tests." She tried to hide it, but she was miserable not hearing.

When the kitchen phone rang, her mother picked it up. "Hello, Keenan Inn." She paused and smiled. "Justin, it's good to hear from you. Yes, she's right here. We're all praying for your father." She held out the receiver to Morgan. "I think someone's anxious to talk to you."

"Thanks, Mom." Morgan took the phone, walked into the hall and sat on the carpeted stairway. "Justin."

"You have no idea how much I need to hear your voice. God, I miss you."

Her heart soared. "I've missed you, too."

"I'm sorry I haven't called sooner, but between the hospital and getting Lauren settled in, there hasn't been time, or it was too late last night."

"That doesn't matter, Justin. You can call me anytime." She hesitated, before asking, "How is your father?"

"He's still stable, and they've been running a barrage of tests. It's going to be another day or so before we know."

"That's good news."

"Dealing with my father when he's confined to a hospital bed has not been fun. He's grumpy with everyone."

"That's a good sign, right?"

"It's hard to tell with that man."

"I wish you could come home."

"You don't know how much I wish that, too,"

he said. "But it's not likely. My father's recovery could take quite a while. And it isn't as if there is anyone else who can run the company. At the moment, it's up to me."

Just as quickly as her mood had brightened by his voice, it now sank low at the thought he might not be returning. "What about your father's assistant?"

"I have power of attorney, and I know the operation. My father didn't trust many people. Except me."

She hadn't trusted easily, either. Until Justin. "It makes sense since you were supposed to take over the company someday." She felt like her entire life was starting to crumble. "So I take it Marc will be running the resort project on his own."

"He can do it, Morgan. Nothing has changed on that. I don't want anything to change, especially us. I'm crazy about you. In fact, when things settle down, I want you come to Denver. Once the resort project breaks ground and construction starts, you should have some free time. You could come here and be with me."

"Justin, I can't do that. I have responsibilities as mayor. I take my job seriously."

"I know." He sighed. "I hate even asking you, but I can't walk out on mine, either. Hilliard Industries employs thousands of people, people with families. The stockholders want someone who knows the business."

Justin was asking for something she couldn't give him. Destiny was the only place she'd ever felt she belonged. "I can't move, Justin. I'm sorry…"

"At least think about it, Morgan? Right now, it's the only way we can be together."

She wanted desperately to be the woman he wanted, but she couldn't move into his world. "Let's not talk about this now."

There was a long pause. "I need to get back. I'll try to call you again. Bye, Morgan."

Before she could speak, she heard the click, then the dial tone. It sounded so final. Had she lost Justin?

She returned the phone to the kitchen to find her family all waiting expectantly for news.

"Justin's dad is still in ICU. So Justin won't be back for a while. He's had to take over as CEO for the company."

"For good?" Paige asked.

Morgan shrugged. "I don't know. I don't think Justin knows for sure."

"I'm sorry, Morgan," her sister said. "But I have no doubt he'll be back. He has the resort and his house here."

Morgan didn't want to talk about this anymore. She couldn't share her feelings for Justin. She'd spent so many years hiding them and acting like the big sister that she didn't know how to share her own problems.

"I'm not very hungry, so if you don't mind, I'll pass on supper."

Before anyone could convince her to stay, Morgan grabbed her coat and was out the door. Pulling up her collar, she took off walking down the street, trying to think positively, but her fears prevented it. She traveled several blocks and realized she was at Justin's house.

She'd come to love this place more and more with every little detail Justin had restored. It was the home she'd always wanted, but she realized she didn't care about the structure, without the man. She used the key Justin had given her. She told herself that she was just checking to see that everything was turned off and locked up tight.

She walked through the main floor, seeing the progress. The living room had new crown moldings, and the workmen had replaced the mantel. She continued into the kitchen to find it empty. New cabinets were ordered and scheduled to be installed next week. But no one would be here.

Her heart was breaking, she hurt so bad.

The doorbell rang, bringing Morgan out of her reverie. She went to answer it, wondering if it was Marc, but was surprised to find Father Reilly on the porch.

"Father, what are you doing here?" She stepped aside to let him inside.

The middle-aged priest smiled sadly as he came into the entry. "I've just heard about Justin Hilliard's father. I wanted to come by…"

"Justin is in Denver."

Of course Father Reilly studied her for a moment. "I can see you're worried. Has his father taken a turn for the worse?"

"No. Mr. Hilliard seems to be holding his own.

But Justin will be staying in Denver, indefinitely, to run the family business."

"So your unhappiness has nothing to do with the resort project."

She shook her head. "Justin assures me that his project manager is more than capable of handling the job." The priest was the only person Morgan had confided in about what happened to her in college. "I don't think Justin will come back here."

Father Reilly took her hand and led her to the stairs. They sat down. "It sounds to me like he didn't have much choice."

"He didn't." She felt so many emotions. "It's all happened so fast…"

"And even more for Justin. He's had to pack up his life here and rush back to handle things." The priest paused. "I take it the two of you have feelings for each other."

Morgan thought back to their night together and nodded. "We had just started seeing each other when this happened." She looked at him. "He asked me to move to Denver."

His understanding blue eyes held hers. "And that's a bad thing?"

"I can't leave here, Father. I have commitments to the town, and it's my home. My parents live here."

He watched her for a while. "It's more than that, isn't it, Morgan?" He sighed. "You're still letting what happened to you hold you prisoner, letting it keep you from making a life for yourself."

"I have a life."

"Not a relationship. Have you ever talked with anyone else?"

"Justin knows."

A slow smile appeared across his rounded face. "So you've trusted Justin enough to let him help you with your biggest fear. That's a big step, Morgan. He must be a special man. And a lucky man. I doubt he's going to let a pretty lass like you get away."

CHAPTER TEN

THE next day, Morgan was in her office with Marc, discussing the hiring of local workers. They decided to give the community a head start on the hiring for the project.

"I'll have the office set up by tomorrow." The young project manager smiled. "I have Kaley helping with handing out applications. The construction company will do the screening of the subcontractors…"

The phone rang and Morgan answered it. "Morgan Keenan."

"Good morning, Mayor," Justin said.

"Hello, Justin." She flashed a look at Marc. "How is everything there?"

"Not bad. My father's been moved into a regular room. They found some blockage and plan to correct the problem. How are things there?"

"Busy." Seems he wanted to keep this business. "Marc's here. We're going to begin hiring tomorrow."

"Good. I don't want any delays. Let me talk to him."

She handed the phone to the project manager, telling herself it was better that he hadn't gotten personal. They didn't need that right now. Justin had too much to worry about as it was. On the other hand she couldn't stop thinking about him.

"Okay, Justin. I'll be in touch. Bye." He held out the receiver to her. "He wants to talk to you again."

Surprised, she took the phone and watched as Marc walked out. The door clicked shut, leaving her alone.

"Justin, was there something else you needed?" she asked, her heart beating in double-time.

"Only you, green eyes."

She closed her eyes. "Justin, this isn't a good time." This was only making it worse. "We both have a lot to deal with right now."

"Can't we do it together, Morgan? I think we make a pretty good team."

"It's different now. Your life is different. Your immediate future is there in Denver. Mine is here."

"This is only temporary. My concern is still the Silver Sky project…and you and Lauren."

Morgan bit her trembling lip. "Justin, please, you can't make any promises now. Your life has to be there…"

"We could if we're willing to compromise."

She didn't want to argue with him. "I think we should put this conversation off for a while."

There was a long pause. "If that's what you want."

No! She wanted more than anything to be with Justin, but that wasn't possible right now. Maybe never. "It's probably better for both of us."

"I guess there's nothing more to say."

"I guess not," she said.

There was a long pause and Morgan almost begged him to come back to her, but she couldn't do that. She couldn't make him choose.

"Goodbye, Morgan."

"Goodbye, Justin."

She hung up first, not wanting to hear the final break in the connection that meant the end. She blinked back the tears, knowing if she started she might never stop.

Morgan went back to work for the rest of the afternoon until a commotion disturbed her. Suddenly Lyle Hutchinson barged into her office, with Beverly close behind him. "Sorry, Morgan. He slipped past me."

"It's okay, Bev," she told her, then looked at her intruder. "You need to see me, Lyle?"

He nodded. "And I think you know why."

Morgan motioned for the town controller to leave them alone. "I'm not in the mood for guessing. Maybe you should just tell me."

"Word's out, Morgan, that Hilliard deserted us."

Morgan got up and moved around her desk. "Deserted?"

"Justin Hilliard pulled out. He's gone."

"That's not true. I just talked with Mr. Hilliard this morning, and I assure you, he's not pulling out of the project. Besides, he's signed a contract, and he'd lose his investment."

"I doubt that matters. The man has plenty of money to lose."

Outside of the investment for the resort project, Morgan hadn't paid much attention to Justin's financial worth. "Whether he does or not doesn't concern me. My only concern is that his project manager can handle things here. But I assure you, Mr. Hilliard is in close touch with everything concerning the project."

Lyle gave her a cold stare. "I don't believe you," he said. "I think you're trying to cover for him. And I'm sure the city council would be interested in the situation."

That did it. Something in Morgan snapped. She was so tired of this man dogging her every step, questioning her every move. Lyle Hutchinson had tried everything to discredit her for the past two years. He hadn't succeeded because she hadn't done anything wrong. In fact, she was doing a good job as mayor.

And she wasn't about to let him smear Justin's good name.

"Well, you go and tell the council whatever you want, Lyle," she began, her anger rising. "I'm tired of your threats and accusations." She walked toward him, suddenly feeling empowered. "You're only ticked off because I beat you in the election. Well, get over it, Hutchinson."

The older man actually backed up, but she didn't stop.

"The citizens of Destiny wanted me—not you— as their mayor. And that's because I do things for the good of this town, not to line my own pockets."

His nostrils flared. "How dare you?"

"It's about time someone told you off. You and your father aren't running this town anymore. So stop coming in here thinking you can frighten me into quitting." She drew a breath and placed her hands on her hips, feeling her energy soar. "Okay, Lyle, give me your best shot."

"You can't talk to me that way."

"Looks like I just did." She smiled. "Now, the next time you want to discuss something with me, you call and make an appointment. I'm busy trying to build a ski resort." She was shaking, but refused to back down. She turned and walked to her desk. Surprisingly all she heard was the door opening and Lyle's retreating footsteps.

Suddenly there was a sound of applause. Morgan swung around to see Beverly. "It's about time someone told that man off."

Morgan began to laugh. "Oh, it did feel good." For the first time in years, she felt free. She'd been hiding behind her fears for so long, she hadn't known her own strength.

Then it dawned on her who had made this possible. The man who gave her her freedom so she'd have the courage to go after what she wanted. And she wanted Justin. Nothing else mattered. But first, she needed to get rid of her other demons.

Later that evening, Morgan sat at the Keenan kitchen table. She'd done what Father Reilly suggested and told her parents what had happened with Ryan.

Morgan reached for her mother's hand, knowing that she desperately needed that loving contact now.

Since that first day she and her sisters had arrived here all those years ago, Claire and Tim Keenan had always been there for them. This time wasn't any different.

"I'm sorry, Mom."

"Don't you ever say that—you have nothing to be ashamed of." Claire Keenan leaned closer, unashamed of the tears in her eyes. "This was out of your control, Morgan. I'm only upset because you went through this alone." Her mother continued to study her. "Please, don't tell me you still believe it was your fault."

"In my mind, no…but emotionally I couldn't help thinking that I was flawed in some way."

Her father spoke up. "Your mother or I never saw any flaws in you. From the first day you came to us, you tried so hard to be perfect. You had the cleanest room, did the most chores and were the top student in school. We always worried that you expected too much of yourself."

Morgan knew what they said was true. "I was so happy to be here. And I was scared that you wouldn't love me if I did anything bad." She felt so childish telling them all this now. "My biological mother gave me away… I thought it was something in me that she couldn't love."

A tear ran down her mother's cheek as she and her husband exchanged a look.

"How could we not love you," Tim asked. "We

prayed for years for a child and suddenly we were blessed with three little girls." Her father cupped her cheek. "From the moment I saw you huddled with your sisters…those big green eyes and wild red hair, you stole my heart. You tried to act so brave. I had to tread so carefully…to earn your trust…your love."

Morgan let a tear fall. "I love you both so much."

"Have you told Justin about what happened in college?" her mother asked.

Morgan nodded. "At first I tried to keep him at a distance, but he wouldn't let me." Sadness washed over her. "But I let him down, Mom. I let him down when he needed me the most. I thought I couldn't handle leaving here…it's been my safe place for so long. Then I realized that Justin is my safe place, too. I love him so much."

Her parents both smiled, then her father said, "Tell us something we don't know."

Morgan smiled, too, hoping one day she and Justin would have a relationship like theirs. "I need to tell him how I feel."

"Tell who how you feel?"

Morgan looked up to see Leah and Paige standing in the doorway. Both expectant mothers should be home and in bed at this late hour.

"What are you two doing here?" Morgan asked as she got up from the table.

"Since no one called us with any news," Paige began, "we decided to come to the source. Mom. And we got this feeling that you needed us."

Morgan hurried over to her siblings and they exchanged hugs. Then Leah added, "And we got this feeling that you need someone to tell you to latch onto that guy of yours. Justin Hilliard is a keeper."

Morgan laughed and it felt good. "I guess you better help me go and pack my suitcase, I'm going to Denver."

"You need to set up a meeting with the office staff," Marshal Hilliard told his son. "Then contact the key stockholders to assure them that Hilliard Industries is on solid ground. The list is in my files."

Over the past five days, Justin had promised himself he wasn't going to let his father rile him anymore. It had been forty-eight hours since he'd been released from the hospital, since the doctors had informed him that his father hadn't had a heart attack, but a severe angina condition. Not that it wasn't serious but they had found some blockage that had been handled by a successful angioplasty procedure.

The doctors expected Marsh Hilliard to make a complete recovery in about six weeks. The overworked CEO still needed to make drastic changes in his lifestyle, but that wasn't going to be at Justin's expense.

Justin paced his father's study, promising himself he would never turn into Marshall Hilliard. He had entirely different plans for his and Lauren's life…and hopefully that included Morgan. And if he was lucky enough to have her in his life, that life wasn't going to be in Denver.

He thought back to the night they'd made love. It had been incredible. Morgan had been so loving and so giving of her body…and her soul. He'd been humbled how easily she put her trust in him. The first man in years. He could still see the look on her face when he left her…

He knew now, coming back here was toxic. How could he ask her to come into this life? That was wrong, especially when there wasn't anything here that he wanted.

God. He had to talk to her. He had to tell her how he truly felt, that he was coming home to her. But not just yet. First, he had to organize things with the company before he could make her any promises.

It wouldn't take long, maybe twenty-four hours. This had affected Lauren, too. She started reverting into her shell. No, this wasn't the place for either of them.

He glanced at his father sitting behind the desk. The man was going over the quarterly figures. He never stopped working. "I'll hold the meeting in the morning, but I'm going to turn things over to Carlton Burke. He's an excellent candidate to take over permanently."

"You can't be serious."

"I'm very serious," Justin said. "The man has worked for you for ten years. He's practically been your shadow."

"He's not my son," Marshal countered. "For three generations a Hilliard has been at the helm of the operations."

"Then you should adopt him."

"Don't be impertinent," his father said.

"Then listen to what I'm saying. I am not running Hilliard Industries now, or ever. I have a new life in Destiny where there's a special woman that I love very much. And if I'm lucky, she'll share my life and Lauren's. We're going to be a family." How he hoped for that. He still needed to convince Morgan.

"Now, if you'll excuse me, I'm going to put Lauren to bed. If you need something, I'm sure your nurse will help you. Good night, Father."

Justin's shoes echoed on the Italian tile floors as he hurried toward the staircase to the second floor. He wanted to call Morgan, to tell her how much he loved her… He paused. He'd never told her. He cursed.

"Oh, Daddy. You said a bad word."

He looked to the top of the stairs to see Lauren dressed in her nightgown with her favorite stuffed animal in her arms.

He smiled. "I'm sorry, sweetie."

"Are you mad at Grandfather again?"

He reached the top step and swung her up in his arms. "Yes, but I shouldn't be because he doesn't feel good."

"He has a bad heart," Lauren said.

"Yeah, he does." In more ways than one, he thought.

"I hope he gets better real soon so we can go back home to Destiny. I miss my friends and school. And Delaney is having a birthday party in two weeks. She's my best friend in the whole world. I got to be there." She laid her head on his shoulder. "And I miss Morgan the most."

"Oh, honey, I miss Morgan, too. And trust me I'm going to try really hard to get us back where we belong." He carried the sleepy child down to her old bedroom and laid her on the bed. He kissed her. "Night, sweetie."

"Night, Daddy. I love you."

"I love you, too." He shut off the light and closed the door. He wasn't waiting any longer. He was returning to Destiny tomorrow. He'd run Hilliard Industries by phone if he had to. He walked to his room and began searching through his desk. He wasn't going back empty-handed, either.

This time he was going to keep his promises to Morgan.

Morgan knew it was late, but she was afraid if she waited until morning she'd lose her nerve and just fly back home. The taxi pulled up in front of the rolling estate. Floodlights lined the long circular driveway as the cab stopped in front of the huge house.

"Oh, my." Her eyes widened as she tried to take it all in. She knew Justin's family was wealthy but she hadn't expected this.

"Hey, lady. You stayin' or what?"

"I'm going in…but please wait for me." She gave him an extra twenty dollars to stay put. What if she came all this way and Justin didn't welcome her with open arms? It had been five days. Maybe his old life had been too strong a temptation. No. She believed he cared about her, but old insecurities were hard to ignore.

Morgan stepped out of the back seat and brushed her hand along her taupe slacks and straightened her black sweater. The outfit that Justin liked so much, hoping his tastes hadn't changed. She walked up the large porch and rang the bell. Her heart pounded loudly in her ears. After waiting several miserable seconds, a woman answered the door.

"I'm here to see Justin Hilliard," Morgan said.

"I'm sorry, Mr. Hilliard has retired for the night. You can leave your name and come back in the morning…"

Her heart sank. "I'm Morgan Keenan."

"The mayor of Destiny?" The housekeeper smiled. "Miss Lauren talks about you and your family all the time." Before Morgan could say any more, the woman ushered her inside. "Now you wait right here," she told her. "Mr. Hilliard just went to put Lauren to bed." The woman ran off.

Morgan glanced around the darkly paneled area and heavy ornate furniture. Original artwork covered the walls, but no family pictures, or flowers. Was this where Justin had grown up? She realized how lucky she'd been having the Keenans.

Now, she just had to let Justin know how much she loved him, whether he lived here or in Destiny.

"Who are you?" a gruff voice called to her.

Morgan swung around to see an older man with thick gray hair and the same silver eyes as his son. He was wearing a dark silk dressing robe and slippers covered his feet.

"Hello, Mr. Hilliard. I'm Morgan Keenan," she said as she held out her hand. "I'm happy to see that you're doing so well."

He ignored her gesture. "You still haven't answered my question, Miss Keenan."

Morgan was taken aback by his rudeness, even if she were in his house. "I apologize for disturbing you, I only came to see—"

"She's here to see me," the familiar voice called from the stairs.

Morgan turned to see Justin. "Justin…" She drew in a breath as she tried to take in the sight of him. He had on jeans and a hunter-green colored sweater. His hair was mussed, and he looked tired…and wonderful.

"Hello, Morgan," he said as he walked toward her. Never taking his eyes from her, he said, "Father, I thought you'd retired for the night."

The older man grumbled something. "As you can see there is a visitor." He looked her over. "It's a little late for business."

"Morgan's visit is personal." Justin placed a protective arm around her waist.

"I'm not here on business, Mr. Hilliard," Morgan told him. "I'm here to see your son, but I do apologize for the late hour."

Justin couldn't believe it when Nancy had come to him and said Morgan was here. He couldn't get down the stairs fast enough.

"Father, Morgan and I have matters to discuss."

The older man stared at Morgan. "You're not

going to talk my son into leaving here. His place is running Hilliard Industries."

"I know, Mr. Hilliard. That's why I came here." She turned to Justin and smiled. "I want your son to know that I'll support any decision he makes, whether it's here in Denver, or back in Destiny."

Justin didn't want to have this conversation in front of his father. "Father, if you'll excuse us, I need to talk with Morgan…in private."

As if he'd arranged it, the hired nurse arrived and escorted the older man out, but not without some more grumbling. Then all at once there was silence.

Justin's gaze roamed over her face. She was so beautiful. Her hair brushed her shoulders in curls, so soft he ached to touch them. "I can't believe you're here."

"I can't believe it, either," she said timidly. "You really don't mind?"

Justin lowered his head and, inches from her mouth, he said, "Does this seem like I mind?" He covered her mouth with a searing kiss. By the time he released her, they were both struggling to breathe. "This has been the longest five days in my life. God, I've missed you." He kissed her again…and again.

"You're starting to convince me," she teased.

"Well, the last thing I want to do is leave you with any doubt…" He pulled her against his body. "I want you to know exactly how I feel about you." He gazed into those sparkling eyes. "I love you, Morgan Keenan…with all my heart."

She gasped. "Oh, Justin, I love you, too. I'm sorry I told you I wouldn't come to Denver… I was afraid."

"Afraid of what? Me?"

"No. That I wouldn't fit in here. That you were going to come back and decide you wanted the life you had before. And if that's what you really want…"

He placed a finger over her mouth. "No, I don't want anything from my old life, except for Lauren. In the last five days, I realized how much I missed you and Destiny. I consider it my home now. What I didn't expect to find was you." He cupped her face. "I think I fell in love with you in the cave that night. But I knew to win you, I'd have to be patient. I had to get you to trust me. We have nothing without trust."

She nodded. "I know. And I'm sorry it took me so long to realize that. I couldn't trust your love until I trusted myself." She lowered her eyes. "That's why I came here…to you."

Justin had thought of so many things he wanted to say, but suddenly he was speechless. Everything he'd ever dreamed of was right here. "I need to make a phone call."

She blinked. "Now?"

"Believe me, it's important. You'll understand in a few minutes." He drew his cell phone from his pocket and punched in the numbers. He waited, then heard, "Hello, Keenan Inn."

"Hello, Tim, it's Justin."

"Justin, it's good to hear from you. Is everything okay?"

"Yes, it's very okay. Morgan is here with me." His

arm tightened around her as he took another breath. "I love her very much, sir, and would like to ask your and Claire's permission for Morgan's hand in marriage?"

He heard Morgan's gasp, but couldn't look at her.

"I have to say I'm not surprised. Morgan is a special woman." There was another pause. "You have our blessing, son. Tell Morgan we love her very much, and we'll talk later. Goodbye."

"Thank you. Goodbye." He set the phone down on the table and looked at the woman he loved more than he'd thought possible.

"I'd already decided I was leaving Denver and coming home to Destiny…and you. I realized that nothing is more important than us being together." He reached into his pocket and pulled out an antique ring.

"I never dreamed I'd find someone like you. Someone who made me feel…the way that you make me feel…someone who wants the same things." He held up an antique emerald ring circled by diamonds and saw the hue mirror in her eyes. "This was my grandmother's, and I think it's perfect for you."

Never breaking eye contact, he knelt down on one knee. "Morgan Keenan, I love you. Will you do me the honor of marrying me and becoming my wife and mother to Lauren, and more children?"

Morgan all but stopped breathing. Tears flooded her eyes and she could barely see him, but she knew her answer. "Oh, Justin, yes, I'll marry you."

He immediately slipped the ring on her finger,

then stood up and pulled her into his arms. "I want to give you the world."

She pulled back and smiled. "You already have. You helped me find me." He'd given her what mattered the most. "I love you, Justin Hilliard." She kissed him.

"Daddy, you're kissing Morgan…"

They broke apart to see Lauren climbing down the steps. "Morgan, you came to get us." The child rushed into her arms.

"Yes, I did," Morgan said as she knelt down. "And I'm going to take you and your daddy back home to Destiny."

Those big blue eyes widened. "Really?" She glanced up at her father.

"And there's more news, sweetie." He picked her up in his arms. "Your daddy and Morgan are going to get married."

"Oh, boy! Delaney said you would because you guys kiss so much."

"How do you feel about Morgan being your new mother?"

She nodded. "I want that the most." She turned to Morgan and kissed her. "I love you, Morgan."

Morgan hugged her new daughter. "I love you, too." She suddenly understood what her parents had been trying to tell her. You didn't need to give birth to a child to love her.

Lauren straightened. "And can we have sleep-overs?"

Morgan fought laughter. "We'll see, but right now

you need to go to bed. We have to go home tomorrow."

"Yeah. Can I see Delaney, too?"

"Sure."

The five-year-old wiggled out of her arms and got down. "You have to take me to bed, Morgan. Come on, I'll show you how to do it…"

Morgan looked back at Justin who shrugged. "I guess you should learn the ritual." He'd started after them when there was a knock at the door. Justin opened the door to find the cabdriver.

"Oh, my, I forgot about him," Morgan said. "I had him wait in case…"

Justin pulled out some bills and paid the driver handsomely for looking after her. Then he took her bag and followed the girls up the steps.

When they got to the top of the stairs, Lauren said, "Maybe Morgan can sleep in my bed tonight?"

Morgan glanced at the hopeful look on the child's face. "How about I stay with you until you fall asleep?"

"I like that." The girl walked ahead of her parents and into the bedroom.

"Welcome to parenthood. Be careful, she'll steal your heart."

Morgan looked at the man with the silver eyes. "Why not, her father already has." She kissed him. "But I think my heart is big enough to go around."

He hugged her. "How did I get so lucky?"

"It must have been the sweet proposal I sent that lured you to Destiny."

He grinned. "Oh, yeah, and I seem to remember something about some fringe benefits you promised me."

She winked. "I'll discuss those terms later…when we're alone."

EPILOGUE

IT TURNED out to be a perfect day for a wedding.

The mid-December morning had produced a dusting of snow for the noontime nuptials that had been performed by Father Reilly at St. Andrews Church. Since Morgan couldn't choose, both her sisters, Paige and Leah, acted as her matrons of honor, along with Lauren as the flower girl.

It was a holiday theme, but with hundreds of white roses trimmed with silver ribbon. The girls wore winter-green dresses. But when Morgan walked down the aisle on her father's arm, she wasn't seeing anything but her groom standing at the altar. Justin looked handsome in his dove-gray morning coat. There were tears in both their eyes when they'd changed their vows, then he drew her in his arms as Father Reilly pronounced them man and wife.

"Hello, Mrs. Hilliard," Justin whispered then he kissed her with a promise of life filled with love.

The reception had been held at the Inn where

family and friends toasted them in their new life together. Finally by midevening—with Lauren staying with her new grandparents—Morgan and Justin were about to escape the party.

Although the honeymoon had been delayed until after the holidays and Paige giving birth, they had their own special plans.

A thrill raced though Morgan as Justin opened the door to the newly remodeled Hilliard home. He swung her up in his arms and carried her over the threshold.

"Welcome home, Mrs. Hilliard," he whispered as he brought her into their new home and their new beginning. He set her down and kissed her, slow and deep.

"Very impressive welcome, Mr. Hilliard."

"You're the one who's impressive…and beautiful," he said as he eyed her hungrily.

"Thank you."

Morgan wore her grandmother's ivory wedding dress. The antique lace over satin had a fitted bodice with scalloped edging just above her breasts, with long, tapered sleeves that ended in a v-point at her wrist. The trim waistline flared into an A-line skirt that went all the way to the floor.

He pulled her back into his arms. "It's a beautiful dress, but I can't wait to get you out of it."

A shiver went through her as he kissed her, then they walked up the stairs to their bedroom.

Justin wanted everything to be so special since their honeymoon had been put on hold until after the first of the year. That was all right with him as long as he could spend some time alone with his new bride, and he didn't care where.

He opened the bedroom door to expose the lit candles, a fire going and a chilled bottle of champagne beside the bed.

She walked around the room, touching all the flowers. "Oh, Justin. It's…beautiful."

"I had a couple of elves come in. I wanted tonight to be special for you."

She came back to him and slipped her arms around his waist. "Just being with you is all I need. You made it all possible. No one has ever been so patient…so giving with me. You helped me become the woman I always wanted to be."

"No, Morgan. You were always that woman. You just needed someone to help you find her."

She rewarded him with a bright smile. "Well, you've got her now."

He kissed the end of her nose. "That was my plan from the moment I first saw you. You saved me, too. I've never felt this way about anyone… ever."

"I feel the same way about you." She placed her hand against his chest, right over his heart. "I want to give you a part of me that I've never shared with anyone else."

Justin remembered their first time together. How her faith and trust in him had humbled him. "That night was so special to me, to us, and we're going to have many more. Starting tonight." He kissed her.

She broke it off. "There's something I have for you."

His eyes searched hers. "You're all I need, Morgan."

She smiled. "And you're all I need. But I want to carry on tradition. Besides, we can share this gift." She went to the large chest at the foot of the four-poster bed, knelt down, opened it and took out a large quilt.

Justin went to her and examined the multiblue colors displayed in the pattern. "This is the one you were quilting the day I met you." He knelt down beside her, his fingers tracing the intricate pattern of circles.

She nodded. "It's called a wedding-ring quilt. Lauren helped me with some of the stitches, and in the last few weeks, Paige, Leah and my mom helped me finish so it would be ready for today." She looked at him. "For a long time, I'd never thought I'd ever sleep under a wedding-ring quilt."

He shook his head. "I'm just glad you waited for me, too." He pulled her closer as his mouth covered hers. She melted into him at once, her arms snaked around his neck as she opened her lips, welcoming him into a deeper intimacy.

"I love you, Justin," Morgan said as she began to work the studs on his shirt.

"And I love you, Morgan Keenan Hilliard."

He kissed her again, eager to start the honeymoon. He also knew that he needed to pace things, to make everything perfect for his bride on their wedding night. "Why don't you go and take off your gown? I'd hate for anything to happen to it.

Who knows, maybe Lauren or one of our other daughters will want to wear this dress on her wedding day."

He saw the tears as he helped his bride to her feet, then with a soft kiss, turned her around and began working the many buttons down the back. He took several calming breaths as he exposed his wife's slender back.

"All finished," he said and placed a kiss against her neck.

Morgan turned around, holding the loosened dress to her breasts. She raised her loving gaze to his. "I want a baby, Justin. Your baby."

His chest tightened. They'd been so busy getting the wedding together and the project started, they hadn't talked much about children…

"You want a baby…now?"

She nodded. "I know we have the resort project and Lauren needs to adjust to us, but all I can think about is how much I want to be pregnant with your child."

His mouth went dry with the image of her large with his baby. It was so overwhelming he couldn't speak. He pulled her into his arms and kissed her. In no time her dress was removed, then his clothes began to fade away as they found their way to the bed. No words needed to be spoken as he lowered her to the mattress. "I'd love a little girl with your green eyes…" He bent down and brushed a kiss against her mouth, then down her neck, continuing the trail along her sensitized skin.

"Or…" Morgan sucked in a breath. "A little boy with silver eyes and dark curly hair would be… perfect."

"You're perfect…" His mouth returned to hers in a deep, soul-searching kiss that nearly drove him over the edge as his arms tightened, pulling her against his heated body.

They were lost in each other when suddenly the phone next to the bed rang. Justin groaned as he rolled away from his bride. "I can't believe this." Justin grabbed the receiver. "This better be an emergency."

"I'm sorry, Justin. It's Tim. We just wanted to call and let you know that Paige went into labor. She's on the way to the hospital. We've taken Lauren over to Delaney's house for the night. I thought you and Morgan would want to know."

"Of course, Tim. Thanks for the call. I'll tell Morgan."

Morgan sat up in bed, the sheet pulled up to cover her nakedness. "Who was that?"

"Your dad. Paige is in labor and on the way to the hospital."

A smile appeared. "She's having the baby." She let the sheet drop. "I guess Mom will call us with the news."

Justin was getting his first lesson on family, and how important it was to be together. "I guess we better get dressed so we can go welcome the new addition to the family."

"But what about our honeymoon?"

"It's also our family…and Paige is having a baby. She needs you there." He leaned closer and kissed his bride. "I'm never going to come between you and your sisters. I know how close you are."

"Oh, Justin," she said. "I love you so much."

He grinned. "Oh, yeah? I guess you'll just have to show me how much when we get back home."

An hour later, Morgan and Justin rushed into the hospital waiting room where her father and Holt sat. "Where are Mom and Leah?"

"They're in with Paige and Reed," Tim said. "Go on in. Even though she asked us not to call you, your sister wants you here. Room 304."

Morgan kissed Justin. "I'll be back with some news. Thanks for this…"

"This is important, we'll have our time later."

"Later," she whispered. She took off down the hall where Reed was coaching Paige through a pain and Mom and Leah were encouraging her. When it passed, Morgan walked into the room.

"I hear my niece is going to make an appearance today."

"Morgan!" Paige held out her hands. "I told them not to disturb your honeymoon."

"And I'd never forgive you," Morgan said as she went to her sister. "You can't have this baby without your big sister here. Remember, we always stick together."

There were tears in Paige's eyes. "Always. But I wish she'd hurry up."

"Me, too," Morgan agreed. "Then little Ellie can share her birthday with our anniversary."

Paige and Reed had decided to name their daughter after the sisters' biological mother. Eleanor Bradshaw. There were tears in Paige's eyes.

Another pain gripped Paige, and Morgan took her sister's hand and helped her through the breathing. When it passed, Reed fed his wife some ice chips.

"I bet this wasn't how Justin planned to spend tonight," Reed teased.

"Don't worry about Justin," Morgan told him. "I'll make it up to him."

Suddenly realizing what she'd said, Morgan's face reddened but another labor pain drew her immediate attention.

Over the next hour things progressed rather quickly. And in the end, it was the doctor, a nurse and Paige and Reed who were in the room when their daughter arrived into the world.

At the sound of the vigorous cry, Justin squeezed Morgan closer to his side. Then Reed came out with a big grin and tears in his eyes. "Eleanor Claire is healthy and weighed in at six pounds eight ounces and twenty inches long. And she's just as beautiful as her mother."

Everyone cheered, then quietly filed into the room to see Paige beaming, looking too good for just having a baby.

Justin held Morgan close as they looked at the new addition to the family. A precious little girl. They seemed to run in the Keenan family.

Morgan and Leah gathered at Paige's bedside, exchanging hugs while Reed and Holt stood next to Justin. "They've always been close," Holt remarked. "And marriage hasn't changed anything."

They turned their attention to the infant in the crib. "Congratulations, Dad," Justin said. "She's a guaranteed heartbreaker."

"Like her mother and her aunts," Reed agreed.

Reed looked at Justin. "If I hadn't said it yet, welcome to the family."

"Thank you, but I think you've been a little busy." Justin glanced at his wife across the room. As if she sensed his gaze, she turned to him and smiled. She said something to her sisters. They hugged and she came to him.

"We should go," she whispered.

Justin didn't have to be asked twice. They said their goodbyes to everyone and walked out the door. At the elevator they waited until the doors opened and they stepped inside the empty car.

When the door closed Justin pulled his wife into his arms and kissed her. When he broke away, he refused to release her.

She smiled. "Wow. You sure you can wait until we get home?"

He took a breath. "I am home. Whenever I'm with you."

Her green eyes searched his, showing her emotions. "Oh, Justin, I feel the same way. I'm so happy that you didn't give up on me."

He kissed her again. "Never. I would have waited for you as long as it took to win you."

She touched his cheek. "The wait is over, Justin."

"For both of us. We have our family." Who knew, when he'd come here just months ago, he'd find his true Destiny.

* * * * *

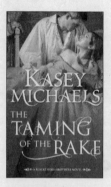

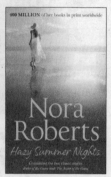

Have Your Say

You've just finished your book.
So what did you think?

We'd love to hear your thoughts on our 'Have your say' online panel
www.millsandboon.co.uk/haveyoursay

- Easy to use
- Short questionnaire
- Chance to win Mills & Boon® goodies